NEVER
CLOCKED OUT

FullTimeTony Season One

TONY GRUENWALD

Contents

For my Jill,
Let's go talk about our superior relationship.

"This raft is hard to steer, the water's low this time of year."
- *Sibling Rivalry* by Pup

Included Stories

FullTimeTony and the Planet Playground
FullTimeTony and the Royal Riders
FullTimeTony and the World Song
FullTimeTony and the Broken Stick
FullTimeTony and the One Small Step Former Man
FullTimeTony and the Sister Sigil
FullTimeTony and the Forever Gone

PART I

FullTimeTony and the Planet Playground

One

In a small area of the woods behind the playground, the branches on the trees swayed, yet the wind had not blown. Something unseen was pushing them aside. There was the sound of something shattering. A tense creak of stretching against resistance. And slowly, the air cracked and separated.

The kids were mad at Tony because they had to go to Garbage Playground. They wanted to go to The Good Playground. The Good Playground had the good slide and the good maze and lots of the good swings. It had bouncy rubber chips on the ground, not that cheap rough mulch like Garbage Playground had.

The Good Playground was their favorite and if you went there, you had better prepare to stay awhile. The Good Playground meant at least two, maybe three hours of playing, because the kids loved it and never wanted to leave. No one wanted to play that long at Garbage Playground. It had pretty suspicious looking slides, monkey bars that went nowhere, and only three swings. There were weird brown pools of water everywhere at Garbage Playground. Instead of just squeaking the way most well-used playground equipment did, at Garbage Playground the equipment screamed horrifically every time someone hopped on the seesaw. The kids tolerated it there, but they got bored quickly and would want to leave after about forty-five minutes.

Bored and restless was the general theme after only a few weeks of summer break, Tony did his best to keep the kids busy every day. His daughter was having a hard time with suddenly having her two brothers around the house all the time, when she was used to them leaving for most of the day. The house had become a ticking time bomb of tantrums and arguing. This morning during breakfast, one of them simply looked at the other and that set them off. That was all it took. The entire day was now going to be miserable. Just because someone looked at someone else. So it was blindfolding everyone or getting out and doing some activities. Even for just a little. Today was a playground day.

But all the morning crabbiness had drained him already, and while they needed the break and distraction, Tony only felt like being out for the bare minimum. Which was the reason he picked Garbage Playground. He also didn't want to reward their bickering with a better playground. Which, of course, is a primary principle of advanced parenting: finding the laziest path to passive aggressiveness.

"Well, I'll go but I'm not having any fun." Quint, age eight, said sitting in his booster seat with his arms folded. Refusing to get out as Tony unbuckled the other two out of their car seats.

"My man, I'm not asking you to go to your ex-wife's wedding, let's just go play for a while and see what happens. I bet you'll have fun. Zip your sweatshirt up, it's kind of chilly out here today." Tony said as he struggled with Quint's younger brother Brody's car seat straps.

Six-year-old Brody was quietly waiting for Tony to unbuckle him. Brody is autistic with low support needs.

"I want to swing!" Brody shouted.

"What? There are no swings at the onion farm." Tony smirked.

"This is not the onion farm! This is a playground!" Brody rolled his eyes.

"Uh, I drove the van. I think I know where we are. We're going to work on the onion farm for the day." Tony told him.

"Daddy. You think you are so funny, but you are not." Brody said, scooting out of his seat.

"Yeah, everyone tells me that." Tony nodded in agreement.

Brody was holding his blanket with the cartoon lion pattern. It was once the soft muslin swaddle blanket that they had wrapped him in as a baby, but now it was his very worn and perpetually filthy comfort object. The blanket went everywhere he did.

"I want to swing too!" Quint barked, making sure as the oldest child that he always pivoted attention back to himself. It was a unique trait that was common in eight-year-olds and reality dating show contestants.

"Yes, we will all get to swing, but we cannot do that until I take your sister out of the van. Just a second guys." Tony said as he moved around the van to the opposite side to unbuckle Hooper.

She was sitting quietly with the headphones for the van's built in DVD player still wrapped around her small four-year-old head. As Tony slipped off the headphones and unclasped the buckles in her car seat, she yawned, and Tony regretted coming at this time of day. He may have blown the window for her to take her nap. She didn't take one very often anymore, and when she did, she never slept for long, but she clearly still needed one on most days. She famously had both the most chill and the shortest fuse of the three kids. She could be the sweetest thing and then just turn on a dime and lay siege to entire civilizations.

"Will you watch me do the slide?" She asked.

"I would love to watch you go down the slide." Tony asked back.

"Great!" she told Tony. As the youngest, she sometimes lost out on attention because of her older sibling's tomfoolery. He would have to make sure he gave her the time she asked for, as it was really important for her emotional growth at this age. He had read about it in a parenting article online and, like all online parenting articles, it immediately made him feel like a terrible parent. Tony thought some websites shouldn't have age restrictions but anxiety restrictions.

Tony slung his cheap backpack, filled with toddler essentials, over his back and lifted Hooper out of her seat.

"Okay, gang, let's do this! Boys, you can jump down now." Tony said. Then the two boys hopped out of the van onto the parking lot pavement. Tony had drilled a routine into their head that they couldn't get out until he told them to. His extreme anxiety about them getting hurt or run over had turned him into the minivan exiting safety sheriff. This was one of about four things he told them to do, that they actually did. The other ninety-six thousand things he asked of them, they of course ignored with extreme prejudice. "Partner up, guys." Tony told the boys, and the two brothers held hands as they walked from the parking lot to the playground.

"Daddy, can I pick the show when we get home?" Quint asked.

"We just got to the playground and you already want to talk about TV when we get home? You've had your morning screen time already, my man. Besides, didn't you just watch the DVD in the van?" Tony explained.

"Daddy, that was a minivan TV, that doesn't count." Quint said.

"Wait, so minivan TV doesn't count towards your daily screen time?"

"Yeah Daddy, it doesn't count. Because like, you could say that the window by my seat is also a kind of screen. Only instead of shows, it's showing me the outside. So when I watch the minivan TV it's like a window to the outside, too."

"Well, I'm not sure that's correct, but strangely, I understand your logic." Tony said.

They walked down the grass to Garbage Playground. Brody immediately picked up someone's discarded fast food cup, and Tony swatted it out of his hand.

"Don't touch, bud. Yucky." Tony said, grossed out.

"Yeah, disgusting." Brody said and then picked up another piece of trash. This one dripped something on his hand and he tossed it down himself. Tony made a mental note to dump a thousand gallons of hand sanitizer on Brody's now disease ridden hand before he took off to play.

"What are we doing first, gang? Slides? Swings?" Tony asked as the boys made a beeline toward the swings. Brody waved his gross garbage juice hand and threw his nasty blanket at Tony to hold. Tony just let them go.

He walked Hooper over to the smaller of the suspicious slides Garbage Playground offered and set her down. There were three other small kids taking turns going up and down the slide. She ran to the line and waited for her turn to climb up. Hooper did her best to be patient. If nobody dawdled or lingered, she would be fine. If they took too long, they'd hear about it.

Tony watched her go down the slide a few times and then glanced at the boys on the swings, who were giggling about flying as they swung back and forth. Tony was glad he and his wife had already taught them how to pump their legs and swing themselves. Painfully boring, being a swing pusher was the second worst parent job on the playground. The first worst job is when you have to dry off a piece of wet equipment, usually with your sweatshirt, because no one has invented playground towels or subsequent playground towel cleaning and delivery service yet.

Garbage Playground wasn't very busy today. Tony found a bench near Hooper's slide and took off the backpack and sat down next to a young woman on her phone. He did the Midwest smile and head nod hello as he opened the backpack and shoved Brody's blanket inside. He suddenly remembered he had brought coffee, but forgot it in the van, and got really annoyed about it. He took his phone out to check the time. It was nine-forty. Tony gave it twenty minutes before someone told him this is boring.

The young lady he shared the bench looked like she was in her early twenties. She wore a college sweatshirt and leggings that had a weird pattern on them that reminded Tony of those old hidden image books. She wore immaculately clean, huge white sneakers, and she knotted her hair about a foot above her head. She was taking pictures on her huge phone and then mindlessly poking the screen. Tony was great at spotting nannies.

"Yay! Good job Rykden!" She shouted at a small girl who had just slid down the slide. Hooper started getting mouthy with a boy while waiting for her turn.

"Hooper, be nice! Wait your turn." Tony said to her.

"Hooper, that's a cute name!" the nanny said to Tony.

"Oh, thanks. Rykden is an adorable name too!" Tony said, concluding that the letter k was a privilege, not a right.

"I nanny four days a week. She's the sweetest. And her parents are, like, the nicest people."

"That's awesome. She's super cute." Tony said, completing the ritual of speaking to someone else with a child. You must blindly complement each other's child for seventeen minutes before speaking about anything else. It was the law.

"I love little Hooper's shoes, they're super cute." She said back. And after everyone had declared everything super cute, she went back to poking at her huge phone.

Tony glanced over at the boys and they were off the swings and had chased each other to the rickety plastic climbing dome. They cackled as it unsafely rocked back and forth while climbing it onto it.

"Off work today?" the nanny asked Tony.

"What?" Tony said, confused.

"Not working today? Your day off, so you've got the kids?" She clarified.

"Oh. Oh! No, no, this is work." Tony finally got it.

"Oh, you nanny, too?" she asked.

"Oh no, they're mine." Tony said. He thought about joking that he couldn't be a nanny because he looked terrible in leggings, but didn't. "I stay at home with them full time. I'm a stay at home dad." Tony stammered out.

"Oh, good FOR YOU!" the nanny said. People always said the 'for you' part of that phrase like they were giving Tony a present. Like: 'I got these new socks FOR YOU!'

"It's not a big deal. Just made more sense for me to stay home when Hooper was born. It's fun. I feel very lucky. It's me and Hooper and my two boys…" Tony said and then

9

turned to acknowledge the boys but could not spot them. "Aww pickles," Tony said instead of the word he really wanted to use. "I lost them."

He stood up and scanned all of Garbage Playground but didn't see them. He'd have to go look for them. He put the backpack on again and went over and took Hooper's hand. "Come on Hoop, we lost the boys."

"Aw pickles." Hooper said.

"Yeah, that's what I said, too. See you around." He said to the nanny.

"Good luck!" she giggled.

"Thanks! If you find one, you can keep it." Tony stupidly joked and wandered over to the climbing dome. He just knew the nanny was judging him. Tony worried constantly that people were judging him. Probably would help if he didn't actually lose his children in public all the time. He did his best to shake the feeling away and he and Hooper walked away faster before someone added a k to their name too.

Tony wandered around the climbing dome and didn't see them anywhere. He didn't see them over by the bigger slides or by the monkey bars. He squinted his eyes and focused on just listening for them, because you could usually hear his kids before you ever saw them. They had almost no volume control. They would make terrible ninjas. He heard Brody laughing. It was his high pitch giggle and Tony zeroed in on it over in the trees behind the playground. There was a small but dense section of woods that separated the playground and some houses on the other side.

His first impulse was to get upset because they know to not leave the playground. But it was Garbage Playground, and he didn't blame them for finding absolutely anything else more interesting. He prepared himself to be serious, but not angry with them when he got over there. Hooper spotted the boys, too.

"Quint! Brody!" She said and pointed. "Hey, you boys!"

"You found them, Hooper. Thanks!" Tony said, letting go of her hand. She ran over to them as Tony followed behind her.

As he got closer, a foul odor drifted through the air. Now, Garbage Playground always smelled a little gross, but this was different. It smelled kind of like sulfur or some kind of burnt metallic smell.

"Daddy! Come here!" Quint yelled over at Tony.

Tony walked a little closer and deeper into the trees. Then he noticed the light. There was light projecting on the boys' faces. It brightly changed from blue to orange to red to yellow to green over and over like a disco light. It got more rapid and vivid as Hooper and he got closer.

"What are you guys doing? You know you're not supposed to be back here." Tony said, walking up behind them. Then he saw what they were looking at. Above their heads there was a crack in the air.

A flawless crack split the air about six feet across and about a foot wide. Maybe not. Tony had no experience at eyeballing the size of floating air cracks. It was from the crack that the smell and colors seeped out of. The rotating hues bled through the crack like sunlight through partially opened window blinds.

"Everyone get back. Behind me. Come on!" he blurted. Tony worried about almost everything. He lost his mind when they got too close to the stairs at home and couldn't help but to issue a safety warning every time they jumped on the couch. You throw being the parent of a child diagnosed with Autism Spectrum Disorder in the mix and forget it. He was a hot mess. His anxiety was pretty relentless, but confronted by a floating air crack spitting out rainbow colors and a burning metal smell, it was in maximum overload. "We have to go!" He herded the kids back and picked up Hooper, who was jumping and grabbing at the light.

"Doesn't it smell funny Daddy?" Quint asked. "It smells super gross, but looks so cool. Brody and I were playing and Brody saw the rainbow, so we came over here and found this. It's pretty cool, huh Daddy?"

"It's super weird, Quint!" Tony said. "We should just go back now and get away from it. Come on!"

Brody heard the noise first. He was very sensitive about sounds. It started as a hum and quickly became louder and higher pitched. He put his hands over his ears.

"Too loud, Daddy." Brody said, huddling closer to Tony's leg. It sounded like something scraping against a violin's strings. An eerie tone that rose higher and higher.

He motioned to Quint to come closer and with Brody on his leg and Hooper in his arms; he started backing away. The noise got louder and the rainbow lights flashed faster. The light smoothly drifted over their bodies, like it was reaching out, and surrounded them. There was a loud blast of noise. The family screamed in surprise as the colors suddenly pulled them all into the crack. The noise stopped. The smell stopped. The colors stopped. The crack faded away and the split air joined again.

They were gone.

Two

As they were getting sucked through the air crack, rainbow lights wrapped tightly around them like a blanket, Tony saw stars. Not like cartoon-got-hit-on-the-head stars, but real life ones. Billions and billions and billions of actual stars rushing past them. He saw planets and moons and suns zoom by as the rainbow light carried them through space. He was having trouble being amazed by it all. His fear refused to let him. His children, however, were laughing and hollering like they were on a roller coaster. Like this was something fun. Tony thought they were crazy. This was not fun.

"This rules!" Quint shouted.

"We're really, really flying!" Brody belly laughed.

"Faster!" Hooper added.

They felt speed as it pulled them along, but obviously not the full force of which they were actually traveling. Tony thought they had to be going some kind of speed of light or sound or something, but to them it only felt like sledding down hills in the winter.

Then it turned. It changed speed. The stars and

planets turned into millions of brightly blurred lines of motion. They were going faster. Suddenly, the pull was stronger. Tony's breath quickened as he became more afraid.

"Woo-hoo!" Quint shouted.

"Quint, hold still!" Tony gritted his teeth and squeezed the kids tighter.

"Faster!" Hooper yelled.

Brody stopped laughing. He had a death grip on Tony's forearm.

"Everyone, stop it!" Tony snapped.

As the word left his frustrated lips, they fell.

The rainbow colors dropped them off about three feet in the air. Tony landed with a messy thud on the hard dirt. He gasped as he hit the ground. The kids dropping on top of him knocked all that air he sucked in, immediately back out.

Panting and catching their breath, no one moved for a minute. The sudden drop had shocked the kids and Tony wasn't feeling so great after landing on his back, then turned into a crash pad. Tony, lightheaded and dizzy, slowly opened his eyes. Looking past his kids' heads at the air above him, his vision came to focus on the crack sealing up. The rainbow colors dimmed. They slowly faded away entirely as the sky smoothed itself back out.

"Pickles!" Hooper swore, rubbing her messy hair out of her eyes. She rolled off of Tony.

"Ow!" Tony said as she smashed his arm. "Pickles is right, Hoop." He groaned. "Boys, can you get off of me, please?" Tony begged. The boys cautiously scooted off Tony and onto the dirt. Tony sat up slowly, making many old man noises as he rose. "Is everyone okay?"

Quint nodded his head and looked around nervously.

Brody didn't reply. He was staring off to the side, panting hard. Those last few seconds of the trip shook him up.

"Brody you okay? Brody?" Tony said, sliding over to Brody. He moved his head low and bobbed it around until he finally met Brody's darting eyes. "Brody, are you okay, bud?"

"I'm o-kay." Brody's eyes wiggled for a second before settling on Tony's. He smiled at Tony, but it was his fake smile.

"It's okay, buddy. That last part was pretty scary, huh?" Tony said sweetly and rubbed Brody's back. He didn't know if he said it to calm Brody down or to justify his own fright. It was hard to tell sometimes. He slipped the backpack off and unzipped it. He handed Brody's lion blanket to him. Brody happily took the blanket and snuggled it. His fake smile faded into a more natural one.

"Daddy, look. The sky." Quint said.

Tony turned away from Brody and looked up. The sky itself was pitch black, but littered across it, punching infinite holes through the darkness, were gigantic stars. Dazzling diamonds of light covered the sky, glowing down upon them. They seemed so close you could reach out and touch them. They went on forever in every direction. Tony got to his feet, his eyes never leaving the sky, and spun around slowly. It was magnificent.

"Whoa. That's a lot of stars, man." Hooper said, her head pointing straight up into the sky and her arms at her side. She looked like a little girl-shaped pillar.

"Yeah, it's totally sick." Quint agreed.

"Sick?"

"Yeah, so sick Daddy."

"So, sick is... cool? Like, good?"

"Oh yeah, 'so sick' is cool." Quint explained.

"Well, one." Tony scrunched his forehead and nose up

and shook his head subtly, back and forth. "And two, I'd really prefer you wait until we get you a skateboard before you call things 'so sick'."

"Where did we go, Daddy?" Brody, a bit more comfortable, stood up and asked.

Tony brushed the dirt off of his pants and the front of his sweatshirt, and finally inspected the place they had landed.

It was the most boring thing he'd ever seen.

While the sky was a stunning sight to see, the ground was dull, dried up, brown dirt and scattered gray rocks. Some rocks were as big as golf balls, others boulders looked as big as houses. Perhaps it just looked boring because it was the follow up to the rollercoaster rainbow light and cosmos show they had just experienced. Like how your yard looks after a week's vacation in the tropics. It was a deeply boring and depressing landscape. Just brown and gray that went on as far as Tony could see, the only light coming from the nearness of the shimmering stars above them.

"It looks like a burnt cornfield. Maybe it sucked us to Iowa?" Tony said out loud.

"Good thing it has the same air as Earth does, Daddy!" Quint said, hopping down from a small boulder he had climbed. "Good thing we can breathe, huh, Daddy?"

Tony hadn't even thought of the air, or considered at all how it was they were breathing or alive in this place. There was apparently gravity, too. And of course leave it to his eight-year-old son to point all this out to him. Tony felt like an idiot. To make himself feel better, he remembered that Quint still put his shoes on the wrong feet at least sixty percent of the time. So there.

"Yeah, we're lucky, I guess. Wherever we are, it's enough like our planet that we can walk and talk and breathe." Tony said. Brody and Hooper had picked up small rocks and started digging in the dirt. Earth or a different planet, it didn't matter. If there's loose dirt, his kids were going to dig in it.

"Where are we Daddy? Is this the moon?" Quint asked while climbing another small boulder.

"Man, I don't know." Tony said, scanning the neutral landscape.

"Check your phone. Your GPS." Quint said.

"Oh yeah, great idea, Quint, you're a genius!" Tony's face lit up. He'd got him again. The eight-year-old was quicker than Tony was. Hopefully, it hadn't broken when they landed or when the kids used him to break their fall. He patted his jeans pocket and pulled the phone out. To make himself feel better, he remembered a time when they pulled into the garage at home. Quint didn't get out of the van right away because he said he 'didn't feel it stop'. So there. Some genius.

Tony thankfully didn't see any obvious cracks or dents in the screen. He touched the side of the phone and the screen lit up. His network displayed no bars or signals. He tried calling his wife, anyway. The call did not even finish dialing before it disconnected.

He tried to text her, not really knowing what to type. He thought for a moment. What to say to not freak her out, but show cause for alarm, and also not sound insane. He simply wrote: 'Hey are you there? Something crazy happened.' He hit send. The message progress just spun and spun. He got a 'failed to send' alert. He'd try it again in a minute. It may be still looking for the network. Also, he was wondering if this was really a text situation. Maybe he should keep trying to call, too. He wanted to let her know that something stranded them on what he assumed was another planet, not asking if she could check and see how much milk they had left.

He paced and wandered, opening the map apps he had. Nothing would load. The map would just be blank. After searching for where he had hidden it, he opened the compass app. The arrow of the digital compass just spun wildly in all directions, never stopping. Tony wasn't even sure what he would have done with the compass information, but it felt like something he should try.

No internet and no service. The mustache app worked just fine though. It put a funny mustache on a selfie you took. It worked just fine. Such innovation was humbling. This must be what the pilgrims felt like. Nothing but fear and mustache apps to keep them alive.

"Does it say where we are, Daddy?" Quint asked, standing next to him suddenly.

"No buddy, it's not working right. No signal, no internet." He pulled Quint close and gave him a reassuring squeeze for the both of them. They walked over to the spot where Brody and Hooper were digging, under the shade of a large grouping of boulders, and sat on the dusty ground.

Tony slid the backpack off and tugged at the back of his shirt where it got sweaty from wearing. Quint crawled over to the other kids and started digging with them. They were already filthy from the dirt. Space dirt. Great, Tony thought.

He thought it best to wait here for now. Maybe the air crack would return to this same spot and suck them back the other way, back home. Like some kind of bus. A magic rainbow space crack transit system. Hopefully.

SO THEY STAYED PUT. He pointed out a perimeter for the kids, and they could not go farther than a grouping of rocks he'd chosen nearby. They knew not to put anything in their mouth and be careful with what they touched. They laughed as they ran around. They climbed and hopped off the small boulders. A game of hide and seek broke out, but it didn't last long as there were so few places to hide. The real draw was the thin, sandy, brown dirt. In a short time, they had built a trench worthy of a Spartan army attack. They were having a great time. Tony sat and worried. He fiddled with his phone, begging it to reach out to his world.

He estimated it had been less than an hour before they told him they were hungry. His children had many talents, chief among them was their ability to eat snacks and to ask for more snacks. He, of course, had some in the backpack, but did not think they should eat yet. He didn't know how long they would be here. They may need those yellow fish crackers and fruit snacks to keep from starving until they can get back home, where they can just die of diabetes instead. He prepared himself for breaking the bad news, but as he explained, Brody gave him the frown. Brody could form the saddest frown, perfectly proportional, since he was a baby.

And with that, under the starry shade of the giant boulder, they sat and ate rationed yellow fish crackers, while Tony wondered which one would try to eat him first when the time came. Probably Hooper. They also shared one of the three juice boxes he found in the backpack. He was angry with himself, picturing the kid's water bottles he forgot back in the refrigerator. Everyone was mad they had to share, but Tony insisted. He took a few small sips to just be putting something in his body, but was happy to let the kids drink the juice, as it was disgusting. These poor kids nowadays had it bad. Modern juice boxes tasted like semi-sweet frog pond water.

Brody stood and walked over to Tony. "Can you zip me, Daddy?" he asked, pointing to the hoodie he was wearing.

"Sure, buddy." Tony zipped him up, and Brody took off to play. It suddenly dawned on him he didn't know if the weather would get colder or hotter the longer they stayed there. Maybe it would rain or a dust storm would come? Or maybe the rocks and stars turned to boiling acid? He just did not know. They were just more fears to add to the long list that Tony kept track of in his head. A master file and checklist of horrible things.

He kept checking the phone. Calls still wouldn't go out. Texts couldn't send. Maps wouldn't generate. Websites wouldn't load. The app that made your voice sound like a robot worked perfectly. Tony did what he was best at, he sat and he worried.

Three

They all heard it, but Brody, being sensitive to noise, was the first to react. Tony watched him stand straight up from playing with Quint and frantically turn his head, searching from where it was coming from.

"What's that sound?" Hooper asked.

Tony focused and heard what sounded like engines. Engines in the distance, but getting louder. Like vehicle engines. Big ones.

"Go stand by your brother and sister." Tony barked at Quint. Tony climbed up on a taller boulder. He balanced on top and scanned the distance, looking, his eyes desperately trying to locate the sound. Then he saw them. Far off, large objects kicking up a lot of dust and making a lot of noise. And they were moving faster towards them. Very fast.

Tony slid down the boulder back to the ground. He threw the backpack on and herded the kids together and knelt down with them.

"Okay. Okay. Okay." He frantically tried to think of what to do.

A hundred billion thoughts spread through Tony's head like a grease fire as the things inside of the tubs stepped out. Randomly, the thought that suddenly beat out all the terror and concern was that he should try not to stare.

LIKE THE VERY BLAND looking planet they lived on, the creatures that walked toward them were not the most glamorous looking. Tony was more than aware that genuine beauty had no definition or standard and taught his kids that, but these guys were pushing it.

There were six of them. Two to each of the floating bathtubs. They waddled out of the tubs on short, stubby legs and gathered in front of Tony and his kids. They were all squat and stocky, no taller than Brody. Their equally small but thick arms stuck out of horribly stained orange and red jumpsuits. They covered the jumpsuits from top to bottom with dozens of pockets and pouches, each one holding something inside that glowed through the fabric. Their skin was spotty and a pale oatmeal color, like they hadn't seen sunshine in… ever. They were thick with shiny, greasy sweat. They had heads shaped like ant hills. Thick at the neck but thinner as you get to the top.

Standing up, Tony tried not to judge, but the weirdest part was the hair. On each one's head, a different, but perfectly done hair style. Curled. Combed over. Spiked. Man-Bun. PonyTail. Pompadour. Thick, smooth, and soft dark hair. All perfectly, excellently styled. Not a single strand out of place. Tony guessed there were worse places in the universe for him and the kids to land than on a planet of amphibian hairspray models.

Stretched wide across their plump mound heads were huge white, toothy mouths. It was astounding how big their mouths were. Their mouths may have only looked so big because their eyes and noses were much smaller in comparison.

One of them spoke. Tony was always certain his children only spoke in one loud constant volume, but these guys made them sound like librarians. It sounded like a cross between a dog's bark, a clown's horn, and the microwave beep. So Tony, with no uncertainty, instantly concluded it was roughly the most annoying noise he'd ever heard. Another one joined it and also started talking. Then another. All of them began yapping.

When they spoke, they moved the tops of their heads in big, wildly arching movements. They opened their mouths very wide and very far back. It reminded Tony of how a puppet talks. Moving cartoonishly, as if they had a hand inside their head, only moving the top half. Also, moving the needle on the super-weird scale was that they had perfect teeth. Not fangs or monster teeth. But immaculately well taken care of human teeth. Movie star teeth. Magazine model teeth. They had these huge wide gaping puppet mouths filled with these amazing, dream come true teeth.

They were the weirdest looking creatures. Short toad aliens with perfect hair and teeth. This was truly the dumbest planet, Tony thought.

They didn't speak to Tony and the kids, but to each other, occasionally pointing in the family's direction. They didn't even really talk to each other as much as at each other... and all at the same time. The noise they made was roughly as loud as the engines on their flying tubs.

As they spoke, they suddenly started shoving their small chunky hands in the pockets and pouches of their ugly jumpsuits. They pulled out small, illuminated blocky machines, spoke into them, and put them right in front of their small beady eyes. Then they would return them to the pockets and pull different ones out of other pouches. They held them right up to their faces, yelled into them, and then put them back and got some more. This went on while they occasionally turned to each other and barked something. This was similar behavior to what Tony witnessed a table of teenagers doing with their phones at a pizza restaurant the other night.

The noise ceased when Hooper yelled at them again.

"BE QUIET!" Hooper shouted at them. "Too loud!" Her fist turned into a finger and pointed to her mouth. Tony did that occasionally to the kids. He wondered if she was making fun of him.

Again, the noises stopped, and all the creatures took a step back. They looked at Hooper and then at each other. The one with the comb over pulled a rectangular device out of its shoulder pocket and whisper-yelled a few phrases into it and then returned it. It then pointed at Tony and the kids and woofed at them. When it finished, it motioned toward its flying vehicle.

"What's it saying Daddy?" Quint asked.

Comb Over waved its arm wildly at Tony and back at its vehicle.

"I think it wants us to get inside its flying bathtub car." Tony said for the first time in his life.

"Yeah, but, Daddy, I know you and Mommy told us it doesn't matter how people look. But, I'm sorry Daddy, but these guys are weird looking." Quint asked. "Where do they want to take us?"

"I do not know." Tony said. He took a deep breath, trying to push oxygen to his brain. To process this. "Buddy, I don't know what to do. I don't think they'll let us stay here. But they also don't seem, I don't think, to want to hurt us. I don't know. Honestly? I think Hooper scares them."

His daughter was still scowling at them.

"Why's their hair like that?" Quint wondered.

"It's great, right? I'm kind of jealous. I can never get mine to look that nice." Tony admitted.

"Should we go Daddy? Do you think they can get us back home?"

"I don't know. I guess. Maybe. They've got things that fly. We don't have that on Earth. That means they have better technology than us. And clearly, they've invented hair care products." Tony rubbed his throbbing head. "Buddy, I wish your mom was here. So bad." Tony took another deep breath. She wasn't here, though. He was going to have to decide himself. "Okay. Well... pickles. Why not? Come on gang. Let's go for a ride." Tony wiped his sweaty forehead.

"Yeah, this will be so sick!" Quint excitedly shouted.

The little creature with the comb-over shouted noisily. It pointed at his vehicle again, very annoyed.

Tony bent down to poor Brody, who looked as uncomfortable as he'd ever seen him. Brody's hands were white from the pressure he was putting on his ears. Tony thought for a second, and then gently took Brody's sacred lion blanket from him. He folded it a few lengthways a few times until it was a thin strip. He pulled Brody's hands away from his ears. It was not very easy. Then he quickly tied the blanket around Brody's head like a headband and made sure it covered his ears. Tony placed his forehead against. Brody's breathing became less labored, and he seemed to relax a little.

"You okay?" Tony asked.

Brody, now looking like a nursery room commando, mumbled quietly for a few seconds.

"It was too loud, Daddy." He finally whispered.

"It was, buddy. It was too loud." Tony told him. He lifted his head off Brody's forehead. "But check it out. I made you some cool headphones. They're not like your ones at home, but we made these out of your lion blanket."

Brody reached up and rubbed his hands smoothly over the blanket around his head. He smiled.

"These are cool, Daddy." Brody said.

"Alright! Hey listen, we are all going to go for a ride with these guys. We're hoping they can help us get home."

"I want to go for a ride, too." Brody said. He was much calmer now.

"Okay let's go for a ride." Tony said, tightening the lion blanket headband a little more. He scooped Brody up in his arms. "Hooper, follow Quint. Go on, Quint." Tony told them. He couldn't believe he was doing this.

Quint walked to Comb-Over's vehicle. The small creature motioned for him to walk up the small step that popped out the side. Quint stepped up and over into the tub. The closer Hooper got to Comb-Over the farther it backed away. She seemed to freak it out. She did a cute brief wave at the small creature, which may have been genuinely friendly or super aggressive. Tony was never sure of Hooper. She got on the step.

"Help her up, Quint." Tony said as Quint reached over and held Hooper's hand as she climbed inside. Then Tony and Brody stepped over. There were no seats inside. Only a front console with switches and buttons and some sticks that looked probably steered the thing. Tony motioned for the kids to sit down. He sat criss-cross applesauce with Brody on his lap. He pulled the other two kids close to him and put his arms around them. The tub was entirely too small for all of them. He felt squished with the kids right on top of him.

Comb-Over seemed super annoyed by Tony's size as well. It loudly grumbled and grunted as it hopped over Tony's legs to get to the dashboard console. It shouted at its friends as they got into the other vehicles. It pulled a small box out of the dashboard and yelled in it for a while. The creature's hair softly bounced as the top of its head jerked up and down as it spoke. Its amazing teeth sparkled in the light of the stars and dashboard. Tony really wanted to ask what teeth whitener and shampoo it used.

Instead, Tony and the kids tumbled back as Comb-Over suddenly yanked the control sticks down. The tub sprang into the air with a jerk and then revved up like a race car. Brody shifted in his seat and grimaced, but didn't get as upset by the noise. Tony knew the headband blanket wasn't keeping the noise out, but it was comforting Brody.

The vehicle revved its engine a few more times, and then it lunged forward at an amazing speed.

"This is AWESOME!!!" Quint yelled.

A powerful wind from the speed rushed over Tony and the kids, blasting them in their faces and blowing their hair everywhere. The little alien creature's hair… didn't budge.

Four

Tony and his three kids were flying in a bathtub over a vast alien wasteland. He didn't recall this being in any of the parenting books and websites he had read. Now, he would trade all the pages upon pages of advice on how best to pick an umbrella stroller for just a single suggestion on how to deal with ugly alien planet ride sharing.

"This is so sick!!!" Quint shouted. He was having the time of his life. He was half hanging out of the vehicle, gawking and pointing at every rock formation or mountain range or canyon they dangerously zipped past as they flew through the sky. Tony always seemed to have to be pulling him back or shouting at him to sit down.

Tony was annoyed. He had to do this with him back home, too. He felt Quint was always trying to do things that were going to get him hurt, because he was never careful or paid close enough attention. Tony knew he was being too overprotective. It was super futile to ask an eight-year-old to settle down, but here he was, saying it over and over again. Kids are going to be kids and Tony had to remember that.

"Daddy, watch this!" Quint shouted and then turned his head and loudly spit out of the side of the flying vehicle.

Never mind, Tony thought, he's a monster and I'm right.

"Quint! Stop! Just sit!" Tony yelled.

Brody giggled hard at Quint's disgusting spit. Hooper and Brody both were both sitting still and looking around at the blur of land and sky around them. Brody, with his blanket still tied around his head and his eyes squinting to deal with the breeze whooshing in his face, was calm and content on Tony's lap.

Hooper seemed much more annoyed with the wind as she kept having to brush her hair out of her face. Tony told himself to put her hair in a ponytail when they got to where it was they were going. Although, that was easier said than done. Hooper screamed and threw a terrible tantrum whenever he tried to put her hair in a pony. Tony had serious concerns that his neighbors thought Hooper was being regularly murdered and that his daughter's pigtails would inadvertently start a true crime podcast. Again, it was his own fault. He just was not good at putting her hair up. His patient wife showed him how, over and over. He watched video tutorials on the internet, but he still had not gotten the hang of it. The poor girl left the house looking like the end of a party, instead of the beginning.

He probably could have asked the driver for hair care tips, since it weirdly had the most meticulously taken care of hair he'd ever seen, but he didn't want to distract it from flying the vehicle. Not that it had been paying the closest attention, anyway. It couldn't seem to go over thirty seconds without taking one of the little boxes out of a pocket and staring at or screaming into it. When it did, the vehicle would swerve and jerk around in the air. Apparently this was not a 'hands free' enforced planet.

It still terrified Tony. His mind raced as he tried to imagine where this thing and its frog salon squad were taking them. He didn't have to imagine for very long as the vehicle suddenly lurched, sputtered, and shifted gears. It slowed down and descended into a large canyon.

Tony stretched his head out to see what was coming below them. So far, all he could see was that it was gradually getting brighter. The dark brown and gray all around them was slowly getting more colorful. Very similar to the rainbow colors Tony and the kids had seen when they were being pulled here. The vehicle moved slower and slower as it descended. The driver pulled a box out of the dashboard and started barking into it.

The terrain shifted from rock to metal. Jaggedly reaching out from the light below, metal structures and buildings grasped onto the sides of the canyon. Long slender antenna poles and to what Tony looked like satellite dishes appeared everywhere. Hundreds and hundreds of them all pointed to the stars. Tony was certain they were going to hit them, just as Comb-Over maneuvered through a small gap between them.

Tony saw lights everywhere, coming from inside and around more buildings. The rock wall of the canyon disappeared, and the terrain transformed into a strictly urban one. Densely packed buildings surrounded them, all propping up the countless antennas and dishes. The buildings were shabby and seemed to rot away. There were holes and chunks missing from the sides and corners of the structures. The exposed metal that stuck out the holes was soggy looking or all rusted and stained.

The area was falling apart. Tony didn't understand how the buildings were not collapsing under the weight of the machinery on top of them. Some buildings appeared to be held together by actual wire. Giant thick wires wrapped around the high rises, with more lights hanging off of them. The city looked like wet cardboard with Christmas lights strung through it. A shanty town built by your local cable provider. Tony was having a harder and harder time convincing himself that these things could get him and his kids back to Earth.

The flying bathtub went further down. There were cords hanging from everywhere. Comb-Over weaved the vehicle in and out and through the strands and around the buildings. A spider's web of cable and wire all tangled and wrapped around each other. It was a mess.

"Oh cool, this planet is located underneath a dad's computer desk." Tony said.

"What Daddy?" Quint asked.

"Nothing. Listen, Quint. I don't know what's going to happen when we land, so stay close to me and keep quiet."

"Okay okay! Sheesh!"

"Don't sheesh me, this is serious! Listen to me and if I say run, move as fast as you can! Got it?" Tony said.

"Okay okay! Sheesh!" Quint grumbled.

"Sheesh is a bad word from now on. I just decided that right now. Sheesh and So Sick are the new 'S' words. Just stay with me and do what I say, okay?" Tony snapped back.

"Okay, Daddy." Quint pouted and suddenly looked anxious. Tony realized he was being too harsh.

"I'm sorry. I'm just really nervous about all this. It's going to be alright. We're all going to get through this. But we have to stick together, okay?" Tony said, pulling Quint close and hugging him.

"Can I say the OTHER 'S' word sometimes?" Quint asked.

"We get out of this, bud, and we will stand in the middle of the mall and yell bad words until they drag us away." Tony said and made Quint laugh.

"I'm going to say bad words too! Like butt and poop!" Brody giggled with his brother.

"You bet we are!" Tony said and hugged Brody.

"And pickles!" Hooper joined in, starting the family swear party early.

It was the first time Tony had smiled in hours.

THE TUB STOPPED SUDDENLY. Landing with a rough thud and then bouncing a few times. The driver pulled another device from a pocket in its pants leg and babbled loudly into it. Then it stepped around Tony's legs and hopped out of the flying tub. Tony leaned up and saw that the two other vehicles that had found them in the desert had landed as well. He watched as the driver waddled over to its group. They all started barking and talking, gesturing wildly and pointing at their tiny screens.

"Stay here gang, I'm going to see what it looks like." Tony said as he slid Brody off his lap onto the floor next to Hooper. He stood up and stepped out of the vehicle.

They were on some sort of landing pad, in a clearing of what Tony guessed was the middle of a city. The cables and wires from above were hanging everywhere, like vines in a jungle. Ancient and frayed cable dangled and sagged low right above Tony. The city planner must have been a carny because the ground was covered in drop cords like a summer fairground. Tony could hear a steady hum coming from the wires. Sparks would randomly burst out of a grouping or from one hanging above.

The constant whir of the cable and wires were competing against the general noise of the strange city.

Tony could see more of the loud flying bathtubs tooling around, both high in the air and over the cables on the ground. And there were hundreds more of his new little alien buddies.

All of them had different, but beautiful hairstyles and all of them were staring or yelling loudly into a brightly lit device in their hands. Tony would watch them walk into one another, not even notice, and then keep walking. They would shove the machine into one of their jumpsuit pockets and pull out another. They all wore similar jumpsuits, but some were cleaner or a different color. The creatures all had the same wide, toothy mouths that clasped open and shut as they blurted into their screens.

The air in the city smelled like a burning odor a computer let out when it's been running for too long. It also had a garbage stink, which made sense, as there appeared to be trash everywhere. Tony felt bad for thinking it was trash. They may consider it to be gold or something. But to Tony, it looked and smelled like trash.

The entire planet was a disaster. There was no way any of those cable TV home hunting shows would ever come here. He could hear the show's terrible couple now: 'this is quaint, but the city is loud and smelly and we hate the color of the wires and the yard is too big and we wish the flying bathtubs were a bit more modern... but those granite countertops are to die for.'

Tony snapped back to reality when he saw that all three of his kids had climbed out of the flying bathtub and were running around.

"Hey! Hey, what did I say?! I said to stay put!" Tony shouted, and jogged over to his kids.

"Waiting is so boring, Daddy." Quint said.

"Yeah, waiting is boring, Daddy." Brody agreed.

"I am so sorry this never-before-seen alien civilization

is a big snooze to you two but I do not know what is going on and…"

The screams of terror interrupted him. Tony spun around to see Hooper had playfully run over to the aliens who had brought them here, and that really freaked them out. They stumbled around, shouting and making panicked noises as she chased them around, laughing. The aliens were running in circles and into each other, all while nervously barking into their hand-held devices. Tony hurried over to Hooper, trying not to trip over any of the cables or trash on the ground, and picked her up.

"I'm chasing them, Daddy!" Hooper said, giggling.

"You are, I know." Tony mouthed 'I'm sorry' to the jumpy little aliens. "Man, you really scare them." He said.

"Ugh! Not scary, Daddy! I'm funny!" Hooper corrected.

She wanted to be put back on the ground, but Tony held on to her. From around the corner, a large group of the squat aliens were marching toward them. The one that was in the front leading the group stomped angrily with its fists clenched. It had a shiny symbol on the front of its jumpsuit, and its big soft hair was slicked straight back. Tony sighed. This one looked like a cop.

The group of aliens that had found Tony and the kids ran over to the approaching mob. The large mob stopped and Comb-Over started wildly pointing at Tony and the kids. Then they all started talking at the same time again, their mouths flopping up and down like the lids of a foot pedal trash can. It sounded like a hostile gaggle of geese, all honking simultaneously. Brody had his hands on the blanket over his ears again, and Tony didn't blame him.

Sheriff Slick-Back held its tiny hand up and the screeching conversation stopped. It pulled a box from the side pocket of its jumpsuit and shouted something into it.

It stared at the screen for a moment, then returned it to his pocket. It motioned for its large party to continue forward. Tony gathered his kids close again, not sure what was about to happen.

Tony knew it had to be a cop, or some kind of authority figure, because it pointed its stubby little finger before it spoke. If a broken tuba could have a scolding tone, that's how the alien officer spoke to Tony and his family. It seemed angry and accusatory.

After everything that had happened, Tony was falling into some kind of oddly comforting middle ground between horrific anxiety and the confidence of being totally unimpressed. Still scared, but he was also starting to not care anymore. He just wanted to get his kids back home. He didn't know if the thing would ever stop shout-honking at him so Tony just started talking.

"Hello." Tony said.

It ignored him. Wagging its pointed finger and still scold-barking at him.

Tony sighed again. Fine. The hard way. He nudged Hooper in his arms.

"Hey Hoop, ask them to be quiet." Tony said to Hooper. He pointed the little girl at the alien.

"HEY! STOP TALKING!" she shouted and smiled.

It stopped speaking.

"Thank you." Hooper said.

"Hello." Tony said again. "Hi there. My name is Tony, and this is my family." Tony motioned to Hooper in his arms and the boys standing next to him. "We don't belong here." Tony looked directly into the Sheriff Slick-Back's beady little eyes. Back on Earth he would never have stared down an authority figure so harshly, but if he was going to get everyone home, he was going to have to do whatever it took. "Maybe you can help us."

. . .

THE ALIEN BOSS listened to Tony explain what had happened. Tony told them they had gotten sucked here by the rainbow light and that they needed to get back home. Sheriff Slick-Back kept quiet until Tony finished. It seemed to think.

It quietly blurted an order into a box from its pocket. It casually moved its arm up and pointed down a busy and cable strewn street. It wanted them to go that way. Tony nodded.

They moved. Sheriff Slick-Back suddenly stopped them. It put its small hand as close as it could to Tony's face and held out its finger. Pointing at Tony, it issued a quiet series of grunts and barks. Tony got the feeling he had just been giving a warning.

They escorted Tony and his family to what must have been a pretty important building. Tony guessed this, because all the cables on the ground and all the wires in the air led to this building. It was a great big, rickety complex with ridiculously large antennas and satellite dishes on top of it. As they walked towards it, all the city's squat alien inhabitants barely looked up from their devices to notice them. Even when they did, Tony and his family registered barely more than a squint.

As they walked, Tony had to keep waving his arms at the kids to keep from either wandering off or to instruct them to walk faster. If you want to kill some time, ask an eight, six, and a four-year-old to walk in a straight line. Hopefully, you don't need to be anywhere, because you will be late. Luckily their hosts walked just as bad as the kids, between their tiny legs and screen time distractions. Tony wondered what they were looking at all the time.

"I'm hungry." Brody said to Tony. His blanket had

slipped from over his ears, down to his shoulders, so now he looked like he was wearing a cape. He seemed to have adjusted to the loud noises.

"I'm hungry too, bud. The next time we get to sit down, I'll give you more yellow fish." Tony leaned over and told Brody. Brody looked satisfied and then ran over to where Quint and Hooper were jumping onto a pile of cables and joined them. Hooper yelled at Brody to go away, and they bickered.

Hooper was hitting her wall. The lack of nap and the insane shift from routine was getting to her. Tony blamed himself for sticking too rigidly to a routine he created. He was clearly setting his kids up for meltdowns whenever it deviated, whether it was an extra long grocery trip or an unexpected alien abduction. He would have to work on creating a looser environment when they got back. If they got back.

It led them up a set of cord littered steps into the gigantic building. Inside, they stepped into a spacious lobby. It was just as trashed as outside. Cable and wires hung everywhere. Trash thrown all over the place. The occasional spark jumping from a coupling of wires.

The fluorescent lights were overwhelming, and the walls were the color of dirty eggshell. There was a large circular desk in the center of the room. The squat aliens sitting at the desk did not appear to be working, but all staring at the four different screens in their tiny paws.

Sheriff Slick-Back waved them over to a bank of elevators near the back of the room. Tony rounded the kids together and followed the little boss and its squad inside the open doors. Tony had to duck down a little to fit inside.

"I get to push the button!" Brody immediately shouted. Kids find elevator buttons to be shaped like delicious candy and just as irresistible. They will fight to the death for the right, no, privilege of pushing an elevator button.

"No Brody, it's MY turn!" Quint fired back and lunged crazily towards the strange shaped buttons, all bearing symbols which Tony had never seen before. Tony reached out and restrained them both to the back of the elevator.

"Boys! Stop! You don't even know where we're going! And you do not know what those buttons say!" Tony attempted logic.

Sheriff Slick-Back barked at its group and they all replied with a series of grumbles and hacking. Tony felt the disapproval coming off of them. Maybe if they ever got back Tony could write a paper for NASA about intergalactic embarrassment.

The boss alien reached towards a button at the top of the panel.

"No! It's my turn!" The little girl shouted. The aliens rushed to the back of the elevator to get away from her. She quietly stepped over to the button and reached up to push it. The doors closed as she smiled naughtily at the group. Hopefully, Hooper could have this planet under control by sundown.

The elevator didn't feel like it was moving up or down, but more like it was being pulled. It felt like being dragged backwards. It was a strange sensation. Tony's mind continued to race over to where they were being taken.

The only thing motivating Tony to keep putting one foot in front of another was that with all these signs of civilization, was the slim hope that they could send them home. The buildings were rickety, but they were still buildings. They had flying vehicles. They had tablet devices and electronic cables. They had elevators. They clearly all owned and operated blow dryers and hair straighteners. Surely, somewhere in this strange place, there was a machine that could send them home. Or something that he could use to contact his wife, at least.

The elevator stopped moving; the doors opened to a gaudily lit hallway with doors on both sides. Sheriff Slick-Back ushered them out and motioned for them to follow it. It was the longest, dullest hallway Tony had ever seen. They walked down the never ending hallway, passing hundreds of doors that all looked exactly alike. After a few minutes, they finally stopped, seemingly at random, and Sheriff Slick-back pressed a panel and the door slid open. Tony ducked down and he and the kids walked through the door.

It was not a jail cell. Tony was thankful for that. The room was still small, but at least it was not a jail cell. There was a small set of cushioned chairs and an empty desk. It had an enormous window that looked out at the remaining edges of the city. Just past the city skyline was the vast bland brown rocky desert they had landed in.

Sheriff Slick-Back loudly jabbered at Tony. Its body language suggested it was giving instructions. Tony stupidly nodded, like he knew what the heck it was saying. It then turned and shuffled out the door, his squat little crew following him. The door slid shut.

Tony could hear it shouting outside the door. Then they noisily marched back down the hallway. Tony pushed the panel on the wall, the same way the Sheriff had. The door slid open. There were still two space cranberries posted outside the door, but they didn't even turn around when the door opened. They weren't carrying weapons, and they didn't seem interested in anything that Tony or the kids were doing. They just stared at their devices. Tony and the kids could run out, and he doubted they would even notice. Tony made the door slide shut again.

Instead of making a break for it, Tony and the kids had

snacks. The kids insisted they were starving, so Tony cautiously brought out more of the fish crackers and juice boxes that were in the backpack. As they sat on the floor and snacked, the kids told Tony about everything they had seen and done, as if Tony had not been there all along.

"There was a spaceship!" Brody told Tony. "It was going so fast and I got to ride inside!"

"Me too, Brody! And did you see me climb all those ropes and wires, Daddy? Did you see those aliens? They love their phones right? Hooper was screaming at them and they were so scared, right Daddy?" Quint recounted. For them this was significantly better than Garbage Playground.

"The spaceship was loud!" Brody added.

"They have magnificent hair!" Hooper yawned.

They kept on talking. The room was the quietest place they'd been since leaving the desert. Hooper soon fell asleep on the small couch, bathed in fish cracker crumbs and a juice box squeezed dry. Tony took off his hoodie and covered her up with it. It was not long after that the two boys were also out like a light. Quint on the floor and Brody right next to him. Tony covered them both with Brody's lion blanket.

Tony himself yawned and sat on the floor against the wall. He faced the big window. The view was not much to look at. It was an ugly cardboard city and boring muted desert. But for more than a while, Tony stared at the infinite stars above it all.

It was the most beautiful view he'd ever looked at. But he couldn't help being terrified by it all. He wished his wife could see it, too. He wished she were here, too. She was probably going insane, wondering where they were. He missed her so much. His body slipped into a sleep, his brain fighting against it with anxiety. He was about to fall asleep when the door loudly slid open.

It didn't wake the kids at all, but it made Tony jump to his feet. A small group of aliens burst into the room. A few of them together started talk-yelling, and then one walked out into the hallway and came back in moments later. He was leading someone else into the room.

"I'm coming, I'm coming! Good gravy, hold your dang horses." The man being led into the room complained.

It was a person. Another human! He looked over at Tony.

"Oh, hey there! My name's Cliff."

Five

"Your name is Cliff?"

"Yeah. Well, mom calls me Heathcliff, but I told her not to because it's super lame, you know?" The man said.

The aliens shuffled out of the room and the door slid shut. Leaving Cliff alone with Tony and the sleeping kids. Tony was in shock.

"You're a human? Like from Earth?" Tony struggled to ask.

"Well, yeah, you goof! What do you think, I look like the bacon bits that just left? Man, what's with you?" Cliff said, walking to the window.

The first thing you noticed about him was his hair. His head seemed to be overtaken by a messy nest of hair. He looked like shrubbery with a face. The hair was long, high, and tangled. He had dark circles under the bright eyes that poked out from under the snarl of hair. His teeth were dirty, but they were all there. He had beard stubble on his cheeks and under his nose, but the greatest concentration of facial hair was directly on his chin. He had one of those chin-only beards. A big, bushy patch of hair that grew only out of his chin and under his lip. The gross island of hair was full of crumbs and had grown out to the size of a long john donut.

He was a little taller than Tony, but not by much. His faded, tattered t-shirt stretched tightly across a rather large, protruding belly. The shirt had words and a logo, but Tony could not make out what it was or said. The jeans he wore were no longer jeans, but cut and turned into shorts. Unlike the shirt, which was being pushed to its limits, the homemade shorts were still big and hung loose. He was barefoot, and Tony was more than taken aback by the terrible odor that radiated from his filthy feet.

He clearly had been here for a little while. Tony had so many questions, but before he could ask…

"So, you play bass?" Cliff turned from the window and asked.

"What?" Tony said, surprised and still in shock at seeing another human.

"Bass, you goof. Can you play the bass guitar?" Cliff said and then held his hands up and made motions like he was playing an invisible bass. He even made some 'bong bong' noises.

"Uh, no. I don't." Tony said, not understanding. His brain finally snapped into action. "Wait, how did you get here? How are you here?"

"Well, that stinks. We really need a bass player. I could do it, but I'm already tied up doing lead guitar and vocals. And I can only do so much, you know? Plus, now I'm handling the bulk of the rapping." Cliff continued.

"Are there more of you? Like more of us, more humans up here?" Tony said, struggling to understand what was happening.

"What? No, you complete idiot!" Cliff snapped. "I've finally got something going with some of the little nugget guys with the hair and teeth." Cliff waved the question away and rambled. "Yeah. It's taken a while, but J-Bone can finally keep a beat on the drum kit I made. Oh, and DJ Butterfingers can really slice on the homemade turntables we put together. Now, I can handle the vocals and guitar and rhymes, no sweat my pet, but we still are missing a bass player. And frankly, you can tell. We just don't have that hard and deep sound I'm looking for yet. Yeah. And we need just a little more slap bass. Not like that California sound though, that's way too much funk for me thank you very much."

Cliff babbled on at Tony like they were standing outside a bar instead of stranded on an alien planet. Clearly, he had lost his mind in the time he'd been here and wasn't processing seeing Tony. That had to be it.

"Anyway. It's not the first time I've had to do practically everything. I was in this one band, The Caffeine Fairies. Bunch of hot chicks. It got a bit too much riot girl for me, thank you very much. But they were all super hot and wore roller skates, and they needed a guitar player. We did some pretty good shows. And after each show, they always made me load the gear back into the van all by myself while they sat at the bar drinking with these dudes! I couldn't believe it! So I got out of there. I said, 'sorry ladies' and got out of there. They were so upset. I bet."

All small feelings of hopefulness Tony had were being buried by shovelfuls of idiocy and nonsense. He did not know what was happening or what Cliff was talking about.

"Oh well. Maybe we could do one of those two lead singer bands? You know where one sings and one raps? Although, I don't know which one I'd pick because I'm friggin' awesome at both, right?" Cliff said.

Two lead singers? Tony could feel a panic attack

coming on. The mere proximity to this person was causing a panic attack.

"Well, just so you understand, I handle all the lyric writing. I mean I'm no monster, you can throw out a line or two here and there but don't expect credit if I decide to use it! And we only do dark and moody material! I'm not trying to be some poppy radio number one hit like all those lame boy bands on the radio right now." Cliff explained.

"Boy bands? On the radio?" Tony scrunched his face up.

"Yeah, man, I'm not about all that safe, bubblegum baloney. My stuff is raw. Deep. Kind of more like: 'I'm MAD! /And everything is DARK! /And I don't need you, MOM! /Because I'm SO MAD!'" Cliff half sung and half screamed. And during the pauses in his scream-singing, he would make 'wshh wshh wshh,' noises and move his hands like he was a DJ scratching on a turntable. "You know, something like that. Actually, that's not bad, right? I should actually write that down. Can I borrow a pen?" Cliff said.

Tony couldn't believe what was happening. The only human in billion trillion zillion miles and he acted like he was in some terrible rap metal band from the early two…

"Oh, no." Tony said out loud. "Cliff? Cliff?" Tony had to get his attention. Cliff was silently repeating what he had just sung and aggressively pointing into the air. "Cliff? What year did you come here?" Tony asked. "Like, what year was it when you got taken?"

"Uh… let's see… 2002? Yeah. Why?"

"2002?" Tony gasped. "Cliff, do you know how long you've been here?" Tony pressed.

"I don't know. Couple months, probably. I know we missed our gig, which makes me mad, let me tell you. There were going to be like twenty people there!"

Tony was now panicking. This guy had been here for

almost twenty years. They took this guy in 2002 and didn't send him back. And he's super annoying, so you'd think they would want to dump him as soon as possible. This wasn't good. Cliff was currently air guitar-ing and making 'rocking out' faces. Tony watched him mime and suddenly felt bad for him.

"Cliff? Listen man, this might be a shock to hear, but… it's 2021." Tony said delicately.

Cliff was quiet for a moment. His mouth dropped. First, his face looked shocked, then slowly the drooping mouth formed into a gigantic smile.

"Heck… yeah… I can… BUY BEER NOW!"

Exhausted physically and mentally, Tony rubbed his face. "Cliff?"

"And I can go to twenty-one and over shows now! None of that all ages, baby crap anymore! Heck, frigging, yes!" Cliff said, pumping his fists.

"Cliff, no one is going to any shows because we're stuck here! We're on a different planet!" Tony was losing his patience. It was like talking to the kids when they were being as difficult as possible. So Tony just pulled out his 'Big Parenting' voice. "Cliff? I am HEARING your words and THANK YOU for explaining things to me." Tony sighed. "BUT, I'm still having some TROUBLE. So can you ANSWER some QUESTIONS I have, so I can better UNDERSTAND?" Tony said slowly and theatrically. He made eye contact with Cliff. This was a pretty effective way to talk to the kids. Hopefully, it worked on Cliffs too.

"Oh. Okay. Fire away." Cliff smiled. He leaned against the window.

"Okay." Tony paused, trying to organize his thoughts and questions. Still thinking in 'Big Parenting' mode, he figured Cliff might respond best to chronological questions. "Cliff? Can you tell me how you got here?"

"Oh, sure. Well, I remember I had just gotten off work. It was pretty late. We had finally closed the kitchen, after the rest of the line got off their lazy behinds and did their closing routines." Cliff said.

"The line? Like a kitchen line? Like you worked in the kitchen of a restaurant?" Tony asked.

"Oh yeah, Tom Tom's Nom Nom's!" Cliff answered. Tony had heard of it. It was a chain of restaurants that used to be scattered all over the Midwest. One of those places with more appetizers than entrees and all kinds of stupid junk nailed to the wall. Tony was pretty sure they'd all closed years ago. Tony finally recognized the restaurant's name and logo as the faded and stretched one on Cliff's shirt.

"Okay, so you worked on the kitchen line as a fry cook or something?" Tony asked.

It was like a switch went off and Cliff snapped.

"Not fry side! Fry side sucks! I worked broiled, man! Broil side for life! Those punks on the fry side are nothing compared to me and my broil side brothers! Bunch of no talent burners! Broil side! We're the 'fry side killas'!"

"Okay! Okay! Sorry. Broil side. Got it." Tony said, not realizing the severity of chain restaurant kitchen turf wars.

"So anyway, those losers finally got their act together, and we closed up. I was waiting outside for my ride. I don't drive since my license got taken away from you know, all the speeding tickets. So yeah, I was waiting to get picked up by my friend Good Buddy. He plays drums in my band and we were going to go to practice. Maybe you've heard of us? Nemesis Control?"

Tony thought that's the worst name he'd ever heard. Rykden was a better name than Nemesis Control. Tony rolled his eyes. "No, sorry Cliff. Where was all this at? Where did you live?"

"Oh, just a real heck-hole town named Shanks in central Illinois. It's about two-and-a-half hours south of Chicago."

People from Illinois always told you how far from Chicago they were. Always. It was the law.

"Okay, so it's late and you're in Shanks, Illinois, waiting to get picked up by your friend? And then what?" Tony said, trying to keep Cliff on track. It didn't work.

"They were going to be a Christian metal band before they asked me to be in the band. They were called Praiser Beams. But then I came in and it was like, whoa! You know? Because, my vocals and my lyrics are pretty out there, you know? Like, whoa, what he'd say?" Cliff went off the rails again.

"Cliff, Cliff stop man. Get back to the night you got taken!" Tony rubbed his face in frustration some more.

"Oh yeah. So, we were going to practice because we had a gig on Saturday. We were going to play at Gina's graduation party, but then Gina didn't graduate."

"Cliff! Focus!" Tony shouted. He noticed his kids were finally stirring awake.

"Cool out, man. I'm getting to it!" Cliff held his hands up reassuringly. "So I'm standing outside work with my guitar and mini amp waiting for Good Buddy to come get me. When suddenly, there's this loud snap. And suddenly, there's this hole in the air in front of me. Then all this disco light shooting out of it, suddenly."

"So, would you say it happened suddenly?" Tony said without realizing.

"Oh yeah, what are you, some kind of joke guy? Yeah, real funny. Uh, sorry to break it to you but there are no open mic nights on this planet. I mean, I see the dummy but where's the ventriloquist?" Cliff snapped back.

"Okay, okay, sorry. We saw the rainbow lights, too. So did it just pull you here? Like it did for us?"

"Basically, I guess. I flew through outer space for a while. It gave me some real cool ideas for a music video. Then, it dumped me out and the little walking tater tots found me." Cliff said.

"And you've been here the whole time? This place is so weird. Can you understand the little hair things? All they seem to do is bark and make loud grunts." Tony asked.

"Not at first. But after a while you get the gist." Cliff said.

Tony suddenly got very sad. He leaned against the wall. Quint and Brody had sat up. Both were making scrunched up confused faces at the sight and smell of the strange man. "Cliff, have you ever tried to get back home?" Tony finally just asked.

"No."

Tony slid down the wall and sat down on the floor. He was exhausted. Physically, mentally, emotionally drained. "No? Never? You've never asked or even tried to get them to send you back to Earth?" His voice cracked.

"No. Why? Earth is full of jerks. And you know, so is this place, but not as bad as back home. The only thing that stinks is that their music doesn't rock at all. But I have my guitar and amp. And we've made drums and the turntables. So some of the hair macaroni dudes and I are going to dominate the scene. Oh yeah! Get ready! ARE YOU READY???!!!" Cliff said and then made turntable scratches, quick grunts, and guitar noises.

Quint, Brody, and the just awake Hooper cracked up at the ridiculous man. The weight of everything crushed Tony. If this guy never gets sent home, what hope did they have? He lowered his head and put his hands behind his neck.

Cliff stopped air performing for a moment. "And the food is awful. Tastes kind of like beef jerky and taffy candy, you know? Luckily it got better when the little sponge guys stole the Takeout Machine."

"What's a Takeout Machine?" Quint stood up and asked.

"You know. It's this thing that can go grab food from anywhere in the universe. I've finally been able to get pizza rolls and burgers and Chinese food." Cliff explained. "It doesn't always work though, because the hair guys don't always know how to work it right. But when it does work, I get to stuff my face, you know?"

"It can grab anything from anywhere?" Tony raised his head. His brain was trying to figure out what that meant. His heart started racing. "Anything from anywhere? Wait, why don't they know how to work it?"

"Well duh. Because they stole it."

"Stole it from where?" Tony stood.

"Well duh. From the other guys."

Suddenly, an alarm went off. The lights in the room flashed red.

Six

The lights in the room were flashing red, and an alert siren was wailing. Tony quickly got the kids together and slung the backpack over his shoulders. As an automatic reflex, Tony carefully redid Brody's blanket across his forehead and over his ears. The poor kid couldn't catch a break on this annoying loud planet. Tony gathered Hooper and Brody close to his legs. Quint was at the window next to Cliff.

"Daddy, the funny hair guys are running all around down there! The lights are flashing everywhere." Quint said, staring out the window. A few flying bathtubs flew right outside the window at a wild speed. "Whoa! Did you see that?" Quint yelled.

"Yeah buddy, step back, okay? Come over to me." Tony said nervously. "Cliff! What the heck is happening?"

"Looks like a rave to me! Did you bring some glow sticks?" Cliff said while doing a little raver dance and making bass noises with his mouth. He stopped and laughed. "Just kidding. I hate techno. More like tech-NO, right?"

"Cliff! What is happening?!" Tony yelled.

Just then the door quickly slid open and Sheriff Slick-Back and a small group of its gel and mousse posse ran into the room. Sheriff gestured at Cliff and Tony and began barking and honking frantically.

"Cliff, what's it saying?" Tony asked.

"It's talking too fast, I can't really tell. Something about the other guys know about you. They're coming here now. I think we're supposed to follow him." Cliff smoothed his chin beard and said.

Sheriff motioned with its small arms to follow and ran out of the room. Some of its squad left with him, and a few others stayed behind, waiting for Tony, Cliff, and the kids. It seemed Tony wasn't being given a choice and they would have to leave the safety of the room and go out into whatever this was. Tony knelt down beside the kids. Cliff knelt down with them.

"Okay, gang, we're going on the move again. It looks like we have to be fast so I want you to keep up and stay together okay." Tony said quickly to everyone. He had an idea. He switched into 'Big Parenting,' mode. "Quint, I need you to be Operations Leader and keep everyone together, okay? Will you help me keep Brody with us? Don't touch or grab or pull him, but if he wanders or looks down too much, will you try to motivate him to keep going? You know how he gets distracted, right? Can you stay with him and keep him with us? Make it kind of like a race, okay?"

"I'll be Operations Leader!" Quint said and did a weird salute.

"Brody? Brody?" Tony moved his head around until he caught Brody's eyes. "Hey buddy, can you run with Quint? Hooper is going to be my running partner. Can you be Quint's running partner?"

"I am way faster than Quint, Daddy." Brody smiled. "He can be my partner, instead."

"Well then, tough guy. Can you show me?" Tony said, smiling back. "Stay with Quint, okay?" Tony stood up.

"And what should I do?" Cliff said.

"Just, uh, stay with us. Okay, Cliff?" Tony said and stood back up. Great. Another kid to take care of. And by far the worst smelling one. "Ready?" Tony called back, and they all ran out of the room with the squat, hair-sprayed, pear-shaped escorts following them.

Tony spotted the Sheriff and its group ahead of them. Their stubby legs hadn't made it too far. Tony and the kids quickly caught up. The hallway crowded with more of the alien toads with their perfect hair, running past them, shouting and barking at one another. The boys were keeping up just fine and were both giggling hysterically as they had to dodge past the little hair styled creatures running around them. Just another game, Tony thought. The Sheriff turned and led them to the left, down a new brightly lit corridor. Cables hung from the ceiling and poked out of the walls.

Tony looked back and found Cliff. Tony and Hooper slowed down to Cliff's pace. Cliff was clearly struggling.

"Cliff, what the heck is happening? What are these 'other guys'? It looks like the little gel models are freaking out!" Tony yelled over to Cliff.

"Yeah, they always do this. I don't know why." Cliff said in between huffs and puffs of breath. "The little dweebs always overreact when the other ones show up. I don't know why. The other ones are pushovers. Don't worry, they don't even fight back." Cliff said, wheezing, as the group took a right turn down a new hallway.

"Fight? There's going to be a fight?" Tony asked, imagining many terrible things coming.

"Maybe. Sometimes. Not really. Who knows?"

"Cliff, you are a wealth of knowledge and reassurance let me tell you." Tony said.

"Thanks, man!" Cliff replied.

Sheriff Slick-Back and the blow dryer brigade turned another corner and headed down yet another long cable strewn hallway. More of the little aliens were coming out of doors and running and stumbling by the group, staring at their devices and shouting. Lights in the hall were still blinking red and the warning siren continued to wail annoyingly.

The boys were still behind Tony and Hooper. They were laughing and giggling. It seems they were playing some kind of tag game, catching up to each other and touching one another's arms and then cracking up. Tony was grateful they were keeping up. Usually the family didn't get anywhere quickly as Quint gets distracted and Brody could go into his slow motion mode and just zone out. Hooper seemed annoyed at all the running. Tony could tell she was getting tired. He bent over and picked her up. She jostled in his arms as he ran.

Sheriff Slick-Back turned and shouted something at Tony and Cliff and then pointed ahead. Tony saw they were running into a brightly lit area. They ran through a tall arched doorway into what looked like a huge airplane hangar. There were two giant doors opened wide to the outside. The vast, starry sky lit the hangar up like it was daylight back on Earth. In the back of the room, there was a little command center with a group of computers and machines and little jellybean aliens furiously working the controls. Up towards the front, near the open doors, were rows and rows of flying bathtub vehicles, all being loaded up and then taking off.

The little frog-like aliens with their perfect hair and

teeth were jumping into the vehicles and blasting off, rocketing out and into the sky with little regard for where they were going and if they were going to run into one another. It was chaotic and seemed to have no organization. Tony was sure they would destroy each other before they ever had the chance to face whatever was coming.

He noticed all the little aliens looked shiner than they used to. They all glistened in the bright light of the stars outside. He looked closer and saw it was what they wore that was reflecting the light. They had new outfits on. Tony watched, and before the aliens jumped into the flying bathtubs, they would run to the side of the hangar and grab a square screen that was hanging on the wall. Tony first thought it was just a new device for them to stare at and talk into, like all the other ones they carried. Then Tony saw an alien, with a beautiful pompadour, take the square screen and drop it on the ground and step on top of it.

Almost immediately, a shiny metallic silver spilled up out of the screen and wrapped itself around the squat legs and enormous belly of the creatures. The silver then snaked up their fat torsos and up and down their stubby arms. Eventually it covered over their small round heads. Then, like a wiper blade wiping rain off of a windshield, their faces appeared underneath the newly formed metallic helmet. They were wearing suits of armor. Then some would jump into a flying vehicle and others would run back down the corridor.

"Not going to be a fight, huh Cliff? Look! They're wearing battle suits!" Tony yelled over at Cliff, who almost fell over while catching his breath from running.

"What? Oh yeah. I'm telling you, don't worry about them. They always overreact like this. The other guys are so stuck up they won't even do anything." Cliff took big gulps of air.

"Really? Because the way these things are scrambling, you'd swear there's some kind of invasion about to happen!" Tony said, setting Hooper down next to him so he could give his aching arms a break.

"Daddy, I want one of those." Quint said, literally hypnotized by watching the little aliens putting their battle armor on. "Daddy, can I wear one?" He pleaded.

"What? No way, Quint. Just stay by me, Operations Leader."

"But Daddy it will fit, I know it will!" Quint whined.

"It's not the fit I'm worried about! Buddy, I don't know what those suits are or what they do!" Tony shouted and waved Quint closer to keep him from wandering.

"Oh, come on, let the little dude wear one. Nothing's going to happen. The Snobs won't do anything." Cliff reassured Tony.

"Snobs?" Tony said, confused. It was getting more chaotic all around them. Sheriff Slick-Back was running from station to station, getting barked at by its fellow beauty school soldiers and looking at screens.

"Yeah, they think they're so big. So much better than the rest of everyone else. And yeah, they're smart. But they won't even look at us or talk to us or do anything with us. The little chicken nuggets and them used to live together, you know? Then the snobs gave the little guys the boot and now they just stay over on their side with all the cool things they make. Like, they made the Takeout Machine, but they wouldn't even share it. So we took it!" Cliff explained.

"Well, maybe they're mad that you stole it and are coming to take it back." Tony said. Cliff seemed to know more than he was letting on. But Tony didn't think he was doing it maliciously. Tony just thought Cliff was an idiot. Tony looked over at an overwhelmed Brody. All the commotion in the hangar was a lot for him to handle.

Tony knelt down, rubbed his back, and reassured him everything was alright.

"No, that can't be right." Cliff said. "They really didn't seem to care that we were using it for food and snacks and stuff. They're probably just mad that we used it to bring you here."

"What?!" Tony stood up like a shot and stared at Cliff. "What did you say? You used it to bring us here?!"

"Well yeah, I needed a bass player."

Tony grabbed Cliff by the shirt and was about to tear him apart when Sheriff Slick-Back suddenly appeared next to him in its full shiny silver battle gear. The Sheriff's dumb little face stuck out of the tiny helmet opening and it bark-shouted something at Tony and pointed to the open doors.

"He says they're outside." Cliff slapped Tony's hands away. He turned towards the open hangar doors.

SHERIFF SLICK-BACK LED TONY, Cliff, and the kids slowly towards the front of the hangar. The chaos and commotion settled down in the base when word had spread that the others were outside. Ships were still taking off, and the aliens were still scurrying around, but they seemed to be much more focused and cautious. The Sheriff's battle armor made a loud clang with every step it took towards the outside.

A visibly anxious Tony was holding Brody and Hooper's hands. Hooper would squirm her hand out of his and he'd have to grab it again. Quint was no fool. He walked behind Tony. Cliff was just following along with the same goofy grin on his face.

They stepped out of the huge hangar doors, out into the open air of the planet. The bright stars shimmered over everything and lit up the sky. As they walked further out, Tony saw they built the hangar doors into some kind of very tall border wall that surrounded the city. The tip tops of the shanty city poked out from behind it. The ends of the wall ran right into the canyon that they built the city into.

The hangar had let them out into a wide open area and there the desert wasteland began again. The aliens had set up their defenses in the open space. The tiny Sheriff led the group down the center of rows and rows of its fellow fashionable alien residents. They were all suited up in their shiny silver battle armor and all standing in straight lines of military formation. There were over two dozen very long rows of them. For the first time, Tony saw the size of their population. There were over a thousand of them all suited up. Tony couldn't imagine the hairspray bills.

As they walked out farther, they heard the rumble and blast of engine noise coming from above them. Tony looked up and saw the same formation on the ground being mirrored in the air. The flying bathtub vehicles had flown into a series of long rows. They all hovered in place, pointed towards the desert. Tony found it unnerving to see such a previously chaotic civilization suddenly go quiet with patience and focus.

They finally reached the front of the formation. The Sheriff stopped. Tony knelt down to the kids' height.

"So where are they, Daddy?" Quint asked.

"I don't see them. I don't see anything at all." Tony said.

"They're coming. They're so slow." Cliff said, unimpressed.

Tony's eyes kept scanning the vast desert in front of them. There really was nothing out there.

"Daddy. This is boring." Hooper said.

Tony rolled his eyes. "Sorry the monsters are taking so long, Hoop."

"Daddy, I see something!" Quint shouted and pointed off into the distance.

"Yeah Daddy look!" Brody repeated.

Tony stood up and saw them, too. Slowly, coming from behind a series of large rocks, was a group of four figures.

Sheriff Slick-Back barked some orders into a box on the gauntlet of its armor. Tony could hear the suited up aliens behind him shuffle and steady themselves. The flying vehicles high above revved their engines up mightily.

The four figures were approaching. They walked slowly, almost deliberately. Moving like they had to think about each step before they took it. As they got closer, they were much taller than the squat, toady aliens with the perfect hair and teeth. It was hard to tell with the distance, but they looked to be even taller than Tony and Cliff. They slowly got closer and closer. Tony could feel the tension coming from the army behind him.

As the four figures approached, Tony huddled the kids together. He could see the figures more clearly now. Their heads were completely bald, exposing a soft, light pink skin. Their skin was very smooth and delicate looking. They wore very large robes on top of visibly skinny bodies. The robes were big enough to be long and flowing, but wide belts cinched tightly around their waists.

In the center of the belt was a golden circle the size of a paper plate, with a series of smaller patterned circles inside of it. The robes looked heavy. Each figure wore a different color, but they were all in the cool color scheme. Some were blue and silver, and some were green and purple. They each walked with their arms crossed softly on top of another. Like the way you hold your body when your stomach hurts.

They looked at the ground as they walked. When they did briefly glance upward, their faces were very calm and passive. Their large round eyes were wide and darted around as they looked at the army. Their body language expressed one of caution and curiosity rather than one of aggression. All was silent as they approached closer and closer.

"These gentle looking things need all this firepower?" Tony asked Cliff. "Look at them. They look so nervous. You say everyone used to live together?"

"I mean, I guess. That's what they told me once." Cliff replied, biting into a gross fingernail. "They said they got kicked out for being too loud. Or something. I don't know. They just said that they didn't want to have to keep changing how they liked to live for those out there."

Sheriff Slick-Back broke the quiet tension by suddenly yelling at the four beings. The sudden noise made Tony and the kids jump. The others in the desert stopped walking and looked at one another. The Sheriff was pointing with one hand and the other was making a fist and shaking it at them. The tall creatures kept glancing up at the intimidating army and then back at each other. They were clearly getting more and more uncomfortable.

"Cliff, what is it saying to them?" Tony asked a very bored-looking Cliff.

"Oh, it's yelling at them."

"I can see that, Cliff. But what is it yelling?!" Tony said, ready to murder Cliff.

"Oh, you know. Usual stuff. To go away and that they can't come here and that they're going to attack them if they don't get out of here. The usual stuff. Chill out, man." Cliff said.

Tony shook his head. This didn't seem right. Something about these things didn't seem dangerous or worthy of this massive military overreaction. They gave Tony a very peaceful vibe. He didn't even really understand why he felt that. There was something about the cautious way they moved and the way they kept their heads down. They didn't make eye contact or noise. They just didn't seem to pose any kind of threat.

Tony was pretty good at reading body language. Maybe it was dumb to trust these four things, but Tony had a child who is autistic. And like a lot of parents of ASD children, Tony and his wife had learned to read all kinds of body language. Tony saw these things out in the desert and he saw them not wanting to hurt anyone. They reminded him of when Brody just wanted to keep more to himself, rather than being outwardly expressive or participating.

The four beings took steps backwards. The Sheriff's loud screaming and gesturing had done its job, and they were going to leave. Tony felt sorry for the creatures. This wasn't a show of force for defense. It was bullying. They were being bullied. Those creatures' simple curiosity was being rewarded with only fear and unkindness.

"Where are they going, Daddy?" Quint asked.

"I don't know, Quint, but I think they're scared." Tony said.

The Sheriff turned and put its armored wrist to its mouth and shouted. Its voice suddenly echoed over the entire army, above and on the ground. A microphone or radio was amplifying the shouting among the population. As it barked orders, the little stubby aliens in their robot armor suits suddenly shifted and raised their arms at the four beings standing in the desert. From out of their forearms, the liquid armor formed a rectangle the size of their cell phone, and it started glowing red. The flying bathtubs in the air revved their engines as they all drifted downwards at the four.

"Cliff? Cliff? What's happening? What's it saying to them?" Tony panicked. He scooped Hooper into one arm and Brody into another, grunted with the additional weight and stood up.

"He's going to fire on them." Cliff said, looking all around.

"What? No! Why? They haven't done anything! They're just standing there!" Tony shouted as he took steps backwards away from Cliff and The Sheriff. Quint followed right next to Tony, matching his steps.

"Daddy, I know. Stay with you. Go fast." Quint said, before Tony could.

"Yeah, but they hate them real bad." Cliff answered.

And then they started firing.

Seven

Tony appreciated that the army of alien amphibian hairdressers didn't all fire at once. He was thankful for their disorganization in this situation. Randomly and chaotically, groups of the armored aliens fired large laser blasts from the rectangle weapons that had grown out of their forearms. The blasters made a large mechanical 'whoosh' noise as they fired.

As soon as Tony heard the first blast let loose, he turned and took off back towards the hangar. He ran holding Brody in one arm and Hooper in the other. Quint dutifully followed as fast as he could. It was like running a marathon while holding two giant bags of uncooperative and smelly cement and a third following right behind you.

"Hurry Daddy, hurry!!" Quint shouted over the sounds of intensifying laser blasts, his hands moving over his ears.

"I'm trying, buddy, I'm trying!" Tony yelled back, desperately out of breath and his arms aching from the weight of his other two children. Brody had his face buried in Tony's shoulder and his blanket over his head, terrified of the noise and commotion. Hooper was gripping Tony's other side and scowling at the scene behind them as they ran.

They had only been running a few seconds since the firing began, the hangar still far away. Suddenly, a bright streak of light flashed over their heads and exploded into the ground about in front of them. The squat aliens closest to the explosion went flying up into the air. Tony and Quint skidded and fell to the ground. Tony landed on his back, his backpack cushioning his fall only slightly, and then quickly rolled over onto Quint and moved the other two kids underneath him.

Smothering his crying kids to the ground with his body, Tony looked up just enough to see clouds of dirt and the catapulted aliens falling back to the ground with a thud. The armor on the dumb little aliens appeared to protect them from the blast and the fall, as they just got back up and ran away.

More explosions started going off everywhere. Rapidly and randomly, streaks of light crashed violently into the dirt and rocky ground. It blasted groups of the armored aliens into the air, screaming. Then they landed with a dusty thud and went running in terror.

Tony saw a few of the flying bathtubs also crash into the ground. The tub's alien passengers leapt out of them, right before it exploded in a fiery crash of metal and dirt.

Tony assumed the four creatures from the desert had enough of the bullying and somehow started firing back on the squat little aliens. He turned back to the front of the formation. The four tall creatures weren't firing back. They had their hands over their faces in recoil and fear.

Tony saw the laser blast that the squat aliens were firing was simply bouncing off of the tall creatures and then ricocheting back. The lasers weren't recoiling off of their bodies. There was a bubble that was around each of the tall creatures. The shields were invisible, but when the protective bubbles jiggled with a laser blast, you could see their shape. The blasts would then recoil backward and either hit the ground and send a cluster of the little grunts flying or it would zing upwards at the flying bathtubs and send them crashing to the ground.

"Stop firing, you idiots! You're doing this to yourselves!" Tony shouted, but knew that they could never hear them or even do what he asked. He looked forward again, toward the hangar. It was still far away, but he knew they couldn't stay out here any longer. He arched his back until he was on his knees, but still hovered over the kids.

"Okay, we're going to move again." He said as he gathered Brody and Hooper in his arms again and turned towards Quint. "You ready, bud? We can do this. Just need to get into that building up there. Don't wait for me. You just run as fast as you can, got it?"

"Okay, Daddy." Quint said, wiping tears from his eyes. Then, without another word, he sprinted off.

Tony struggled to his feet, holding the heavy kids, took a deep breath, and then ran. He slowed his pace down, which wasn't difficult with two kids in his arms. He stayed just a foot or two behind Quint to watch him. Blasts and crashes were still going off, but luckily none had come near them again. But with each explosion the family's bodies would clench up and they'd briefly slow down, waiting for the next one to be right on top of them.

Tony watched Quint jump over newly made holes in the ground and around burning pieces of vehicle wreckage. Tony followed his path, his chest burning and arms weakening. Fleeing armored aliens running in the same direction shoved Quint down, but he sprang up and kept going. They were almost back into the hangar. Quint turned and checked on Tony. His eyes grew wide.

"Look out, Daddy!" Quint shouted and then dived to the ground.

Tony dropped to his knees and bent over, doing his best to keep from dumping the two kids on the ground. Tony heard a loud screeching over their bodies and glanced up just in time to see one of the flying vehicles on fire, spiraling over them, and heading straight into the hangar. Once inside, it crashed straight into a cluster of parked vehicles and machines. One explosion followed another and another. The noise and heat were huge and overwhelming. The little aliens got tossed all over the place. They bounced off the ground and off the walls and off of each other. Then, as if nothing happened, they would leap up to their stubby little legs and take off running.

Tony put the two kids down on the ground next to him, no longer able to hold them in his aching arms. Quint scooted backwards to his father as more alien soldiers ran around them in retreat.

"Pickles! This is not sick, Daddy." Quint said, spitting some dirt out of his mouth.

"You okay?" Tony asked, brushing dirt off of Quint's face and hair.

"Yeah, I'm fine. These guys are kind of stupid. Where do we go now?" Quint asked, ducking as he heard another explosion.

"Kind of stupid." Hooper said, scowling.

Tony saw the hangar was a burning wreck and no longer safe to hide out in. He looked around to see where they could go.

"Daddy, let's go where they go!" Brody yelled out, pushing up his now extra filthy blanket bandanna from over his eyes and ears to his forehead.

Tony looked at him and saw that he was talking about the dozens of little armored aliens running just off to the side of the burning hangar. Surely they were taking cover somewhere safe.

"Good job looking, Brody!" Tony found Brody's eyes. "Thank you, buddy."

Tony rose and picked up Hooper. She squirmed and shouted.

"Put me down Daddy! No more holding me! I will do it."

"Okay, you run with Daddy and the boys, but we hold hands, got it?" Tony said to her. He set her back on the ground.

"Okay, Daddy! Fine!" Hooper yelled, irritated. "Kind of stupid."

Hunched over and holding the two little kids' hands, he followed Quint. The family speedily jogged around wreckage and flame and into the mob of running aliens. The aliens were all hollering like normal, but this time with fear. Tony saw they were all herding themselves through an enormous hole in the wall that separated the city and the desert.

Tony turned around and saw that far ahead there was still a dedicated group of the dumb little soldiers shooting at the four beings in the desert. The armored army was still firing blasts that bounced right off the force field bubbles and skidded right back at them. The sound of explosions and blasting lasers rang through the air. There were a few flying bathtubs that somehow had maneuvered behind the four creatures and were firing at them from behind.

The retreating crowd slowed as they bottlenecked through the smoking opening in the wall.

Tony guided his kids through the hole and over the piles of debris on the other side. It looked like they were on the streets of the cable wrapped shanty city. Tony sighed. It didn't look any safer here.

The little aliens with the perfect hair and teeth, some still in their armor and others back in their dirty jumpsuits, were running all over the place. The aliens were screaming at each other and screaming into their devices. Some were scuffling with one another. They were throwing boxes and machines out of the building's windows onto the ground. There were some fires. Random flying bathtubs skidded wildly through the low airspace, bumping into one another and into the close clusters of buildings.

"Don't worry kids, we'll be safe in this burning macaroni and cheese box." Tony said out loud. They shoved themselves against a building near the opening in the wall. Hundreds of the tubby little armored aliens passed by them, streaming in through the hole.

"Gross. No macaroni." Hooper said.

Tony looked down at his kids, caked in dirt and dust and grime. He bent down and used his also filthy sweat-shirt sleeve to get it off their faces and out of their eyes, at least.

"We've got to go hide somewhere. And figure out how to get out of here. Maybe try to get a hold of mommy. Maybe she can help us." Tony said as he wiped their faces.

"What about that pickup food machine that weird smelly guy was talking about? Can that get us home?" Quint asked as pushed Tony's hand away from his face.

"That's what I was thinking too, bud. Cliff said they used it to bring us here, so I bet it can get us home. You're good at this stuff, buddy." Tony said, smiling at him. He stood up and looked at the maze of shoddy buildings all around them. "Now where do you think it is?"

"There you jerks are!"

Tony spun around just as Cliff was squeezing his tall

frame through the hole in the wall. Also covered in dirt, he had a cut on his forehead that was bleeding.

"Where'd you guys go? Man, that got nuts, didn't it?" Cliff said as he pushed through the crowd over to Tony and the kids.

"Cliff, what happened out there? Why'd that little cop shoot at them? They weren't doing anything! They were just standing there!" Tony yelled.

"Yeah, he's in a real mood today, isn't he?" Cliff said, leaning against the wall. "He usually just puts on a big show and yells and they take off. Maybe today he was showing off because you're here. I don't know. That was wild, right? It reminds me of this wicked pit I was in at this show once. There was this guy with a green mohawk who…"

Tony grabbed him by the shirt. "Cliff shut up! Shut up! That was no mosh pit, it was a war zone, you moron! Now listen to me! Where is this Takeout Machine thing? Because you're going to help get us back home!"

"Okay okay, geez. Lighten up, will you? I'll show you where it is." Cliff said. "But first we should probably hide, because all of that…" Cliff hooked his thumb back towards the hole in the wall. "… is about to come in here."

The rest of the wall with the hole exploded. Tony let go of Cliff and used his body to shield the kids just as chunks of wall and rock flew at his back. It catapulted cartoonishly more squat aliens through the air.

Tony's ears rang as he turned his head. He watched two of the four tall alien creatures from the desert gracefully glide through the air past them. Behind them ran a small platoon of the dumb little armored aliens shooting at them from the machines in their arms. Tony guessed it was the bubbles that protected them that made them float, too. The bubbles flashed briefly with light as lasers collided with it. The lasers being fired were still bouncing right off the bubbles and careening into the surrounding buildings and streets. Chunks of the structures exploded and burst onto the ground.

The tall bald pink aliens in the bubbles floated quickly, zig-zagging up and down the street in a panic. The platoon of soldiers underneath them fired upwards and then dodged the random returning blasts. Even higher above, a few flying bathtubs joined the chase. The more the soldiers and the vehicles fired, the more the ricocheting beams took out buildings and vehicles and cables and streets. Explosions and crashes everywhere. The rubble and rock swept over Tony's body as he did his best to cover the kids up. The bubbled pink aliens speedily turned a corner farther down the street and the little army followed them. They went out of sight, but you could still hear the destruction being done.

Tony stepped away from the kids and checked them out. Tony's own back hurt, and he could feel something on the back of his neck and head. He reached back and touched the bleeding. It was light and just felt like some scrapes. He was lucky. He ignored it.

Tony found Cliff on the ground, covered in rocks and debris. He brushed everything off of him and shook him. "Cliff? Cliff!"

Cliff sat up and shook his head back and forth. "Whoa." He said. "Did you see that?"

"Yeah I caught it, Cliff. Come on, get up. Get us out of here. It's not safe out here in the streets." Tony said, helping Cliff get to his feet. In the distance, Tony could see the top of a building explode and then crumble down. Then another. The pursuit was going deeper into the city. "I don't think it's safe anywhere."

"My drummer J-Bone lives a few blocks away. We can

go hide out there. Come on!" Cliff said, running. Then he tripped hard over a block of rubble and fell to the ground. The three kids busted up laughing. Some of the fleeing chunky little aliens had seen and started laughing too. "Oh, whatever, you think you're so cool!" Cliff said, getting back up. "Follow me, jerks!"

Cliff ran down the street, and Tony and the kids followed. They ran around pieces of building and immense craters in the ground. They dodged standing fires and falling debris. Cliff led them left, down a side street.

As they turned down the street, another two tall pink aliens appeared. Safe in their floating bubbles, they came streaming over the wall and into the city. Just like the others, they were being pursued on land and air by the squat, armored hairdressers. With them followed the same chaos and noise and damage caused by the mindless firing on the indestructible floating bubbles.

Cliff took another turn down a narrow street. Then another. Tony and the kids kept up as the locals crowded the street, also fleeing the destruction. In the distance, you could hear explosions and laser fire. Crashes and explosions. This city wouldn't last much longer. Cliff turned again. They tore this street to bits and the burning buildings were hanging threadbare.

"How much farther, Cliff?" Tony yelled ahead at him, pulling Hooper off her feet and into his arms. "These idiots are destroying their own city!" Tony saw Quint was straying off away from the group. "Quint! Closer to us! Come on!"

"Just another block or two, over that way." Cliff yelled between huge gasps of air. The running was doing a real number on him. "Hey, listen. So if it's really 2021, then what's the music like now? Like, how amazing is the rock? It has got to be great, right?" Cliff shouted back at Tony.

"Cliff, in 2021 music is just sad kids with computers. The best rock you can get is when a band reunites to play the anniversary of their second best album." Tony told Cliff as they ran around a crashed burning flying bathtub.

"Oh. Well, that's a bummer." Cliff said.

One of the tall pink aliens appeared to their left. It floated between two burned-out buildings. Cliff, Tony, and the kids skidded to a stop and watched as it floated above them. The alien had its hands up over its head in fear and was desperately looking behind it as it floated across the street. Then its attackers burst through the buildings, firing their lasers. Bathtubs zoomed over the buildings and dived at the floating bubble.

"In there!" Tony yelled and with his free arm pulled Brody over to the nearest standing building.

Cliff followed behind him. Hooper in one arm and grasping Brody's shirt in his hands, Tony stepped into the building through a hole in its front. Inside, piles of junk and broken machines scattered all over. There was a wide flight of stairs that led to a second floor. Underneath the stairs was a low, empty space. It was an open enough cubby that Tony, Cliff, and the kids could squeeze into. Tony dropped Hooper down next to him in the tight space. He looked up at the big hole in the building's front.

Quint was still outside. Gazing up at the action above him.

"Quint!" Tony yelled and immediately darted out after him.

Quint turned his head at Tony's shout.

An explosion went off above the building. Then a loud crash. Pieces of the ceiling tumbled down on Tony as he slipped backwards into the spot under the stairs. Then the entire building came crashing down all around them.

Tony grabbed the two kids with him and pulled them

into his chest, covering their faces with his hands. His head down and eyes tightly shut, he felt bits of building sweep past his face and knees.

It stopped. The collapse was over as quickly as it started.

Tony opened his eyes. The room was darker, almost black but for small pinholes and narrow shafts of light. It looked like the roof and second floor had completely caved in, but the stairs they hid under had saved their lives. The standing stairs held up the ceiling before it could crush them. Directly in front of them were stacks and piles of rubble from the broken building.

Tony checked the kids. They were panting and whimpering.

"Quint!" Tony lunged forward and tried moving the pieces of the broken building that trapped them. It was not budging. Who knows how many tons lay on top of them? Cliff was stirring, moaning. "Cliff! Help me move it!" Tony said, trying to lift a piece of wall. Cliff pushed an area in front of him, but nothing was happening.

"It's not moving man!" Cliff said through gritted teeth.

"Come on!" Tony shouted as he tried to lift with everything he had in him.

Quietly, he heard a voice.

"Daddy? Daddy?"

It was coming from the other side of this mountain that trapped them.

"Quint! Quint! Where are you?" Tony shouted as he moved around, trying to see through the debris to the other side.

"I'm here Daddy, I'm here!" Quint yelled.

Tony found a small opening at the top of the pile, the size of his fist, that was letting a shaft of light through. He yelled through it.

"Quint! Quint! Are you okay?"

"I'm fine Daddy! Where are you? Are you okay?" Quint yelled.

Peering through the slight break in the debris, he saw Quint wander past, looking for him.

"I see you Quint! Stop! I see you! We're under here! We're okay, but we're stuck!" Tony shouted through the hole. Quint couldn't see Tony, but was looking toward where he heard his voice.

"You're stuck Daddy? Those guys are all gone. They went the other way. Daddy, I can help you!"

"No Quint! Don't move! It's not safe! You stay there until we can figure out how to get out!"

"Daddy, I can do it, I can get you out! Don't worry!"

"No Quint, no! It's too dangerous! Just stay put until I can get out!"

"I can do it!" Quint yelled at the sound of Tony's voice.

Quint ran out of sight. Tony couldn't see him through the opening any more.

"Quint! Quint! Don't! Quint! No! QUINT!!!"

But he was gone.

Eight

"No! Quint, no!" Tony was screaming through a gap in the rubble that trapped him. He moved to a different spot where a shaft of light shone through the piles of collapsed building. He fumbled around in the cramped space under the staircase that had saved their lives. "Quint! Quint! Where are you? Quint?" No answer. Just the sound of his own frantic breathing.

Tony slammed his body against the pile of building that stood between him and his son. His arms reached and prodded around the debris for loose spots. He looked for anything that would move. Anything that would give way so they could escape. He told himself he didn't need much to shift away. Just enough to squeeze himself and his kids through. He lifted. He pushed.

"Cliff. Cliff. Help me." Tony said desperately.

"Okay, man, okay." Cliff said as he pushed against the rubble from his side.

"Daddy? It's very dark, Daddy. Where is Quint?" Brody asked. He and Hooper sat huddled close to each other on the ground. Frightened from the darkness and the yelling. From seeing their father so worried.

"Yeah, where's Quint, Daddy?" Hooper also asked.

"He's out there. He's out there and we're stuck in here." Tony shouted. His face had become shiny with sweat. It dripped from his chin as he tried lifting a beam. Through gritted teeth and labored, anxious breathing, Tony ranted out loud. "He's out there and we have to go find him. But we're stuck. We're trapped here. Cliff, try this one with me."

Cliff shifted over to where Tony was, and together they attempted to lift another pile of wreckage. But it did not budge. After a moment, Tony and Cliff collapsed backwards with exhaustion. Tony got back up and tried another area.

"He always does this. He never listens. Never listens. He's always wandering too far away." Tony said. It was Tony's voice and words, but it was pure panic and mania that was speaking. "Always off doing something he's not supposed to. He never tells me what he's doing. He doesn't listen at all."

Tony turned around and was now pushing with his back. His arms felt like jelly. He was panting hard. He continued to rant in between big gulps of air. "He needs to stay with the rest of us. We've got to stay together. Stay safe. Look what happens. Look what happens."

Tony, unable to push any longer, slumped to the ground. Gasping for air. "He thinks he can do things all on his own. All by himself. But he can't. He can't. He's too little. He needs my help. He needs my…"

And then he started crying. The anxiety and the exhaustion finally collapsed on him, just as the building had. He sobbed as he thought of his boy out there all alone. The danger out there. Those pony-tailed frogs out there destroying their own city.

He cried as he pictured his wife. Worried sick about where they were. Confused. Wondering what had happened. He wished desperately she were here with him. He missed her so much. She would have known what to do. She would have stopped Tony from letting this happen. She would have helped Tony keep them safe. All this time. Every day. All this time and he still doesn't know how to do this. He can never do it right.

He was breaking down.

Brody leaned forward and threw his little arms around Tony's neck and squeezed. Tony wrapped his arms around the little boy.

"Not sad, Daddy. Be happy. You are not sad, Daddy." Brody said, hugging Tony. Brody's hand lightly patted Tony's back as he hugged. Just like they did to him when he got upset. It only made Tony cry more.

"Hooper's turn." She said as she scooted over to Tony and hugged his side. Then… WOOSH. The sound of a laser being fired.

Then… CRUNCH. A sound like a can crushing under your shoe.

Then another WOOSH and another CRUNCH.

WOOSH. CRUNCH.

Suddenly, to their left, the top of the pile of the rubble got shaved clean away by a laser blast. Tony, Cliff, and the kids threw their hands over their eyes as the fresh light from outside blinded them. After a second, Tony slowly stood, his hand covering his eyes as they adjusted. Still squinting, he looked out of the newly made exit. He saw a figure.

There stood Quint.

"QUINT!" Tony screamed in surprise.

"Told you I could do it, Daddy." Quint said. And then he lowered his arm. The laser blaster that was poking out slowly disappeared back into the armor he was wearing.

Tony bent over and lifted Brody and Hooper and set each one on top of the wreckage that they could now climb out of. He climbed out of the hole that Quint had made. Brody and Hooper hopped down the pile of building and to the ground. Tony followed, and they all ran towards Quint.

He stood there looking as proud as Tony had ever seen him. Standing in his shiny metallic armor, that he knew would fit him. His face beaming through the clear face-plate in his helmet. Tony slid over to him and tried to lift him up in joy, but the suit of armor made him too heavy. So instead he bent down and hugged the cold, hard armor as tight as he could. He doubted Quint could even feel it.

"Quint, you did it! You saved us!" Tony said, tears running down his cheeks as he let him go.

"Yeah Daddy. Because see, I had this idea, and I remembered where they had all the squares of these suits hanging on the walls. So I ran back to the building where they were. And it was on fire. But I was really careful Daddy, I promise. And I found the last one hanging on the wall so I put it on the ground and stepped on it like I saw them doing and the armor just started going up all around my body, Daddy." Quint said so proudly.

"What's it feel like? How are you moving around in it?" Tony asked, his breathing finally slowing at the relief of seeing Quint safe and sound.

"It's tight but not too tight. Kind of snuggly like my winter coat, you know? But it moves really easy though. Like, I know it's heavy on the outside, but it doesn't feel heavy inside here. It made me run super fast to get back here. And I think the helmet reads my brain, Daddy.

Because I just wanted to shoot the laser blaster and it just popped out of my arm. It shot when I thought about it." Quint rambled quickly. Brody and Hooper each curiously patted and poked at the back and arms of brother Quint's cool new suit.

"Well, don't think about it right now. I don't want you to blast your brother and sister away." Tony sternly warned. Then he stopped himself. This was the problem, he thought. Tony, this is the problem. This is what you do. He knelt back down to Quint and looked him in the eyes. "Quint, I'm sorry I said that. I know you know what you're doing. Sometimes my brain just won't stop worrying. About everything. I trust you, buddy. Your idea was exactly perfect. Thank you for saving us." He hugged Quint again.

"Whoa! Sweet suit, man!" Cliff said as he stumbled out of the fallen building. "They won't let me wear one, the jerks."

A FEW STREETS OVER, you could still hear explosions and laser blasters being fired. Tony stood up and watched the skyline and saw another tall building come crumbling down.

"Cliff, this place will not last much longer. The little hair guys... wait... WAIT..." Tony stopped talking. He closed his eyes. He held up his hands. "Hairsprayliens." He opened his eyes. "They're Hairsprayliens." Tony smiled. "Why did it take me all day to think of that?"

"Wait? Did you just make that up? That is brilliant. No, it's fantastic. Hairsprayliens." Cliff said with wide eyes. "Whoa. I think I need to sit down."

"This city is going to be burning rubble soon. Cliff, tell me they keep this Takeout Machine somewhere safe? Can you take us there?" Tony said.

"It should be back in the building where they first took you. It's close to here. My guitar and amp are back there, anyway. Let's go get it!" Cliff said.

"We'll sneak in and use the machine to finally get us back home." Tony said.

"And save the guitar, too!" Cliff said.

"Daddy, wait!" Quint said and put his hand on the side of his helmet. "I can hear their walkie-talkies in here. They're really yelling about something right now. I can hear that one police officer that doesn't like you, shouting."

Then, down the street from around one of the burning buildings, one of the tall pink aliens ran out. It was frantically poking at some buttons on its large, round belt buckle. It mashed a button and sparks flew out of the belt's front. The belt looked broken.

"Looks like his bubble burst." Cliff chuckled.

"Cliff, not now." Tony said.

"Oh sorry. I didn't know you were the king of deciding who makes dumb jokes."

It heard them. It stopped running and stood there. Panting heavily, its eyes were wide as it briefly stared at the group. Then it quickly looked down, not making direct eye contact but watching them out of the corners of its eyes. Its bald pink head dripped with sweat. It looked absolutely terrified.

Out from the same place the tall alien had come from, a small group of Hairsprayliens came running. There were six of them and when they spotted the tall alien they had been chasing, they each barked something.

"Daddy, I could hear them in here." Quint told Tony. "There are lots of others talking now."

"Pickles, they probably called for backup." Tony said. He'd had enough. "Hey!" he yelled at the small mob. "Leave it alone!" He put his arms out to show he meant it no harm and started walking toward the tall alien. He could see it was getting ready to run again.

The armored Hairsprayliens ignored Tony's shouts, and they each lifted their arm cannons.

"No! Stop! Don't!" Tony said, now taking off into a run. He did not know what he was going to do. "Leave it alone! That's enough, do you hear me! That's enough!" Tony shouted.

He noticed Quint was running quickly alongside him, his own laser blaster out, and pointed at the short aggressors. Tony was going to have to trust him.

The tall alien's mouth quivered as it quickly backed away from the approaching Hairsprayliens. It held one arm up in defense while with his other hand he pushed the useless buttons on the broken belt.

The rectangle cannons on the short aliens' arms glowed red. They were going to fire on the helpless creature.

"THAT'S ENOUGH!!!"

The armored Hairsprayliens stopped dead in their tracks. Frozen. They lowered their weapons. Tony and Quint hit the brakes and stood in place. It was suddenly silent.

Slowly, the Hairsprayliens turned to Tony and Quint. The tall alien also stopped moving and was looking at Tony.

But Tony didn't yell that.

Hooper did.

SHE WAS MARCHING TOWARD THEM. Big steps. Her feet crunched on the ground. She had one arm pointed at the Hairsprayliens and the other was resting on her hip.

She was in full scolding mode. And it was terrifying to behold.

"THAT'S ENOUGH! NO MORE! YOU GO AWAY!" Hooper yelled as she stomped towards the armored Hairsprayliens.

They all turned to each other and then back to the approaching Hooper. Then they all screamed and took off running back in the direction they had come.

Tony turned to Hooper. Her eyebrows arched and her messy face was in a scowl.

"No more, Daddy." Hooper said as she stood next to Tony.

"Uh… good job, Hoop." Tony squeezed her into his side.

Cliff and Brody came up running and joined them.

"Man, your kids are hardcore." Cliff said.

"I guess so." Tony said, still in shock.

The tall pink alien was still standing motionless. Its enormous eyes darted back and forth, sometimes stopping to briefly focus on the family. It held its long arms out defensively in front of itself. Tony struggled to meet its wandering eyes so he could wordlessly convey that it had nothing to fear from them. He was trying to think of another way to comfort it when Brody stepped forward and walked towards it.

"Brody, buddy…" Tony said. But he stopped himself. Today was clearly a learning day for him. As much as he wanted to fight it, he needed to keep rolling with these things.

Brody quietly moved toward the tense and quivering alien. He stopped directly in front of it. The tall, pink alien looked at Brody.

"Hey! Are you scared?" Brody quietly asked.

Its face relaxed a little. Its wide eyes stopped moving so

much and got narrow and more focused. Its body straightened out, and it stood up tall again. It lowered its arms.

"I was scared, but then my daddy hugged me. I was still scared, but I felt a little better."

Brody walked up to the pink alien and hugged it around the legs. And with one hand, he softly patted the back of its thick robe. Just like what they did to him when he was upset. The tall alien slowly reached its large hand down and started to awkwardly pat Brody's back.

"Daddy, I can still hear them all shouting in my helmet. I think they're coming here soon." Quint guessed.

"Pickles." Tony said. "What do we do?"

Cliff suddenly spoke. "Man, back home, I used to have this wicked microphone setup I stole from this guy. It was so crazy loud. Man, I wish I had that right now, then we could make that mean little girl yell at all of them at the same time."

Tony suddenly looked over at Quint.

"You say you can hear the rest of that army or cops or whatever they are in your thing, Quint?" Tony asked.

"I guess so." Quint answered.

"When we were outside the wall, the Sheriff talked into one of his boxes and they all heard it. Do you know where that radio is on your suit, Quint?" Tony said, kneeling down and patting his arms and chest.

"Not really."

"Well, you said it could read your brain. So think of a radio and maybe it will pop out somewhere." Tony said.

From up the street, Tony could hear heavy footsteps. Marching feet. Lots of them. They were coming.

"I'm trying Daddy!" Quint said. Then a round, hollow cylinder popped out from the side of his leg.

"That looks like a cup holder, Quint. I need the radio, buddy. Maybe try thinking of a walkie-talkie?"

The alien army appeared down the street. Armored Hairsprayliens at least fifty strong. In the air, a small squadron of flying bathtubs circled. Standing front and center of the army, Sheriff Slick-Back shouted some orders.

"Quint…" Tony started.

"I'm trying Daddy. I'm thinking of a radio. I'm trying." Quint promised.

A large pink hand appeared next to Tony. Its long finger extended and softly touched a smooth spot on the shoulder of Quint's armor. Tony turned to see the tall alien standing next to them. Brody was right alongside it, grasping the pinky finger of its other large hand.

Out of that spot on Quint's shoulder, the armor slowly formed a small rectangular screen. It popped up like a finished piece of toast. Tony reached over and pulled it out of Brody's shoulder. It lit up in his hand. Tony heard the loud and sharp whistle of feedback echo from the army ahead of them and also throughout the standing city.

"What are you going to do?" Cliff asked.

"Steal their wicked microphone setup, Cliff." Tony turned to Brody and the tall alien. "Buddy, cover them up. It's going to get loud."

"Hardcore!" Cliff said, clapping his hands in delight.

Brody pulled his blanket from his shoulders back up and over his ears. He looked up at the tall alien and mimed covering his ears. The alien moved its hands up and rested them over the sides of its head.

Quint must have also been thinking the same thing. Slowly and fluidly, his helmet melted away into the rest of his armor. He covered his ears.

Tony turned to Hooper. She was smiling. It was the most mischievous looking smile Tony had ever seen.

"Hoop? Tell them…" Tony pointed to the approaching

army. "... tell them all to stop it." And then he held the small rectangle radio to Hooper's tiny lips. She squeezed her little hands into fists. She let them have it.

"STOOOOOP IIIIIITTTTTT!!!!!" she screamed into the rectangle.

It was like a bomb going off. Hooper's scream blasted through the city. It ripped through the radios of every single suit of armor and vehicle. Tony saw Sheriff Slick-Back spasm itself into a building to escape Hooper's terrifying voice. The noise vibrated the buildings and shook the ground. The entire army in front of them dropped to the ground and withered in pain. The few flying bathtubs either sank quickly down or spiraled backwards. The echo and feedback rang over and over and over.

"NOW GO AWAY!!!!!" Hooper yelled.

Again, the noise shattered through their bodies over the city. Terrified beyond understanding, the small, stubby aliens scrambled to their stocky little legs and started running away. Any flying bathtub still airborne turned and flew off. Retreating in fear of the little girl with the big voice, the street was almost empty.

The echo lasted another few seconds. Tony and the kids watched the last of the retreat. The small Hair-sprayliens stumbled over each other and ran into walls. Then they were gone. It was quiet again.

Tony, ears ringing, bent over again and squeezed Hooper tight. "You did it!"

"I am so funny!" Hooper said, delighted.

"You are Hoop!" Tony said. He stood up and looked at Cliff. "That should buy us some time. Take us to the machine now, Cliff."

"What about them?" Cliff said and pointed above Tony.

· · ·

TONY LOOKED up and saw them floating in the air. Tall, pink, bald, and hovering above him in their invisible bubbles. They drifted softly to the ground. Each of them touched a button on their belt. Tony assumed they turned their force field off.

They cautiously shuffled over to the tall alien that the family had saved. They each looked extremely anxious and tired. None of them would look directly at the family. They were hunched over with tension. Their eyes were wide and scared and always moving.

Their rescued friend turned to each one of them. It appeared to be smiling. The rest of them suddenly relaxed their bodies and stood up straight. They also smiled.

The first tall alien turned back to Tony and his family. It wouldn't make eye contact, but it glanced at them. Then he stopped on Brody. Brody stood there with his filthy blanket tied around his head, looking back at him. It reached out and pointed at Brody.

"This one." It said softly.

Nine

"It talks like we do, Daddy!" Quint shouted in surprise.

"Yes." It mumbled. It turned back to Tony. It kept its eyes either on the ground or looking just beyond Tony. "You are from planet Earth?"

Tony was in shock. He wasn't sure why. This planet kept throwing the dumbest curveballs at him, so why should this surprise him as well.

"Yes, we are." Tony said. He motioned to his family, including Cliff. "All of us are."

The tall creature glanced up at Tony and Cliff and then back at the ground.

"Yes. We know Cliff."

"Hey, Kow." Cliff waved.

"We brought him here. During our research." The tall alien quietly said. "Him? Why?" Tony said. He forgot Cliff could hear him. He turned to Cliff. "Sorry."

"Oh, don't worry about it." Cliff stepped forward and said. "Yeah, it was funny. When I got here, they told me they had made a big old boo boo and that they'd work on sending me back. But then I was having such a great time just chilling with them in their super cool city! Just hanging out and stuff! I finally told them it was no big whoop, I'll just stay here, no problemo. But then one day, out of the blue, they went and dropped me off here with all the little hair guys. The weirdest thing." Cliff rambled.

"Yeah. That's weird Cliff." Tony said to Cliff. Then he turned and leaned in to the tall alien. "Didn't want Cliff crashing on your couch, did you?"

The tall alien furrowed its brow at the expression, but seemed to understand what Tony meant.

"We thought Cliff might find it more... suitable to live here. More comfortable." It said slowly and quietly.

"Yeah, it rocks a little more over here. You guys were too quiet." Cliff said with a wave. "Plus, you never wanted to listen when I was trying to teach about all the ways of my planet for your dumb research."

"You told us your planet is named Cliff World. We found your information to be... inaccurate." It replied.

"Yeah well, whatever." Cliff said and then shuffled off to the side.

Tony was still paranoid that they weren't entirely out of danger just yet. They had to get somewhere more safe. He stepped forward to the tall pink alien.

"My name is Tony. What is your name?"

It glanced up at Tony for a quick second. Then back at the ground.

"You may call me Kow." It answered. "These are my friends. We are Tessons."

"Cow! Like, moo, get it?" Cliff said, laughing.

"Cliff, shut up!" Tony turned and snapped.

"Daddy, don't say shut up. It's a bad word." Quint butted in.

"Sorry Quint." Tony apologized. The bad word list

was getting longer by the second. Tony rubbed his face in exhaustion.

"What is… this one's name?" Kow asked Tony, not looking but gesturing at Brody.

"This is Brody." Tony answered. "Say hi, Brody."

"Hello." Brody said in his little voice and pulled on his blanket.

The tall creature named Kow smiled for a moment again. He seemed to relax.

"There is a… gentleness about Brody that is quite calm. A comfort here in this chaotic place. It is a similar energy we feel, when our people are safely within our own city." Kow explained softly. "I felt it from him after you rescued me."

"Yeah we like him, too." Tony said. He was pretty sure he knew what they meant. The lack of eye contact. The quiet voices. The tense bodies. These were all things Brody did.

"And I'm Quint!" the boy shouted, making sure he wasn't getting left out. Eight-year-olds love to talk to new grown ups. "And that's my sister Hooper. She's the one who did all the loud screaming."

"I'm Hooper." She waved.

"Yes. They are quite frightened of Hooper. She radiates a strength and confidence that they are incapable of. So instead, they are afraid." Kow replied. "Also, she is very loud."

"Yeah she's super loud, listen Kow. I'm not entirely sure that our Hairspraylien friends will not come back and take another shot at you and your Tesson friends. Or us. So why don't we get off this street and somewhere safe." Tony said, trying to stay on track.

"Hairspraylien?" Kow said, confused. "That does not

quite make sense. They take great pride in the hair they have on their head, but..."

"Well, it's the best I could do." Tony cut Kow off. "Look. Cliff said he thinks he knows where the machine they used to bring us here is. If we find it, can you send us back?"

"Of course. The Tessons created the machine." Kow said. "However, we will have to inspect it to make sure it is working properly. We fear they modified it after they took it from us."

"Yeah, Cliff said they were using it to find fast food." Tony said, smiling. He felt the tension leave his shoulders, and his stomach fluttered. He could barely contain his excitement at the thought of him and the kids getting back home. Back to his wife.

Kow looked at the ground beside him. "We found it odd that they would steal the device for such a purpose. The Tessons and the ones who live here usually have an... understanding between one another. But we learn there has been a change of leadership here in recent times." Kow softly said.

"Oh yeah, sure. Maybe that one that looks and talks like a cop. With the slicked back hair? It seems totally out of control." Tony told Kow.

"Its corruption and hatred runs deep, that is true. But it is merely the head of the city's law and defense systems. Its position rarely comes with the power that could authorize all of this." Kow motioned to all the destruction. "There is another above him." Kow said. His eyes moved up from the ground.

And he looked at Cliff.

"What?" Cliff said in surprise. "What, me? Look pal, I'm not... oh yeah, they elected me mayor a few months ago."

"What!" Tony shouted.

"No! Just listen!" Cliff threw his hands up in front of him. "It was all that cop, man! They got me a job as mayor or governor or something, but I don't actually do anything. Just hang out and play guitar! They asked what I wanted, and I said I wanted something else to eat than that gross slop we always have. A few days later, they showed up with that machine and we started looking for some pizza. That cop guy does everything else around here. I sometimes sign some papers, but I don't know what they say!"

"They made you a strawman, Cliff. A puppet so the Sheriff could take control." Tony told Cliff.

"What? Lame." Cliff huffed.

"The machine's purpose was not to find... pizza." Kow said, almost scolding.

"Yeah, yeah whatever. But you jerks never share all the cool things you have. I was hungry, dude." Cliff said. "But then we got bored and started looking for someone who knows how to play bass. Because this time, man, this band is going to go all the way. This time..."

The ground next to him exploded. A cloud of dirt and rock in the air.

Tony pushed the kids away and spun around to see Sheriff Slick Back suddenly standing there, its arm cannon pointed at all of them. Its armor was filthy and dented all over. Its helmet was off and a bruised and beat up face. Its hair, however, was still perfectly slicked backwards, not a single fiber out of place.

It had a crazed look in its beady little eyes. It started to hoarsely bark orders or threats. It may have been just having the last word before it killed them.

"Hey man, watch it!" Cliff yelled from the ground.

Tony pulled Hooper forward. He knew this was dangerous, but he hoped she could scare him off again.

Hooper seemed to read his mind and was already yelling at the crazed Sheriff.

"No! You go away! You are mean!" Hooper shouted and waved her little arms.

But the Sheriff did not move. It scowled. It looked too far gone. Past fear. Living on only anger. It raised the arm cannon higher at the family and the tall pink aliens.

Kow and the other Tessons were all huddled together. Tony looked over for help and saw Kow make brief eye contact with the Sheriff, and then turned to one of its friends and whispered. The Tesson broke away from the group, hesitantly walked forward, touching a series of buttons on its large round belt buckle. Tony thought Kow told it to put up a new force field.

But instead, the rectangle blaster that was on Sheriff's arm stopped glowing red. Then it quickly receded back into the suit of armor. The Sheriff was furious. It shouted and yelled, and then a different rectangle smoothly formed out of its opposite arm. This one faced the Sheriff and lit up with soft light.

Almost immediately, the Sheriff's expression changed. The rage drained from its face and changed into a blank expression. Its eyes narrowed and its mouth fell wide open as it stared at the glowing rectangle that faced it. It looked passive.

"What's it looking at?" Tony shouted over at Kow.

Kow and its group relaxed and separated again.

"It is looking at its own image. Admiring how it looks."

Tony didn't understand. The Sheriff stood frozen with focus on the rectangle.

"You sent it a picture of itself?" Tony said, standing up and helping the kids.

"Yes. They like to look at themselves." Kow said. "We shall be safe now."

"That's it? That's it! You ended the war by texting it a selfie?" Tony said, exhausted. He took a deep, frustrated breath. "Is that what they're always looking at on those boxes?"

"We believe so. The Tessons invented them as a means of communication, but they mainly use it to look at images of themselves. And also to share their opinions of the images with one another."

"Ridiculous! That's ridiculous. We found the only other planet in the universe that lives on social media?" He wanted to lie down. His head hurt. What an honor. He was so thrilled he got to visit the other dumbest planet in the universe.

The Sheriff suddenly seemed to snap back to reality. It jumped up into the air. When it landed, the metal armor smoothly slid off its body and formed back into a square on the ground. The Sheriff was back in its dirty jumpsuit. It reached into its pocket and pulled out another small device and shouted into it. Then it ran off in another direction and out of sight.

"What just happened?" Tony asked.

"I believe it sent the image off to other devices throughout its population. The image shall occupy the rest of the city for the time being. We are out of danger now." Kow softly said while looking down.

"Well, while they're all distracted with their likes and favs, we can go get the Takeout Machine, right?" Tony said.

Kow walked down the street. The other Tessons followed. "Come. Let us find the machine so we may send you back to your home."

Cliff led them into a tower of the main building. Like Kow had promised, no one paid any attention to them walking around. The little Hairsprayliens seemed to have forgotten or just no longer cared they were there. Tony, Cliff, The Tessons, and the kids were all ignored the whole way there. The Hairsprayliens just walked around, staring at their devices and yelling into them. Tony could not believe these were the same creatures that were shooting at them minutes before. The city was literally burning, but these things were too busy looking at their screens to put out the fire.

After an elevator and some hallways, they found The Takeout Machine sitting in a large room. It sat next to a gigantic pile of empty fast food packaging. It was a piece of technology that looked clearly out of place when compared to everything else Tony had seen in the city. Smooth and slim and expertly built. It was shiny and clean and pretty.

Also in the room was a shoddy slapped together drum kit, a crudely built keyboard, and what Cliff swore was a set of homemade turntables. Homemade, like duct tape and string holding it together, homemade. Tony did not know how they possibly worked. Cliff ran over to the guitar that was lying on the floor and scooped it up. He appeared to be hugging it.

Kow and his friends examined their machine and told Tony that the machine needed some minor repairs. That if they took the machine back to their Tesson home, Kow and his people could do the repairs and send Tony and his family back to Earth. They then disassembled the machine and broke it down into smaller pieces. After pressing some buttons on their large belts, invisible bubbles made the pieces float in the air.

Tony, trying not to get his hopes up too high, fought back tears of joy. They were going to get back to Earth. Back to his wife and a safe place for his children.

"Come. We shall take the device back to our home.

Our transport is waiting for us back in the desert." Kow said. As his tall pink friends walked, the floating pieces of machine followed them like balloons.

They made their way out of the building and back through the ruined city toward the desert. The kids were having a great time jumping off pieces of broken rock and buildings. They bounced and slid down huge rolls of the surviving cable that still ran through the city. Each time they picked some random thing up off the ground, they demanded that Tony look at it. And then to look at this. And look at this.

"So what exactly is… that thing?" Tony asked Kow about the floating pieces of machinery behind them. He was curious, but mainly it was an excuse to take a break from all the looking.

The machine Cliff had called the Takeout Machine and used to get fast food from throughout the universe, the Tessons invented to study other worlds and civilizations. Kow explained the Tessons engineered a device to observe places in time and space to gain knowledge. It was only through a series of unrelated upgrades did they find the machine could physically breach the reality they were observing. The Tessons found they could suddenly zero in and remove objects from the world they were looking at. Kow explained that anything that was brought here from other planets and times got studied and then always returned.

"Did you guys ever send yourselves through? Visit the places you were looking at?" Tony asked as they walked through the tattered remains of the hangar command center that opened up into the desert.

Kow didn't answer that question. It looked off into the distance of the desert.

"Well, how did the Hairsprayliens know about it? How did they know what it did?" Tony asked.

After a long silence, Kow answered, "Because we used to co-exist in the same city. They knew about it before they left."

"So Cliff wasn't lying. You did all live together." Tony confirmed.

"Long ago, yes."

"He said you kicked the little guys out?"

"They were asked to leave." Kow said and then made eye contact with Tony for the longest time since they had met. It then broke away. "And they agreed. It was mutually concluded that it was too difficult to exist in the same space."

"Because you are so different from each other?" Tony asked. "I mean, I get it. They are, well... obnoxious, frankly. You guys like it more orderly, I would imagine."

Kow's very monotone voice suddenly contained some emotion in it. "They are loud and they are concerned with nothing but themselves. They strive to maintain a way of living that only suits those already like them." Kow said. "They work tirelessly to ensure that nothing questions or threatens those ways they want to live. They made it quite clear that there was no place for those like us. That if we wanted to co-exist, it would be us that would have to change. We would have to learn to live how they lived. We would have to adapt to them. They found that to be more convenient than to just welcome us as we are. More convenient than to simply change some of their behaviors and their lifestyles to make the world safer for us. You do not understand."

Tony looked back at Brody. He was pretty sure he understood perfectly.

"So it was decided that we should exist separately. The

Tessons provided them with technology to build their own city. They dug this place here out of the rocks above us. They did it using the very suits and vehicles that they turned upon us today."

"So that's not military armor?" Tony asked, looking at Quint bouncing up and down in his metal suit.

"They used them for mining the mountain of rock down in order to build the city. The Tessons also provided them with a means of communication. The small boxes you see them speaking into and looking at. They used neither technology for their intended purpose any longer. So, The Tessons stopped providing them with things they would not use properly." Kow said.

"That would explain why now most of their city looked like they tied it together from pieces of trash." Tony said. He smiled. "And I guess since you changed the Wi-Fi password, they had to revert to hard wire. That must be this rat's nest of wires that are everywhere here."

"They resent the Tessons. They resent the way we make them feel. So they try to hurt us. And they refuse to co-exist. Look at this destruction," Kow said. "They would rather burn their own city to the ground than change how they live." Kow raised its arm and pointed. "Look there. Our transport." Kow said, avoiding any more discussion of the subject.

Tony and the kids looked ahead. From behind the series of boulders the Tessons had first walked out of, a tall and very long vehicle suddenly materialized. They had cloaked it invisible this whole time. It looked to be thousands of feet long. It shined softly in the light from the stars above. And it didn't seem to sit on the ground, but hovered in place just above it.

"Space train!" Brody yelled and pointed. "Look, Daddy it's a space train!"

"Whoa, that's sick." Quint said. "Do we get to ride in that Daddy? Please, can we?"

"We shall take you and your family back to our home. Repair our technology to send you back to Earth. Come." Kow said as it walked to the floating train.

Tony smiled as he turned to look back at the city behind him. This dumb weird place. With its loud, terrible people. They had set fire to and knocked down their own city.

Tony felt very sad when he should have been happy.

"Wait! Kow? What about them?" Tony said, pointing to the destroyed city.

"They did that to themselves." Kow said, looking past Tony.

"But come on, you said they needed you to build that city the first time. If you don't help them, they're never going to get that back up and running. They had the place held together with string and spit." Tony said. He walked right up to Kow. He found his eyes like he does to Brody. "I mean… they're actively, physically hostile towards you. They are terrible, terrible creatures with dumb stupid hair-cuts. I don't blame you for wanting to leave them out here to rot." Tony said. He gulped and tried to think of the words. "But that's what they would do to you, wouldn't they? They would leave you out here to suffer. And you are not them. You can do something. You can help them. You might even change them! Beat it through their thick perfectly styled skulls that being hateful little monsters is an enormous waste of life." Tony said. "Come on, Kow. Be petty, but don't leave them out to die. They don't stand a chance without you." Tony pleaded.

Kow did not respond. It broke eye contact with Tony and then just looked off into the distance. After a few seconds, Kow shuffled over to its friends, who were loading the pieces of the floating machine into the space train. Tony watched as they gathered together.

"What's going on Daddy?" Quint asked Tony.

"I think they're deciding if they are going to help or not." Tony said. He hoped.

"Well, see ya later, I guess." Cliff said dramatically.

Cliff stood there with his beat up guitar slung around his body and was holding his small amplifier. Tony had forgotten he was following them. Cliff turned around and headed back towards the charred hangar.

"Cliff, wait!" Tony said. "You've got to come back with us. They're going to send us back home, man."

Cliff shook his head. "Man, I don't want to go back there. Nothing but a bunch of jerks back home. Used to get nothing but laughed at all the time. Here they like me. I mean, I think they do. Besides, I got a new band, man. We rock, you know?" Cliff explained.

"Cliff, you are a fascinating and infuriating person." Tony told him. "Well, if you're going to stay, please think of a new band name. Nemesis Control is the second worst name I've heard today."

"What was the first?" Cliff asked.

Kow and a Tesson appeared next to Tony and Cliff.

"This city is uninhabitable and dangerous. To rebuild it would be a waste of time and resources." Kow said. Tony's heart sank. "Instead, we shall offer sanctuary to its inhabitants in our own city." Kow said. "Temporary, until all parties reach a more permanent solution. One of us will stay here to assist in the transportation." Kow softly said.

Kow's friend pushed a button on its belt. The front half of the floating space train broke away and separated from the back. It hissed as it separated.

"We will need help in convincing them it is not safe to stay here. To tell them they need to come to our city. And that they need to adhere to some rules and standards for sanctuary. Minor ones, but necessary, in order to remain a peaceful co-habituation." Kow said.

Tony turned to Cliff.

"Sounds like a job for a mayor, right, Cliff? What do you say, man? I hear you're a great front man. You can get the crowd all pumped up. Maybe you can rally these guys together."

Cliff thought about it. He grinned.

"I mean, it makes perfect sense for a man of my abilities. A lot of rock stars eventually get into politics right? Might as well use these smooth moves for something useful." Cliff said as he did a revolting little dance.

"I mean, sure Cliff." Tony said.

"My friend will assist you in your leadership." Kow said. Then it turned and walked to the front half of the space train. "We must return now. We have much work to do to get you home."

Ten

The space train made no noise. It was like gliding over the ground in a dream you were having. Peaceful and serene. But fast. Really fast.

Inside the train cars, it was large in space but minimal in design. A few rows of seats. Some tables. Low lit lights hung on the walls between spotless windows. The colors were cool and the seating was soft.

Tony and the kids had a whole passenger car to themselves. Good thing too, because now that Tony could see himself and the kids in a clean environment, he realized how disgusting they all looked. Their clothes were filthy and torn up. Quint's once shiny metal suit was now dull and dusty. Their faces were covered in dirt and soot. Sand fell from their hair as they moved their heads. No one would have wanted to sit by them. Kow and its friends had gone to the engine room to pilot the speeding vehicle. At least, that's what they told Tony. They may have just been grossed out.

Tony, Brody, and Hooper sat on one side and big shot Quint sat by himself on the other side. They wordlessly watched out the windows as the hovering train barreled through the desert. The speed rocked them back and forth. After only a few minutes of riding, Tony saw Quint was passed out, sleeping with his cheek against the window. Hooper was snoring soundly on his lap, drooling on his arm.

Brody, though, was wide awake. Staring intensely out the window as the desert and boulders blurred past them. His face made a small smile. His lips slightly curled up. Tony and his wife called it the 'TV face'. Not specifically for television, but just the face of being content and focused and calm. That face you make when you watch TV or read a book. Brody, for the first time since coming to this weird place, was comfortable.

Tony stayed awake with him. They sometimes talked about what they were looking at. Sometimes Brody would tell Tony his version about what they had just experienced. But mostly they just sat and looked out the window. Brody, with the warm feeling of being safe and Tony at the thought of going home.

THE SPACE TRAIN went through a tunnel and when it came out the other side, they were slowing down out of the desert and into civilization. Like the other city, this one also had a wall around it. But unlike the Hairsprayliens city, this city was well built. Just like the train they were on, the city was elegant in its design. Buildings were tall and lean. The streets were clean and clear. There appeared to be trees rising in between the sleek buildings. The city was not scattershot and congested like the Hairsprayliens were. Not like the ones on Earth were. The buildings and roads seemed to be well organized and each part specifically placed. A city built with function and purpose. It was obvious they had the time and resources to think about and properly build a city to suit its citizens and their needs.

Tony and Brody could see many hundreds of Tessons going about their day. The Tessons were walking on the streets and riding along in other trains. You could see them working through windows of the buildings. There were many of them on the ground tending to several enormous gardens in the middle of the city. It was jarring to see such colorful plant life after nothing but brown and gray everywhere else on this planet. And especially different to see such large functioning gardens in the middle of a metropolitan city. Tony knew they would use those spots as parking lots if this were Earth.

The space train slowed and quietly stopped moving. Quint and Hooper did not stir at all. The doors slid open and Kow leaned in and motioned for them to exit. Tony stood and briefly suffered the death stare of an abruptly awakened Hooper. He shook Quint awake and they all walked off the train together. The platform appeared to be built in the busy lobby of a building. Kow's friends were unloading the pieces of the Takeout Machine and carrying them down a corridor.

Kow led Tony and his kids down the platform and into the soft and clean lobby. It looked like a hotel lobby. Kow met several Tessons and greeted them with affection. They spoke wordlessly for a few moments. Then Kow told Tony to follow a friendly looking Tesson and it would take his family to a safe place to rest and relax while they got the machine ready.

THE TESSON HAD TAKEN them to the coziest looking room that Tony had ever seen. They filled it with more soft furniture and calming low light. There was no noise. The sparseness of its minimalism was made up for by the vast-ness its huge window provided. The giant window faced out into the city. The tall buildings and trees. The hovering trains floating by. And as always, the stars. The infinite night light shining down upon the metropolis.

The Tesson that showed them the room told Tony in quiet, broken up English that they had prepared a bath in a side room and that there were robes they could change into afterwards. It said that if they needed anything to press a button that was placed by the door. Then it left the family, the doors softly sliding shut behind it.

After a few minutes of exploring and running and jumping on all the furniture, Tony wrangled the kids to stand still long enough to get them changed out of their filthy clothes. Quint finally took off his stolen battle armor. It slid off of him like running paint and into a perfect square on the floor. Tony put it up and away from the kids.

A room off to the side had a big bathtub in it. Tony was never so excited to see a bathtub that didn't fly. The water was warm. All three kids hopped in and splashed around. Tony found strange shaped bottles of what he assumed was soap next to the tub. They could have been filled with toilet bowl cleaner, he supposed, but all he knew was it smelled better than his kids did. He soaped them up and rinsed them off and let them play for a while. Outside the tub, he used the water to wash his own face and all the splashing from the kids took care of the rest of him. When the water looked like a swamp, he made them get out and dried them with soft towels he had found. At least he hoped they were towels.

THEY ALL PUT on the soft, clean robes that the Tessons had left. Tony piled their filthy clothes together off in the corner. He was pretty sure they were a health hazard. The robes were snug and warm. He wished he had tooth-brushes, because their breath was just as rank as their clothes were. They all sat together on a large sofa by the window. They were all fast asleep in a matter of minutes. Dreaming, as the city continued to softly breathe outside their window.

TONY WAS NOT sure how long they had slept, but when he woke, he felt completely rested. The kids were already awake and sitting on the floor. They looked out the window and showed each other what they saw. Tony noticed that on a table by the door were all their clothes neatly folded. He picked them up and saw that they were completely clean. Like they were brand new. The holes in the knees and shirts were fixed. Even their ratty shoes. They looked immaculate. The detergent on this planet must be amazing, Tony thought.

After he got himself dressed, he helped the kids put their things on. Quint, while looking out the window, shouted over to Tony to come and look. Tony looked out and saw a few rows of the space trains pull into a station. Exiting the trains were hundreds and hundreds of the Hairsprayliens. They were carrying boxes and bags. They looked to be in just as much awe of the city as Tony and the kids had been. The Tessons set up groups and led them off the trains and into several buildings.

They were all watching out the window when the doors slid open and Kow walked in. Kow commented on how rested they looked. Tony expressed gratitude for how comfortable it had made them and for taking care of their clothes. Kow nodded, and then motioned for them to follow. Tony asked where they were going.

"It's time to send you home." Kow said smiling.

TEARS SOFTLY ROLLED down Tony's face as they walked down a long hallway. He silently cried as his kids bounced up and down and said hello to the Tessons that walked by them. They always said hello back. The family went down a set of hallways and then up some stairs. The building was clean, not a thing looking out of place.

They arrived at the top of the stairs. It looked like a very organized machine shop or laboratory. There were rows of computer looking devices and tables of machines and tools. There were groups of Tessons working together on projects at the tables. Set up in the back of the room was the reassembled Takeout Machine. A large group of Tessons greeted them. With a tear-streaked face, Tony thanked them over and over for helping his family get back home.

"It's okay, I didn't help or nothing… it wasn't me who came up with the idea or found the machine for you, or nothing."

It was Cliff. He was standing there in one of the Tessons long robes. They were too big on him, but he didn't seem to care. His face was clean shaven except for the stupid, gross chin beard, but at least it had been groomed. They had trimmed his huge hair down and was now slicked completely back. Apparently, the slick back was the power haircut of choice around here.

"Cliff, it's your fault we're here in the first place." Tony said back.

"Oh man, it's a broken record with you, jeez louise." Cliff replied and rolled his eyes.

"Nice outfit, Cliff."

"Do you like it? I think they're all jealous of how good

their clothes look on me. And the little fellas did my hair, see? I've got to look the part now that I'm an ambassador."

"He is not an ambassador." Kow said.

"We're still talking about it."

"You are not an ambassador."

Cliff winked and nodded.

"So how does this work?" Tony asked Kow.

"We shall send you back to the moment and location seconds after you would have left." Kow said, leading them closer to the machine.

"Wait… so, it will be like we never left? This thing does time travel?" Tony asked.

"It does many things." Kow said.

"Yeah, except get milkshakes at the drive thru after nine p.m." Cliff butt in.

"We shall send you back at the same time as you left." Kow repeated.

"Won't that mess up like timelines and stuff?" Tony asked, pretending he could understand things like time and space.

"Something like this should not cause a problem." Kow reassured as he looked at his fellow Tessons.

He pushed a button and the machine came to life. Lights flashed. Slowly, in front of them, a rainbow of light materialized. It started as a tiny pin sized hole and slowly ballooned in a crack, growing larger and larger and larger. The colorful light spread wider and wider and eventually the crack opened up into a doorway.

Tony had to squint his eyes to see through the bright light. He peered into the doorway and saw what looked like the brown grass back at Garbage Playground. He'd never been so excited to see that brown grass.

Kow held his arm out to the doorway.

"It is safe. You may walk through and you shall land back on Earth. Safely."

"Can I go first Daddy?" Quint excitedly asked.

Tony thought for a moment. He thought about everything that had happened. How terrified he'd been this whole time. Quint smiled at him.

"Go ahead, buddy. Be careful." Tony winced. He'd said it automatically. "I mean, have fun. We'll be right behind you." Tony told Quint.

"Sick." Quint said. He walked up to the doorway. "Bye everyone! Your planet is weird, but I had a great time!" He leapt into the rainbow doorway.

Tony peered through the door nervously. After just a second or two, Quint was standing back on the grass, waving back at everyone and laughing.

"I get a turn! Me!" Hooper shouted. She barreled past Tony and Brody. She turned and did a cute little wave, and then walked into the doorway. Seconds later, she was right next to Quint, and they were jumping around in excitement.

Tony laughed. He reached down and grabbed Brody's hand and was ready to follow the other two.

"He could stay with us." Kow suddenly said.

"Stay? Who?" Tony asked. Then he looked down at Brody.

"We have looked at Earth before. We know it is… difficult for Brody there. The same as it would be difficult for us." Kow said. "If he stayed here, he would be safe. He could be more comfortable with us. He could stay." Kow said.

Tony looked at his little boy.

"But then he wouldn't be with me." Tony said, looking back at Kow. "This place is amazing. I can tell that Brody would thrive here. He could grow and live more peacefully than on Earth. Things wouldn't be such a struggle for him here. He wouldn't have to listen to all the people who are constantly pushing him to be more like them." Tony said. "It's never going to be easy. But, maybe we try to change that?" Tony pointed to the doorway. "Earth is not the best for Brody, but Brody might be the best for Earth. What if we push back? Make everyone else work just as hard as they expect him to? Maybe they all start trying to meet his standards, instead of theirs? What if everyone did that full time?" Tony looked back at the smiling Brody. "He would be great here. But I wouldn't get to see it. And neither would they." Tony pointed to the doorway again. "And they need to see it." Tony said. "Thank you Kow, but we'll stick together."

Kow nodded. "Very well. If you ever change your mind…"

Tony turned to Cliff. "You sure you're not coming, Cliff?"

Cliff, with his slicked back hair and robe two sizes too big, shook his head. "No thanks man, I'm good here. Got political responsibilities now, you know."

"Any messages you want me to give anybody back home?" Tony asked.

"No." Cliff shrugged.

"Nothing? You don't want me to tell anyone where you are or what happened?"

"Nah."

"You're sure? Nothing at all?"

"Nope." Cliff scratched his upper lip.

"Okay, man, you take it easy." Tony waved.

"Oh yeah, I always keep it sleazy." Cliff smirked.

"Yeah, Cliff, I know." Tony looked around the lab and at Kow one last time. He leaned close to Kow. "Can I ask you a question?"

"Of course." Kow replied.

"Since we got here in the city, I've been thinking. When those little things were shooting and trying to crash their bathtubs into you all? When all their laser beams were doing nothing but blowing up their own town? I was thinking. You could have sent them that selfie anytime, right? Maybe, before they destroyed where they live?" Tony raised his eyebrows.

"Well. Like you said. Sometimes you have to push back a little." Kow said quietly, looking at the floor. It glanced up at Tony and narrowed its eyes.

"Must just be overthinking it. I'm a worrier, you know. Thank you for everything, Kow." Tony said.

KOW NODDED.

"Bye! See you later!" Brody yelled.

They jumped into the rainbow doorway. Tony and Brody were floating through space, past billions of stars and planets. They were speeding past different galaxies and unknown solar systems. Then... they were at the Garbage Playground.

Quint and Hooper ran up and hugged them. Tony embraced his kids. They were back on Earth. They were home. He breathed a sigh of relief. Tony looked over and watched as the rainbow doorway melted away into a crack. Smaller and smaller, it shrank. Then it was gone.

Tony stood up and looked around. It really was Garbage Playground.

"Can we play Daddy?" Quint asked. The boy was relentless.

"I don't know about you guys, but I'm starving. Who wants an early lunch? We'll go through the drive -thru on the way home." Tony asked. They all excitedly agreed.

They started walking out of the woods, back into the playground. As they passed the slide, Tony saw the nanny he had talked to earlier.

"Oh good, you found them!" The young nanny laughed when she saw Tony and the kids.

"Yeah, they didn't get too far." Tony replied.

Meanwhile...

A couple billion trillion galaxies away…

"Okay okay guys. Let's try this again."

Cliff had a flawless looking guitar strapped on and plugged in. There was one Hairspraylien with a mohawk sitting at a brand new drum kit. Another Hairspraylien, this one with long curly hair, stood on a crate behind a state-of-the-art set of laptops and turntables.

On the opposite side, there was a tall Tesson standing at a large keyboard. Fiddling with the knobs on a brand new amplifier, another Tesson had a brightly colored bass guitar across its chest. Both Tessons had on tight headphones.

The air was filled with the hum of feedback.

"DJ Butterfingers, we talked about this, you're getting too far ahead of yourself. Let's focus up now. J-Bone, you too. Come on guys, you know this. We've gone over this a hundred times. Now let's try again." Cliff paced around and lectured. "Okay, new guys? Fellas, don't think I'm cutting you any slack here. You've got to keep up. We've got our first gig next week and I don't want to blow it. Come on now, let's do this. Let's try it one more time."

A bouncy beat blasted out of the turntables, and the keyboards added some flourish. The bass joined in. The drums slowly banged faster and faster. Cliff threw his hand across the strings of his guitar. He leaned into a microphone and yelled.

"Thank you, ladies and gentlemen! We are Rykden! Are you ready? Are you ready?! ARE YOU READYYYYYYYYYYYY???!!!"

The End.

PART II

FullTimeTony and the Royal Riders

One

The bus picked Quint up every morning right down the block. Then, as soon as Quint left, Brody's bus came. They both went to the same school, third grade and kindergarten, but Brody rode specialized transportation. After he got picked up, Tony had to drive Hooper to her morning preschool. About two hours later, he'd go pick Hooper up. Tony would meet Quint and Brody when their buses dropped them back off around three-thirty.

A joke he was thinking of trying out on people was that he was 'going to change his job title from stay-at-home dad to stay-in-car dad'. He didn't get to say it to anyone yet, because he hadn't spoken to another adult outside of his wife in weeks. She didn't give him the best feedback about it.

Still Fall, the cold weather was bitter but had not turned hateful yet. That meant that Tony could just throw sweatshirts and light jackets on the kids, before they rushed out the door in time for the first bus. Brody had his lion blanket tied around his neck like a hipster scarf. He got to hang on to it until his bus arrived, and then he would turn the blanket over to Tony for safekeeping during the day.

Today they had gotten out of the door with little conflict, except for the one they were having with each other. At breakfast, the argument over who got to sit in the center right chair at the dining room table had started up again. Tony and his wife's long national nightmare about the chair had been going on for years now. The war had taken a heavy toll upon the family. Tony's wife said that when they were both dead, the kids would only kill each other over who was rightful heir to the stupid chair, so they should just spend all the money now. Tony sat in it one time when they were at school. He didn't get it. Not that great.

"No, not you, Quint! It's my turn!" Brody shouted at Quint as they all stood on the corner waiting for Quint's bus.

"No way Brody! You got to sit in it yesterday!" Quint fired back at him as he readjusted his backpack.

"You two! We're not even in the house anymore. Why are we still arguing about this?" Tony said. Then he smiled at them and threw some gas on the raging fire. "Besides, Hooper gets it next, right?"

"Yeah! Not you boys! I get a turn!" Hooper said, tossing a handful of leaves into the air.

"No!" both boys whined.

Tony heard the bus's loud engine coming from around the corner.

"Okay, okay. You can duel each other in the name of cheap furniture later. I hear your bus coming." Tony said. "Hey! Have a great day today, bud!" Tony said as he bent down and hugged a pouting Quint.

But instead of the bus, a dirty yellow spaceship came around the corner and stopped right in front of the family.

"New bus? The school just emailed saying the budget got cut." Tony said.

The floating ship was yellow but covered in dirt and grime and soot. It was about the same size as a cargo van or the small buses that pick up Brody. It had strange looking tubes and attachments on its roof and back. Its engine rattled shakily. Brody covered his ears up as it parked loudly in front of them.

The ship was hovering about three feet above the street, so when the side door slid open the creature had to hop down to get out. It was fuzzy and had horns that folded back like a ram. Long and sharp teeth poked up out of the bottom half of its scowling mouth. When it stood up straight after leaping to the ground, it was the size of a full-grown grizzly bear. And it was wearing a bright neon yellow vest.

Tony took a step back and pushed the kids behind him.

"Good morning?" Tony said, his eyes wide.

The big fuzzy beast ripped the bright vest off and tossed it to the ground. Then it turned and stomped away from the ship and family.

"I'd get out of here if I was you mister, this group is nothing but trouble." The creature said, pointing back at the ship with its huge thumb. "Get away while you still BLARK BLAF BARG YOOG MURP GART VARM." It grumbled as it got farther from the ship. It was still talking nonsense words as it went down the block and turned the corner. It was gone.

"Where's it going?" Brody asked.

"I don't know, man, but it's going to wake up the entire neighborhood with its weird swear words." Tony replied.

"Blark Blaf Barg!" Hooper swung her arms and parroted in a silly voice. The two boys busted up laughing.

"Blark Blaf Barg!" the kids all repeated and giggled.

"Great." Tony said, shaking his head.

"Excuse me." A tiny voice said.

They all stopped space cussing and turned. Standing in the spaceship's doorway was a little purple octopus with thick glasses on. It was shorter than Hooper. Four of its arms stuck out of a white polo shirt and its other four hung out of a navy blue skirt. It had a pink bow in its quick puff of auburn hair on top of its round head.

"Look Daddy!" Brody shouted.

"Hi, there. Uh… can you drive us to school?" The little octopus said in a squeaky voice as it adjusted its glasses.

"This is your school bus? Awesome!" Quint asked in amazement.

"Yes, it is! I think our driver just quit?" It pointed two of its arms to Tony. "Can you finish driving us to school, please?"

Tony couldn't believe what he was seeing. Surely this was not really happening. Maybe he should cut back on all the coffee.

"I'm sorry, what is going on?" Tony said cautiously.

"We all go to a special school far, far away. Our driver just quit and I'm not sure why. Maybe all the pressure probably got to him." It said.

"The pressure?" Tony asked.

"Well, yes. We are all kind of special, I guess." It suddenly looked embarrassed. "We are all members of royalty, if I can say that without sounding stuck up." It said, rolling its eyes behind the thick glasses.

"Royalty? Like kings and queens?" Hooper asked.

"Yes! Our parents are the rulers of the Four Realms of the Infinite. We are all next in line to take over each of our empires, someday. I am Princess Chara of the Harmony Realm!"

"Hi Princess Chara! I'm Quint and this is my brother Brody and my sister Hooper!" Quint said warmly.

"I'm sorry, the rulers of the what of the what?" Tony said, confused.

"The Four Realms of the Infinite. It's kind of like everything in the Universe. There's an infinite number of different galaxies and planets and people. Our parents are rulers of the realms that keep watch over them." Princess Chara explained.

"So, the future heirs to the entire universe are all sitting on that space bus?" Tony said, pointing at the dirty yellow ship.

"Yes! Come aboard and meet them!" Princess Chara said, and turned back inside.

Quint and Brody immediately leapt up and climbed into the doorway.

"Boys! Stop!" Tony shouted, but they were already on the bus.

"Come on!" Hooper said and followed them.

"I must be out of my mind. Tomorrow, just one pot of coffee. Wait. Maybe more? Three pots." Tony followed her inside.

AN OVERSIZED DRIVER'S seat was directly across from the door like on a regular Earth bus. The dashboard, however, looked insanely more complicated. It had hundreds of touchscreens and switches and buttons on all three sides of the seat. Lights blinked and tiny displays flashed with symbols of alien language from the front and side and behind. There was lots of beeping.

Tony was so hypnotized by the technology that when he turned and saw that his kids, the octopus girl, a robot, and a velociraptor were all staring at him. He jumped in surprise.

"Ah! Pickles!" Tony squealed.

"Scared you, Daddy!" Brody laughed.

"Okay, uh, hi everybody." Tony said to the very odd-looking group.

"Who's this guy?" The dinosaur kid said in a loud snarl.

Even slightly hunched over in the cramped space bus, the lizard child was still taller than Quint. It had the face, skin, and claws of a velociraptor. Its hair resembled a lion's mane, big and flowing up and out. When it stood still, it breathed heavily, panting hard like a wolf. It wore a solid navy polo and a pair of khaki pants. The school uniform really took a bite out of the scariness.

"Come on Chara! Don't tell me this meatbag is going to drive us to school. He's pathetic looking." It growled.

"Be nice, Chomar!" Princess Chara yelled back. "We need his help!"

"Meatbag? So you speak English, but just the rude words?" Tony said to the dinosaur kid called Chomar.

"We're not speaking English, you moron. It's the bus." Chomar snarled.

"The bus?" Tony said, adding another stamp to his recently issued 'nope, not getting it' punch card.

The small robot child spoke up. Its voice sounded like it was coming from a tin can.

"Through a combination of highly advanced technology... BEEP... and carefully curated and complicated magic... BEEP... they built the bus with a multi-universal translator. None of us speak the same language... BEEP... yet we can all hear and understand each other when in and near the bus. That is why you no longer understood the bus driver… BEEP… the further away from the bus he walked."

Shaped like a series of small metal boxes stacked on top of a larger box, the small robot kid had thin tent poles for arms and legs. It had artificial eyes that moved around as it looked at Tony, but its mouth was simply a series of lights that activated when it spoke. There were more lights and buttons scattered around on its chest. There was an ID tag stamped near its shoulder. It was wearing a pair of khaki uniform shorts.

"Okay… Dig?" Tony said, reading the ID tag.

"Ha! Dig!" Chomar laughed and pointed at the little robot.

"Actually… BEEP… it's D16. I am the sixteenth upgrade model to, when my time comes, assume installation as head program of… BEEP… the Machine Collective Dataset. It is a pleasure to meet you." D16 said.

"It's nice to meet you too, D16." Tony smiled at the little robot. He looked around the bus again. "Magic and technology? So whenever we talk, you guys all hear it in your own language. And we hear you talk in ours." Tony said.

"Oh, man. This one catches on quick. Don't worry everyone, we don't have to go to school, we can just stay here and learn from this genius." Chomar mocked.

"Take it easy, kid." Tony said. "I guess you're what? Destined to be the king of space-lizard bullies?"

"King? I am her royal highness, Chomar The Firefury, Future Reign Of The Bloodhorde! You should watch it with your misgendering, pal. Last one to do that now has to be spoon fed by the surviving members of his family." Chomar growled.

"Oh, no! Okay. I am sorry, Chomar. I should not have done that. Thank you for telling me. I won't do it again."

Tony apologized. He turned to Princess Chara. "Wait, didn't you say there were four kingdoms? I mean, you're the peace world. And Dig…"

"D16… BEEP."

"Sorry, D16 is the technology one. The dino queen here is some kind of war kingdom, I guess. You said there was a fourth?" Tony asked.

Princess Chara, Chomar and D16 all slowly turned around and looked at the back of the bus. Tony and his kids craned their heads around them to see what they were looking at. In the back, in a seat all by itself, hovered a small swirling circle.

It looked about the same size as a large pizza hanging vertically. The spinning circle floated just above its seat. Its center was absolute black. But spreading out from the dark middle, soft light and tiny colorful stars delicately drifted and churned around and around. The colors changed and faded in and out as they spun. It was quite hypnotizing to look at.

"Who is that?" Quint asked.

"He's a black hole. Created by the dark wizards and witches of the Ancient Lands. They've controlled and watched over most of the magic that happens in the universes." Princess Chara explained. She turned to Tony. "All of our realms didn't always get along, you see? They've been at war with each other more or less forever." Princess Chara pointed at the swirling circle with one of her tentacles. "Recently, the keepers of the dark magic summoned that black hole to destroy the rest of us once and for all. But something went wrong. It was alive. But, it was like a newborn, just a child like us. That's when things changed." Princess Chara said.

"It is because of it BEEP… that peace finally came. Frightened by it and its ability to end absolutely everything should it choose... BEEP... they decided that the future generations should learn to live peacefully together. They all agreed to a peace treaty. The rulers of each of our worlds decided we should all... BEEP... go to the same school. To grow up together, so that the universe may live in peace forever. They combined their resources and built this bus. A combination of... BEEP... science and magic." D16 continued. "But... BEEP... if we don't make it to school on time, then that violates the peace treaty and..."

"Then it's war. For the last time." Chomar grunted and folded her arms.

"That is why it is so important that we get to school!" Princess Chara said.

"Daddy, help them!" Quint pleaded as D16 brushed past him and waddled to the bus's complicated dashboard.

"Help? How? I can't fly this thing? We can't go to some planet! I've got to get you two and your sister to school!" Tony said, not believing this was happening. "Look, nowadays all kids have cellphones. Come on Chomar, you can't text your folks to come pick you up?"

"No, idiot. We're not allowed to have our phones at school." Chomar snapped back.

"Yeah, that's a good rule, actually." Tony sighed.

"My bus driver sometimes talks on the radio!" Brody said.

"Yeah, good call Brody. Isn't one of these fancy buttons a walkie-talkie that you can radio for a ride home?" Tony pointed to the dashboard.

"Normally yes... BEEP... but it appears all of our outgoing communications have been... BEEP... disabled." D16 said, standing at the dashboard, pressing buttons and screens.

"Disabled? Like turned off? But why? Who would do that?" Princess Chara asked.

"The driver. The bus driver turned it off, I bet. That horned, fuzzy creep." Chomar snarled, turning to look out the window. "I'd say he didn't quit because of the pressure. He straight up sold us out."

"What are you talking about, Chomar?" Princess Chara furrowed her little brow.

"Four future heirs to the universe. One of whom has the power to end absolutely everything. We're worth quite a bit of money, I'd imagine."

"You mean… BEEP… we are in danger?" D16 said, turning away from the control panels.

"It's what I'd do. Buy off the driver to leave us somewhere unprotected. Swoop in and grab us. Ransom us or blackmail our parents. If it's not for money, believe me, the peace treaty didn't thrill absolutely everyone in the universe." Chomar said, crossing the bus's aisle and looking out the other windows.

"Wait, wait, wait, wait, wait. What's happening?" Tony said, waving his hands, trying to catch up.

Suddenly, a loud ringing started coming from the dashboard. Several lights were flashing rapidly.

"What is it, D16?" Princess Chara asked.

D16 turned back to the panels and started pressing more buttons and screens. The ringing and lights stopped.

"A group of ships just entered… BEEP… this planet's galaxy. A big Harmony System Transport cruiser and what appears to be five or six… BEEP…. Bloodhorde Gun Cruisers." D16 read out loud.

"Chomar? Maybe it's our parents?" Princess Chara asked her. Chomar just shrugged her big shoulders in confusion.

"It is strange… BEEP…" D16 said while pushing more buttons. "They outfitted the ships with my programmer's Machine Collective tracking software… BEEP… and I can also see Dark Magic protection spells radiating off of them?"

"It could be all our parents coming to get us?" Princess Chara said.

"Our parents would have radioed or tried to contact us the second we went off route." Chomar looked out of a window up at the blue morning sky. "No, I think some angry members of each of our realms are looking to cause a lot of trouble."

"What is happening??!!" Tony yelled.

"Trouble, daddy. We've got trouble." Brody reached up and said.

Princess Chara grabbed Tony with her four top arms. "Please, mister, drive us to school! It's safe there, we're protected! We can contact our families once we're there and they can take care of those guys!" She begged.

"But I don't know how to drive this thing! I can barely handle my minivan! Ask my wife!" Tony said.

"The bus's engine and flight controls are mostly automated... BEEP... it has a built-in guidance system... BEEP... that will show you which way to go. You really just... BEEP... need to steer it. It won't move without a driver... BEEP." D16 said.

"Well, can't you drive it?" Tony asked.

"Seriously, dude? You're going to let a bunch of kids drive a bus alone, up there with a pack of traitorous kidnappers after them? Your parent of the year award must have gotten lost in the mail." Chomar mocked.

"Hey! Listen! I never win anything, kid!" Tony yelled back.

He looked down at Hooper, Brody, and Quint. They all looked very concerned about what was going on.

"Please, Daddy." Quint said softly.

Tony took a deep breath. He thought he must be out of his mind.

"Fine." Tony said.

"Alright Daddy!" Quint shouted.

"Woo-hoo!" Brody leapt up.

"Hooray for Hooper!" Hooper said.

"Okay. Kids, sit down and stay sitting. Same rules as on your busses, got it?"

"Got it!" Quint shot him a thumbs up.

"Hey, Dig?"

"D16… BEEP."

"Right. You seem to know what these buttons do, so I want you sitting up close to me in these front seats." Tony told the robot as it sat down up front. Quint politely asked the robot if he could sit with it. Tony leaned down to the octopus and whispered quietly. "Princess Chara, please understand I'm not throwing you the babysitting job because you're one of the girls, but I'm honestly afraid if I ask Chomar, she'll try to eat them or something. Can you help keep an eye on my kids?"

"I will try, yes!" Princess Chara giggled and hurried to her seat.

"Chomar, you sit over there and be as negative as possible about everything. Maybe make some mean sarcastic comments now and then. That would help A LOT."

"Whatever." Chomar said, sitting alone. Brody picked a seat across from the bored warrior princess.

"What about your, uh, magic black hole buddy back there, is it going to be okay?" Tony motioned to the swirling dark void sitting quietly in the back.

"He doesn't talk much here or at school. One time, he whispered he likes to be called Kevin. So that's what we call him," Princess Chara said, scooting Hooper closer to her on the bus seat. Hooper smiled at her new friend and snuggled in.

"Magic black hole named Kevin, got it. It's the least weird thing about all of this." Tony said. He walked to the front of the bus and took a deep breath.

SITTING down in the oversized driver's seat, Tony noticed new lights and screens turning on in the dashboard. As he sat down, the dash slid open and a series of small bars folded out smoothly and joined to form a steering wheel.

Symbols and charts appeared along the edges of the windshield. Tony watched as the glass slightly tinted. Then, through the windshield, a thick bright yellow line appeared from the front of the bus and extended down the street. At the end of the block, the line tilted into the air and up to the sky and clouds above.

"That is… BEEP… the destination path to the school. It is not really there and only… BEEP… we can see it from inside the bus. Just follow the line to get us to school!" D16 happily explained.

"Okay, sounds easy enough. But how do I get this thing going?" Tony asked.

"I think that one?" D16 said, pointing to the hand lever near the steering wheel.

Tony cautiously and slowly pulled the lever down and the bus's engine revved up louder and he could feel them going forward. He felt the lever suddenly pulling itself, and he let go. The bus was moving faster now, like it was in its proper gear.

Tony guided the big vehicle carefully down the yellow line, feeling its heavy weight in the pull of the steering wheel. The bus went faster and faster. Then he could feel it getting higher and higher, like when a plane was about to take off. Down the yellow line the bus went, then up into the air.

They were ascending into the sky now, feeling the push of the acceleration against their bodies as they got higher and higher into the clouds. Tony looked out the side windows and watched the street, block, neighborhood, and city getting smaller as they flew up.

"Woo-hoo!" Quint joyfully yelled. All the other kids joined him. They all shouted in excitement.

Above the clouds, the sky was shifting from the bright blue to a much darker color as they approached the upper atmosphere. Sweat was forming along Tony's forehead. He gripped the steering wheel, trying to stay on the yellow line as best he could. He was stressfully trying to keep the bus's heavy weight from drifting them off course. Higher and higher, they rose.

Then, as simple as passing through a tunnel, they were in outer space.

It was pretty anticlimactic. Tony didn't know what he expected. Flames or a boom or something? He was almost disappointed.

"So, uh, space. I guess. Woo-hoo?" Tony said underwhelmed.

He kept following the yellow line. Tony saw it stretched far and turned and looped around up ahead.

"This rules!" Quint yelled, his nose pressed against his seat window, watching the Earth get smaller and smaller.

"Wee." Chomar mocked.

"Ha! We're flying!" Hooper said next to Princess Chara.

"Daddy, I see the stars!" Brody called up to Tony.

"I see them too, bud!" Tony replied. He was wildly looking all around him to see it all. It was absolutely breathtaking.

D16 tapped Quint on the shoulder. Quint turned away from the window.

"Quint, what is… BEEP… your father's name?" D16 asked.

Quint smiled at his dad flying the space bus.

"His name is Tony. And he's awesome." Quint said.

Tony had heard. He turned and looked lovingly at his proud son. He thought he was going to cry.

"Tell awesome Tony that he's about to run into the moon." Chomar said.

"Huh?" Tony said, turning to see the moon directly in front of them. "Pickles!" He panicked and jerked the wheel. All the kids yelped and slid over to the side. He quickly got the bus back on the yellow line.

"Everything's fine. It's fine." Tony said.

Everything was not fine.

Two

Not counting almost running into the moon, Tony was a pretty good space bus driver. All you really had to do was keep the bus on the line. The bus's windshield displayed a yellow GPS path that seemed to steer clear of the planets, moons, and other space potholes. He couldn't guess how fast they were going, but at the rate the stars were passing by, it had to be an incredible speed. You could feel the strength of the ship in the pull of its steering wheel. Tony was gripping tight with sweaty hands.

It was hard not to hold your breath at the majesty of outer space. The bus cruised through Earth's own solar system quickly. Quint told everyone to wave at Pluto as it sailed by. Beyond was an infinity of unseen space. They passed new systems and planets. They watched comets and asteroids dance around each other. They saw massive, blazing stars that made their own sun look like the light in the fridge. Tony was trying to stay laser focused on keeping the bus on the floating yellow line guiding them through the universes, but it was hard to keep your eyes from wandering.

All the bickering in the back also wasn't helping his concentration. Tony's kids were behaving pretty well. Everything around them was too distracting for them to be their usual monster selves. It was the space kids. They were driving Tony crazy with all their fighting.

"Chomar! Stop kicking our seats!" Princess Chara turned and yelled. The little octopus princess sat with Hooper and was getting annoyed with the classmate behind her.

"I'm not! It's not my fault they built this bus for whiny little babies like you, Chara." The large reptile warrior princess snapped back. In her defense, she was a good three feet taller than the other kids, but Tony thought that she really didn't have to be a jerk about absolutely everything.

"Do not call Princess Chara... BEEP... a baby." D16, the robot prince, told Chomar.

"Did you say something, you Wi-Fi wimp?" Chomar leaned over to where D16 and Quint were sitting.

"Why are you so... BEEP... mean all the time, Chomar?" D16 sniffed. Quint stopped gawking out the window and patted his metal seatmate on the shoulder.

"Because it bites that I have to go to this wimpy school with you losers. My kingdom could have conquered all of yours, ten times over, if it wasn't for this dumb peace treaty." Chomar waved her arms around.

"Oh yeah? Then why didn't they?" Princess Chara adjusted her glasses. "It's because your realm needs the peace treaty as much as all of ours do." Princess Chara leaned closer to Chomar. "You're not as strong and scary as all of you pretend you are."

"You want to find out how scary Sally Squid?" Chomar reared up.

Then from over the seat, Chomar saw Hooper creepily rise and give the dinosaur princess a death glare.

"Lookit me. Lookit me." Hooper pointed to her face, mocking Tony when he sometimes did this to the kids. "Stop being mean. Sit down. You're in time out. Five minutes." And she held up her open palm, showing Chomar five fingers. "Five. Minutes."

Chomar's eyes narrowed at Hooper. They stared at each other. Then slowly Chomar's mouth formed a smile, exposing her razor-sharp teeth.

"I like this one. She's scary. You must be one of Earth's warrior classes." Chomar nodded at Hooper.

Hopper kept her death glare, but turned and sat back down next to a beaming Princess Chara.

"Thanks, Hooper!" Princess Chara said and hugged her new friend with her top four octopus arms.

Tony's clear favorite of these bratty space kids was the one who didn't speak. The fourth student, Kevin, the small magical sentient black hole, still hadn't made a sound. He just floated above his seat in the back. Small stars and cosmos colorfully swirled around his perfectly dark center.

Brody was sitting by himself in a seat across from Chomar. He had been snuggling his lion blanket and zoning out at all the space scenery. He suddenly shouted up front at Tony.

"Daddy? Are we almost there yet?" Brody asked.

"Yeah, that's actually a good question. Do you guys know how far we have to go? I don't want a universal war to break out because I'm Sunday driving and missed the first bell." Tony called back.

"Landing on Earth did... BEEP... take us off route but... BEEP... it does not matter because the school... BEEP... changes location every day. Sometimes hourly. It randomly teleports itself around for... BEEP... security and our safety." D16 explained.

"So we don't even know where the school is right now? No idea at all where we're going?" Tony turned back, confused.

"Well, the bus knows... BEEP... where it is. They update its coordinates as needed."

"Okay, I guess. Moving school. That's got to be a zoning nightmare." Tony said to himself.

Chomar leaned over the seat in front of her.

"So, what's your weapon of choice? You like an axe? Or maybe a double-sided spear? You definitely look like a blade type of girl." Chomar genuinely inquired about Hooper.

"Ugh. She's not a warrior jerk like you, Chomar. Back off. Your breath stinks." Princess Chara said, rolling her eyes.

"Does not, Princess Perfect-puss!"

"Leave her alone... BEEP... Chomar!" D16 shouted in his tinny voice.

"Make me you megabyte moron!" Chomar turned to D16.

"Everyone! Can we stop fighting, please? Can we not scream at Chomar for every little thing she does or says? And Chomar, your mastery of bully's alliteration is astounding, but can you please give everyone some space?" Tony shouted back.

"Yeah! My daddy is trying to drive!" Quint thought he should assist in the scolding.

"Yeah, thanks, Quint." Tony said and turned back to the space in front of him. "Is there a radio on this thing somewhere? Some music we can play? Maybe really loud? At least in my minivan, I can drown out and ignore my kids when they are bickering."

"What type of… BEEP… Earth music do you listen to?" D16 asked.

But Tony didn't answer quickly enough.

"My dad listens to ska music." Quint said to D16.

"WHAT?!" Chomar suddenly sat up.

"Ska music. Like with horns and stuff." Quint repeated.

"You've got to be kidding me. Like what? Old jazzy type stuff?" Chomar was giggling.

"Well, no. More like the punk ska stuff from the nineties. Like punk rock, but with horns. Trumpets. Trombones. Played really fast." Tony reluctantly answered. He already knew what was coming.

"Third wave? You still listen to third wave ska? Oh man, that is hilarious! Ska sucks!"

"Yeah, my mom says my dad fell off his skateboard in high school and broke his musical taste." Quint said, smiling.

"HAHAHA!" Chomar pointed at Tony and cracked up.

"What? Your mother said that? When did she say that?" Tony turned in disgust.

"Hey, digital dork!" Chomar shouted at D16. "Play some ska punk for our super cool driver. Maybe he'll start skanking." Chomar said, making fun of the way ska kids danced.

D16's body made little sorting chirping noises. Then, he started playing some 90s ska punk music out of himself, like a speaker. It was loud and fast. Tony exhaled. He knew this song. It was actually one of his favorites.

"BBBWWWAAAHAHAHAHAHAHAHAHA!" Chomar said, dying with laughter. "This is clown music, you nerd!" She was wiping tears from her eyes.

Chomar's contagious cackling made all the other kids

laugh, too. Giggling and slapping the seats hysterically. Earth and space children laughing together. Peace and harmony achieved through making fun of Tony. He should get a medal for this.

"I don't only listen to ska music!" Tony shouted back, trying to keep some bit of authority.

"Buddy, I don't think it matters anymore!" Chomar chuckled. "Your street cred just got blown to bits!" And then she started laughing again. Tony swore he saw some of them high fiving.

"Oh yeah? Well jokes on you! I never had street cred to begin with, so there! And how's a rude dinosaur alien like you even know about ska?" Tony said, shaking his head.

"We use it to torture prisoners!" Chomar said, and they all howled with laughter again.

SUDDENLY... a loud alarm went off. The lights on the bus flashed red.

"Okay, okay, okay. What the heck is that?" Tony panicked as the alarm and lights intensified. In his panic, he loosened his grip on the steering wheel and the bus waved around. "D16! Get up here and help me!"

"We are not... BEEP... allowed to stand while the bus... BEEP... is moving." The robot warned.

"I'm giving you permission! Come on!" Tony shouted.

"Okay... BEEP!" D16 said and waddled shakily to the front of the bus, next to Tony.

"What's going on? Make this stop!" Tony yelled, trying to control the bus.

D16 quickly pushed a combination of buttons and screens. The alarm and flashing lights stopped.

"Okay, thank you. Now turn down the ska." Tony told D16.

"Okay… BEEP… shutting off."

"Well, hey now. I didn't say off, I just said, turn it down. Now, what just happened? Are we out of gas or something?"

The ska music got quieter as D16 rapidly started turning switches and poked at displays. Tony thought he heard him gasp.

"Worse. It appears… BEEP… that transport and those gun cruisers that had entered your galaxy… BEEP… have doubled back around and are going to be in our range shortly."

"But you said no one knows where the school is. So they don't know where the bus is going. So how did they find us?" A confused Tony asked.

"Obviously they're tracking us somehow. Maybe that turncoat driver let them hack into the navigation." Chomar shouted from her seat.

"So what do we do? I mean, what…"

The dark voice coming from a speaker on the dashboard suddenly cut Tony's anxiety off.

"Attention Earth Man." A sinister voice crackled from the speaker. "Your communicator has been disabled. But you can hear us. Please listen." The voice instructed. "Your own family will not be harmed. We will return you to Earth after you hand the transport and the royal children over to us. It is your only option." The gravelly voice said. "Well, there is another way. But you will not enjoy it." The speaker went silent again.

"That's them. This is really happening. They're really coming to get us." Princess Chara worried.

"They're incoming… BEEP… three minutes." D16 read off of a monitor.

"What do we do? Does this thing have weapons or anything?" Tony asked.

"It's a school bus not a warship, idiot." Chomar said.

"Then can we outrun them?" Tony wondered.

"Well, yes, this bus is capable of quantum speeds... BEEP... but..."

"But it would take a seasoned fighter pilot to outmaneuver them in a chase. You've been driving this thing for what, twenty minutes?" Chomar growled.

"Then what, Chomar? I'm not letting them take us!" Tony turned and shouted.

Princess Chara and Hooper were hugging each other tight. Quint hopped back to Brody's seat, and they were sitting together and looking worried. Chomar stood and stalked to the front of the bus.

"Okay. So they know where we are, because they know where we're going. So... what if they don't know where we're going? What if we shut that off?" Chomar said and pointed out the windshield at the yellow guidance line.

"Two minutes... BEEP."

Tony looked out at the thick yellow line that showed them which way to go.

"So we turn off the yellow line and they can't track us anymore? Then what?" Tony wondered.

"Go really fast. Right now. Before they get here. Get somewhere else. Turn in a bunch of random directions. Try to lose them." Chomar squinted out the windshield.

"I don't know." Tony started.

"I've run the numbers... BEEP... it could work. If we put enough distance between us and those ships... BEEP... we could eventually switch the guidance system back on and... BEEP... hopefully make it to school before they track us again." D16 said.

Tony looked back at his kids. They all stared wide-eyed at their father. Tony sighed.

"Okay, do it. Turn off the guidance thing, so they can't

track us. D16, can you make the bus do the, go fast speed or whatever you called it?"

"I'm activating the… BEEP… quantum speeds now. I'm switching the controls to manual." D16 said. A small section of the floor by Tony's feet slid open, and a step elevated out slightly.

"Right. Gas pedal." Tony said. "Wait, what if I hit an asteroid or a planet or something?"

"Try not to." Chomar warned.

D16 glanced at the display again and shouted. "One minute until they're here… BEEP… they are going to be right on top of us!"

"Turn off the yellow line and go sit down. Hold on tight." Tony instructed everyone.

"Uh oh, Daddy's going to go fast!" Brody warned.

D16 quickly punched a series of buttons. Suddenly the windshield was no longer tinted and the bright, thick yellow line was gone. Tony could feel the space bus drift around on its own. He readjusted his hands on the wheel and gained back control. Chomar and D16 rushed back to their seats.

Everyone braced themselves. D16 leaned over and looked at a display.

"Thirty seconds… BEEP!"

"Hold on everyone! We're about to do something stupid." Tony shouted. Then he slowly and carefully put a little pressure on the new pedal with his feet. He felt the bus shimmy with more power and his body felt even more pressure of being pulled forward.

"BEEP… ten seconds!!"

"Come on, rude boy! Pick it up, pick it up, pick up!" Chomar screamed.

"Stop making fun of ska!" Tony yelled and stomped on the pedal.

The space bus and its occupants lunged forward like being shot out of a cannon.

The exact second the bus sped away, six stolen Blood-horde Gunships appeared. Behind them flew a gigantic, dark magic retrofitted Harmony System Transport ship.

Surprised by the sudden disappearance of the bus, two of the Gunships panicked and ran into each other, exploding upon impact.

Another two fired their weapons upon a target they could no longer see. They were firing so blind and wild that they only ended up hitting each other, which resulted in another set of explosions.

A FEW MILLION light years ahead of the pursuers, Tony was barely maintaining control of the bus rocketing through the universe at unfathomable speeds. The steering wheel and the rest of the bus were shaking with the tremors of moving so fast.

"Remember to be turning, Mister Tony! So they can't find us!" Princess Chara shouted up from her and Hooper's seat. They had a tight grip on one another.

"Right! Hold on!" Tony said, and pulled the heavy wheel over to the right. The bus drifted to the side and then hurdled forward again. The kids all slid around in their seats. Tony let the bus speed ahead in a straight line for a few seconds and then turned the wheel to the left. The bus jerked around and then straightened out again. Tony kept changing directions every few seconds. Each second speeding through millions of miles of space.

Brody and Quint huddled together. They were trying to hang on and sit still against the amazing speeds and sharp turns. After a minute of his father's crazy driving, Brody leaned up and looked at the seat behind him. There, hovering silently, was Kevin, the magical living black hole. He was also bouncing in his seat; his mini solar system shaking around when he did. Brody made a worried face at Kevin.

"You can come sit with me and Quint." Brody told Kevin.

Kevin remained quiet.

Then, wordlessly, Kevin floated out of his seat and around to Brody and Quint's seat. Quint and Brody scooted over closer to the window to make room for Kevin. The small, sentient force of destruction settled in next to Brody. Kevin's tiny system of swirling stars and colors brushed up against Brody's shoulder. But he didn't seem to mind. The bus made another tight turn, and the three slid into one another. A nervous Brody suddenly threw his lion blanket over his head, making sure some of the blanket covered the top of Kevin, too. They both hid under the blanket together.

"What do you think? Think we've put enough road between us and those guys?" Tony yelled, while turning the wheel again.

"We should stop and see where we are!" Princess Chara shouted to the front.

Tony slowly eased his foot off the gas pedal. The bus decelerated. The force and pressure on the bus lessened. After a few moments, it was going at its normal speed again. Tony loosened his tight grip on the wheel. He took a few deep breaths.

"Okay, D16, come up here and let's find out if that bought us any time."

The small robot slid off his seat and clanked to the front. He poked and swiped at some displays.

"Nothing in... BEEP... range. It appears to have

gotten us out of… BEEP… immediate danger." D16 said while pressing more buttons.

"But what will happen when we turn the guidance system back on? They'll find us again, won't they?" Princess Chara wondered.

"It bought us some time, but unless the school is right around the corner, then yeah they'll catch up to us, eventually." Chomar stood in the aisle.

"So, if they track us through the bus's directions, can't we just go a different way than the computer tells us?" Princess Chara looked at Tony and suggested.

"Yeah. Yeah! Why not? Princess, that's a great idea." Tony looked down at D16. "On my phone's GPS app it always gives me different route options. Can't we try to find out what the bus's route is, then look for an alternate and take that instead?"

"I can try to patch into the bus's guidance system… BEEP… its security is weak… BEEP… since they already hacked into it. One moment." D16 said before furiously moving his metal arms and hands along the controls on the dashboard.

Tony shouted back at his kids.

"Everyone okay back there?"

"Yeah Daddy, we're good!" Quint said, giving the thumbs up.

Brody and Kevin were still under the lion blanket. From underneath, Brody's hand poked out, also giving the thumbs up.

Hooper stood in her seat next to Princess Chara. She dramatically gave the thumbs down.

Tony pursed his lips. "Are you really not okay? Or are you just bored with this?"

"This is boring." Hooper scowled and slid back down into her seat and folded her arms.

"Hahaha! I love it! This girl is so cold-blooded!" Chomar laughed.

D16's arms stopped moving.

"You find out where we need to go?" Tony asked.

"Yes... BEEP... but I am afraid it does not help us. The school is close; it is just around the Linden System over there." D16 pointed out the windshield.

"Wait, the Linden System?" Chomar said. Then she unhappily sank back to her seat.

"Oh, no." Princess Chara said and her arms went over her mouth.

"Great driving, you moron. You've driven us to the worst place in the universes." Chomar yelled up at Tony.

"Yes." D16 quietly replied. "The bus wants us... BEEP... to go the long way around this system. Which, in the time it would take to get around the system... BEEP... our kidnappers would catch up to us."

"Yeah, but just won't go that way, remember? You figured out where the school is, so now we'll just take a different way and trick those guys." Tony said.

"But the only other route... BEEP... is to go directly through the Linden System and..."

"No one gets through the Linden System. Ever." Chomar said. The dinosaur princess looked absolutely defeated.

"Why? What's in there?" Quint leaned forward and asked.

"The Raging Widows." Chomar almost whispered.

The whole bus went silent.

"What? What is that? That sounds like something you'd name a rollercoaster in the Midwest."

"Most galaxies and systems comprise planets... BEEP... but the Linden System is a system made up of six gigantic matter-eating black holes.... BEEP... that, for reasons no one has ever figured out... BEEP... have all settled right here. We refer them, throughout the known infinities, as the Raging Widows." D16 explained.

"If anyone flies through there, you will get pulled apart and erased from existence!" Princess Chara said. "All four realms stay away from this place. Except for the pirates."

"The pirates." Chomar whispered, recalling the stories.

"She is correct... BEEP... because the realms won't come near here... BEEP... they say that the pirates... BEEP... will try to make runs through the Linden System. Through a stretch of space in there called The... BEEP... Widow's Corridor."

"Again? Great name. What is the Widow's Corridor?" Tony said, anxiously slumped over the steering wheel.

"The pirates that get captured say that there's a path of space that runs through the Raging Widows, a long corridor that they use to get through." Princess Chara explained.

"Yes... BEEP... the corridor is the exact distance from all six black holes that... BEEP... keep one safe from being immediately sucked into any of the Raging Widows BEEP... Provided that your ship is powerful enough... BEEP... to stand the almost apocalyptic conditions... BEEP... one could make it through the system and to the other side... BEEP... where the school currently is!" D16 said.

"But most pirates can't make it all the way. Their ships aren't strong enough and break down or get taken out by flying debris." Chomar added. "The stories say that the corridor is packed with the wreckage of ships that weren't able to get through. But, they are still far enough away from the Widows that they don't get sucked into them. They're just stuck there. Forever. And any of the pirates left inside, go mad with hopelessness."

Tony closed his eyes. His head throbbed. His hands were sore. And he desperately wanted for him and his kids to be absolutely anywhere else than this place. He exhaled loudly.

"So, let's see if I'm getting this right. We got rebel kidnappers on the way to capture us and do unspeakable things in the name of money and revolution. If we go the long, but safe way, they'll catch up to us." Tony checked off. "Our other option is to go the way that virtually no one can get through, because it's like a stretch of country road running between a group of huge, hungry tornadoes. And also, that road is a traffic jam graveyard of busted spaceships that may or may not have insane tortured pirates still inside of them."

"Don't forget the school moves, Daddy! It might be gone soon!" Quint shouted up.

"Thanks, son!" Tony yelled back, wanting to die. "D16? My very astute son has just pointed out to me that the school may move again soon. So, I'm going to guess that we have only a limited amount of time to get there before it disappears on us again?"

"Correct... BEEP." D16 answered.

"Well!" Tony said, clapping his hands together. "I'm just going to step outside into the airless void of outer space and think about it." Then slumped over the steering wheel again.

"I don't want to get taken." Chomar said. Her voice cracked a little. "Any of us. It's not our fault." Chomar started tearing up.

Princess Chara stood up in her seat and put four of her arms on Chomar's shoulders.

Chomar balled her enormous fists up in anger. She clenched her long, sharp teeth together. "It's not our fault our parents screwed everything up. We didn't ask for any of this. I don't care about being queen someday or whose turn it is to take over."

D16 stepped away from the dashboard and went over to Chomar. He put his tiny metal claw on Chomar's other shoulder. Quint also hopped over the seats to Chomar.

"I just want to go to school. With my friends." Chomar looked at everyone who was comforting her. "Sorry I'm such a jerk sometimes, guys. You are my friends, though, you really are." Chomar sniffed and wiped her eyes.

Tony looked at the kids. This wasn't their fault. They just want to be kids. They don't care who gets the special chair.

"Why, not?" Tony said in his bravest voice. "Everyone sit down and hang on. D16, give me directions, first."

D16 darted back up front and moved some buttons and screens. After a moment, the windshield dimmed once again. This time, two different paths appeared from the front of the bus. The familiar yellow line extended out far ahead of them in a straight line. Another line, this one the color red, curved off sharply to their right.

"Okay… BEEP… the yellow line is the route the bus wants us to take… BEEP… the long way around the system. The red line will take us on the shortcut… BEEP… using the Raging Widows Corridor." D16 explained.

"Are those kidnappers going to follow us, when they catch on that we're not where we say we are?"

"The Bloodhorde Gunships most definitely can not… BEEP… they are too small and light. The Harmony Transport ship may… BEEP… it has been so heavily modified it's hard to say for sure!" D16 said, sitting down in his seat.

"Daddy?" Quint pointed out the windshield at the red line and looked worried. "Uh, you're not going to…"

"I sure am, boy! We're taking the murder road to school!" He looked at Quint. "I think we can do this, buddy."

Quint smiled and nodded. He sat down in the seat in front of Brody and Kevin. They were both still quietly sitting underneath the lion blanket.

"Alright, here we go. D16! Crank that ska up buddy!" Tony said. The music got loud again.

"Ugh. I changed my mind. Let's just let the kidnappers take us." Chomar groaned as Princess Chara sat down next to her and smiled.

"Shut up, Chomar!" Tony said. "Here we go!"

Everyone cheered. Hooper just silently gave the thumbs down. Hooper was right.

Three

One time, back when Tony was nineteen or twenty, he and his best friends drove around in the worst snowstorm they'd ever seen. Cars were abandoned in ditches. Zero traction on the roads. No visibility. Even the snow plows stayed home. Except for Tony and his friends. They wanted to sit at the truck stop diner and drink coffee. It was a dumb idea, but when you're young, dumb ideas make the most sense.

It was truly a miracle Tony and his friends made it out alive that night. Too many close calls to count. But they had a place to go and a lot of blind determination. They thought that if you had the music loud enough, it could protect you like armor. If the people you loved were with you, it would make you invincible.

This is what Tony kept reminding himself as he was about to drive a space bus through the apocalypse.

As soon as they had entered the system, Tony could feel the bus being pulled in different directions. The back would drift one way and the front would go the opposite. Every turn felt like they were going to tip. It's what he imagined it was like trying to float with competing under-tows grabbing at you. Tony did his best to stay on the red GPS line, but it was difficult.

Then Tony saw the Raging Widows and knew it was going to get much, much worse.

Up ahead, there were six monstrous black holes, three on each side of the long corridor. Each black hole's outer disc aggressively churned with colorful gasses and swirling debris of the surrounding system. The Widow's centers were a dark nightmare of collapsed matter.

In between both sides of the Raging Widows, running down almost the entire length of the corridor, was a junk-yard of broken down spaceships. All of them were different sizes and shapes and markings. Just floating in one place, too weak or broken to escape, but too far away to get sucked into the Widow's oblivions.

"You're sure the bus's calculations are right, D16?" Tony asked nervously. "That if I stay as close to the red line as possible we won't get sucked into any of these?"

"Yes... BEEP... the bus will know to keep at a safe distance, so it will show you the proper path to take... BEEP... It will also take control of the engine... BEEP... to combat the high suction and resistance as we experience it. The bus should be small enough to go quickly through here... BEEP... but also just heavy enough to not get sucked immediately." D16 answered from his seat. He was still playing Tony's loud ska music.

"Okay. So just stay on the line. Simple." Tony whispered. "You can do this."

"Probably would be easier without this music." Chomar said.

"No, it wouldn't." Tony said. The music would form a safe bubble around them, Tony thought. Or that's what he used to think when he used to do dumb things like this. The music would distract him from being terrified.

Tony guided the bus along the line as it dipped downward. It looked like this was it. It was guiding them directly through the Widows now.

Upon entering the corridor, it blasted the space bus with gusts of wind from all directions. The bus rocked side to side. Tony felt the steering wheel wanting to move on its own. He tightened his grip as they shakily glided further down the Widows runway. The red line was getting harder to see. The deeper they got down the corridor, the more flying debris there was. Colorful gasses got much thicker, like fog. It was now like driving in equal parts tornado and snow storm.

The bus auto adjusted speeds as it tugged along. Usually, the Widow's gusts and vacuums were too strong, so the bus would slow to a crawl and drift safely through the currents. But occasionally, the bus took advantage of whenever the conditions were even slightly safer, and it would rocket as fast as it could forward. It made for a lot of jerking back and forth, but Tony was grateful for any extra second they didn't have to spend inside of here. It was claustrophobic being sandwiched between the Raging Widows, especially when the walls can eat you if you get too close.

The kids in the back were dead quiet. It was the first time they weren't fighting with each other. Each of them were staring out their windows at the giant swirling black holes that wanted to suck them in and chew them up. Even Kevin and Brody had come out from under the lion blanket to watch. Brody was, anyway. Kevin was still just floating quietly. Tony wished the black holes outside were more like Kevin was. Quiet and passive.

Tony's hands hurt terribly, but they were making excellent progress, so he gripped the wheel tighter as he guided the bus over the red line.

"Almost past the first two, Mister Tony!" Princess Chara called up to Tony.

This was a relief, but this was also where a new challenge started. This was where the broken down spaceships littered the corridor's path. The ships that never made it past the Widows. Tony was now having to steer the bus around these floating wrecks. Some were quite large, and it frustrated Tony as they slowed them down. It was disturbing to see all the discarded ships. Like being in a cemetery.

"Look at them all, Daddy." Quint said, mesmerized by what he thought were cool looking spaceships. "They're all just stuck here." Quint backed up from his window and had a scary thought. "Daddy, what about the people inside the spaceships?"

"Buddy, they probably didn't survive being stranded here." Tony said, trying to concentrate on following the red line around an annoyingly shaped star cruiser.

But right after the bus got around the cruiser, a long thin creature crawled up the back of one of the wrecked ships. It had seen the bus when it first entered the corridor. It had already alerted its also stranded brothers and sisters. Another one, it had said. Another chance at escape has come, it told them. They were gathering.

Brody was looking out the window at the color swirling all around them. Blue and silver colors floated smoothly in a thick mist. He was staring at the colorful fog when a faceless helmet suddenly popped out of it.

Brody jumped in surprise. The space helmet stared at Brody, inspecting him. Then, the helmet and the long stretched out body attached to it slowly crawled out of the rainbow haze and leapt over to a nearby destroyed ship.

"Uh, Daddy? I think there's a problem." Brody said, wrapping himself up in his lion blanket.

"Oh no. I knew I should have made you go to the bathroom before we left." Tony said.

Chomar was looking out her window, on the opposite of Brody's side. She sat up straight as soon as she saw a tall and gangly creature crawl out of the broken window of a large ship and down its side. It stopped to look up at the bus sailing by.

"They probably didn't survive, huh? Well, what are those, then?" Chomar pointed and yelled.

Tony looked out the Chomar's side of the bus. There, perched on the side of a ship like gargoyles, were another two super thin and very long creatures. They had dirty reflective helmets on, so you couldn't see their faces. They tilted their heads at the bus as it passed them.

"The pirates! I knew it!" Chomar shouted out.

"Pirates?" Quint asked and ran over to Chomar's side to see.

"Ugh. What happened to their bodies?" A grossed out Princess Chara asked. "Why are they all long and stretchy?"

"I bet they go from ship to ship raiding supplies. It's probably how they survived being stuck in here." Chomar said.

"You're probably right, Chomar…. BEEP… but if you were out in these conditions for long enough… BEEP… the extreme pull of the Raging Widows suction would either jerk you apart… BEEP… or would stretch your body out like that." D16 said, picking up on Chomar's thoughts.

"They look like when I pull my gum out of my mouth in a long string." Quint added. "All long and bendy."

"Look at their weird spacesuits." Chomar said.

"They're like, different suits patched together. Wrapped around their skinny bodies." Princess Chara observed.

"Well, what do we do?" Tony shouted. He spotted another tall, thin pirate crouched on a ship ahead of them. Its long arms, frame, and legs made it look almost like a spider. Its lifeless mask just stared back at Tony.

It cocked its rubbery neck at Tony, then sprang to the bus. Gliding over, it carried two large pointed tools in each of its wiry hands. When it got close enough to the bus, it slammed the sharp tools into its side. Then, like a mountain climber, pulled the tool out, slammed it higher into the bus, and pulled itself up.

"I think he wants a ride." Chomar said as the bus tilted from the extra passenger.

"Don't let him in Daddy!" Quint yelled. "Tell him there's nowhere else to sit!"

Then, from the other side of the bus, two more of the distorted pirates floated onto the bus and began hammering at its hull. And then another from the back, where Brody and Kevin sat. The inside of the bus sounded like a hailstorm on a tin roof as they hit the outside repeatedly.

Hooper screamed in terror when one popped up right by her window. Princess Chara and Quint jumped out of their seats to get to Hooper and pull her away from the window.

"You get away!" Quint hit the window and yelled at the stretched pirate. It clawed at the outside of the bus.

"Mister Tony, do something!" Princess Chara shouted as she slid into the seat next to D16. She held Hooper in her lap and squeezed her tight.

Tony swerved the wheel back and forth to shake them off the bus. He was risking drifting too far off the red line and getting sucked up into the Raging Widows, but he didn't have many options at the moment. The bus wiggled back and forth sharply. The kids inside slid around, but the attackers outside hung on tightly.

There were three of the pirates hanging on the driver's side of the bus. Up ahead, a broken spaceship was sticking out into the bus's path, the red line directing Tony around the obstruction. Instead, Tony jerked the wheel to the right and let the bus slide across the side of the spaceship. It scraped the three pirates off the bus and sent them spinning off into space. It sucked them all into the nearest black hole, flapping their long arms wildly and in terror as the Widow took them

"Hahaha! Got them! Nice one!" Chomar raised his arms and shouted.

"They're going to break the bus! What's the point of all the hammering? What good is a ship to them with a bunch of holes in it?" Tony shouted as the wheel jerked around again.

"They probably want to steal parts from the bus... BEEP... to repair a larger craft in order to escape from here." D16 said, sliding around in his seat.

"Which means, there's probably a lot more of th..."

The bus suddenly rocked back and forth with added bodies jumping and hammering on its outside. More of the stretched pirates had glided over onto the bus. Tony struggled to keep the bus from tipping over or drifting off course. He stared far ahead down the corridor. They weren't quite past the second set of Widows. It was still going to take a while to get out of here. They'd never make it out before these things tore their way inside.

The outside clawing and hammering got more intense. Tony swerved towards more stranded ships, trying to knock the attackers off, but they hooked onto the bus too tightly. Alarms sounded and lights started flashing on the bus's dashboard. Severe damage was being done to the bus.

Tony turned around and looked at Chomar.

"Chomar? If those things get in here, don't make it easy for them. Got it?"

Chomar nodded. She stood up, stretched her arms out, and flexed her razor-sharp claws. She spun around and faced whatever direction had the loudest hammering. Then around to the next loudest. Then the next. She was ready.

A worried D16 hugged Princess Chara, who was holding Hooper in her lap. Quint stood up next to Chomar, scanning the roof and sides of the bus for the loudest banging. Brody and Kevin had retreated under the lion blanket once again.

Tony looked at the scared kids. This wasn't their fault.

A stretched out pirate landing on the bus's hood snapped Tony's attention back to the front. It was right outside the windshield and raised its long stick arm. It was grasping a sharp tool. It was going to break the windshield.

Then something shot it off the hood.

THE PIRATE FLAILED its skinny arms and legs as it floated up and away into the pull of the Raging Widows.

From behind, a continuous, rapid fire stream of laser blasts swept the attacking pirates off the bus. Like using a fire hose to clean mud off your car, the blasts easily peeled the pirates away and sent them flying off into the black holes. The blasting stopped.

The bus straightened itself out again and was flying as it was before. The alarms and flashing lights also stopped.

"What was that?" Tony yelled and turned around.

"It's a… BEEP… Harmony System Transport!" D16 said, looking over his seat.

"My parents!?" Princess Chara excitedly turned.

"I don't think so!" Chomar replied, looking back. "It's them!"

Suddenly, the same dark voice chirped through the communicator speakers once again.

"Perhaps, you can repay us for saving your lives by just simply surrendering?" The voice said.

It was the kidnappers. They followed it through the corridor. It was all alone, which meant the other two gunships once with it didn't make it very far inside.

"You can't escape. You can't outrun us here. Why don't you just give up before you either get stuck here or get dragged into the Widows? We can help you get out." The dark voice calmly said.

The huge transport ship didn't have to maneuver around the stranded ghost ships. It was big enough that it could just ram right through them. But crashing through the junkyard was creating even more wreckage and debris. Now, Tony was having to drive around flying junk hurdling past them.

Tony compared what he saw ahead with a map readout on the side of the windshield. They had two more sets of black holes to pass, then they would be out of the system. The school would hopefully be on the other side. They could get help. He just needed to go faster.

"D16? I'm going to need that gas pedal again. We're going to make a run for it. But I can't do it if the bus keeps controlling my speed."

"Are you sure, Daddy?" Quint asked.

He felt energized by 'dumb idea determination' again. Like when he was young and stupid. He could do this. They could do this.

"I think so, buddy. We can make it." Tony said.

D16 hit some buttons and the gas pedal came back out again. Then he and all the other kids sat back down.

"Hang on everyone! Doing the go-fast thing, again." Tony said, and he slammed on the gas. The bus lunged forward and Tony had to quickly turn the wheel in order to avoid hitting a stranded ship.

The dark voice came on the radio again.

"Very well." The dark voice said. "I suppose instead, we'll just retrieve your bodies." Then the radio went silent again.

Now, the kidnappers' stolen transport ship was shooting at them. They fired their laser cannons. They might have just been bluffing about killing them, but just one direct hit could put the bus in their hands.

Now Tony was having to avoid laser blasts, abandoned spaceships and floating space junk. Like a toy car being chased by a freight train, he had a huge spaceship ten times his size behind him. He was also trying to stay close enough on course, so the six black holes wouldn't suck them up and eat their matter. All while going at a dangerously fast speed. Tony needed to be doing all these things at the same time. Tony, a nerd driver that uses his turn signal when he pulls into his own driveway.

He swerved away from blast after blast, turning away from them just in time so they would hit a junk ship instead. The explosion that followed would send debris crashing all over the place, knocking against the bus. The kids would scream every time something exploded. Tony would ease up off the gas, wrench the steering wheel over back on course, and hit the gas again.

Tony narrowly missed a floating ship by inches and had to swing the bus underneath it. The kids all shouted in terror. The bus got pushed off the red line by a lot, and was drifting over to the Widows. The pull of the black hole was incredible. Tony was using every ounce of strength he had left to pull the wheel back over to the red line, the bus recalibrating and shifting systems trying to help him. He glanced ahead and at his map readout. They were halfway past the last two sisters. They just needed to make it a little farther.

Suddenly, the kidnappers stopped shooting directly at them. Now it was shooting ahead of them at the broken ships in their path. The explosions would break the ships up into smaller pieces and spread them all over the corridor. The kids were screaming.

"They're trying to make it harder for us to get through!" Tony said.

He was frantically trying to fly around all the broken pieces of ships. The junk would hit the bus and knock over everyone inside. It was getting harder and harder for Tony to see around the debris and to see the red GPS line he needed to stick close to.

"Come on! Come on!" Tony was chanting.

A piece of a ship Tony hadn't seen break apart slammed into the bus's back side. The bus spun out. Tony lifted his foot off the gas and tried to straighten out. But the pursuing kidnappers finally had their shot. They fired a single laser blast at the bus, as it was skidding to the side.

THE LASER BEAM zapped the bus, and it shook with impact. The blast pushed them right up against one of the pirate ships. The bus collided and stalled out. The dashboard sparked several times in different spots, then all the lights went out. Tony's ears were ringing and his head hurt from banging it against the side of his window. He still jumped to his feet.

"Is everyone okay?" He asked while stumbling to the back. The kids were laying all over the place and sniffling.

"We're okay Daddy. I think. What happened to the lights?" Quint asked, rubbing his head and standing back up.

"The blast... BEEP... knocked the power out." D16 answered. He stood up and ran to the dashboard. He fumbled with some switches and buttons. Nothing was working. Then he went over to the driver's seat and reached under the steering wheel. Tony heard the loud click of a switch. After a few seconds, a computerized voice spoke.

"Rebooting... Please wait." The computer said.

"There... BEEP... the system is rebooting... BEEP... we just need a minute or two for it to come back online and... BEEP... we should be able to move again." D16 said.

Tony saw lights were slowly coming back on in the dashboard. Alien reboot command code was running on the windshield screen.

"I don't know if we're going to get that minute." Chomar said and pointed to the floating transport ship in the distance. It was just hovering in place. Waiting to scoop up the bus and its passengers.

"What do we do?" Princess Chara asked.

"I don't know Princess; I don't know what else to try to..." Tony panicked. But Brody cut him off.

"Hey Daddy!" Brody, standing in his seat with his blanket over his shoulders, said.

Tony turned and was startled to see Kevin suddenly floating near him in the middle of the bus's aisle. Where before, his center was pitch black, it was now changing color. Kevin's middle was now a wavy, purple-green color. Vibrating and swirling brighter and brighter and brighter.

"What's he doing, Daddy?" Quint asked, burying himself into Tony's arms.

Suddenly, like someone had switched on a spotlight, the same pulsating purple-green color shined through the bus's windows. The bright light blinded Tony and the kids, and their hands shot up to cover their eyes. Tony pulled his hand away slowly and moved closer to the windows.

All the Raging Widows centers were glowing the same colors as Kevin's was. The colors were pulsing in and out. Tony looked back at Kevin. He was just floating there silently in the middle of the bus. Tony turned to the window again.

"What is happening?" Princess Chara asked and hugged Hooper tighter.

"Kevin said he is going to ask for help." Brody said.

"Look!" Chomar yelled.

From out of each Widow's center, purple and green shapes materialized. Bigger and farther out they grew. At first, the shapes looked formless, like giant puddles of grape juice spilling out of the center of the Widows. The longer and larger the colors got, the tighter the shapes became.

Tony looked closer at the shapes. They now looked tube-like. They resembled tentacles. Slithering, glowing limbs reached out to the center of the corridor.

The kidnappers' floating transport ship suddenly rocked back and forth erratically. Like something was shaking it. The black holes farthest to the back had gotten to it first. The Widows they had passed long ago, had stretched out and with their dark matter tentacles and grabbed onto the rear of the ship. The ship shook harder and harder as it was being squeezed from behind.

Then, the center two Widows dark arms wrapped

themselves around the middle of the gigantic ship. The tentacles twisted around the ship tighter and tighter.

Then, the last two Widows, the ones closest to them, slapped the front of the transport ship and grabbed ahold of it. The dark matter started digging into the hull of the ship.

Pieces of the kidnapper's ship broke off. Parts were flaking away as it was being pulled and twisted and dug into. Tony and the kids watched the giant ship crumble apart.

As quick as they had taken a hold of it, the glowing dark tentacles suddenly ripped the transport ship apart.

"Pickles!" the entire bus yelled.

It looked like it was as easy as cracking a peanut shell. The Raging Widows arms had each grabbed a section of the ship and tore it to pieces. Then, with each tentacle still wrapped around a part of the enemy ship, the Widows quickly yanked them back toward themselves. The dark matter tentacles and the pieces of the ship faded away, back into the centers of the black holes.

The kidnappers were gone.

Kevin, still floating quietly in the bus, stopped glowing the purple and green color. His center returned to its pitch black color. At almost the same time, the Raging Widows also stopped glowing, and they returned to their nightmarish darkness. The bright light had faded away.

All the kids cheered.

"Alright Kevin! Woo-hoo! You did it!" They were all yelling thanks and praise for their friend Kevin. Quint and D16 were jumping up and down. Chomar and Princess Chara high fived each other. Brody was clapping and Hooper gave Kevin the all-approving thumbs up.

"Thanks, Kevin." Tony smiled and said to the small

floating black hole. "But next time you can do that, much sooner."

"No problem, Mister Tony." Kevin said in a very quiet, echoing voice. Then he floated over and into the seat with Brody.

Suddenly the bus's interior lights came back on. The dashboard was fully lit up again.

"Reboot complete." The computer voice said.

The bus's engine roared to life.

"We're... BEEP... back!" D16 said.

The bus started drifting again. It floated away from the ship it wedged into.

"Uh, hey. Who's driving?" Chomar anxiously asked.

Tony jumped up and ran to the driver's seat. Sitting down, he gripped the steering wheel and got it under control before it drifted. It wasn't easy, but he kept it from spinning out too far and into the grip of the Raging Widows. Once he had the bus straightened out, the windshield tinted darker and the red line was once again pointing them in the direction they needed to go. The kids all sat back down.

Tony pressed the gas pedal, and they zoomed off, following the red line. The kids all cheered. D16 turned Tony's ska music back up loud in victory.

They didn't have far to go now. It still wasn't the smoothest drive with the Widows powerful pull grabbing at them. The pirate junkyard had thinned out to just a few ships, so there was less to have to drive around. Tony took advantage and flew as fast as the bus would go.

Faster and faster they went. Farther and farther they passed by the last two Raging Widows. Second by second, Tony found it was getting easier to control the bus. It didn't feel like he was fighting near as much resistance anymore. The Raging Widows were letting go.

Then they were out! Away from the Widows and heading out of the Linden System! Tony felt tears welling up in his eyes. He allowed himself to relax his hands on the wheel a little. Just a little. The kids all cheered louder.

Princess Chara suddenly reached out with a few of her arms and pointed to the windshield.

"I see it! I see the school!" She shouted in excitement.

"I see it too!" Hooper next to her mimed.

"We actually made it!" Chomar laughed.

It looked like a castle. A huge castle under a glass dome. Built on top of a flying saucer. There was a lot going on there.

Tony steered the bus towards the school. His leg was shaking up and down with excitement. It elated him that this all would soon be over.

THEN, a hundred different spaceships suddenly appeared from out of quantum speed. Warships, transport ships, gunships. Small ships. Enormous ships. A lot of spaceships, all maneuvering around them quickly. Surrounding the bus.

A voice suddenly came over the speaker.

"Attention! Attention! This is the Peace Collective of the Infinity. Surrender the children or we will fire!"

"It's our parents!" Princess Chara said.

The kids all jumped to their windows and yelled and waved their arms. Tony was waving his arms, too.

"Don't fire! Don't fire! The kids are here! They're safe! I have them! I have them!" Tony yelled. He was waving his arms frantically out the windshield of the bus at a bunch of spaceships when suddenly...

. . .

... THEY WERE IN A PARKING LOT. The bus's engine was no longer running. It was a quiet parking lot full of space buses, just like them. Tony craned his neck and looked out the windows. The parking lot was in front of the huge castle. They were in the school's dome. They just appeared there. Like someone had magically teleported them inside.

"We're... BEEP... here!" D16 said. He stood up and clanked over to the doors. The bus doors opened up and the small robot stepped down. Chomar and Princess Chara followed him out. Then Kevin floated by Tony. His own kids hopped down into the parking lot.

"Wait? That's it?" Tony said. He was alone on the bus. He looked down at his hands. They were red and raw and blistered. He flexed his fingers and winced from the sharp pain. He stood up, grabbed the kid's backpacks they'd forgotten, and stepped down out of the bus.

Tony couldn't say for sure, but he ball parked at least four different looking armies staring at him and the kids. They were lined up in different formations, waiting for them when they got off the bus. The robots pointed cannon arms at them. The huge dinosaur warriors had axes, spears, and arrows. There were tall octopus people holding small laser guns in each of their long arms. And the wizards either had fiery hands or glowing staffs. None of the armies looked happy to see Tony.

"Father! Mother!" Princess Chara shouted and ran toward the Octopus people.

"Chara!" A pair of crowned octopuses pushed aside their soldiers and rushed to meet her. They both scooped her up in all their arms. "Oh, my sweet darling!" one of them said.

"Moms!" Chomar also shouted, and she zoomed over to two huge raptors in battle armor.

D16 joined his robot family and even little Kevin floated over to the section of wizards.

"Who is this?" One of Chomar's moms pointed her axe at Tony and his kids. "What is the meaning of this? Why are our children late to school??" she hissed.

"No... BEEP... it's not his fault!" D16 jumped up and said. "Mister Tony saved... BEEP... us!"

"Yeah!" Princess Chara joined. "The bus driver sold us out to a bunch of creeps who wanted to kidnap us! Our own people! All of ours!"

"It's true Mom! This guy got us here. Got us away from the traitors. He even drove through the Raging Widows Corridor to get us here." Chomar explained.

"You drove through... BOOP... the Corridor?" one of D16's robot parents asked.

"Uh, yeah. I guess so. I know it was dangerous, but it was the only way to get away from those guys." Tony held out his hands and said. Quint, Brody, and Hooper gathered around him. They stood in front of him like bodyguards. He looked down at his kids. "I had help, though. Your kids are all pretty special." He pointed to the space kids. "They're smart, brave and kind. All I had to do was steer this thing." Tony said, hooking his thumb back at the bus. "Never would have made it through those black holes without Kevin's trick, though. He asked the Widows to help us out."

"Kevin's trick?" A tall and mysterious looking wizard said. His cape was blowing majestically, although Tony didn't feel any wind in here. He looked down at the tiny floating black hole. "You spoke to the Widows? Very interesting. Fascinating." He stroked his elegant and long beard. "Well done, Kevin. I'm proud of you for helping your friends."

Then the dark wizard simply lifted and twitched his

hand slightly. With a quiet pop, the fuzzy and horned bus driver that had abandoned the kids on Tony's street suddenly appeared next to everyone. It had an oversized Hawaiian shirt on. But it was also wearing glowing restraints on its wrists, ankles, and over its mouth. Its eyes were wide in shock and terror.

"We shall investigate further into these matters." Chomar's other mom snarled, waving her spear in the traitorous driver's direction.

"Yes." Princess Chara's father said. "Thank you for bringing our children safely back to us. You have our most sincere gratitude." He said and slightly bowed. "Our wizard friends shall teleport you back to your planet."

"Unless you want to drive back on the bus? Maybe you could be our new driver?" Chomar said.

"Oh, I'm good. I think I'll retire from bus driving. I've got a job already. I'm a stay-at-home dad." Tony's eyes lit up. "Although these days, it's more like stay-in-car dad." He joked, looking at the adults.

No one laughed.

"Okay, then." Tony said, disappointed. "Thanks anyway, Chomar."

"Thank you... BEEP... Mister Tony." D16 said. He waved his tiny metal hand.

"Thank you, Mister Tony. And Quint and Brody and Hooper. We shall miss you. Maybe we can get together and play sometime?" Princess Chara hugged her new friends. Her little tentacles wrapped around all three at the same time.

"That would be awesome!" Quint said excitedly.

"Bye Princess Chara! Thanks for sitting with me!" Hooper said and waved.

"See you later, Kevin!" Brody shouted over to Kevin.

"Bye Brody." Kevin said in an echoed whisper. His

wizard parents looked down in surprise at the small black hole. Then they smiled proudly.

The tall, dark wizard raised his hand again. "Ready?" He said.

Tony gathered his kids close together.

"Uh, sure." Tony said.

"Hey mom, guess what? This guy listens to ska music!" Chomar turned to one of her moms and said.

"What?! Ska sucks!" His mom said, howling with laughter.

"Hey!" Tony said.

The wizard twitched his hand slightly. Tony heard a small popping noise.

THEY WERE BACK ON EARTH. On their street. At their bus stop.

Tony stepped back, disoriented. He looked at his hands. They were still red and raw.

"You guys okay?" Tony asked his kids.

"We're okay, Daddy." Brody said, wrapping his blanket around his waist.

Hooper and Quint smiled giddily at each other.

"That was fun, Daddy!" Hooper said.

"Oh, you think so? Glad something finally impressed you, Hoop. Well, sorry to disappoint you but things are going back to boring." Tony said. He rubbed his face, exhausted.

The kid's backpacks were laying on the sidewalk.

"Buddies. Pick your backpacks up." Tony's eyes suddenly got wide. "Wait. Your backpacks. Your backpacks! What time is it?"

Quint shrugged.

"School! Pickles! We're late! We got to get you to

school!" Tony bent over and scooped the backpacks up. "We've got to go! Come on! Hurry!"

And they all took off running back towards the house. Tony would have to rush to get them to school. Things were never boring around here.

THE END.

PART III

FullTimeTony and the World Song

1

The Once Was

Ori couldn't remember the last time she had seen the sun. It stopped rising. It seemed to have forgotten about them.

Ori stopped running to catch her breath and looked up. The stars had also left them behind. Now the only thing in the sky was an endless blanket of gray clouds. The air was nothing but smoke and soot.

Ori wiped the sweat from her forehead with her blood-stained arm. The heat that hung dead in the air was oppressive.

Ori and her siblings used to climb the trees that lined these hills. The hills and its forests had once been beautiful and lush. Now they were scorched black from the fires. Only smoldering stumps remained now.

Ori was exhausted. Exhausted from the fighting. Exhausted from the heartache. Exhausted from seeing all the death.

Ori was exhausted from trying to remember. Trying to remember what life was before her friends and family faded away. Before all the machines stopped working.

When the magic still brought hope. Before the kingdom fell.

Ori's arms ached from dragging her wounded brother up the hills. She was not sure where the rest of her brothers and sisters were. She saw them just before the Shadows broke through the blockades. Then they lost each other. She later found Kuna face down in the mud. He was alive but badly wounded.

Ori remembered the last orders given. If they could no longer hold the Shadows off, they would retreat to the hills. Hide in the caves.

Ori didn't want to stop fighting. She was bullheaded and too proud to let these monsters take her home and her people. But she knew trying to fight them off at this point was useless.

Ori knew it was the end of the world.

Ori bent over to drag Kuna up the hill again. She strained as pulled him up. Kuna groaned in pain and confusion.

Ori heard them before she saw them. The coals and embers crunched under their claws as they darted out of what used to be the forest. They were so fast. The Shadows.

Ori dropped Kuna and slid her spear off of her shoulder. Even after all the battle it had seen today, her weapon was still sharp. There were four of them. They were so fast.

Ori dug her feet into the dirt as the first Shadow leaped at her. It was snarling and screeching wildly right until Ori ran her spear through its body. She quickly pulled her spear back and spun towards the other that was diving toward her.

Ori stepped to the side and stabbed the Shadow in the back as it stretched out trying to grab her. It pinned the creature to the ground. Ori twisted her spear as it shook, dying on the ground.

Ori pulled her spear out of the dead monster, but not quick enough. A Shadow was dragging Kuna away from her. She screamed Kuna's name. She flipped the spear in her hand so she could throw it at the creature taking her brother.

Ori was knocked over by another Shadow. She landed hard onto her back as the Shadow pushed down on her body and raised its arms to claw at her. Ori jabbed her spear into its now unprotected side. The Shadow howled in pain.

Ori rolled out of the way of its lifeless body before it fell on top of her. She got to her feet as fast as she could, but Kuna was being pulled farther and farther away. Into the darkness of the former forest. She ran after him, but an arm was suddenly around her waist, stopping her.

"Ori! No!" A voice said as it pulled her back. "He's gone, Ori. Let him go. He's gone."

Ori turned and looked to see who was holding her back. It was her best friend, Maur. He was retreating up the hill with the rest of the surviving soldiers. He had seen her being attacked and hurried to help her.

Ori turned back to Kuna and screamed and stretched her arms out at the body of her big brother being taken away. She screamed and screamed. Maur struggled to keep her restrained. She was so strong.

Ori finally collapsed and sobbed. She remembered Kuna taking her fishing when she was little. Just the two of them. Just Kuna and Ori. Much later she tutored him in the math for the machines. Kuna never said, but she knew she was his favorite. Kuna was hers, no question. And now he was gone. Just like the others.

"Ori. We thought we'd lost you too. When they broke

through, I turned and you were gone." Maur said. "Ori, we must keep moving. They're coming, Ori. Our families are all gone, too." Maur helped her to her feet but kept his arms around her.

Ori could tell that Maur felt the same dread as her. "Why is this happening?" Maur said as he looked at the smoky sky.

Ori spoke with tears in her eyes. Ori spoke with rage. "I know why."

Ori broke free of Maur's embrace and scooped her spear back up off the ground. Ori did not walk up the hill. She furiously stomped. Maur and the rest of the surviving fighters hurried to keep up with her.

Ori trudged up the ever more steeping hill and towards the caves. They hid the remaining population of the kingdom in the caves. It was their last resort. A once advanced and hopeful world now reduced to hiding in the rocks.

Ori brushed past the warriors that protected the entrance to the caves. They were young, untrained, and weak. They wouldn't stand a chance against the Shadows and other monsters. The guards anxiously called after her, asking to know what was going on below.

Ori only bluntly said, "It's over."

Ori marched into the caves and looked over the young children and the sickly that lined the cave walls. The lights from tiny fires flickered in their eyes as they looked at Ori for hope. But they could quickly see there was no hope she could offer. Maur and his troops followed her.

Ori finally saw who she was looking for sitting in the back. All huddled together. Fools seeking solace in the company of other fools. The Elders of the kingdom. The old and the wise. Ori spat on the ground.

Ori shouted as she approached them. "Traitors! Is it

true what they say? Is it true?" She threw her bloody spear on the ground. "Before the Shadows broke the barricades, they taunted us from over the wall! They laughed at us! They said we did this! That we let this happen! Is it true?"

Ori's grandmother rose and stepped over the thrown spear. She answered the angry girl. She spoke with reserve. She spoke with disappointment. "Such an ungrateful girl. You watch the way you speak to us, child. We do not deserve such disrespect."

Ori lunged at the old woman. Her Grandmother stumbled backward. Maur yelled, "Ori, stop! What are you doing?" Ori stopped and steadied herself. She must have answers. She must know. They would all be dead soon, anyway.

Ori said, "What about The Song, old woman? They said we stopped singing The Song and we let them back in."

Ori's grandmother snorted in disgust as two warriors helped her to her feet. "The Song?" she said as she brushed herself off. "That Song was foolish. It served no purpose."

Ori couldn't believe it was true. "We were only children! It kept us safe! Don't you see that?"

Ori's grandmother sharply raised her finger at Ori. "No! It kept you from providing! From joining the community! It served no purpose other than to distract silly and ungrateful children from what they should be focused on. No time for ridiculous songs when there's work to be done. The machines needed to be kept running."

Ori was in shock. "We weren't ready. You were supposed to teach us The Song. To let us enjoy it and its protection. To let us enjoy being young." Ori leaned against the cave wall and slid to the ground. "You took that from us because you needed our labor. You needed us to work so you could keep what you already had."

Ori's grandmother leaned over and put her withered hand on Ori's shoulder. "Child. Kingdoms demand function. For the wheel of the kingdom to remain turning as it was, we needed you to join it sooner. You weep because you think you've lost what? Games? Playing? Singing foolish Songs? Child. There was no time. We'd gained so much."

Ori slapped the old woman's hand away and jumped back to her feet. "And now it's all gone. It's burning, and they have torn it apart. Because you didn't let children be children!" Ori wiped her eyes. The rest of the cave wasn't making a sound. "Did you not care that The Song was magic? That it was The Song that kept the monsters away?"

"Ori, my child. We decided we had grown past it. We no longer needed it. It was unnecessary. There was no longer any time, child. All we had gained…" Grandmother was cut off by one of the warrior guards from outside the cave. He was shouting.

"Ori! Maur! Come quick! Something is coming!" The young warrior was shouting. Ori and Maur ran to the entrance of the cave. They looked out.

Ori watched The Monster come out of the sky. Its claws broke through the gray clouds and shook the world as it landed. The hill and the cave rocked back and forth. It had finally broken through. The millions and millions of Shadows on the ground had destroyed and burned enough of the world that it was finally time. The Monster was here.

Ori couldn't see where the Monster's body stopped and started. It wasn't just giant. It was everything. As it stomped, the world exploded. Fire sprouted on the ground like weeds and fell from the sky like rain.

Ori felt Maur's hand take hers. She turned and looked at him. Maybe she would have taken him as a partner. Let him raise her children while she devised new calculations for the growing city. But that would never happen now. She closed her eyes. It was the last dream Ori would ever have.

Ori's grandmother emerged from the cave, steadying herself on the rocks as the ground shook beneath her. She looked around at the destruction. Her cracked lips formed a desperate and pathetic brief smile. "It will all come back someday, you know. We'll be back someday. It might take billions of infinities, but we will rise again. It will happen. It always does. The once was… will be again. And no silly little Song will help us do it, I promise you." Ori's grandmother rambled.

Ori wouldn't look at her grandmother. Ori said: "Grandmother? You suck."

Then the world ended.

BILLIONS OF INFINITIES LATER…

Tony and the kids were in the van. Tony had gotten so sick of them arguing over what DVD to watch on the six-minute drive to the grocery store that he made them listen to music instead.

They were listening to the music on his phone. He was trying to remember when he downloaded the song they were listening to right now. One kid must have requested it at some point. He felt stupid he had bought it, because it literally played everywhere.

Kids loved it. Grown ups also thought it was cute at first. But then it didn't go away. Eventually, everyone not still in grade school despised the song. Now the song had apps and videos and games and toys and clothes. It was everywhere.

Tony didn't get all the hate. The song was annoying and repetitive and an earworm, but it was for kids. Tony listened to songs for adults that were just as annoying.

Tony thought eight-year-old Quint had grown out of it because Quint had recently discovered pop music. He was obsessed, like everybody else, with that girl the radio played nonstop for the last few years. But Tony caught the now too-cool Quint still singing the kid's song every now and again. The song finished playing.

"Play it again, Daddy!" Hooper shouted from her car seat.

"Hey! Yeah, let's play it... maybe three more times!" Brody agreed and held up three fingers.

"It's okay, Daddy. You can play it again." Quint said with no enthusiasm and continued to stare out his window.

Tony reached over and pushed the back button on his phone. The most popular kid's song in the world played again.

Pizza Party Hip Hop was The Song.

The Worst Ever

Tony was supposed to be folding laundry. He was playing on his phone instead.

The two boys, eight-year old Quint, and six-year-old Brody were at school. Tony's four-year-old girl Hooper was napping. This was usually his time to get some chores done, but he was on his phone instead.

It was a common misconception that, as a stay-at-home dad, Tony was on his phone all day. In reality, Tony barely had time to use the bathroom, never mind play a stacking jewel game or take an online quiz to find out what kind of chip dip he was.

(He was French Onion. Pretty boring and disappointing, honestly.)

Today, he absently picked his phone up to check the weather and now forty minutes had passed. He was looking at his news and social media apps, reading headlines and scrolling robotically.

The laundry quietly waited to be folded.

(Scroll.)

WWW.DAILYSTORIES.COM - @DAILYHEAD-

LINES – Double oil spill off San Francisco coast. Two tankers improbably collide. Still developing…

(Scroll.)

CWN NEWS - @CWNNEWS – Riots continue in Hong Kong. Nine more injured by police.

(Scroll.)

US INFO NEWS - @USINNEWS – Treasury Secretary to hold press conference over looming Wall Street crisis.

(Scroll.)

WORLD NEWS DAILY - @WND – Huge sinkhole suddenly appears in Paris. City investigators baffled.

(Scroll.)

APW SOURCE - @APWSRCE – Entire blocks of buildings collapsing in Brazil.

Officials are unsure of the cause. More updates.

(Scroll.)

WORLD NEWS DAILY - @WND – Britain to Brexit from the Brexit's Brexit.

(App swiped shut.)

Somehow, the laundry looked less depressing than the headlines. Tony put his phone down on his lap and stared at the overflowing basket. Then he sighed loudly and picked his phone back up. He thought he would switch to the Science and Nature topics. Maybe there would be some cool pictures of outer space or lions or something.

(App tapped open.)

WWW.TECHREPORTS.COM - @TECHCOM – Facial recognition software giant adds three more countries to its growing client list.

(Scroll.)

NATIONAL INFOGRAPHIC - @NATILIT – Where are all the birds migrating to? Researchers are asking why birds are not arriving at their usual migration points. Where are they? Click to read the full story.

(Scroll.)

MAJOR SCIENCE MONTHLY - @MAJSCI-MONTHLY – Did anyone else feel that? Is the Earth rotating differently than a year ago? Our report continues.

(Scroll.)

WWW.TECHREPORTS.COM - @TECHCOM – Massive data breach occurs again in Silicon Valley. It affects two hundred million users. Senators call for another round of investigation hearings.

(Scroll.)

WWW.SCIENCEWEEKLY.COM - @SCIWEEK – Hold your breath! Air quality tested as 23% poison! Details inside! Click here!

(App swiped shut.)

Good gravy. Maybe instead of reading his phone, he should just hit himself in the face with it repeatedly. He put the phone down again and started folding clothes. After two shirts and a pair of leggings, he had his phone in his hand again. Maybe Entertainment and Gossip news wouldn't make him want to curl up and cry.

(App tapped open.)

CHECK IT OUT! – @CHECKITOUT – Pop Superstar Vikki Dean Grace U.S. tour sold out in every city! More dates and cities being added! Click here for details!

(Scroll.)

HOT GOSSIP FIRE - @HOTGOSSBURN – Guess who's back on drugs? Click to find out!

(Scroll.)

CELEBRITY R BETTER - @CELEBSBET-TERTHANYOU – Paparazzi catch Action Hunk Jake

North high fiving everyone's favorite TV Nurse Angela Woods… is a baby on the way next? Click for the pics!

(Scroll.)

TUNES TALK - @TUNESTALK – LA's Too Cool Party festival expected to bring in record numbers both in audience attendance and live stream.

(Scroll.)

TV REVIEWS DAILY - @TVREVDAILY – Last night's episode of 'Falling Down The Stairs With The Stars' sends two celebs home in a shocking judge's decision! Read the recap here!

(Scroll.)

BOX OFFICE UPDATES - @BOXUPDATES – Weekend BOMB! 'Pizza Party Hip Hop' animated film cannot bring in the audiences! Studio in trouble!

(Scroll.)

WWW.MOVIETALK.COM—@MOVIETALK—
Please let this just go away and die. Our 'Pizza Party Hip Hop' review.

(Scroll.)

FILM REPORT NEWS - @FILMREPORTNEWS – 'Pizza Party Hip Hop' film adaptation huge bomb at the weekend box office. Is the phenomenon finally over?

(Scroll.)

MUSIC HEAR NOW - @MUSICHEARNOW – Volume 4 of 'Say That's What I Call Pizza Party Hip Hop!' barely cracks the top 100. Are kids finally over this garbage?

(Scroll.)

COOL MUSIC DUDE NEWS - @COOLMUSIC-DUDES – 'Pizza Party Hip Hop' album compilations dropped by record label. Hopefully gets dropped off a cliff next. Click for more snark and badly spelled reviews!

Tony looked up from his phone. Apparently, today's

news cycle was death, destruction, and annoying kid's songs.

(Scroll.)

CWN'S WAKE UP EVERYONE! AMERICA'S NUMBER ONE MORNING SHOW! - @CWN-WAKEUP – Pizza Party Hip Hop: Are parent's worst nightmare finally over? <u>Click the link for the full video.</u>

Tony furrowed his brow. Might as well.

(Link clicked.)

(30-second ad for insurance.)

(Video freezes.)

(30-second ad for insurance plays again.)

(Video starts finally. Three morning show anchors sit on a brightly colored couch in front of a coffee table. A busy city street is out the window behind them.)

"Good morning again everyone and wake up! Haha. It's twelve past the hour. We're still waiting for continuing developments on the double oil spill off the coast of San Francisco, and we'll be giving you updates as we receive them. I'm Ted Pear and with me, of course, are my co-hosts Amy Reynolds and Ronny Peters."

"Good morning."

"Wake up, everyone!"

"Haha. Good one, Ronny. Well… it's been a rough day already this morning but… this…"

"Haha."

"… this… might be some good news. Haha. Finally, right?"

"Finally! Oh, my husband and I are so thrilled! Haha."

"I bet Amy! My wife and I too! Everyone… it's over. Haha."

"Haha."

"The popularity of the cultural phenomenon Pizza Party Hip Hop may have finally run its course. After almost two long years... wait... are we playing it? Oh no, please stop playing it! Haha."

"Haha. Our producers are trying to torture us! Stop!"

"We're going to ruin everyone's morning! Haha."

"Maybe we should let it play one last time. Haha."

"Yeah, a final send-off. Haha. Roll it, I guess. Haha."

(The video cuts to the music video for Pizza Party Hip Hop. A computer-animated cartoon pizza slice, wearing a backward baseball cap and sunglasses, dances around in repetitive dance moves. The animation is very cheap and generic-looking. The song plays.)

Pizza Party Hip Hop!

Pizza Party Hip Hop!

Pizza Party Hip Hop!

Pizza Party Don't Stop!

(The pizza with the backward hat and sunglasses continues to do the same dance moves over and over. Some cheaply animated star wipes occur in the background.)

Pizza Party Hip Hop!

Pizza Party Have Some Fun!

Pizza Party Hip Hop!

Pizza Party Everyone!

(The pizza continues to dance.)

Pizza Party Hip Hop!

Pizza Party Get It, Janet!

Pizza Party Hip Hop!

Pizza Party Save The Planet!

(Fireworks appear and the pizza pulls down his sunglasses and winks at the camera.)

(Cut back to the morning show anchors. They are goofily covering their ears and eyes.)

"Oh, man! Turn it off! Turn it off! Haha."

"Hopefully that is the last time we ever have to see and hear that! Haha."

"The worst. It's the worst. And my kids… will… not… stop… playing… it. Haha."

"Well Amy, apparently they're getting over it! The big-budget animated movie adaptation hit theaters this past weekend. And guess what? No one saw it! The film opened to a meager one-point-six million dollars of its over one-hundred-ninety-five-million-dollar budget."

"Wow."

"Wow."

"Wow. Yes, not even the star power of Action Hunk Jake North as the voice of the pizza could bring in the audience. The failure of the movie has apparently trickled down to its record sales as the popular compilation albums of the song have also been let go from its record label."

"Good riddance. Haha."

"Analysts report that it was the parents who finally did in the song's popularity. The parents are saying, they just flat out refused to take their kids to see the movie or buy any more copies of the song!"

"Yes! Solidarity!"

"Haha."

"Haha. We did it! Haha."

"The earworm nature of the song has annoyed children's parents and grandparents and guardians since it first appeared on VideoHang over two years ago. That same catchiness mesmerized children and quickly the song racked up over eight billion views on VideoHang."

"Wow."

"Wow. And a hundred million of those have to be just from my kids. Haha."

"Haha. Views on the video have since plateaued and numbers have not increased. The song and video's popularity led to more videos, apps, and of course those awful albums. Endless merchandise including stuffed animals, books, video games, toys, and branded apparel, and school supplies. The identities of creators of the video and song have never been confirmed or located. Well guys, can we breathe a sigh of relief?"

"Yes. YES! Haha. They have held my husband and me hostage by this song for months. MONTHS! Haha."

"Haha. Same here, Amy. It just never stops. Even when my kids aren't playing the song, they're singing it over and over and over. Haha. Finally, I told them if they sing it one more time I was taking their devices away! I laid the law down. Haha."

"They asked me to go see whatever this movie was and I said no! No! I am not taking you to that! I'm not spending any more on this stupid song! Now all they have to do is get it off the internet. Can we do that? Haha. I mean, enough is enough, right? Haha."

"It's truly the worst ever. I mean it was cute at first but enough is enough, right"

"Enough is enough, right? Haha."

"Haha."

"Haha. Coming up next... Farmers in the Midwest report that crop growth is down 75% from last year and many of their cows are no longer producing milk. We'll have that story and more from Ronny about the rising missing person reports out of Los Angeles. We'll be right back."

(Video ends.)

Tony swiped the app closed and put his phone down again.

The song got stuck in your head sometimes. But the kids liked it. And if something kept kids happy and silly and occupied, why was it such a monstrous thing? Tony's kids liked the song, but they did FAR MORE annoying things than just singing a silly song.

Pizza Party Hip Hop played regularly in the evening dance parties they sometimes held in the living room. Although lately, Quint was making them play his new favorites. Quint had recently fallen in love with all kinds of pop music. His favorite, as was everyone else's in the world, was anything by that Vikki Dean Grace girl on the radio. She ruled.

Tony was a hot mess of anxiety and overreactions pretty much twenty-four seven, he just didn't have the energy to add 'terrible children's music' to his daily emotional struggle. All these terrible things happening and these people are complaining about a song? It was bizarre.

He stared at the laundry basket. He shrugged and got up and went to the kitchen to eat some of the kid's afternoon snacks instead.

The laundry wouldn't finish getting folded until tomorrow. But what did folded pants and sorted socks really matter at this point? It clearly had already begun. Things were falling apart. Everything was dying. The world was once again without its Song. And the Shadows were making their moves.

And only one person knew why.

3

The Professor

Tony wouldn't say someone had kicked them out of the library's story time… but that's what happened.

It was Hooper's fault. She kept whistling. Really, she was just making a high pitched "wee" sound with her voice because Hooper didn't know how to whistle. Tony had adjusted to ignoring it. But he forgot that other people can hear her too.

So Miss Abby kindly asked them to step out of the group so the other people could hear the story. It was a riveting tale of a steam engine who gets a fresh pair of sneakers just in time to win the big slam dunk contest! Brody had looked bored with it, so it wasn't terrible they got booted.

The crowd was enormous today for story time. Tony guessed there must have been about fifty or sixty people there. It made sense. They had canceled school for the fourth day in a row, and people were dying to take their kids some place. The blackouts were still occurring. Long periods of time where there was no internet or no power or both.

There was also a new super-flu going around, a food and supply shortage, and lots of random unexplained missing persons. Schools and most of the city were shutting down. The rest of the country wasn't in much better shape. It was happening all over the world.

"Okay, where do you think your goofy brother is?" Tony said once they were out of the crowd. Quint was old enough to wander the library by himself. Tony just asked that he behave and not bother anyone.

"Maybe he is looking for a new book?" Brody said as he twisted his lion blanket around.

"Maybe he is looking for... for... diaper!" Hooper added, and then she and Brody both cracked up. The newest, funniest thing in the world to all three of the kids involved saying someone was wearing a diaper, had eaten a diaper, or was a diaper. It seemed to be interchangeable as either insult or satire or wit. Their comedy was very advanced.

"Alright, you two. He said when we got here he wanted to look at the graphic novels, let's go look there." Tony said.

They walked past a frustrated mother. "No. No. No. We are NOT checking out any more of these stupid Pizza Party Hip Hop books." She was saying as she grabbed a small stack of books out of her son's arms and dropped them back on a shelf. "Come on, let's go find a book that is not so annoying."

Tony and the kids strolled over to the graphic novel section, but Quint wasn't there. He also wasn't by the DVDs or the computers. Tony didn't see him in any of the fiction aisles either.

"Where'd you go, Quint?" Tony said out loud. They had looked around the entire first floor of the library and hadn't found Quint. Tony was anxious, but not panicked.

Tony guessed he must have gone upstairs, but that was all reference and non-fiction. The kids rarely wanted to go up there.

It was much quieter on the second floor as they stepped off the elevator. It was only one floor up, but the kids insisted on taking the elevator. It was all business up here. Right off the stairs and elevator, there was a small media section. Just a few computers. But there were rows and rows of long aisles of reference books and materials. In this quieter space, Quint's voice could be heard easily. It sounded like he was somewhere in the back. Like always, you could always hear Tony's kids before you could see them.

They found Quint in the back corner of the library. There was a large table and about two dozen books opened and messily spread across the table. There were also large maps, both rolled and unrolled, hanging off the ends of the table.

Quint seemed to be chatting up an older gentleman who was hunched over the table intensely running his fingers along the pages of two books at the same time. His three-piece brown tweed suit looked like it had been slept in. The thin gray hair on his head was messy and uncombed. It looked like he had not groomed his beard in a few weeks either. There were reading glasses balanced on his nose. When he looked up from his table at Tony, the glasses magnified the swollen dark circles under his sleepless eyes.

"Hey, Daddy!" Quint said when he finally noticed Tony.

Tony was hit with another wave of anxiety. Pointless, stupid anxiety over this stranger thinking Tony was a bad dad because he let his kid run around and bother people.

Now Tony would have to perform 'Parenting' for this stranger.

"Hey, buddy! Where'd you go? We couldn't find you? You aren't bothering this gentleman, are you? We should let him work, buddy." Tony's customer service voice said in one quick, long burst to cover all his bases and let the old man know he was handling it.

The dumbest part of parenting is having to show your work like it's some kind of high school math test.

"Professor, this is Tony, my Dad, and my brother Brody and my sister Hooper," Quint said introducing everyone. "I was helping the Professor, Daddy!"

"Oh, I don't think he needs your help, man. Let's not bother him." Tony said, starting to lead Quint away.

"No, no bother at all. The young man saw me attempting to carry too many of these books at the same time and assisted me in bringing them to my table here." The disheveled man said. He had a 'smart person,' accent. "In fact, I should commend you, sir. Your boy not only has excellent matters but quite a refreshing curiosity about things." The man leaned over the table with his hand out.

"Yeah, well, Quint must have come here after that kid left." Tony joked and shook his hand.

The old man took his glasses off and smiled. He chuckled.

"I must thank you for that." The old man said and set his glasses down on a book. He looked so tired. "It has been quite a while since I have smiled." He put his head down and stared at the floor, defeated. "And I am afraid I don't know when I shall again. When any of us will smile again."

"Okay. Well, thanks for putting up with my son here, we'll get out of your hair." Tony said, trying to duck out of whatever this was turning into.

"Daddy, The Professor is a real scientist!" Quint said. Then his voice got serious. "He says that the world is in big trouble."

"Well, you need not be a scientist to know that!" Tony replied, pressing his luck at a second joke landing. It didn't.

"Indeed, you are correct, sir. One needs not to have any higher education to see what is happening out there." The Professor said, walking around the table towards Tony and the kids. "The blackouts. The rioting. The sickness. Structures both physical and societal breaking down. The world is falling apart and I fear I have found the cause." He gestured to the piles of books on the table. "But unfortunately, I am having difficulty getting anyone to take my claims seriously."

Great. This guy must be one of those guys that think the Earth is shaped like macaroni or something. "Well. Sorry to bother you again. Come on gang, let's go grab a couple of books and head home." Tony said to the kids. The old man seemed nice, but clearly crazy. Tony wasn't in a 'nice but crazy' headspace today.

"Daddy, it's true. The Professor used to send rockets into space!" Quint said, still clearly fascinated by the man.

"Oh boy, that's… wait, really?" Tony said mid-humoring.

"Yeah, really Daddy!" Quint said.

"It's true. I was a part of the Experimental Science and Rocket Division. Although that was a while ago. I'm afraid funding and a general lack of national passion and priority have relegated me to a teaching and advisory position. I still assist in the satellite program. And that… is how I discovered the tones. Those blasted tones." The Professor said.

"The tones? What's that mean?" Tony regretfully asked.

"Well over the past decade, as the technology of the satellites has become more advanced, I made an astonishing discovery. And after many years of research, I concluded that there is a previously undetected atmospheric layer." The Professor said, walking back around the big table.

"Like the gasses that surround Earth, Daddy. You know, like the Exosphere, the Troposphere, the Stratosphere..." Quint said to Tony, counting on his fingers.

"Yeah yeah, man I remember," Tony said, forgetting his eight-year-old could out-adult him sometimes.

"But unlike the already known atmospheres, this one is not a gas. After carefully studying the data, I found this new atmosphere to be... tones. Sound. And more specifically... music." The Professor said.

"So, you found space music?" Tony asked.

"Not in space. Around the Earth." The Professor replied. Then he quickly went to the desk and unrolled a large map of the planet Earth. Tony and the kids stepped closer. "An invisible bubble made up of a series of tones and notes surrounding the planet Earth," The Professor said. He took a pencil from the table and started circling the picture of Earth with it. He sketched a series of thick lines along the curve of the entire planet.

"So what's that got to do with never smiling again?" Tony asked.

"Well, just recently I found I no longer had much of a sample size to collect data from." The Professor flipped his pencil around and erased the thick lines he had drawn around the Earth. "From what I could analyze, the tonal atmosphere was getting thinner and starting to disappear. One or two years ago it seemed as dense as London fog, but as of a few months ago it was no thicker than the steam that rises from a boiling pot of water." He stopped erasing. There were little to no lines left around the Earth.

"Why?" Quint asked.

"I didn't know. But... that is almost precisely when all the madness out in the world began." The Professor said, standing up straight again.

Tony furrowed his brow.

"Why?" Quint asked again. The old man better be ready. Quint had been known to ask why for seventeen hours in a row.

"It doesn't make any logical sense. But I could not let the theory go. Like something was speaking to me about it." The Professor gestured to his books. "I started looking into the histories of past civilizations. Diving into ancient texts and stories that speak of important songs in different cultures. Trying to find some kind of correlation. The research is as endless as the starry sky." The Professor sounded exhausted again as he absently tapped on the cover of a book.

"Don't talk to any teenagers, then. They have a song for everything." Tony said.

No one laughed.

"Daddy... don't," Quint said, shaking his head.

"In almost every society I have studied, I have found texts that describe songs passed down from generation to generation central to the very being of that culture. Usually either songs or poems or prayers. People who felt that without their songs, they would cease to exist. I even found writings that describe ancient but advanced cultures, maybe older than even recorded time, that disappeared after they forgot their songs." The Professor continued.

"There are some songs from the 2000s I wish I could forget," Tony muttered.

"Daddy! What did I say?" Quint snapped.

"The way they are written about, it's almost as if... these songs are magic. Magic spells for protection, spoken by an entire civilization. Stop casting the spell and then you open yourself up to danger or even annihilation." The Professor said.

"Okay, but no offense... magic? Songs as protection spells? That's a stretch, isn't it?" Tony asked in disbelief.

"Well, if you'd rather, think of it as a code for a program. Inserting the correct information to get a system to properly function. Coding and magic spells aren't that different from one another. They are both words, numbers, and phrases to make something appear out of thin air. Maybe the code you are singing is creating something like a firewall, but instead of on your computer, it goes around the entire planet. What happens when you forget to keep the firewall on?" The Professor asked.

"Something could get into your computer," Quint replied. "Like a computer virus or something. Or sometimes little pop-up boxes of annoying ads for like, I don't know, singles in your area."

"Right. Wait... where are you seeing ads like that?" Tony asked Quint.

"At the very least, you make yourself more vulnerable. And maybe you inadvertently let something in... that is normally kept out." The Professor said gravely.

"So, we stopped singing the magic firewall song and the music cloud around the planet disappeared. Now, something bad got in and now all of sudden everything on Earth is falling apart? Sure. So, what's the magic song? It's not classic rock, is it? You know, nineties grunge is considered classic rock now." Tony joked.

The Professor did not smile.

"It was one of the most difficult problems I've ever

attempted to find a solution for. It took me months… years… of putting the data together, but I finally could sequence the atmospheric tones in an order. I ran it again and again and again. It was the only answer that kept coming up."

The Professor reached into his coat pocket and pulled out a small tape recorder. He hit play.

The notes were very hollow and tinny sounding. Like an old computer trying to imitate an instrument. A metallic melody.

It took a few seconds. But Hooper caught it first.

"Huh?" Hooper perked up. "Yay!!!" She shouted.

Then Tony heard it. It was unmistakable.

"Pizza Party Hip Hop!!!" Hooper jumped up. She started doing a little dance to the robot-like music box cover of her favorite song. Brody laughed and joined her.

"Aw, why did it have to be Pizza Party Hip Hop?" Quint said disappointed. "Do you have any Vikki Dean Grace songs? She's my favorite!" Quint asked The Professor.

Tony was done. "Come on, man. I listened to your whole rocket story, the thing with the pencil around the map, and that magic firewall comparison. Like, you had me, and then this?" Tony said. He was disappointed in himself that he fell right into the crazy trap.

"Your reaction to my story is quite normal, unfortunately. When I brought my findings to my superiors, they dismissed it immediately. They let me go from my position. They said they were no longer confident in my abilities."

"Pizza Party Hip Hop! Pizza Party Hip Hop! Pizza Party Hip Hop! Pizza Party Don't Stop!" The two little kids danced around and sang. They looked like they were having fun. Quint smiled and joined them.

"Grown-ups hate this song," Tony said, watching his

kids dance around. "I'm serious. The hot small talk between parents right now is the weather, appropriate screen time amounts, and how much they hate Pizza Party Hip Hop. That's it." Tony said, holding up three fingers.

"And worse… I… I feel I'm being watched." The Professor shakily continued. He shut off the tape recorder. The kids all stopped dancing.

"Aw!" They whined.

"Or being followed. Or in my most paranoid moments… stalked. I have this unshakeable feeling that something is trying to keep me quiet. To silence me." The Professor put the tape recorder back in his pocket. He smoothed the front of his jacket and straightened his tie. "I've been moving around from city to city. Sleeping whenever I can. Stopping only to do more research. Trying to find out how to fix all of this. To restore our protection. But I always have this feeling that I'm being pursued. Something just out of reach, trying to stop me." The Professor leaned against the table with defeat.

Brody tugged at Tony's shirt. Tony leaned down to him.

"Daddy. This is boring for me again. Can we go now?" Brody said.

"Yeah, buddy," Tony replied. He straightened back up and looked at the Professor. "Well, it was nice talking to you… I think. Sounds like you have some marvellous stories, but we have to get going now. If I don't get these kid's lunch soon, they'll turn into monsters."

Then there was a loud pop.

The power in the library went out.

The kids shrieked with the surprise of the darkness. You could hear the rest of the library's shock.

"It's okay, it's okay. Everyone freeze. We're okay, gang." Tony reassuredly said as he reached into his pocket and pulled out his phone. He swiped the phone's flashlight on. "There, we're good. It's just another power outage."

He shined the light onto the kids. They were all huddled together. Quint had his arm around Brody's shoulder. Hooper ran over and hugged Tony's leg.

"It's okay. It's okay. Let's just slowly go back downstairs and we'll go home, okay?" Tony said. "You okay, Professor?" Tony asked, shining his light on The Professor.

"Yes, I'll be quite alright. Thank you." The Professor said.

Then, the shadow that The Professor was casting on the wall reached out and grabbed him by the throat.

4

The Last Warning

Darkness.

Somewhere in the darkness.

Suddenly.

"Massster! It's him! The old man!" A voice hissed.

"**Take**. **Him**." A deep reply thundered with echo and hate.

"Yesss Massster!" The hiss obeyed and tore away.

The hissing voice swam up through the darkness.

Floating upon the opposite of everything.

Up up up.

Weaving and in and out between the dark and light.

The hiss twisted itself and blew out their precious power.

There.

There you are.

"It's okay. It's okay. Let's just slowly go back downstairs and we'll go home, okay?" Tony said. "You okay, Professor?" Tony asked, shining his light on The Professor.

"Yes, I'll be quite alright. Thank you." The Professor said.

Then, the shadow that The Professor was casting on the wall reached out and grabbed him by the throat.

The kids all started screaming.

Tony jumped and almost dropped his phone. Then he shoved the kids behind him.

The Shadow slowly stepped off the wall, grasping The Professor's throat. The shocked Professor was choking and frantically grabbing and pulling at the pitch-black grip around his throat.

Tony started pushing his terrified kids backward.

Then, as quick as flipping a switch, The Professor suddenly absorbed his attacking Shadow. Like a sponge sucking up water, the dark shape flowed into the Professor's body. And almost instantaneously The Professor turned into something else.

Dark gray smoke suddenly engulfed his body. His neck, torso, arms, and legs increased in length by about three feet. His limbs made crunching noises as they stretched out. The Professor's body fell forward and propped itself up on all four of its now long and lanky limbs. The thing raised its head and looked at Tony and the kids. They got to see the smoky darkness cover the rest of the Professor's face. It was replaced with blank white slits of eyes and a huge grin of twisted and gnarled teeth.

The creature spoke in a rough hiss.

"Flesssh." The Shadow snarled.

"Pickles. Run kids!" Tony yelled.

The kids took off running. Tony scooped Hooper up in his arms.

He kept his phone's flashlight up and facing forward so they could see where they were running in the darkness. The boys were up front, leading the way. But Tony's kids rarely ever came up here. They didn't know how to get back downstairs to the front doors.

"No, not that way!" Tony shouted, holding Hooper.

The boys immediately turned and darted down the nearest long aisle of reference and non-fiction books. The mistake saved their lives. Just as they all turned the corner, the Shadow monster lunged like a tiger and just missed them. It slammed hard against the floor and tumbled over on its side.

There were just a few library visitors that were still upstairs, gathering their belongings in the dark using the lights on their phones. When they saw the giant gangly dog monster jump out of the back, they all started screaming and frantically rushed for the stairs.

Tony and the kids were running down the tall, but thin, aisle of books as fast as they could. The light from Tony's bouncing phone waved from the shelves to the floor.

The monster scrambled to its feet. It leaped into the same aisle that the man and the children had run down. But it barely fit because of its newly stretched-out size. The shelves rocked back and books tumbled to the floor as it squeezed through. It snarled and growled.

Tony and the kids turned the corner and ran up the next row.

Stupidly, they were now running towards the monster, with it on the other side of the bookshelf. Tony's eyes went wide as they passed the lumbering, smoky-colored beast going the opposite way. He ducked down as the shelf tipped towards them. He reached over and covered the top of the kids as a bunch of books fell off onto his back. He winced in pain, wishing that thick Russian poetry criticism that just fell on the back of his neck could have been summarized in a thin pamphlet.

"Keep going! Run! Run!" Tony shouted. "Boys, don't go down another aisle! Go out and to the left and head for the stairs!"

But they instead went out and turned and ran down yet another aisle of books. Tony's kids were always brilliant listeners.

As they took off down the next aisle, a member of the library's staff was walking up the steps. He had been coming to check on the upstairs after the power went out, but was greeted by terrified visitors running past him. He was holding a large flashlight and was waving it around in the darkness.

"Hello? Is everyone okay? What's going on up here?" He yelled into what he thought was an empty upstairs.

He heard with a loud hiss. Startled, he shined his light right where he heard the noise. The light shined on the end of the aisle right as the Shadow monster clumsily leaped out.

"What is…?" The staff member said right before the Shadow monster took a running leap at him.

The Shadow knocked the man down and they both skidded back by the computers.

Tony and the kids watched this terrible thing happen while crouched down around the corner of an aisle.

"We've got to get downstairs," Tony whispered to his kids. "The stairs and elevator are just over there."

Up ahead were the stairs and the elevator right next to it. The light from the downstairs windows was shining up the stairwell. The problem was that Tony couldn't decide if it was better to run there or to tiptoe there while the monster was busy with whatever horrible thing it was doing to that poor man.

"Daddy, can we take the elevator?" Quint asked quietly.

"What?" Tony turned.

"I get to push the buttons," Brody announced not so quietly.

"Wait…" Tony said.

"No! I get to push the buttons!" Hooper demanded absolutely not quietly.

"Stop!" Tony shushed them. He checked around the corner again. No monster. He looked back at the kids. "Kids, don't. Please be quiet. Quint, I don't know if the elevator is a good idea. Aren't we supposed to take the stairs in an emergency?" Tony said, checking the corner again.

"That's a fire, Daddy. In a fire, you don't take elevators," Quint whispered.

"But surely this counts too, right? I mean, there's no circle with a line through a big smoke dog monster on the elevator wall. But if one is chasing you, getting in a small box is probably not a great idea, right?"

Tony had no idea what to do. He could carry Hooper down, but it could be dangerous to make his boys rush down a flight of steps. He closed his eyes for a moment. He took a breath.

"We're going for the stairs." Tony turned to the kids and said. "It's only one floor. And the doors to get outside the library are real close by once we get down there. Boys, I'm going to carry Hooper and you're going to get down those steps as fast, but as safe as you can." Tony said, tying Brody's lion blanket tight around the little guy's waist.

"We're ready, Daddy," Quint said and held his hand up for Brody to high five. Brody smiled big and high fived him.

"Okay, here we go," Tony said, lifting Hooper. Still scared with her eyes shut tight, she tucked her head into Tony's shoulder. "Ready… set… go!" Tony quietly counted off.

They all quietly sprinted towards the stairs. Tony could

hear the boys huffing and puffing. Hooper bounced roughly in his arms and against his shoulder.

At the top of the steps, Tony let the boys get a head start down, while he kept watch on the area where the monster had gone. The light from the downstairs windows was making the stairwell bright enough to easily see. The boys hopped down the steps, taking some two at a time. Tony started down the steps and turned back again to check.

Suddenly, the heads of TWO Shadows popped up from behind the computer table.

The Professor turned the staff member into a Shadow. It looked just as large and just as terrifying. Their blank white eyes narrowed at Tony. They both snarled and hissed. One leaped up onto the table and the other jetted around it. They both started lunging towards the stairs.

"Go boys go!" Tony shouted to Quint and Brody. They were almost to the bottom and Tony started jumping down the steps to catch up. He gripped Hooper tight in his arms as he quickly made his way down.

They made it back to the first floor. The boys stopped at the bottom, waiting for direction.

"The front doors, boys! Get outside!" Tony shouted as he leaped down the last few steps.

They took off for the front doors of the virtually empty library. Tony turned to check behind them. But then he stopped. The boys noticed Tony stopped running, and they stopped too.

"Daddy?" Quint asked.

The monsters weren't behind them. They didn't chase them down the steps.

"Where are…"

DING.

The elevator doors opened and the two giant creatures lumbered out. Snarling and hissing.

"Boys. Outside. Go!" Tony yelled.

"Itsss no ussse, flesssh," The Professor's Shadow hissed.

Tony and the kids stopped again.

The Shadows claws clicked as they gently walked across the floor.

"Itsss over... we have had an infinity to prepare... we made sssure thisss time it would lassst..." The monster spoke.

Tony pushed the boys behind him, and they stepped backward again. While the one Shadow spoke, the other hunched lower to the ground like it was going to pounce. It was getting ready.

"We found a way into the sssong itsssself... changed it ssslowly note by note... it took endlesss lifetimesss upon endlesss lifetimesss... but we tricked it... poisssoned it... itsss oursss now." The monster hissed, getting closer and closer.

"Okay, get ready to run," Tony said to the boys.

"Itsss perfect... turn the adultsss againsssst the children... change the sssong into what they would hate... what happened before will happen again... they have turned their backsss on the sssong... There isss nothing protecting you now, flesssh... itsss over," The Shadow spoke and smiled its twisted smile.

"You changed the song. But the song still works, right?" Tony said. A stupid idea popping into his stupid head.

"Yesss... for now," The monster hissed.

"Okay," Tony said. He slipped Hooper off his shoulder and turned her around. "Hoop? What's your favorite song?"

The little girl's eyes opened with a shot.

"Pizza Party Hip Hopppppp!" She yelled. She belted out the song. "Pizza Party Hip Hop! Pizza Party Hip Hop! Pizza Party Hip Hop! Pizza Party Don't Stop!"

The monsters suddenly stopped moving.

Tony set Hooper down on the ground. She danced as she sang.

"Pizza Party Hip Hop! Pizza Party Have Some Fun! Pizza Party Hip Hop! Pizza Party Everyone!" Hooper sang and threw her arms up, dancing like the pizza in the video.

The two monsters quivered. Their legs gave out. They fell to the ground. They began to violently shake and drool. Hugs gusts of their smoky flesh rose off their wretched bodies.

The boys ran around Tony and joined Hooper's singing and dancing.

"Pizza Party Hip Hop! Pizza Party Get It, Janet! Pizza Party Hip Hop! Pizza Party SAVE THE PLANET!!!!!" They all yelled.

"You've ssstopped nothing!!! Thisss isss the lassst warning!!!" The Shadow hissed before it blew away like a fan blowing away smoke. They were gone.

Tony crouched down and hugged his kids.

"Great job, everyone! You did it!" Tony said.

When the last of the smoke cleared away, the bodies of the Professor and the library staff member lay on the ground.

"Stay here," Tony said and walked over to the two bodies on the floor. They looked normal again. Tony slowly bent down and checked them for any signs of life.

Miraculously, they were still alive.

The Professor slowly opened his eyes. He looked at Tony. Clearly weak, his breaths were quick and shallow.

"You must stop them," He quietly pleaded. "You must stop them."

Tony stood up. What the heck was he supposed to do? How do you fight ancient demon monster things? Especially when your only weapon had been taken away?

Quint walked over.

"Daddy, I bet lots of kids are going to be sad about the Pizza Party Hip Hop song. But honestly, I'm just glad they didn't infect one of the songs that I really like. You know, like the new songs I make you play in the car and at the dance party?"

Tony looked down at Quint for a second. Another stupid idea popped into his stupid head.

He pulled his phone out of his pocket. Tapped on it for a second or two. His eyes got wide.

"Okay, gang. Question? Would you all rather we used your college fund for college in about a decade OR should we use it to go to a concert next weekend?"

The Pop Star

She's seventeen.

The first time she plays in front of other people is also the first time she ever punches somebody. A boy makes fun of how she is holding her guitar. She knocks him to the ground. Three months later, he begs her to be the bass player in the band.

She plays church basements and halls and parties and bars. Eventually, another punk band takes her out on tour with them. A little record label signs her band. She records an album in an afternoon. Fourteen tracks that last a whole thirty-one minutes. Everyone loves it.

She's eighteen.

The little record label gets bought by a bigger record label. They let her record another album. It does well enough that they send her out on a tour around the country and the world. She plays festivals. She opens for everyone.

She gets in a fight with her record label. They drop her band from the label. It devastates her.

She's nineteen.

To cheer herself up, she plays acoustic shows on her VideoHang channel. A new audience that lives on the internet proves that you don't need a record or a label for people to enjoy and love your music.

She's twenty.

One day to make a few bucks, she sings the hook on a hip hop song for a young rapper she'd met before at a festival. The song blows up. She does another hook for him. Then does one for another rapper. She shows up on their tours to come out and just sing the one song. Crowds go insane when she comes out. Hip hop falls in love with the former punk rock girl.

An ally at her old record label starts quietly selling songs she's writing to artists in Nashville. Word spreads around there's a new girl in town. Her songwriting becomes high in demand. The songs she writes dominate country radio.

The label that dropped her tries to sign her again. She instead finds a new label that helps her buy back her publishing. They tell her that can do whatever she wants. She makes a new album.

She's twenty-one.

She tries a new sound. A pop record wrapped in alt-rock. Pretty, but messy. Catchy, but loud. Songwriting you dance to. Stories with hooks. The album opens big and stays there.

The bands she used to open for are now opening for her. The festivals that had her playing at nine in the morning are now having her headline. She has seven hit singles on four different genre charts. She dominates radio airplay in at least three genres. She still goes on the internet every few days to sing for her fans for free.

She has a foot in pop, rock, hip hop, and country. She's an internet embraced artist with punk rock roots.

She's the biggest and rarest thing in music. Loved by everyone.

She's twenty-two.

Her name is Vikki Dean Grace, and right now she's wondering why these little kids are eating her food.

She opened the door to her dressing room and saw three kids. Two boys and a girl. And they were digging into her snack table like it was an all you can eat buffet. She wasn't sure how they got backstage after the show, never mind in her dressing room.

"Uh. Excuse me?" Vikki said, drying off her sweaty face with a towel.

The three kids turned around, their faces covered in chocolate and bits of banana and cake.

"Oh pickles, it's really YOU!" The tallest kid said with eyes as wide as the plate he was eating off of. He was wearing one of her new tour t-shirts, even though it was about two times too big. She made a mental note to tell somebody to get more child-size stuff for the merchandise booth. "Great job tonight, Miss Vikki! That was an AMAZING show!" The boy had an enormous smile on his face.

"Uh, thanks. How'd you all get back here?" Vikki asked, shutting the door behind her. "There's security everywhere." She grabbed another towel and continued to wipe the sweat off her arms.

She was right. There were hundreds of mean-looking men and women all over the place. They'd be in here too if she didn't insist on getting at least fifteen minutes to herself after every show. After that, her entourage would come in. Then her managers, some media, security, and VIP's who wanted to say hello. In a half-hour, it would be a zoo in here. So, she demanded at least fifteen minutes of alone time after a show. What she didn't ask for was three little kids eating all her candy.

"Well, if you keep your 'cute face' on you can walk into most places," The boy replied matter of fact while taking another huge bite of Vikki's cake. He was right. They were cute.

The other little boy next to him was eating a banana. He was wearing big thick noise-canceling headphones and had a baby blanket draped over his shoulders. He had on one of those Pizza Party Hip Hop shirts. He raised his banana to her.

"Hey. How's it going?" The little guy mumbled with a mouthful.

"Uh, good, little guy, thanks," Vikki said. She sat down in front of a big mirror and started taking off her show makeup. The little girl skipped to her.

"Can I have some makeup?" The little girl sweetly asked. She was also wearing a brightly colored Pizza Party Hip Hop shirt.

"Oh... I don't know, hon. I think you have to be a big girl to put on makeup?" Vikki said, making something up.

The little girl tipped her head back and just replied with the biggest eye roll Vikki had ever seen. She stomped back over to the table of food.

Vikki heard the toilet flush in her private bathroom. She spun around to see a tall man walking out, drying his hands with one of her towels.

"Sorry everyone, the line to the bathroom was too long out there. Those sodas were huge. Okay Hoop, do you need to g... oh? Hello there," The man said when he finally noticed Vikki was in the room. He was wearing a homemade Pizza Party Hip Hop shirt under his black hoodie. It was a white t-shirt that had Pizza Party Hip Hop written on it in marker

"These belong to you?" Vikki asked, motioning with her makeup wipe to the three cute scavengers.

"Uh. Yeah. They're mine. Sorry. This is your food," The man put the towel back and walked over to the kids. "Kids, she's going to think I don't feed you. Come on, let's leave her food alone. Come on," Tony said, waving the kids away from the table. The kids all started wandering around her dressing room.

"So, first question, two parts. Who are you and how did you get in here?" Vikki said, wiping her face.

"Oh, boy. This is not how this was supposed to happen. Okay. Um… okay. Um…" The man flustered.

"Daddy. Relax. Keep it together. Stick to the plan," The oldest boy reassured from across the room.

"Gee, thanks, Quint. You've got cake on your face there, life coach," The man said sarcastically to the kid.

"Okay, since two-part questions are overwhelming for you. Let's take them one at a time, then. So? Who are you?" Vikki said, putting her makeup stuff away.

She stood up and went to her little mini fridge and got out a bottle of juice. Suddenly, the oldest boy was right next to her. Looking at the juice. She smiled and reached back in. She got out another juice and handed it to him.

"Thank you," The boy said and ran back over to his little brother.

"Yes, thank you. Be sure to share with your brother and sister, Quint," The man said. "Sorry about them. They do this at home too. Uh… I'm Tony. We live here. Well, like an hour away. These are my three kids. The one wearing your t-shirt is one of your biggest fans, Quint. His little brother with the headphones is Brody. And that girl who is currently trying on all your shoes is their sister, Hooper."

"These fit me!" Hooper said wearing huge fancy boots that did not fit her.

"We are, of course, all big fans. You are a regular staple at our weeknight dance parties," Tony said.

"Thanks for playing 'Happily Never Catch Her' tonight! It's my very favorite. You did such a good job!" The boy named Quint said, handing the juice to his brother.

"Thanks, Quint," Vikki replied, sitting down on a fancy couch.

The little girl named Hooper waddled over the couch wearing Vikki's enormous boots, a feather boa, and Vikki's cowboy hat. She could barely see under the hat. She climbed up next to Vikki and sat. She didn't look at Vikki but stared over at the table with Vikki's makeup.

Quint started gently strumming Vikki's acoustic guitar in the corner. Brody ran over.

"I want to play the kintar too!" Brody said.

"No Brody. Not kintar. Gui-tar!" Quint corrected.

"Yeah, Quint. I know! I know! Kintar!" Brody said. And then they started taking turns strumming and plucking the strings.

"And you played 'Duck and Roll'. It's pretty cool you still play your older stuff," Tony said. He made a face like he was unsure he should say something else. "I don't know if you care, but I saw you play, years ago, at the Metro in Chicago. You opened for Boss Bonesauce. You had to be like seventeen or eighteen years old. You blew everyone away. Your band used to play so fast," Tony said, sitting on the arm of the couch next to Hooper.

"Yeah, and I bet you want me to apologize for being a big sellout, huh?" Vikki said, getting defensive. She'd heard the 'used to be punk' complaint all the time.

"Absolutely not. Don't apologize for being good at what you do," Tony replied.

"Thanks. And how about you? You great at what you

do?" Vikki asked, taking her huge necklace off and putting it on Hooper.

"Well, I'm an… okay Dad. I stay home full time with these kids," Tony answered.

"You must be better than okay if you're walking around wearing a Pizza Party Hip Hop shirt like your kids are. That's some dedication there, man. Also very DIY, good job," Vikki said, pointing to Tony's homemade marker shirt.

"Oh yeah, this," Tony looked down. His voice suddenly had hesitation again. "Uh, this is more like when, you know, you wear garlic and crosses to keep vampires away. This is armor. It's protection."

"Sure, man. Whatever," Vikki said, putting her rings on Hooper's little fingers.

"Actually, that's what we came to talk to you about. Now, I know this is going to sound absolutely…" Tony stood up and started saying.

The door burst open.

"Vikki?" Kurt burst into the room. He wore a tailored suit jacket over a t-shirt and jeans. He was carrying two smartphones. Following behind him was Mikey, one of her bodyguards. "What is going on here?"

"Oh hey, Kurt," Vikki said, not looking up. "You know my fifteen minutes of quiet time isn't done yet." She said.

She had inherited Kurt from the label. He handled most of her day-to-day commitments. He could be a jerk, but he was an excellent manager. He was a necessary evil when you got as big as Vikki had.

Mikey normally looked like he could run through brick walls. Right now though, he was gloomily looking down at the ground like they had scolded him. It was strange to see such a big guy look so small, Vikki thought.

"Who are these people?" Kurt asked, motioning to

Tony and the kids. He then turned around to Mikey. "Are these them?" Kurt yelled.

"Don't yell at Mikey or I'll tell him to fold you up," Vikki said, finally looking at Kurt.

"Well, your buddy here let these people backstage and into your dressing room without clearing it with anyone. Says he knows them," Kurt shouted.

"Well, it's not his fault." Tony interrupted. "He was just helping me out. I've never met Mike until tonight. But we know each other from an online group we belong to," Tony said.

"What group, Mikey?" Vikki asked.

"Tony and I belong to the same online ASD Parenting group. It's a group where we share articles, advice, and encourage other parents of children with Autism Spectrum Disorder. Tony and I started talking about a year ago after my wife and I got Ben's diagnosis. Tony has a son with autism too," Mikey explained. He looked over at Brody by the guitar. "You good, partner?" Mikey shouted at Brody. Brody had been diagnosed as autistic when he was three.

Brody stopped banging on the guitar and gave Mikey a thumbs up.

"So I knew what Mike did for a living and knew he'd be in town tonight for the show," Tony stood up. "I asked him if he could help us get backstage and to see you. It's not his fault," Tony pleaded to Kurt and Vikki.

"Relax, Kurt. They're not hurting anyone. Mikey, it's cool," Vikki said, putting her hair back in a ponytail. She loved Mikey's little boy.

"Thanks, Vikki," Mikey said, relaxing.

"Did they eat all your food?" Kurt said, standing over the ravaged table.

"Yeah, uh, that's my fault again. Sorry," Tony moved over to Kurt.

"Why are you here? Meet and greets are for scheduled times only," Kurt said, pointing one of his phones at Tony's chest.

"We're on a very important mission," Quint blurted, standing behind Kurt. "We need Miss Vikki's help," Quint said, looking up at Kurt.

"Very rimpotent mission," Brody repeated.

"Not rimpotent, im-por-tant!" Quint corrected him.

"What is this?" Kurt looked around in shock.

"I don't know some family of vampire hunters. Something about homemade garlic shirts," Vikki said, standing up. She gave Mikey a fist bump.

"Great show, Vikki," Mikey said.

"Thanks, buddy." She replied.

"Yes. Excellent tonight, Vikki." Kurt said, answering a text on one of his phones. "Crowd was a little light. Still empty seats. Worse than the show the other night." He said texting.

"Well, I can't blame people for not wanting to come out. All the blackouts and shutdowns. Things are crazy right now." Vikki said as she looked over what they left on her snack table. She picked up some grapes. Quint looked at the grapes too. Vikki smiled and put some grapes on a napkin for him.

"Boston is talking about canceling," Kurt said, looking up from his phone.

"Boston too?" Vikki said with a grape in her mouth. She was bummed. She loved the crowds there.

"The stadium rep said buildings are just randomly falling down in the city. They say may not be safe to come." Kurt replied.

"My wife told me that the sinkhole in downtown L.A. is getting bigger, too," Mikey said.

"And they're reporting more missing persons in Texas," Kurt said, looking at his phone again.

"All of… that… is why we came to see you, Vikki." Tony interrupted again. "We know why all these chaotic things are happening… and we think you can help stop it."

Well, there it is, Vikki thought. He WAS a lunatic. A crazy man with cute children.

"And how do I stop people from disappearing and buildings from falling down?" Vikki humored him.

"Pizza Party Hip Hop!" Quint shouted, looking up at her.

"Yeah! Pizza Party Hip Hop!" Hooper also yelled and scooted off the couch. She sang the song and danced around in Vikki's clothes and jewelry. Brody ran over to sing and dance too.

Tony took a deep breath.

"So. Kids love the song, right?" Tony said. He took another breath. Vikki thought he looked nervous. "But adults hate it. Loathe it. It's the most annoying thing in the world to them, right?"

"Right," Mikey said.

"Okay, but we just learned that it's all by design. So… just hear me out." Tony said. He wet his lips. "So, there's this force that surrounds the Earth. A protective shell. That keeps these awful things out. Shadows. Ancient monsters, older than time, who want to take over and destroy the world. But the shell… is actually a song. A song that keeps us safe. A song that we as a culture, a civilization, have got to keep in our hearts and keep alive for it to work. Well, these monsters over billions and billions of years have somehow gotten into the very DNA of the song and hacked it. They changed it to this." Tony said, motioning to the kids singing and dancing. "So that the adults would hate it and make the kids stop singing it. We all stop singing the song and all hate it, and then the shield goes away. We all stop saying the very magic spell that keeps these monsters away." Tony explained. "About the same time the world finally turned on *Pizza Party Hip Hop* is when everything outside started failing. The blackouts. The disappearances. The structure failures. The sickness. The riots. Corruption. The Shadows have gotten back in. They're slowly dismantling everything they can. Tearing everything down. Preparing the Earth for something. Clearing space. Getting ready for… well, something." Tony nervously said.

"You're an insane person. Mikey, get this lunatic out of here immediately. And I swear, I will have your job for letting this man and these kids in here!" Kurt yelled at Mikey.

"It's true, mister!" Quint scowled at Kurt.

"You. Have. Cake. On. Your. Face." Kurt said, leaning down to Quint.

"For what? They're getting ready for what?" Vikki asked. His story was insane sounding, but it seemed to draw her in. Things he was saying. She didn't know why.

"Well, we don't know," Tony answered.

"Who's we?" Mikey asked.

"Oh yeah, sorry. We learned all this from an old Professor in our library. He worked it out and then got attacked and turned into a monster for a little bit. We took care of it, don't worry." Tony said nonchalantly.

"Took care of it? Like, is he dead?" Kurt asked, horrified.

"Oh, no, no. He's alive. But you do NOT want to talk to him about all this. Trust me. He is a huge bummer. No. We decided that I would do this part. He's in D.C. right now trying to drum up some help from the government while I do this." Tony said.

"Do what?" Kurt asked.

"We need your help, Vikki," Tony said, moving in front of her. He took a big breath. Vikki saw that he was sweating. "We have got to get Pizza Party Hip Hop popular again. And there is no one more popular than you right now. You can do no wrong. And rightly so, you're great at what you do. No question. You're the only one who can stop this."

Vikki stared at the strange man. Then she walked around the room. There was something about… this.

"You know. About a month ago when we were in New York, I was halfway through the show when I looked out into the crowd. Like you said, Kurt, the audience has been lighter than we're used to. It's been easier to pick things out. When we were in New York, I swore I saw these black spots in the back… like… staring at me. These bright white eyes. Just staring me down. It was creepy. I just brushed it off and kept playing… but… my girlfriend was standing just off stage watching me. She said that several times throughout the show, she felt like something was reaching out trying to grab her. But when she turned around, nothing was there." Vikki said. "When I'm not playing music, my other job is looking out windows. I'm great at it. Out of airplanes, buses, vans. I'm like an office drone staring at a computer screen. These last few months I've seen the strangest things out those windows." Vikki stopped pacing.

"Vikki…" Kurt said.

"You say that it's because of this song?" Vikki asked Tony. She stared him in the eyes.

"It is," Tony said, staring right back.

Vikki was famous. She'd been famous since was seventeen. Someone has lied to her face every five minutes every day since then. She knew a lie. Between what he was saying and what she had been seeing… what she was feeling… he wasn't normal, but he also wasn't lying.

"What do you need me to do?" Vikki asked.

"You can't be serious? Vikki, stop." Kurt stomped over to her.

"You did it, Daddy!" Quint said, and he and Tony high-fived.

"Are you suggesting that Vikki Dean Grace record Pizza Party Hip Hop?" Kurt said, starting to laugh.

"Well, maybe eventually yes, but we need to do something faster. Something that will reach people almost immediately." Tony said.

"Internet?" Vikki asked.

"Kind of," Tony said. "You probably heard they canceled it because of all the blackouts, but they've just rescheduled The Too Cool Party festival. It's in L.A. in a week. They say both physical attendance and the free live stream audience will be record-breaking."

"Those guys are jerks. I always turn down their headlining offer." Vikki said.

"But come on. Surely they'd pull their own eyes out to get Vikki Dean Grace to play." Tony said.

He was right. She sighed. "I need you to make some calls, Kurt," Vikki said.

"The only call I'm making is to the police. To come to arrest this man and take away these awful children." Kurt said.

"Kurt. Come on. You said it yourself. Shows are getting canceled. This will make up some of that lost revenue. You know those Too Cool Party jerks will pay whatever we ask. It's not so crazy, either. I'm going to stop my set for a minute and a half to play a cover of a kid's song, Kurt. This will not ruin me." Vikki raised her voice.

"You don't know that," Kurt said sadly. Then he nodded to Vikki. He'd do what she asked. He opened the door and stepped out. The hallway was getting crowded with people waiting to be let in.

"I'm beautiful!" The little girl Hooper suddenly yelled. She had slathered a bunch of Vikki's makeup all over her face.

"Welcome to the resistance," Tony said to Vikki with a smile.

Quint walked up to Vikki. He had a serious look on his face. He put up his hand for a high five.

"Welcome to the resistance," Quint said.

Vikki smiled. She high fived him.

Brody was suddenly at her side. Looking up at her.

"Yeah," Brody said. "Welcome to the redchristmas."

The Too Cool Party

There is a certain stupid beauty to someone paying a minimum of four to five hundred dollars to stand outside in the oppressive heat with ninety-nine thousand other people and listen to some kid with a rented guitar sing a song where he rhymes "way" with "way" again.

Even before he had kids, Tony avoided music festivals. He just never had the stamina for it. It just always was too much. Too long, too hot, and too many people. It also could have been that Tony was born a complaining eighty-year-old man.

To keep everything as secret as possible, they had code named their plan. The idea itself was shaky enough on its own, they didn't need too much knowledge getting out before it even had a chance to fail. So in the week running up to the festival, when the small team talked and texted about the plan, they used the codename: Redchristmas.

The operation began for Tony and the kids earlier that afternoon when Vikki Dean Grace sent her record label's huge private plane to pick them up at their local airport. The kids were pumped up about the plane. Tony knew that this would ruin his children's tolerance for riding in the minivan again. They would all need a good humbling after this. IF this worked.

After landing in Los Angeles, they were driven to the huge outdoor venue where The Too Cool Party had already been several hours into its varied lineup. They had converted a once barren patch of the desert into a wide-reaching carnival surrounded by several different sized stages. On each stage was a performer playing to the largest crowd of people Tony had ever seen. It was just an ocean of bodies and heads and crushing credit card debt.

They spent a few hours in Vikki's massive trailer waiting for her closing time slot. Earlier in the week, the sudden announcement that they had added her to the lineup and would close the festival, made the entire world convulse with excitement. After all the terrible, strange, and bleak things that had been happening, it seemed to give everyone something to be excited about.

After several hours of waiting and the kids loudly complaining about the waiting, a series of squawks from walkie-talkies said that it was time to head to the stage. Tony put earplugs in the kid's ears. Tony had been to too many shows when he was younger without them and always paid the price afterward. Hooper had fought him about it, but Tony won when he told her she could have some ice cream later. He wasn't even sure there was ice cream here, but that's the gamble you take when you do a Parent Lie.

Tony slid Brody's noise-canceling headphones over his son's already plugged ears and tied his lion blanket tight around his tiny waist. As Tony slipped his worn backpack over his shoulders, Quint made 'hurry' whining noises. The poor kid had been dying to see his favorite artists and bands play today and couldn't wait another second, apparently.

They shuffled their way out of the trailer that was bigger than Tony's house and joined the crowd following the flashlights to get to the main stage. Even at night, the sweltering Los Angeles heat blew like a hairdryer upon Tony's poor Midwest body. He was covered in sweat from both the temperature and the worry over whether this was going to work.

The kids all walked alongside Tony as they followed the giant entourage, and support staff Vikki kept. With them was the rest of Team Redchristmas. Up next to Vikki was one of her huge bodyguards, Mikey. He sweetly told Tony earlier that he would help watch the kids. On the road most of the year already, he missed his own kids and was happy to help.

One of her many managers, Kurt was also with them. He made sure everyone knew he was not thrilled about this idea. He was terrified about what Redchristmas could do to Vikki's career. Her reputation.

Vikki promised Tony that besides Kurt and Mikey, the only other people that knew about Redchristmas were her band members. They needed to know so they could play the song with her. She'd also told her girlfriend Maureen. Maureen had another name on the internet and was one of those famous influencers. She made more money than Tony or his wife would ever see for putting on different kinds of face lotion on her VideoHang channel. She was very sweet and had helped Tony keep the kids entertained by watching videos with them on her gigantic phone.

Tony's pocket buzzed. He'd gotten a text. He pulled it out and swiped it open. It was from The Professor.

. . .

PROFESSOR

I shall watch along with the rest of the world tonight. I have made contact here in Washington D.C. with some high-ranking former colleagues. They may be able to help us in our cause. Please let me know if I can be of any assistance this evening. Good luck!

TONY TYPED back a quick thank you and returned his phone to his pocket. He had a hard time believing any person of power would ever buy that Pizza Party Hip Hop was going to save the planet. But they would need all the help they could get if this didn't work.

They walked up the back steps to the main stage. Tony looked over at Vikki, all made up in a perfectly styled stage outfit. She was so calm. She acted like she was waiting in line to get a new driver's license instead of waiting to play in front of the largest physical and online audience ever. She was so cool.

"You're not going to be able to see it." Vikki's girl-friend, Maureen said. "I've never seen her nervous right before she goes out." She noticed Tony looking. "Hours before, sure. After even sometimes. But she never seems bothered by anything right before she goes out." She said, "It's weird, right?"

"Uh, yeah… I feel like I'm going to throw up and all I am doing is standing here and watching," Tony said. His anxiety had fully merged into the center lane of his stomach and was barreling down it at full speed. "Quint be cool!" Tony suddenly shouted.

Quint could barely hold in his excitement. He was finally going to get to see his favorite artist sing her songs! And from the side of the stage, no less! He was dancing around and getting in people's way.

"Sorry Daddy, but this is SO SICK!" Quint ran up to Tony. "Daddy, look!" Quint shouted.

A bunch more very, very, very cool-looking people turned up on the side of the stage with them.

"Daddy… it's Comma Comma Comma Comma Comma Comedian!!!" Quint was shaking, pointing at another one of his favorite bands.

"I don't really know them. Are they sick?" Tony asked.

"Daddy. So. Sick." Quint said deadly serious. Then he hugged Tony.

Tony hugged him back. "That's awesome, buddy. But let's just stay out of people's way. They're trying to get everything ready."

"Okay, Daddy," Quint said and went and stood by Brody and Hooper. They were all hypnotized by the movement and the army of people getting things ready. Their little heads bobbed back and forth, looking at everything going on around them.

"You're a wonderful dad," Maureen said.

"Well, they're not being total monsters, so they're making me look good," Tony said, refusing the compliment.

"Where's your wife at?" She suddenly asked.

"Uh, she thinks I took the kids to my moms for the weekend since they don't have school."

"You're going to get in trouble." Maureen sang.

"Probably. She's very cool. But… I don't know if she's take-your-kids-to-a-music-festival-across-the-country-to-fight-ancient-evil-cool?" Tony wondered.

"Five minutes!!!" Someone shouted.

Vikki, her band, and her dancers all went to the side and stood together for a pre-show huddle.

Tony took a deep breath. He peeked over and looked out at the crowd. It was massive. If she played a killer version of Pizza Party Hip Hop and got the crowd to love it, then that energy would spread online to the live stream. She could get the song trending on social media, back on the news, and in the papers again. But this time in a positive light instead of a negative one. She just needed to get the song back on their side.

The stage lights dimmed to black. The crowd roared with excitement. Tony pulled the kids closer to him so they wouldn't get lost or stepped on in the dark. He put some earplugs into his own ears.

Here goes nothing, Tony thought.

Tony looked out and saw about a hundred thousand phones go up in the air at the same time. Continuous flashing from the cameras on people's phones. Everyone recording and capturing and streaming at the same time.

After a few minutes of moody synth introduction music to build anticipation, a bunch of fire blasts and fireworks went off at the same time. Brody stepped back scared and buried himself into Tony's legs. Tony rubbed his back reassuringly. Quint and Hooper's eyes were wild with explosion bloodlust.

The crowd, already crazed, went nuclear as lights came on and standing there was Vikki Dean Grace. The noise was louder than the explosions had been.

Vikki Dean Grace.

She put the frenzied crowd out of its misery when she her pick hit her guitar. She started playing her current hit single, "L-O-V-ME". The audience went wild.

After that song, she did her previous hooky single and destroyed the audience. Then she played the first song that got her on the radio and everyone lost their minds again. She played her ballad and everyone cried. She invited out the popular hip hop act T-Money and DJ Swerve, and she sang the hook on their single and had the crowd singing along. For the first time ever, she did one of those enormous country hits she had written for someone else. Then another indie-rock darling, the guy from Stillwell Angel, came out and sang a duet with her.

Tony forgot the reason they were here. He was just another audience member singing along. Even Brody eventually warmed to the noise and the lights. Now he was dancing around with his siblings and Miss Maureen and Big Mikey, shaking his little booty along to the songs.

Tony was snapped back to reality by Vikki's manager Kurt. He walked up to Tony in between songs and waved his phone back and forth. Even leaning over right next to Tony's ear, he had to shout to be heard over the noise.

"The response online is unbelievable! She's trending number one on eleven different social media apps!" Kurt yelled. "If your little stunt hurts her, I swear I will do everything in my power to destroy you!" Kurt shouted.

"If this doesn't work, you'll have to get in line!" Tony shouted back into Kurt's ear.

After she played another crowd favorite, she turned and looked at Tony. She nodded.

She had front-loaded her set. She'd gotten the crowd as worked up as possible. Now it was time.

Tony, Kurt, Mikey, and Maureen all exchanged looks.

Here we go.

She faced the band and they jammed for a bit. A bouncing beat and a tight riff. Something new. The audience didn't recognize or know. They clapped along. Clap. Clap. Clap.

Finally, Vikki turned back to the audience. The riff melted effortlessly into something else... something more familiar. She'd changed it a little. Brilliantly updated some of it. But suddenly, it was there.

Vikki Dean Grace was playing Pizza Party Hip Hop.

In her unmistakable voice, she sang.

"Pizza Party Hip Hop! Pizza Party Hip Hop! Pizza Party Hip Hop! Pizza Party Don't Stop!"

The clapping stopped. The screaming stopped. The frenzy stopped. Almost a hundred thousand people were just staring at Vikki and her band.

"Pizza Party Hip Hop! Pizza Party Have Some Fun! Pizza Party Hip Hop! Pizza Party Everyone!" Vikki sang.

The lack of noise was jarring.

Then, the audience started laughing. They started booing. People started shouting.

The cool bands and artists standing on the side of the stage watching with them were cracking up. Like it was some funny joke. Some took out their phones and were taking video selfies of them shaking their heads. Many of the VIP's just started leaving.

"It's not working, Daddy!" Quint turned and said.

Tony saw Kurt's look up from his phone. Kurt closed his eyes and shook his head. Tony guessed that meant they weren't loving it online either. Kurt started angrily walking over to Tony.

The booing got louder. The yelling got angrier. The camera flashes even seemed aggressive. Then things started getting thrown on stage.

It rattled Vikki. She kept starting and stopping again. She and the band were having to dodge cups and bottles that were getting thrown at them.

"Why didn't it work, Daddy?" Quint asked again.

"I don't know, Quint, I don't know!" Tony said just as Kurt finished stomping over to him.

"I told you nothing could ssstop usss, flesssh." The hissing Shadow said as it finished covering Kurt's face.

It grabbed Tony by the back of the head.

Maureen screamed.

Somehow in one big swoop, Mikey scooped all three kids up and started backing away.

Kurt's body was completely covered in the Shadow's smoky skin and it had replaced his face with the blank white eyes and snarled grin. Its body stretched out in size. It twisted Tony around so he was facing the audience again.

"It'sss too late, flesssh. It'sss time." The hissing Shadow barked, pointing Tony's head at the crowd. "Look!"

They were scattered throughout the crowd. Hundreds of Shadows grabbing people. They were knocking down tents and concession stands and food trucks. They were climbing the scaffolds and lighting rigs. They were everywhere.

The crowd was screaming. They were panicking. They were trying to run.

The long gangly Shadows jumped up on stage and started pouncing on stagehands, onlookers, and even members of Vikki's band.

Maureen was still screaming.

Mikey was in shock, still backing away.

Tony's kids were crying.

The sky suddenly turned from starry black to bloody gray.

The hissing Shadow whispered into Tony's ear.

"The Massster isss here."

The Monster

It was the end of the world.

There was screaming and crying. Panicking and running. Buildings collapsed and fires burned.

The sky was the color of blood and smoke.

The Shadows had invaded The Too Cool Party. They were tackling the fleeing members of the audience and transforming them into more Shadows. The number of creatures was exploding. It wouldn't take long before they turned the entire massive crowd.

The hissing Shadow cackled as it held the back of Tony's head, forcing him to watch all the destruction.

"Watch, flesssh. Watch as your world burnsss!" The Shadow hissed and giggled again.

Big Mikey was still backing away, holding all three of Tony's kids up in his enormous arms. Brody and Hooper were crying.

"Daddy!" Quint cried and reached out.

"Mike... get them... out of here!" Tony struggled to shout at Mikey. The creature's long smoky claws gripped tighter around the back of his head.

"Itsss no ussse… there isss no essscape! The Massster is coming. Your end isss here!" The Shadow roared. It laughed wildly.

Then Maureen slammed her huge phone into the back of the Shadow's head. It crushed like a beer can on a frat boy. But it must have hurt because it let go of Tony to put its claws to where she had hit it.

Tony fell to the ground and without thinking, kicked the legs of the creature.

The startled creature suddenly collapsed to the ground, and Maureen immediately swept a nearby stagehand's stool over its back.

It yelped and slumped to the ground. The Shadow's murky gray body steamed off of Kurt in enormous clouds of smoke. It was gone. Only an unconscious Kurt remained sprawled out on the stage floor.

"Thanks," Tony said, getting to his feet. He rubbed the back of his sore head where the Shadow had been squeezing him. "I think I went down a hat size."

"Where's Vikki?" Maureen panicked as she scanned the stage, looking for signs of her girlfriend.

"Daddy!" Quint, Brody, and Hooper all yelled as they ran into his arms.

"Everyone okay?" Tony said as he hugged them.

"They're good. But look!" Mikey said.

He pointed to a group of Shadows that had Vikki surrounded towards the edge of the stage. They seemed to be teasing her, slowly closing in.

"Stay here!" Mikey said to everyone and took off running to help Vikki.

"Mikey, wait!" Tony shouted.

But the big man was already over to Vikki. He jumped on the back of a Shadow, flattening it on the stage. Then sprang off of it and with both of his enormous fists he pounded the remaining Shadows in their heads. He was so fast. Within just a few seconds they were all knocked out. Their gray smoky skin fizzed off their host bodies like vapor.

Mike led Vikki back to the others. They had to dodge several pieces of light rigs that were falling from the top of the stage.

Vikki ran to Maureen, and they hugged.

"Are you all okay?" Vikki asked.

"Yeah, we're fine," Quint answered for everyone.

"Song didn't work," Vikki said to Tony.

"Yeah, I know. The crowd out-cynical-ed our irony." Tony replied.

"I really hate this festival," Vikki said, rolling her eyes.

"Look at that!" Hooper pointed to the anarchic audience.

The Shadows were everywhere. They were taking over more and more of the terrified crowd by the second. The festival's structures were all almost torn to the ground and burning. The screaming was deafening. It was madness.

"We need to get out of here." Mikey said.

"Do you think this is happening everywhere? Or just here? Can people still see us?" Maureen asked. "Are the live streams still working?"

"There's like a hundred cameras. They put them absolutely everywhere. The live stream has to be up on one of them. Check your phone." Vikki said.

"I broke it over the demon Kurt's head!" Maureen replied.

"Kurt was a demon?" Vikki said. She looked down at Kurt's unconscious body. "You hit him with your phone?" She looked down at him again. "And I missed it?"

"People, we have to go. Come on." Mikey said. "We'll

make our way back to the trucks and vans. We get a truck and plow our way out of here." He said.

"Works for me," Tony said, turning to gather the kids together. Quint and Brody were still staring off into the crowd.

"Dddaaadddddyyy…" Quint said slowly.

"Whoa," Brody said. "We got trouble, Daddy."

"Okay, we've got to g… oh pickles." Tony saw what the boys were looking at.

IT STRETCHED FOR MILES. Like a whale breached the waters, a dark smoky shape was breaking through the fiery gray sky. It was huge but it was shapeless. Tony saw claws pierce the dark sky. Then a long murky arm. The Shadows suddenly all started celebrating.

"What is that?" Maureen screamed.

It was right in front of him, but Tony still couldn't believe what they were looking at. A giant Monster was coming out of the sky.

Another clawed arm appeared on the other side of the shape. Dark clouds and lightning surrounded the arms covering them in thunderstorms. The thing waved its arms over the festival grounds for a moment. It stopped moving its arms just over where the festival's carnival had been. Then, with an enormous crack of thunder, the monster slammed its claws into the ground.

Everything shook as if an earthquake had hit. Tony tried to grab the kids before they fell, but they all tumbled to the ground together. Vikki, Maureen, and Mikey were also rolling around on the stage, unable to keep still. Pieces of the stage were folding in and the lighting frames from above were falling all around them. Tony crawled over the tops of the kids and tried to shove them underneath him as much as he could.

Bodies of hundreds and hundreds of Shadows went flying all over the place as the fists hit the ground. Some of them started excitedly crawling up the fingers of the giant beast. What was left of the festival's carnival setup was smashed and crunched into the dirt by the Monster's giant claws. The Ferris Wheel crumpled like paper. The already burning booths and crushed stands that had surrounded the wheel slid into the collapsed ground the claws had created. The Monster mashed the structures in.

The whole Earth seemed to shake. Tony squeezed the kids underneath him tighter, gritting his teeth and preparing for something to fall on him any moment.

The Monster finally lifted his claws back out of the ground. Everything stopped shaking.

Tony reached down and checked the kids. They seemed okay. Tony looked up and around for everyone else. Vikki, Maureen, and Mike were spread all over the side of the stage and slowly standing up.

Tony felt the heat first. As the Monster pulled its claws out, the giant pit that it created was filled with a raging fire. The claws raised back into the air and fire dripped down from them like rain.

"Who's this diaper?" Hooper stood up and pointed.

"Let's get to that truck. Now." Mikey demanded as they all met up again.

But suddenly, about ten Shadows jumped down from the top and sides of the skakey stage. The creatures blocked the escape route.

They were snarling and flexing their claws.

"Oh. Good." Tony said.

One of the Shadows leapt up at the group.

A punch from Mikey quickly sent it down to the stage

floor. Broken bars and pipes were lying all around from the destroyed parts of the stage. Mikey kicked some over to Tony, Vikki, and Maureen.

"Hit your way out!" Mikey shouted as he decked another Shadow.

The Shadows all charged.

Vikki and Maureen started swinging at the creatures as they got closer. They made contact with a couple of Shadows and knocked them out.

Tony pushed the kids behind him and sidestepped to the stage exit. A Shadow suddenly dropped in front of him. The kids all screamed. Tony swung his pipe down like he was chopping a block of wood and hit it directly on top of its ugly head. It collapsed to the floor.

"Got him, Daddy! Can I have a stick too?" Hooper asked.

"Me too!" Brody chimed in.

"Maybe next time. Stay close to me." Tony said, keeping his eye on two Shadows that were slowly stalking toward them.

Vikki, Maureen, and Mikey were keeping the Shadows away. But no one was making any progress getting off the stage and towards the fleet of vans or trucks.

THE DEAFENING ROAR of helicopter blades and jet engines suddenly filled the air.

Tony turned around to see three huge military helicopters and two fighter jets soaring over the stage and toward the huge Monster in the sky.

"Helicopters!" Hooper yelled.

"Must mean they can still see us! Cameras must be working somewhere!" Vikki excitedly yelled over to them as she swung her pipe at another Shadow.

"Yeah! Go get it!" Quint threw his hand in the air and pointed at the Monster.

The army aircraft sped higher and higher at the Monster. Faster and Faster. Ready to take it out.

The Monster simply swatted them away.

With a single sweep of its giant arm, it swept all the aircraft out of the sky. One helicopter hit another, which knocked into the other one that flipped backward and into the two jets.

All the many millions of dollars of broken, twisted, and useless metal spun wildly back down to the festival. The destroyed aircraft introduced themselves to the ground with fiery explosions.

The remaining normal festival-goers and the deadly Shadows pursuing them were tossed around by the huge blasts.

Tony dropped his pipe and once again pushed the kids backward and covered them up. Vikki and Maureen dived to the ground. Mikey pushed a Shadow off of him and rolled to the side.

Chunks of burning metal and hot dirt scattered hundreds of feet through the air and covered the festival grounds.

Tony looked over just in time to see the severed back half of one of the fighter jets come crashing down directly down into the center of the stage.

The stage split in half with the broken jet cutting it cleanly down the middle.

Tony and the kids screamed as they tumbled down the newly created hill and rolled into the side of the jet.

TONY SAT UP.

"We're okay, Daddy," Quint said, rubbing his head.

"This plane crashed!" Brody pointed out.

The back end of the big jet ran the width of the stage. The very back of it stuck out the front of the now broken platform.

Tony turned and looked up at the slanted stage. It wasn't so bad. They should be able to crawl up the hill and get out.

Tony turned to climb up it when he saw Mikey lean down into the incline.

"Mikey! Are you okay?" Tony shouted up. "You think you can reach down and help me pull the kids back up?"

Two long arms suddenly shot down at Tony. Huge hands grabbed Tony's shoulders, and it yanked him up the broken stage.

Tony's eyes went wide as he saw Mikey's face finish being covered by the Shadow.

"Happy to help, flesssh." The hissing Shadow said and threw him across what was left of the standing stage.

Tony bounced a few times and rolled into a pile of debris. The pain opened his eyes to see the hissing Shadow stomping over to him. Taking over Mikey's body had made it stretch out even bigger than it had been before. Tony gulped.

VIKKI OPENED HER EYES.

She had been tossed to the side of the crashed jet opposite of Tony and Shadow Mikey. She pushed herself to her feet. Her entire body was stinging.

She looked up into the sky. The Monster was moving its giant claws over the destroyed festival.

She looked around for Maureen. She didn't see her anywhere. Vikki stumbled around her side of the stage pushing debris over, looking underneath broken pieces for Maureen.

"Maureen!" Vikki called out.

She turned to see Maureen suddenly standing right behind her. She was being overtaken with the smoky skin of a Shadow. Maureen's face was covered and replaced with blank white eyes and a mouth full of jagged teeth.

"Nooo!" Vikki screamed as Shadow Maureen tackled her to the ground.

QUINT HELPED PUSH Brody and Hooper up onto the back of the plane that had split the stage. After they were up safely, he climbed it himself. The three kids stood on the back of the broken fighter jet.

"Where's Daddy?" Brody asked.

"He got grabbed, we got to go help him," Quint replied.

"That's it!" Hooper suddenly shouted. "I don't like this... this... diaper!" She yelled at the giant Monster floating in the sky.

She walked to the very back of the crashed jet. Facing the destroyed festival grounds and scowling at the Monster in the sky, she started singing as loud as she could.

"Pizza Party Hip Hop! Pizza Party Hip Hop! Pizza Party Hip Hop! Pizza Party Don't Stop!" Hooper screamed at the Monster.

The two other kids joined her. They all bravely faced the sky and screamed Pizza Party Hip Hop at the Monster.

VIKKI STRUGGLED to keep Shadow Maureen from clawing and smothering her. Shadow Maureen drooled and snarled. Vikki was pushing up against the heavy gray smoky body as hard as she could.

Then she heard the kids singing.

The Shadow Maureen heard it too. It stopped pushing down on Vikki. Its head jerked up toward the kids. It twitched. Just a little.

But it was enough for Vikki to use whatever strength she had left to push the creature off of her. The Shadow Maureen landed on its back and then accidentally rolled into a big hole in the stage. It disappeared into the dark underneath.

Vikki rolled onto her stomach.

She was out of breath. She hurt all over. She just wanted to pass out.

Her heavy, closing eyes saw her guitar. It had slid down her half of the broken stage and was laying at the bottom next to the jet. She swore she could still hear the hum of feedback from some still-standing stack of speakers somewhere. Maybe they still had power?

She cried.

"Maureen." She sobbed.

She reached up and wiped the tears from her eyes.

It hurt to move. She noticed her hands and arms were all cut up and bleeding.

She slid her head slowly toward Tony's kids, singing their hearts out at the monster.

The Monster's hands suddenly stopped swaying. And Vikki swore… she saw them twitch a little.

She looked back down the slanted stage again.

The kids were closer to it.

She felt strength rush into her and she pushed herself to her elbows.

"Quint! QUINT!" Vikki yelled at the kids.

Quint stopped singing and turned around. He saw her.

"Quint! Can you get to it?" Vikki yelled and pointed.

He looked down at where she was motioning.

He leaped down Vikki's side of the jet and slid down the broken stage into the ditch. He crawled over and grabbed the guitar.

The feedback echoed across the festival. They definitely still had power.

He couldn't climb the slant and hold the guitar, so he just pushed the guitar as high as it would go. Somewhere, speakers whistled sharply as the guitar banged against the broken stage.

"What are you going to do, Miss Vikki?" Quint grunted as he pushed the guitar up to her.

Her bloody hand grabbed the neck of the guitar.

Vikki smiled.

The Redchristmas

Vikki Dean Grace slipped the guitar strap over her bruised shoulder. It hurt to move, but she had a sudden rush of adrenaline and confidence. She checked her guitar. Like its owner, it was also pretty beat up, but it would get the job done.

Quint finished crawling up the collapsed stage. It was a tough climb for the little guy. He stood next to Vikki.

"What... are you going to do... Miss Vikki?" Quint asked again, all out of breath.

"People get mad if you don't play an encore." Vikki winked.

The other two kids were still standing on the back of the jet. They were screaming Pizza Party Hip Hop at the Monster in the sky.

Their singing wasn't having a major effect, but the Monster had clearly noticed it. It was probably like a fly poking around a rhino's face. Its giant claws had stopped moving. It seemed... unsure.

Looking up at the Monster, Vikki tapped the wireless

mic still taped to the side of her face. Nothing. It was broken.

She looked around at all the debris scattered over the broken stage. There.

"Quint buddy, run over there and see if you can pick up that microphone stand and bring it here." Vikki pointed.

Quint ran over to the fallen over stand, one that Vikki's backup singers had used, and lifted it. Somewhere a speaker squealed as Quint moved the microphone. It was still working.

"Let's put it up here," Vikki said. As she walked towards the edge of the stage she tried tuning the guitar the best she could. It wasn't going to sound great, but she'd played worse before.

As she plucked the strings on the guitar, its sounds carried across the destroyed festival.

Shadows began turning their heads towards the stage. Something was happening.

Quint lugged the heavy microphone stand over to Vikki, its cord dragging behind him. Vikki helped him set it upright in front of her. They set it down with a loud thud that echoed over the field.

"Thanks, dude. You should get back over there and keep an eye on your brother and sister." Vikki told Quint.

"Okay!" Quint said. He backed up a little to take a running start. Then he jumped over the ditch of the slanted stage and back onto the rear of the jet.

Vikki wiped the hair and sweat out of her face. She took a breath.

She strummed the guitar. Looking for the right chords. The guitar sounded rough.

"Pizza Party Hip Hop! Pizza Party Hip Hop! Pizza

Party Hip Hop! Pizza Party Don't Stop!" Vikki sang. The music boomed over the festival grounds.

Her voice sounded unsure. She was hurt and she was scared.

The Monster's giant claws in the sky suddenly clenched into fists. It squeezed them tightly.

"I think it's working! I think it's hurting it!" Quint shouted over to Vikki.

Then The Monster slowly stretched out a single finger. It moved it down through the air. Then it stopped.

The Monster's finger was pointing directly at Vikki and the kids.

"Nope. Not hurting it." Quint said.

The thousands of Shadows throughout the festival all roared together in anger. Then they charged the stage.

"Pickles." Vikki stopped singing to say.

The frenzied army of Shadows all rushed at the stage. A rabid horde of snarling and screaming creatures barreling at top speed.

Vikki stepped back from the microphone.

Quint, Brody, and Hooper all looked over at her. Looking to her to tell them what to do.

Vikki started to mumble out loud to herself.

"SING, Victoria, sing. They're going to kill you all if you don't. You're going to die." She rambled, trying to psyche herself up. "Sing... like if you don't... you'll die." She closed her eyes. "Like... how it used to be. Before you had all of... this. When... if you didn't do this... you thought you would die. When this was all you could do and all you had. Just... sing."

Her hands involuntarily returned to her guitar's strings. She started just playfully plucking notes. Softly drifting from one to another. No purpose. No destination.

In her head, she's sixteen again. She's back in her bedroom. The door is shut. She's learning to play.

She's angry and confused and scared all the time.

She's doing the only thing that makes her feel better.

She's making up songs in her head. She's singing the parts that escape out.

To everyone outside her bedroom door, this is just play-time… but for her, the playtime is all that there is.

Vikki steps forward.

"Pizza Party. Hip Hoppp. Pizzaaa Partyyy Hippp Hoppp." She starts to quietly sing into the microphone.

The song is not in the normal key. Or chords. Or tune of.

"Pizza Party. Hippp Hop. Pizzzaaa Parttty. Hippp Hop." Vikki sings as her fingers swim on the guitar strings.

It's rambling. It's gentle. It's playful.

It's something different.

It's hers now.

She opens her eyes.

THE SHADOWS DROP to the ground. Like she willed an invisible wall to magically appear. The front line of attacking Shadows all collapsed like their legs had been pulled out from under them. The Shadows in the back slam into the ones in front of them. And so on. A wave of collisions and carnage carry all the way to the very back of the violent horde.

"Piiizzzaaa Paaarrrtttyyy Hippp Hoooppp." Vikki continues to sing.

The Shadows begin to wither and convulse. Their bloodlust screams turn into cries of pain and agony. The gray smoky skin of the Shadows lifts off of their host's body in big clouds of smoke and steam.

"Pizza Party. Hip Hop. Pizzzaaa Parrrtttyyy. Don't Stoooppp." Vikki continues to sing. The three kids also start singing the song like she was. Accompanying her the best they could.

ON THE OTHER side of the stage, the opposite side of the crashed jet, Tony was getting lifted into the air by the Hissing Shadow Mikey. It had been a while since someone picked him up. He was not enjoying it. He'd have to remember this queasy feeling the next time he picked Hooper up.

"You will beg for death, flesssh!" The Hissing Shadow Mikey loudly snarled. It tossed Tony back to the ground.

Tony landed hard and rolled backward. It probably would have hurt more if Tony wasn't already numb from this thing giddily beating on him.

"Mikey... if you're in there, man... you've got to snap out of it." Tony painfully pleaded.

"He'sss gone! Sssoon, you'll all be GONE!" The huge Shadow hissed and stomped towards Tony again. It cackled as it moved.

It hurt to do so, but Tony stood as fast as he could. He grabbed a broken plank of wood on his way up. When the Shadow Mikey got close enough, Tony slapped the thick board across the creature's face.

The wood exploded into tiny splinters as it raked across the Shadow. The Shadow stepped back and reached up to its face and howled in pain. But it didn't stay hurt for long. Tony had only made it mad.

"I'll feassst on your bonesss, flesssh!!!" The Hissing Shadow snarled then let out a terrifying roar. Then it started moving towards Tony again. Hissing and snarling and growling.

It was hard to hear. The Shadow gave Tony's kids a run for their money at being loud 24/7. Tony could hear that Vikki was playing the song again. If this dumb diaper would shut up for a second it would hear it too, Tony thought.

"Hey man!" Tony yelled over to it as it got closer and closer. "HEY! I got this song stuck in my head but I can't remember the name of it... think you can help me out?"

Confused, the Shadow quieted down for a second. It wasn't long, but it was enough.

"Pizzaaa Partyyy Hippp Hoppp. Pizzaaa Partyyy Everyooone." Vikki softly sang.

The Hissing Shadow dropped to the stage floor like it no longer had control of its hind legs. It started shaking in pain.

Tony was pretty pleased with himself. But his smile disappeared when the Shadow reached out with its giant arm and dug its claws into the stage. Then, still in pain, it pulled itself forward. Then it dug its other arm into the stage and dragged itself closer again. It was still coming for Tony.

Tony tried to back up farther, but the thing was too fast. It swiftly reached out and grabbed Tony by the ankle and yanked him to the floor. Then it pulled Tony toward its twitching, snarling jaws. Huge puffs of its smoky skin were flowing off of the Shadow's body.

"The Massster will finish you all! You've ssstopped nothing, flesssh!" The Hissing Shadow growled as it pulled a struggling Tony closer.

A metal pipe suddenly slammed down again and again on the Shadow's arm. The Shadow let go of Tony's leg.

Tony looked up to see the pipe was being swung by a finally conscious Kurt.

Tony scrambled to his feet and moved quickly behind Kurt before the Shadow could grab him again. They watched as the last of the creature's dark gray skin vaporized off of Mikey's body. It hissed sharply one final time, and then it was gone.

"Morning," Tony said, taking deep breaths.

"What I miss?" Kurt replied, rubbing his pounding head.

"Uh, not much. Lots of those things there. You were one for a minute. A Big Monster showed up in the sky. Crashed jets and helicopters. Sounds like Vikki and my kids are handling it." Tony said, still catching his breath.

Mikey groaned on the ground. Tony and Kurt bent down to check on him. He was coming to again. They helped him sit up.

"That sucked." Mikey winced.

"I didn't hurt you at all, did I, big guy?" Tony asked.

"What? No!" Mikey quickly replied.

"Well, don't sound so offended by the suggestion." Tony pouted.

"They're getting on the stage!" Kurt said, looking over at Vikki and the kids.

A few of the Shadows on the festival grounds were fighting through the pain and erosion the song was causing. Some of them had made it to the front of the stage and were climbing on it.

"Come on!" Mikey said, getting to his feet.

Tony picked up a long metal pipe as Kurt had, and they all raced towards Vikki and the kids.

They each jumped over the slanted stage ditch and onto the back of the jet. Mikey and Kurt ran across the plane and hopped onto the other side of the stage to keep the Shadows away from Vikki so she could do her job. Tony stopped and stood by the kids.

"Daddy!" Hooper stopped singing to shout.

"Don't stop singing!" Tony said

With all the remaining strength the dying Shadows had, they tried lunging at Vikki. Mikey punched two of them in quick succession back off the stage. With his pipe, Kurt batted another Shadow back down to the festival grounds.

Vikki continued to sing.

"Pizza Party. Hip Hoppp. Pizza Party. Don't Stoppp."

The air was filled with the wafting smoke of the Shadows bodies fading away. No longer possessed by the Shadows, the human-again festival-goers were waking up confused and weak.

THE SHADOWS WERE all gone now, but before anyone could celebrate, the Monster in the sky roared so loud it felt like it was shaking the entire world.

Everyone tumbled to their feet as the ground shook. They all threw their hands over their ears as the great beast in the sky screamed in anger. The shaking continued until the Monster stopped bellowing.

The giant claws in the sky clenched into fists again. Then they slowly opened back up.

"Oh, it's never good when he does that," Tony, helping the kids stand up again.

"Vikki, start playing again," Kurt suggested.

But before Vikki could sing the Monster began to rapidly flick its clawed fingers out. The Monster was shaking big chunks of fire off its claws and down at the stage.

"Look out! Fireballs!" Quint shouted.

As soon as he said it, fire rained down on the stage. Basketball sized bursts of fire pouring down all around them and landing with small explosions.

"Boys! Jump!" Tony scooped up Hooper and yelled. The boys leaped down onto the stage. Tony followed.

Kurt ran for cover behind some fallen scaffolding. A fireball exploded near Mikey and Vikki. The blast threw Vikki and her guitar down. It knocked Mikey backward and unconscious. Vikki landed hard up on the back of the jet.

Tony and the kids slid back down the slanted stage and got as close to the crashed jet as possible. Hopefully, these things were fireproof, Tony tried to reason quickly. Lumps of fire were still bursting all around them.

"Under here," Tony said, noticing a wide crack between the bottom of the crashed jet and the stage. If they could squeeze through, it would take them underneath the stage. Then maybe they could crawl out and away from here.

"Daddy! The fire is hot!" Hooper whined.

"I know Hoop we're going to get out through here," Tony said as he pulled her closer and showed her the gap. Brody slid through it no problem and went underneath the stage. Hooper followed him. Quint flipped on his belly and got his legs through when he suddenly stopped.

"But Daddy, what about Miss Vikki?" Quint asked.

Vikki was still on top of the jet.

She sat up and opened her eyes to see a baseball-sized flame barreling right toward her. Thinking quickly, she pushed her guitar up and covered her face the best she could. The fireball hit the body of the guitar and burst with a tiny explosion. She dropped her burning guitar on the jet and stood up, expecting to get hit with a fire blast at any moment.

But the fire rain stopped.

Then she heard it.

Tony heard it too. He leaned up out of the ditch to see what was happening.

IT WAS THE FESTIVAL CROWD. They were singing.

They were singing Pizza Party Hip Hop.

The entire crowd.

The Monster's giant claws were waving frantically over the crowd. Disoriented. Like it didn't know what to do. Then, the claws and the rest of its body hanging in the sky began to glitch out as the Shadows had. It looked like it was going in and out of focus. Phasing in and out of our reality. It made a confused roaring noise.

"Daddy, everyone is singing! It's working!" Quint said, standing next to Tony. "Let's go see!"

Quint climbed up out of the ditch back onto the stage. Tony gathered the two little kids and followed him out.

The crowd was swaying back and forth. A hundred thousand people. Singing together at the Monster in the sky. Holding their phones up.

"Isn't it awesome, Daddy?" Quint asked when Tony saw.

"Pretty awesome, bud," Tony replied. He couldn't believe it was working. It was beautiful.

Kurt appeared and was holding up one of his phones. He looked like he was in shock. His eyes were wide, and he was taking deep breaths.

"What is it?" Tony asked him.

"Everyone," Kurt said, breathing heavily. "Everyone is singing it. Not just here," He said pointing to the festival crowd. "But here too." And then he pointed to his phone screen. "Everyone watching the stream is singing the song.

The whole world." He held out his phone for Tony to see and started scrolling.

Video after video after video of people singing. They were leaning out their windows. Standing outside their doors. City streets are packed with people. The video of Times Square looked like it did on New Year's Eve. Everyone sang Pizza Party Hip Hop as loud as they could.

ANY EXCITEMENT they felt quickly turned to terror once again as the giant Monster roared angrily in the sky. It sounded painful. Its fading away was happening more rapidly now. The song was doing its job and sending the beast away.

The Monster refused to go empty-handed, though. Its giant claw suddenly extended out and directly down towards the stage. It was coming right at them.

Down, down, down the claw came at them.

"Daddy!" Hooper screamed and grabbed Tony's leg.

Quint and Brody hugged each other.

"Vikki, run!" Tony yelled.

Vikki was still standing up high on the back of the crashed jet.

She didn't say a word. She reached down and grabbed her still-burning guitar by its neck. She held it up like a flaming ax. Then she started running. And jumped off the back of the jet.

Mid-air, the pop star swung her burning guitar at the giant Monster's claw.

The fiery instrument made contact with the beast's palm. The Monster's claw recoiled slightly.

Just as the claw was closing into a fist, it started flashing in and out like a strobe light. Faster and faster. Then, an enormous bright blast of light burst over the entire festival.

The Monster was gone.

Vikki continued to glide down through the air and somehow landed on her feet in a spot the crowd had cleared.

Everything was quiet. No one made a sound.

THEN THE ENTIRE festival burst into celebration. Everyone was screaming and cheering. Jumping and throwing their hands into their air. People hugging one another and crying tears of relief and exhaustion.

The dark blood gray sky faded away. The night sky reappeared and covered the festival with the peaceful light of a billion stars.

Tony picked up Hooper and hugged her tight as his boys high fived each other.

The excited and grateful festival crowd gathered around her and lifted Vikki into the air. They started chanting her name.

Vikki!

Vikki!

Vikki!

She'd done it. She'd saved them all. She saved the whole world.

If she wasn't a legend already, she was now.

RIGHT NOW, Vikki Dean Grace is the most spoken word on the planet.

It didn't take long before the military, first responders, and the news crews flooded the festival. Helicopters flew back and forth in the air over the grounds. Jeeps, fire trucks, ambulances, and news trucks were parked all over the place.

There were some major injuries, but the majority had just scrapes and bruises. The crowd had been lucky.

Mikey woke up with a terrible headache and nothing else. The big man was a tough one.

Maureen crawled out from underneath the stage. She collapsed, crying into Vikki's arms when they found each other.

IT WAS an hour later and Team Redchristmas were sitting on the ground against an ambulance.

Hooper was sleeping on Maureen's stretched out legs. Brody was slowly nodding off in Vikki's lap, his lion blanket covering them both. Quint cozily sat between Vikki and Maureen. Maureen held an ice pack to her head with one hand and had a phone in her other. They were watching The Professor being interviewed live on CWN News. He still sounded too dark and ominous, but he was keeping it together well. He seemed happy that people were finally listening to him.

Kurt was skillfully talking on his phones and to the press and the authorities at the same time. They were being chaperoned by police and men in dark suits. Old men in various military uniforms were asking them a whole lot of questions. The media was dying to find out what was happening. Kurt was handling it all.

Tony walked around the ambulance with a phone to his ear.

"… be home soon. Okay. Love you too. Bye." Tony said and then ended the call. "Well kids, mommy is very proud of all of you. She said she has such brave kiddos."

Tony said to the kids. They all roused awake when they heard his voice.

"Are you in trouble?" A smiling Maureen asked Tony.

"Well, yeah, but I kind of have it coming. It's fine." Tony replied.

"You believe some people think we faked this? That it was a publicity stunt?" Kurt said, circling back by them. "I mean… I WISH I'd thought of it, but seriously?"

"Next album is going to have to be good to top this," Vikki said as the boys got up off of her. "I think I'll take a vacation before I start thinking about it." She said as she stood up.

"Are you kidding me? No, no, no. We have to get you into the studio as soon as possible to record your cover of Pizza Party Hip Hop. The bootlegs of the show are already all over the internet. We need an official version and fast. This is the biggest song in the history of the world, Vikki!" Kurt pleaded. "I wonder if we can get it to replace the national anthem? Can we do that? Think of the royalties." Kurt mumbled and wandered back over to the crowd of reporters.

"You're welcome to the private plane to get back home," Vikki said, walking over to Tony.

"Thanks, that would be great," Tony said.

"I can drive them to the airport." Mikey volunteered.

"We get to fly on the plane again! Awesome!" Quint said.

"Yeah! The airplane!" Brody joined in.

"Of course, the private plane would still be the only thing that impresses you after a night like tonight." Tony said.

Maureen handed a still sleepy Hooper over to Tony. Hooper tucked in and rested her head on Tony's shoulder.

"Told you you're a wonderful dad." Maureen insisted.

"Nah," Tony said, still refusing the compliment. "Uh, your lives are about to get a little bit crazier, though. That's probably the understatement of infinity. You did it. Something like this Vikki... this thing had been in the works for a long time. And you got in its way. You saved the world. Not bad for a little punk rock girl." Tony told Vikki.

"I didn't really, though. I've been sitting here thinking about it. No one started singing the song until it was too late. Until they absolutely knew that if they didn't do something they'd die. It had to get that extreme for them to even consider it. That bums me out." She said, frowning in thought.

"Yeah but that's not really surprising. Humans are the worst. We're destined to doom ourselves." Tony said. He was quiet for a second. "Look. You made everyone come together for just a minute and do something. Sixty seconds of everyone working together? That's a pretty big deal. Maybe for the next thing that comes, it lasts longer than just a minute. I don't know." Tony said and shook his head. He shrugged his shoulders. "You bought this entire planet another day to be alive. Just see what they do with it, I guess."

"Bye, Miss Vikki!" Quint said. He and Brody both high fived her. "This was the best concert I've ever been to."

"Thanks, buddy," Vikki said, laughing. "It was a pretty good show."

"Come on gang, your Mommy said she wants to give her heroes a big hug," Tony said. He nodded goodbye to Vikki and Maureen.

Mikey led Tony and the kids through the large crowd of reporters and authorities towards the fleet of trucks and vans behind the stage. Hooper appeared to get a second wind and wiggled out of Tony's arms down to the ground with the boys.

"Slow down, diapers!" Hooper shouted to the boys.

"I'm not a diaper! You are the queen diaper of the world!" Brody said, laughing.

"Well, I am the biggest diaper in the universe and I am your diaper master!" Quint topped them and they all got hysterical laughing about it.

"What's with the diaper thing? I don't get it." Mikey asked Tony.

"Dude, I have no idea. But after tonight, I think I'm done questioning or judging anything my kids like. They seem to know something we don't." Tony said. "But I swear if next month a giant diaper crawls out of a volcano and tries to eat us all... I'm selling all three of them and getting a dog."

THE END.

PART IV

FullTimeTony and the Broken Stick

∞

The woods were noisy with the scattered chatter of birds and bugs. Branches and leaves scratched each other in the breeze. Somewhere nearby, a creek started to gain speed. The morning sunlight nudged through whatever open spaces it could find in the tops of the trees.

"Daddy? I have to go potty." Hooper said.

Tony and the kids had been on the hiking trail for five minutes.

Exactly five minutes ago they were all at the park's Nature Center restrooms. Unlike her brothers, Quint and Brody, Hooper had dramatically assured Tony that she didn't have to use the bathroom before going on their hike. And Tony fell for it.

"Aw pickles, Hoop." Tony let out an annoyed groan.

"Ugh! Sorry, Daddy, I didn't know!" Hooper furrowed her brow and crossed her arms.

"It's okay, it's okay. It's not your fault." Tony assured the four-year-old. He always tried to make a point to never potty shame, even when it always seemed to happen at the most inconvenient times.

Tony looked around. The trail was a thin clearing between the grass and tall trees on both sides.

He could take her over to the trees. Her brothers loved any opportunity to get to pee outside. For boys, peeing outdoors was euphoric on the same levels as unlimited screen time and throwing things into bodies of water. Tony looked back down at the wiggling Hooper.

"You want to go by those trees over there?" Tony asked.

She narrowed her eyes.

"Daddy. Ugh! Seriously?" Hooper said through pursed lips.

"Alright. Alright. We'll run back to the Nature Center. We can make it. Come on boys, let's hustle." Tony said scooping up Hooper.

"Aw come on, Daddy!" Quint threw his arms up. "We don't want to go back. Can't we just stay here?"

"I will just stay here too." Brody held up his hand and agreed with his brother.

"Guys, I can't just leave you here in the woods. Come on." Tony nixed the idea.

"Why not? We promise not to go anywhere. We can stay here and look for rocks and bugs and stuff. I promise to watch Brody!" Quint pitched again to Tony.

"Yeah, I think I will just stay here Daddy," Brody said, squeezing the knot of his favorite blanket that was tied around his waist.

Tony, holding a little girl in his arms that could begin massively leaking at any moment, thought for what little precious seconds he had. There was next to no one hiking this morning. It was the beginning of the trail, so there was nothing treacherous around them yet. The bathrooms were fairly close. If he rushed there and back, he would be gone maybe less than ten minutes.

"Fine. You do not go off this path. If you have to go anywhere, you go back the way we came and meet me at the Nature Center. You got me?" Tony said, already walking backward.

"Yeah, Daddy." Quint nodded.

"And watch your brother! We'll be right back!" Tony said, breaking into a run and taking off with a bouncing Hooper in his arms to the bathrooms.

"Daddy, Quint will watch me, Daddy!" Brody shouted at Tony as he ran out of sight.

"What should we do, Brody?" Quint asked, wandering over to the tall grass and brush that lined the edge of the trail.

"Maybe we could look for some cool flowers for Mommy?" Brody said, walking to the opposite side of the trial. "She will love that I found her flowers."

"Oh yeah. Why don't you look for flowers on that side and I'll look for some over here? Maybe some cool rocks and bugs too? Oh, wait! Maybe we'll find some fossils too!" Quint said, crouching down.

"Yeah, maybe we will find some dinosaurs!" Brody said excitedly and crouched down on his side of the trail.

"There's no dinosaurs, you idiots!" A snarky voice said.

Brody and Quint both bolted up and turned to see a group of older boys walking out of the woods. The group shuffled back onto the trail.

There were four of them. They looked about junior high age. Their clothes and shoes were all muddy, and their exposed skin was sweaty and red from walking through branches and tall weeds.

"Whoa. You guys hiking through the woods instead of on the trails?" Quint asked, always in awe of older kids.

"Yeah. Whatever. The trails are boring." One of them said.

"Yeah. There's nothing cool on the trails." Said another.

"No dinosaurs either, idiots. But you know these woods are totally haunted." The snarky voiced one said. His friends all chuckled as they walked closer to the two brothers.

"Yeah. My cousin says some weird stuff happens out here." One said very seriously to his friends.

"Careful, you don't want to scare the babies. Nice blanket there, little baby." A kid laughed at Brody. The rest all laughed too.

Quint walked over to where Brody was and stood next to him. Brody absently twisted the knot on his tied blanket. He looked down at his feet.

"It's his favorite. He takes it everywhere." Quint said.

The snarky sounding kid walked right up and stood over Brody.

"Hey kid, all this exploring has got me sweating like a pig. How about you let me borrow that blanket so I can wipe my face? I'll give it back. Promise." The snarky kid said grinning.

His friends all laughed.

"No. Don't, Brody," Quint said.

The snarky kid jerked his head over at Quint and glared. It startled Quint and he took a step back. Brody kept his head down and eyes on the ground in front of him.

"Hey guys, I hear the creek! Come on, I think it's down here. Let's go!" A kid said. He was already halfway into the woods with another.

"The creek? Yeah! Let's go!" The snarky kid straightened up and said. He turned away from Quint and Brody and leaped off the trail into the tall grass.

"Yeah, let's go! There's nothing cool on the trails!" The

last one's voice echoed as he followed his friends deep into the woods.

They were gone. The natural noise of the woods came back up to full volume again.

"Don't worry about them, Brody," Quint said walking back over to the spot he had been. "They're just being jerks."

"Yeah, I think they are just saying mean things to me. But I am not a baby." Brody said. He still spoke quietly.

"Hey, you know what? I bet like they wear diapers like the real babies!" Quint said, trying to make his brother laugh. Trying to Cheer him up. But as his own biggest fan, Quint just gave himself the giggles instead.

Giggles being more contagious than chickenpox, Brody caught them instantly and started laughing with Quint.

Right away they were back crouching and inspecting along the trail for treasures.

"Look at this one Brody! I think it must be a T-Rex skull!" Quint shouted.

Brody stood up and ran over to Quint's side. Together they looked at what was clearly just a very large rock lodged in the mud next to the walking trail.

"I'll have to dig it out. I'll start with my hands, but why don't you find a stick or something I can use to help escalate?" Quint asked. He'd meant excavate, but Brody knew what he was talking about.

"Okay, Quint! I will look!" Brody said and spun around and then ran over to the other side of the trail, looking for something to help Quint. Standing on his tippy-toes and leaning over the edge of the path, he scanned the area around him.

Something bright caught his eye. A quick flash of gold.

Brody looked to where the flicker had been. A little way off the trail and into the thick woods, something was laying in the tall grass. Brody couldn't see what it was because it was mostly covered up by the grass and leaves. Brody thought maybe it was just trash. Sometimes people dropped their trash in the woods, which he knew was not very nice to do.

Suddenly the thing sparkled a bright gold again. Bright gold for just a quick second and then back to normal. It was like a blink. Or a wave.

Brody wanted to see what it was. Maybe it was something that could help Quint dig out that T-Rex fossil. But it was a little farther away. He remembered that his Dad told him to stay on the trail. And he was still a little nervous that those boys were close by.

Brody thought if he was super-fast, he could go see what it was and be back on the trail before his Dad or those mean boys could see him. He didn't know where they had gone, so he cautiously looked around. He also used his listening ears trying to hear them.

When he didn't hear or see anyone, he jumped into the overgrown grass that lined the trail. His little heart racing with fear and excitement, he ran quickly over to where the odd-shaped thing was. When it was at his feet, he stopped.

It was just a broken stick. It kind of looked like that big wooden spoon that his Dad uses to make dinner. Brody had used it to help make cupcakes for Mommy a few days ago.

The stick's one end was a thick lump. The shape was about the size of a baseball. It got skinnier in the middle and at the bottom, there was a sharp jagged part like it had broken off of something.

Confused, Brody narrowed his eyes at the broken stick. He'd never seen a stick like this before.

Then the stick briefly shined bright gold at him again. A quick blink or a wave. Or maybe even a hello.

Brody smiled. Whatever kind of stick this was, it was very cool. He had to show Quint.

Brody bravely bent down and picked the broken stick up. Holding the rough globe end upright and with the sharp end at the bottom, he quickly turned around and hurried back to the trail. He hopped back over the tall grass and onto the path.

Quint spun around as he heard Brody's feet hit the dirt.

"Dude, we're not supposed to go off the trail. You're going to get me in trouble, Brody!" Quint lectured. "Whoa. What's that?" He said, suddenly noticing the cool stick Brody was holding up to show him.

"It's a cool stick, and I found it," Brody said proudly. "And plusly, maybe it can dig out the dinosaur bones!"

"Yeah, good idea! Here, let me have it." Quint said grabbing the broken stick.

"No! Let me go first, I found it!" Brody refused.

"Ugh. Okay! Fine! Try to push the skull out of the mud." Quint let go of the stick.

Brody walked over and crouched down. He started moving the broken stick towards the lodged rock.

Quint crouched next to him to supervise.

"Maybe we can sell it to the museum and use the money to buy some…" He said.

Suddenly, a short bolt of golden lightning shot out of the thick round end of the broken stick. The golden lightning hit the stuck rock and blasted it out of the mud with a loud boom. The rock went spinning off into the deep woods.

The blast had knocked both of the boys backward. They both sat back up at the same time. Their mouths and eyes were wide open. They looked at each other.

"What in the heck was that?" Quint slowly asked as the echo of the boom faded away.

"My stick did it," Brody said holding it up.

The boys stared at the stick for a moment.

"Do it again." Quint suddenly said.

They stood up. Quint silently pointed out a dead and fallen over tree off the trail ahead of them.

Brody cautiously brought the stick up and held it as far out as he could. He shakily pointed the ball end of the broken stick at the fallen over tree.

Both boys squinted their eyes.

A thick golden bolt of lightning blasted out of the stick and flew directly into the fallen tree. The tree exploded in an eruption of small sparks and dead wood. The boom echoed through the woods. Small pieces of the former tree started to rain down gently back to the wood's floor.

The boys turned and looked at each other again. Their mouths and eyes were wide with shock.

"No..." Quint started.

"... way." Brody finished.

"This is amazing, Brody! How did you do that?" Quint asked, hopping around, not being able to stand still with delight.

"I don't even know! I was just thinking of it and then it did it!" Brody excitedly said. He skipped around with Quint. "It was totally amazing!"

Flapping his arms as he jumped, Brody absently waved the broken stick in front of Quint's also jumping body.

Quint leaped up into the air with joy. And then he kept going.

Quint wondered why his feet hadn't hit the ground again. He looked down and suddenly realized he was floating about ten feet in the air.

"Uh... Brody?" Quint said.

Brody quit dancing around and looked over for Quint. But he wasn't there.

"Uh… up here, Brody," Quint said.

Brody looked up and saw his older brother floating in the air.

"Brody. I think this is a very special stick you have found." Quint said calmly.

Brody moved his stick to look at it. Quint suddenly moved around in the air.

"Whoaaa!" Quint said, laughing and holding his arms out.

As Brody slowly moved the stick, Quint would move in the air with it. He moved it left and Quint went left. He moved it up and Quint went up. It was like his remote-control truck at home. The stick was his remote control and Quint was his truck.

"Look at me, I'm flying!" Quint sang as he stretched out like a superhero.

Both boys giggled continuously as Brody slowly made Quint glide back and forth and up and down.

"I'm going to make you go up higher, Quint!" Brody shouted.

"Copy that, control tower, we are taking off on runway five!" Quint said in a funny voice as his little brother made him float up higher.

Quint was hanging as high as the tallest trees lining the path. He looked all around him. The tips of the trees were bright with color. The breeze blew the branches back and forth peacefully.

Looking down from up high, he saw those mean boys from earlier. They were off in the distance, throwing things into the creek. They were deep into the woods off the path. Quint suddenly had an idea.

"Hey, Brody! Can you put me down?" Quint called

down to Brody.

"Okay!" Brody said. "You are clear for a landing!" He traced the stick back down. Quint smoothly glided back to the ground.

"I'm going to see if I can land like a superhero!" Quint said as he got closer to the ground. He prepared himself to do one of those famous three-point landings he saw in the movies all the time.

Except Brody moved the stick too fast, and Quint landed on the trail floor like a sack of potatoes.

"Oof!" Quint grunted as he hit the dirt.

"Oops! Sorry, Quint." Brody ran over apologizing.

"Hahaha! No, that was awesome Brody!" Quint laughed as he stood back up. "Hey guess what? Those big kids are over there throwing stuff into the creek!" Quint pointed off in the direction he had seen the boys. "We should use your stick to make them fall in!" Quint laughed.

Brody looked at the broken stick.

"Or we could shoot some lighting at the trees by them! That would scare them!" Quint said.

Brody looked at the broken stick.

People underestimated Brody. While it is not always easy for him, he is capable of way more than people think. Sometimes seeing results of his therapies can take a long time, but he always works hard and tries to do his best day after day. Still, sometimes other people treat him as if he can't handle or do some things. They're almost always wrong.

Except about one thing. Brody just couldn't be mean.

He got angry. He lost his temper. He had lots of big emotions. But he just didn't seem to be interested in being purposefully unkind. He never wanted to be cruel, as those older boys had been before. Brody was an infinite sky of potential, but being mean was just something he didn't care to do.

"Eh. No thanks. I think we should just leave them alone." Brody said to Quint.

"Okay, that's cool," Quint replied. He had meant well and was only trying to help his brother. "Want to blow up another dead tree?"

"Heck, yeah!" Brody said.

Suddenly, the stick glowed bright gold again. But instead of just a brief flash, this time the broken stick stayed illuminated. The boys looked at each other, confused.

"There you are." A deep rough voice behind them said.

The boys spun around to see a very tall older man suddenly standing there.

The boys noticed his amazing long white beard first. It looked like an upside-down triangle. It was thick at the top and it got skinnier the lower it fell around his stomach. He had long white hair neatly pulled back into a bun behind his head. He wore a long robe that seemed to reflect bright colors in different places, almost like slowly fading Christmas lights. He had several strange looking necklaces on, all different lengths, shapes, and sizes. He wore many shiny rings and bracelets.

"Whoa," Quint said. "Are you the park ranger?" He asked.

"Of a sort." The colorful old man replied. "I keep an eye on things."

"You live out here?" Quint asked.

"No, not here. But your trees and these woods stretch farther out than you can see. From the lowest root to the highest branch, they pass through many worlds beyond this one." The man said.

"Oh yeah? Cool." Quint said. "Why are you dressed like that? You play in a band or something?"

"No." The old man huffed. "I don't play in a band or something." He turned to Brody, who was holding the still glowing stick. "I believe you found something I've been looking for." He casually walked toward them, pointing at the broken stick.

"Yeah, it's a cool stick I found. It was blowing up some rocks and trees. And plusly, it made Quint fly!" Brody said excitedly.

"Yes. It was showing off, no doubt." The old man said, pursing his lips. "It loves attention. I've been looking for it for days now." The old man put his empty hand around his back and held it there for a second. When he brought it back around to the front, he was suddenly holding a long staff. It was also glowing gold.

"Whoa," Brody said. "That was amazing."

"A few days ago, I was… taking care of something…" The old man blinked longer than normal, as one does when trying to make a terrible memory go away. He opened his eyes again.

"… and, I broke the top of my staff off." The old man pointed at the jagged break at the top of his half. "And it thought it would be very clever to sneak away from me!" He finished in a disgusted tone.

Brody's stick twinkled on and off quickly.

"Don't argue with me!" The old man yelled at the broken stick. "I'm not interested in hearing it!"

The stick flickered rapidly on and off a few more times.

The old man held up his hand to the broken stick. "That's quite enough. We shall discuss this later."

Quint leaned over and whispered to Brody. "Hey. If

sticks can talk, we should probably stop using them to get dog poop off our shoes."

"Now Brody, if you would be so kind, may I please have that terribly ungrateful piece of old wood back?" The old man bent over and held out his hand.

Brody made a face like he was thinking about it. It was a very cool stick. But it did not belong to him. He handed the glowing stick over to the tall man with the white beard.

The man took the stick and balanced it on top of his broken half. He closed his eyes and the glow from the two sticks got brighter and brighter. Brody and Quint covered their faces as it started shining as bright as a spotlight. Then, after a few moments, the light dulled again until it faded away entirely.

The two broken sticks were whole again. No longer glowing, the fixed staff was almost as tall as the old man.

"There. Good as new." The man said. The staff blinked gold for a second. "Quiet, you."

The boys laughed as the old man bent over to Brody again.

"Young man, I must thank you for finding my lost friend." The man said. "You know..." He whispered. "... most people could not handle the power it holds. It can be far too tempting to use it in all the wrong ways. But not you. It was no problem for you. You're a good boy, Brody. We thank you."

"No problem. You are welcome." Brody said. Then he smiled.

The wizard smiled back.

"I think I handled it very well." Quint butted in. "I mean, when I was up there flying I..."

"Quint?" The old man interrupted.

"Yeah?"

"Your father and sister are coming." The old man said.

The two boys turned around to see Tony and Hooper come walking back down the path.

"Hey, you boys! I saw a spider! It was a really huge spider!" Hooper took off in a run to her brothers.

Brody and Quint turned back around, but the old man was suddenly gone. Vanished.

"Yes. Hooper saw one of those long leg spiders walking across the trail, and we had to wait until it walked to the other side before we could go by. Your sister is quite the crossing guard. Sorry, that took so long. You guys good?" Tony asked.

"Yeah, Daddy! There was a wizard!" Quint ran up to Tony and said excitedly.

"Yeah! And he was talking to sticks!" Brody added. "And plusly, I made Quint fly!"

"There was a wizard who talked to sticks AND you made Quint fly?" Tony repeated with enthusiasm. "That's amazing!"

"Yeah! And Brody was using the wizard's broken stick to blow up trees!" Quint said.

"No way! Hey! Thanks for watching your brother, dude." Tony high-fived Quint. "Well, why don't we get exploring? Come on, let's check this trail out." Tony said.

The kids all followed him as he started down the path.

"Quint! We can look for dinosaur footprints!" Brody shouted.

"Yeah, good idea, Brody!" Quint replied.

"Daddy? Are we almost done?" Hooper asked.

"Hoop. You're killing me." Tony said.

And as they all turned the trail corner and walked out of sight, the old man was suddenly back where he had been standing.

The wizard quietly chuckled at the passing family. His staff blinked gold at him. "No, there's no time. We have much work to do. His dark forces are gathering for another attack and we must prepare before…"

The four older boys stumbled out of the woods and back on the trail. They were red, muddy, and now all wet from throwing things into the creek.

"Shut up, you idiots!" The snarky one said to his friends as they clumsily stepped out of the overgrown woods.

"Hey. Where are those loser babies?" Another said.

"Yeah, where'd they go?"

"Hey guys, check out that weird old man!" One said, spotting the colorfully dressed and decorated tall man standing close by.

"Nice beard, beardo." The snarky one said, and they all started laughing.

The tall old man sighed and nodded his head in disappointment. He started to slowly walk toward the boys.

"I say, boys, it certainly is humid out this morning. All this hiking surely has you working up quite a…" He took the round end of his staff and gently touched his forehead with it. "… sweat."

Like a faucet turned on, sweat poured from the foreheads of all four boys. A constant slow trickle ran down all their faces.

The boys panicked and whimpered. They frantically wiped their foreheads with their hands and forearms. But it was not stopping. The sweat just kept pouring. Down their faces. Into their eyes. Running down into their ears. Drenching their necks and backs. Their shirts were completely soaked.

They screamed the best they could as sweat dripped into their mouths. Then, they took off running back towards the Nature Center and parking lot. Back up the trail.

"But where are you going, boys? Why not explore the woods a little more?" The wizard shouted to the running boys. He suddenly grinned mischievously. "There's nothing cool on the trails."

THE END.

PART V

FullTimeTony and the One Small Step Former Man

Prologue

World War Three began a month ago. The conflict
erupted a little over two hundred and fifty miles above the
Earth on the Worldwide Space Station. Russian cosmonaut
Dr. Volya Balakin drank the sole remaining coffee ration.
This dangerous action had broken serious official protocol:
mainly... that someone had already called 'dibs'.

That someone was astrophysicist Dr. Rebecca Hackett,
who after going a month without coffee, was ready to dive-
bomb the entire space station into the sun. Thinking about
it made her stressfully grind her teeth. Since Dr. Hackett
and the rest of the American team had come aboard a few
months ago, the entire Russian team had been nothing but
rude and antisocial. The Russians showed the Americans
the absolute bare minimum of professional courtesy, and it
was difficult to get through the daily operations.

Dr. Hackett relied on her daily coffee fix to take the
tense edge off. Dr. Balakin knew that Hackett had called
dibs on that coffee and drank it, anyway. Hackett realized
she must have looked pretty ridiculous trying to violently

lunge at Balakin in zero gravity. She just kind of angry-floated at him.

PILGRIM FOWL PRESS PRESENTS:

It was the last straw of a long time coming. Several months of hostile working and living environments finally boiled over. Her bosses back at Mission Control said there was nothing they could do, and she'd have to work it out with Balakin and the rest of the Russians. Which she knew would not happen. So instead she declared World War Three. Over gross and barely drinkable, but very necessary, nasty freeze-dried coffee.

She fought the initial campaign of the war with food. She snuck into his bunk and angrily scarfed down overly sweet Russian candy she'd found that Balakin had smuggled aboard. Dr. Balakin fired back by cutting the straps on her bed, so Hackett woke up to find she'd been floating around the living quarters in the night. A former teacher of Hackett's called last week so she could speak to her class, but Balakin answered the call before Hackett could get there. He lied and said, "Hackett cannot come to phone right now because she in bathroom. She in there very long time." and then ended the call.

A TONY GRUENWALD STORY

So, of course, Hackett would get paired with Balakin today for docking duty. It was a big day. Mission Control back on Earth had sent up another unmanned supply vessel. It carried more of the upgrades necessary for the new phase of the Worldwide Space Station's operation. The station's team had been hard at work installing the upgrades for months now.

They've been attaching additional outer modules and connecting extensions to the station. They spent weeks modernizing the interiors. Tearing out old outdated parts and putting in new enhancements and add-ons. Today's supply vessel contained not only more materials for the renovations, but a state-of-the-art set of computer servers. Once these new servers were installed, their software would enable the station to move to a higher orbit.

The upgrade would push the station farther up and farther out into space. To eventually act as a more functional hub for the next generation of space travelers that were coming soon. These travelers would not be scientists or physicians or even hotshot pilots in search of the ultimate speed fix. The next wave of astronauts would be just plain old super-rich people. The privatization of space flight was here. And these ultra-wealthy tourists were going to need a place to pull into and stretch their legs. The Worldwide Space Station was getting remodeled into a truck stop.

Hackett and Balakin got picked to do today's grunt work. The rest of the team got to stare at their cushy screens and pilot the supply transport into the dock remotely from the station's terminals. Hackett and Balakin's job was to make sure the transport physically docked correctly and then to begin the unloading procedures. This was probably a punishment from the team for their little war. Hackett gritted her teeth again. At least there was going to be more coffee on this supply run. Mission Control had promised. They swore to her.

QUINT

"Come on. You are still angry with me?" Balakin amusingly called over to Hackett floating on the opposite side of the docking doors. "We should stop the fighting.

Stop all the beefing!" He said in his thick Russian accent.

"Unless it is absolutely vital to the safety of this station and the lives of its crew... I'm not listening to a thing you have to say," Hackett replied, keeping her eyes fixed on the door's signals and warning lights. "Ugh. And please don't say 'beefing'. Ever."

BRODY

"All of this is just misunderstanding. A mistake, I promise you." Balakin said. "You take things too serious."

Their headset radios clicked on.

"That's enough chatter, you two. Eyes open. Transport docking now." The station's commander scolded them through their communicators.

HOOPER

There was a soft crunch on the opposite side of the doors as the supply transport fitted itself into the docking station. Hydraulics hissed and systems recalibrated. Hackett checked the system lights that told her it was safe to open the two sets of dock doors.

"Transport docked." The radio said. "Doors are a green light for unlocking."

The lights changed, and Hackett and Balakin began twisting knobs and handles. The first set of dock doors slid open.

AND TONY

"There is supposed to be more coffee on this run. We have cup and talk this over. Bury hatchet?" Balakin said, pulling the locking levers into place.

Hackett shook her head in disgust as she turned the handle to open the second dock door.

"I can't think of anything less likely to happen on this station today," Hackett said as the dock door slid open.

Floating there was a man wearing a backpack and rubbing a bump on his head. Three grinning children, two boys, and a girl hovered around him.

"Okay... I swear this wasn't my fault," Tony said.

FULLTIMETONY AND THE ONE SMALL STEP FORMER MAN

Part I

Hackett knew she had words, but they couldn't escape her mouth. The shock of seeing a random man and three kids suddenly show up on your space station had rendered the doctor speechless.

"Who are you?" Balakin, just as surprised, asked for both of them.

"It's okay! I can explain!" The man said, still tenderly touching the red bump on his head.

"Commander! Get down here, Hart, now!" Hackett finally spit out into her radio.

"Please don't let the cops take my kids away. I swear I'm normally a good dad." The man pleaded.

"Hackett! What's going on?" The radio squawked.

"There's a man in the supply transport!" Hackett yelled.

"A what?" The Commander said in disbelief.

"A man. In the transport. With two little boys and..."

"... and Hooper!" The little girl announced.

"And... Hooper." Hackett continued. This couldn't be happening, she thought.

"We're coming down. We're coming!" The radio said before it clicked back off.

"Hey, Miss! Watch what I can do!" One of the floating little boys said. Then he barrel rolled in the air. The faded dirty blanket he grasped spun around with him. He looked like a ribbon dancer.

"I can do that too!" The older boy said and copied him.

Hackett, still totally confused, watched the two of them spin into each other over and over again.

"Ow! Watch it, Brody!"

"Move out of the way, Quint! I was here first!"

"How did you get in there?" Balakin yelled at the man.

"Well…" The man began. "… I mean, you know… the kids…" The man gestured at the kids floating behind him. Then held his hands up. "… you know?"

Hackett and Balakin kept staring at the man. Waiting for more. But he just stood there awkwardly, smiling and shaking his head.

"That's it?" Hackett said when it was apparent from the long silence that the explanation was over.

"Well… it's… it's… well… you know how it is? Right? The kids? You try to get the kids out of the house and off their screens and… you know they run around… and it's loud." The man crossed his arms and elaborated.

Silence again.

"Okay." Hackett calmly said. "I know you think you just said words, but that was absolute nonsense." Her voice got louder as she spoke. "How did you get in that supply transport? And how did you survive being in it when it was shot into outer space and traveled here?" She finished in a shout.

"Hey! I bumped my head when this thing launched. And it still hurts!" The man shouted back.

Three more members of the space station appeared from down a hatch. They all audibly gasped when they saw the man and the three kids. They quickly swam over behind Hackett and Balakin.

"What in the world is going on!" shouted Hart, who so far had yelled the loudest. That made him the one in charge. "Who are you?" shouted the commander.

"It's totally cool. My name is Tony." Said the floating stranger. "I'm a stay at home dad. These are my kids, Quint and Brody." He pointed to the still rolling boys. "And this is Hooper." He bobbed his head at the smiling little girl floating criss cross applesauce by his shoulders. "And I am so, so sorry," Tony said.

"We were going so fast!" Hooper said giddily.

"How did you get in there?" Commander Hart shouted louder.

"He says: 'you know, the kids' like that means something," Hackett answered for the man.

"You know, the kids?" Commander Hart repeated in confusion.

Tony pursed his lips, closed his eyes, and nodded his head.

"Mine are same way." The Russian cosmonaut that accompanied Commander Hart suddenly said. "Always get into trouble." He shook his head.

"It's like some days I don't even know what to do!" The other astronaut with Hart exhaustedly agreed. "It's like, are they being just kids or am I doing something wrong?" She said.

"RIGHT? I know. I KNOW." Tony shot his arm out and acknowledged.

Commander Hart exhaled loudly. As he thought, he absently rubbed the fuzz that was growing on top of his bald head. His eyes darted around as he tried to process what was going on and what to do.

"Well, let's get you out of there and up the command hub. We need to call Mission Control. Figure out what to do with you." Hart said. He turned to the two crew members that had come with him. "Sturges? Rogov? You two stay here and start unloading the transport. Get these supplies where they go as fast as you can. Move the new servers first, I'll send Volkov down as soon as I can to help begin the installation. For God's sake, be careful with them." Hart ordered.

"Sir," Sturges replied.

"Da, Komandir," Rogov said.

"Come on, then. Follow me." Hart said to the family.

The family floated out of the supply transport and onto the Worldwide Space Station.

Part II

"Behave yourselves. You are guests." Tony warned the kids.

Awkwardly bumping into and probably breaking more than a few things, Tony and the kids were escorted through the cramped tunnels and corridors of tubes to the crew's command hub. As they passed through each module and volume, a hatch had to be opened. More of the crew trickled in to join them, each one more shocked than the last when they saw the family. A very embarrassed Tony apologized to each new face he saw. They arrived at one of many t-shaped intersections of the station. Tunnel shaped corridors running down the left and right. The command hub was in the center.

After getting situated, Commander Hart and his VERY annoyed-looking Russian counterpart Volkov began turning cameras on and starting the process to make a video call to Mission Control back on Earth.

Tony counted eight crew members. Including the American and Russian back unloading the supply transport, Tony counted four Russians and four Americans. The command hub was already cramped, but with Tony and the kids added, it was downright claustrophobic. So crowded, Tony couldn't ignore all the whispering and worried looks going on between crew members.

"So… you guys like being in space?" Tony lamely attempted small talk.

"Daddy, it smells like feet in here," Hooper said, scrunching up her face.

"Hooper, stop," Tony warned.

"Well! It does!" Hooper insisted.

Hooper's hair was floating wildly all over the place. Tony pulled one of his wife's hair ties off his wrist and fixed Hooper's hair into a terrible-looking ponytail. The ponytail still stood straight up when he let go, but at least her hair was contained now.

"Excuse me, astronauts?" Quint politely asked. "But is there perhaps a button that my brother and I could take turns pushing? Perhaps one that fires a laser?"

"I would also like to push the laser button," Brody raised his hand and added.

"Guys. No. We are not touching ANYTHING? Got it?" Tony said.

As Quint crossed his arm to pout, about five coins sneaked out of Quint's pockets. Quarters and dimes. Floating away.

"My money!" Quint shouted as he and Brody picked them out of midair.

"Where did you get all that change?" Tony asked.

"From the van," Quint said, stuffing the coins back down deep into his pocket. "Your cup holder."

"Dude, that's not your money," Tony said.

"Well, can I have it?"

"You have to ask FIRST, Quint."

"Can we use them if we see a soda machine?" Quint smiled.

"Well yeah, absolutely," Tony said, never one to pass up using a soda vending machine. "But keep those coins safe in your pocket. We don't want them floating off into some computer and breaking something, okay?"

No one in the crew responded to the ridiculousness happening in front of them. They just leaned in and whispered to each other and avoided eye contact with Tony.

"Do you guys have a soda machine up here?" Tony tried again.

Hackett appeared and floated over with a first aid kid. She started looking at the bump on Tony's head.

"Do you have a concussion?" Hackett asked.

"Most of the time, yeah."

"Thought so," Hackett replied, pushing a cold pack against the bump. "Hold this here."

"They really hate me, don't they?" Tony asked, holding the cold pack.

"Who, them?" Hackett looked at the gossiping crew behind her and then turned and whispered. "I think they only came to space for the anti-social benefits. Trust me, it's not just you. They have a super-secret special handshake no one will show me."

"Doesn't sound very nice," Tony said.

"The Russians, I get it. They were here before we cycled up here. But even my crew changed and got all snooty once we stepped foot in this place." Hackett sighed. "Oh well. Stupid of me to come to space to make friends."

"I hear the parties on submarines are much better, anyway," Tony said with a sympathetic smile.

"I'll remember that for next time." Hackett smiled back.

"Okay. We're live, people." Hart called out to the crew.

The video call had been answered and Mission Control was on the line. The crew floated towards the camera and screen set up in the room's front.

"Good afternoon, WSS, what is your status?" Smith, the ground team leader, asked. His voice carried a hint of worry over the unexpected call.

"Afternoon, Control. We have... a minor issue." Hart started. "At about 1300 hours, after we had last spoken confirming the supply docking a success, we opened the supply transport and discovered a little problem."

"Copy that, WSS. Could you explain the problem? Damaged supplies? Are the new servers okay?" Smith asked.

"Negative. No damage, Control. Extra cargo." Hart said.

Then each member of the station crew floated to the sides of the camera and revealed Tony and the kids. Hooper waved.

"Good lord! Who are those people!" Smith shouted. You could hear the commotion at Mission Control break out. In the video, you could see people running around in the background. More people began crowding the camera next to Smith to get a better look.

"This is Tony and his kids. Quint, Brody, and Hooper. They somehow managed to be on the supply transport when it launched." Hart explained.

"On the transport? But how?" Smith shouted.

Everyone turned their heads and looked at Tony.

Tony didn't say a word. He just shook his head, stuck his two thumbs out, and gestured at the kids floating next to him. The kids giggled.

On the video, most staff members were all nodding their heads and rolling their eyes.

"Oh, you're telling me. Mine are teenagers. You have no idea." Smith huffed.

"I am honestly dreading when that day comes," Tony said.

"Control, we're going to need to come up with some kind of plan to get these folks back home," Hart said.

"And soon," Volkov said bluntly.

Before anyone at Mission Control could answer. A young man in a sleeveless t-shirt, shorts, and flip-flops ran into the video frame. He pushed Smith and the others to the side.

"You're kidding me! No way! Oh man, this is amazing!" The man shouted and leaped around.

The entire space station crew groaned out loud.

"Whoa. Hey Daddy? Do you know who that is?" Quint leaned over and whispered to Tony. "That's Nathan Kane! I've watched tons of VideoHang videos about him. He's like a billionaire!"

"I know who Nathan Kane is, Quint," Tony said, pretending to know who Nathan Kane was.

"He's the payroll for this operation," Hackett added. "It's him who's leading the charge for privatized space travel. He bought the station and is paying to have all the upgrades installed and outfitted." She explained. "The station is going to be the primary hub for him and all his billionaire bros to stop at during their Sunday afternoon drives to the moon."

"Ask him if he wants to chip in on paint, I need to redo our living room," Tony whispered back.

"You see, Smith? This. This is what I've been talking about!" Kane ranted loudly on the video from Earth. "Regular people. Regular, everyday people! Traveling to space! It's not only for the military and you scientists anymore! Not only for fruitless experiments and dangerous war games!" Kane got more excited. "Anyone can do this! Anyone can go to space!"

"As long as the check clears," Smith muttered.

"What was that?" Kane turned and demanded.

"Mr. Kane, this man, and his children could have been killed. They are endangering not only themselves but this entire mission! The station doesn't have the air nor food for four more people." Smith said.

"Food? Do they have space snacks, Daddy? I'm hungry." Brody asked.

Tony slid off his backpack, the family go-bag, and got out a little baggie of yellow fish crackers. He was about to pass a handful out when he stopped and remembered where he was. Instead, with a tiny grin, he just opened his hand and let them float out. The kids laughed and giggled as they bobbed around chomping the tiny crackers out of the air.

"Oh, look at them! They're fine. They did great!" Kane giddily said. "I have to get this to the news outlets immediately!" He said taking out his phone and starting to text on it.

"Whoa, whoa! Wait for a second! Before we turn this into a media circus, can we come up with a game plan on getting these people home?" Hart shouted into the camera.

"Easy. Send them back on the supply transport." Kane casually said, not even looking up from his texting. "It's a stage one drone ship. All the Kane Stage Drone Ships return to Earth to be refurbished and re-flown. It's more cost effective." He said, still texting on his phone. "Just send them back on that."

"Mr. Kane, we know the supply transport is marked for return, but it's not outfitted to carry a person back. Not safely anyway." Smith said.

"So have the gang up there rig some car seats in it or something. I don't know, you're the geniuses." Kane said. "I gotta go. I'm on CWN News in two minutes." Kane said, walking out of the video's frame.

"That dude got a billion dollars," Quint said to Tony. "He's so cool."

"Not really, buddy," Tony said.

"Commander Hart? Volkov?" Smith said into the camera. "You think you can look at the supply transport and see what needs to be done to outfit its cab to get that family home safely? Maybe check your inventory for left-over renovation supplies to use. We'll pull some specs and blueprints and see what we can come up with from down here. We also must start the math to find out what engine recalibrations will need to be made. And also, some hull protection and oxygen readings. Let's meet back up again in one hour with what we got. Sound good?"

"Copy that, Smith. See you in an hour." Hart replied and powered off the camera. He took a big breath and absently rubbed his bald head. "Okay. How about this for a plan? Balakin and Petrov, you two go through the left-overs in the empty modules and see if there's anything we can swipe to outfit that supply transport. Seats, straps, padding, safety bars. Anything that's going to keep Mr. Tony and his kids from getting much worse than a little bump on their heads during re-entry. Nelson and I will start pulling data on engine recalibration, oxygen levels, and hull stabilization."

"I'll go get started," Balakin announced and floated through a hatch.

"Good idea, Balakin." Hart said.

"What about me?" Volkov angrily asked.

"Well, we still have a mission timetable we've got to keep. Rogov and Sturges are unloading the supply transport and getting the new servers into position now. Get down there and help get them online. We'll never hear the end of it if this mission gets delayed any longer than it already has. We've got to stay on schedule. Sound good, everyone?"

"Sir? And me?" Hackett asked.

"You're on chaperone duty. Keep Tony and his kids safe and out of the way until we need them." Hart ordered.

"Great," Hackett said unenthusiastically.

"I'm so sorry," Tony said.

"We're going to be BEST FRIENDS!" Hooper shouted in Hackett's face.

"Great," Hackett said unenthusiastically.

"I'm so sorry," Tony said.

Commander Hart's watch beeped loudly.

"Say, that means we'll be passing the moon in about ten minutes. Would you kids like to get an astronaut's view of the moon?" Hart asked warmly.

"What? You guys get the moon up here?" Quint excitedly asked.

"We sure do." Hart laughed. "Hackett can take you up to the observation module to get a good look!"

"Daddy I want to see the moon!" Brody tugged at Hackett's arm. "And eat space snacks!"

"Fine. Come on, follow me." Hackett said and started floating through the entryway.

"Yay!" The kids shouted. "Hackett! Hackett! Hackett!" They chanted her name.

"Please stop that." Hackett groaned.

The kids started swimming behind and followed her out. Tony stopped before exiting the room. He turned around to the crew.

"Thank you, everyone. For all that you're doing. And again... I'm really sorry about this." Tony apologized.

The crew said nothing back. They just stared at him.

Tony nodded and shamefully floated out of the command hub. He shut the hatch door behind him.

The crew was alone.

"They're going to ruin EVERYTHING!" Volkov snapped suddenly.

"Why did you contact Earth so quickly?" Nelson shouted.

"They're going to know!" Petrov yelled.

"Keep your voices DOWN." Hart harshly scolded. "Nothing is ruined. They know nothing. Not yet. We just work FASTER."

"I swear if your foolishness jeopardized mission I will..." Volkov threatened Hart.

"You'll what? What?" Hart aggressively glided into Volkov's face. He gave him an icy stare. "Get down there and get those servers online. Now." Hart said.

Volkov backed up. A nasty grin formed on the Russian's face.

"Maybe soon... someone else is Komandir." Volkov chuckled.

Hart's watch beeped loudly again. He shut it off.

"We need to get moving. Now." Hard ordered. "Just stick to the plan. Work quickly. These problems will be gone soon."

Part III

"Whoa, does that have games on it?" Quint asked as they all floated past a serving tray sized LCD touchscreen surrounded by lots of beautiful buttons just begging to be pushed.

"Don't touch it. That's an access terminal. Gives us information on the station. They're in all the corridors." Hackett felt annoyed that she had to explain.

"I hope I can see that old dune buggy they left on the moon!" Quint excitedly said to Hackett as they floated to the observation module.

"There's a dune buggy on the moon?" Brody asked Quint.

"Yeah, man. They just left it there. Maybe a moon man drives around in it!"

"Yeah! And he goes to the moon store!" Brody giggled.

"Well, don't get too excited," Hackett warned. "While we're closer to the moon, it's still going to look pretty far away. We're not like right up on it. Sometimes it looks as far away as it does on Earth."

"Well, that's lame," Quint said, disappointed.

"Yeah, sorry, the moon is lame." Hackett sarcastically said. "Everyone around here thinks the moon is lame. We orbit the Earth about every ninety minutes. That's about sixteen times a day. And every time… EVERY time… we pass the moon, this entire station clears out. I don't know where they go, but suddenly everyone has something to do or somewhere to be whenever the moon comes into view." Hackett whined.

They pulled themselves into the observation module. The module had several windows lining the sides of the cylinder-shaped volume.

"There it is," Hackett said, directing them.

It still looked distant, but it wasn't any less impressive to see. The family pressed their faces against the window.

"I think it looks closer! I can kind of see the craters!" Quint admitted.

"Hey? Where's the moon man?" Hooper asked.

"Wow! That moon is big!" Brody marveled.

"That's so crazy," Tony said. "How close are we?"

"Give or take about four hundred kilometers. About two hundred and fifty miles." Hackett said. "It never stops taking my breath away. Being this close." She admitted. Her face got suddenly sad. "You know, that trust fund man child back on Earth says he wants space travel to be for everyone. But he doesn't mean everyone. He just means other bloated billionaires like him and his buddies. They're just going to make space another place that's only for the ultra-elite to enjoy. And that bums me out. Everyone should be able to enjoy this. Not just the super-rich." Then her face turned from sad to angry. "They're just going to ruin it. Like they always do."

"You're right but, I've seen videos of how you guys have to eat and drink. They're going to be really annoyed when the olives keep floating out of their martini glasses."

Tony joked. "Oh! And I'm sure trying to find a decent wait staff up here will be rough for them."

"It's hard to fire someone in outer space. You can't have them escorted out." Hackett smiled.

Something in the module beeped rapidly. Then the lights went out. The light from Earth and the moon kept the module brightly lit, though.

"Where did the lights go?" Hooper worried.

"What's going on?" Tony asked.

"No idea," Hackett said, just as confused.

Then the lights came back on and the beeping stopped.

"Weird," Hackett said.

The station began to violently shake and jostle around. Everyone started bumping into one another. The station felt like it was going to shake itself apart. The kids panicked.

Then, as suddenly as it had started, the shaking abruptly stopped. The family and astronaut floated apart again.

"No more of that Daddy." Brody twisted his floating blanket and told Tony.

"What the heck was that? Did we run over an alien?" Quint asked.

"Well... did we?" Tony asked Hackett.

"The only time I've ever felt something like that is when we had to fire the reverse boosters to suddenly slow the station down. There was a supply transport needed to catch up with us. We almost broke the ship. Why would we be trying to slow down right now?" Hackett explained.

"Is it because of us?" Tony wondered.

"I have no idea. Come on, let's go back to the command hub and find out what's going on." Hackett said.

Hackett held the module door open for them as the family floated back down the hatch and into the station's cramped connecting corridor tunnel. She pulled the hatch door shut as she passed through.

"Who's that?" Hooper asked.

Hackett pushed floating children out of the way and saw another member of the crew down the hallway. They were floating in front of one of the many screen access terminals installed at corridor intersections.

"I think that's Nelson. Nelson, what's going on?" Hackett shouted.

But the crew member didn't respond. Didn't even turn around. Instead, with her back to them, Nelson just quickly darted like a fish down the corridor tunnel to the right of the terminal.

"Rude," Tony said.

"Told you. Anti-social." Hackett said. "Here, maybe I can see what happened from that terminal."

"And maybe play some games on it?" Brody wondered.

Hackett and the family soared over the terminal. Hackett poked at the screen. Then she seemed to get frustrated.

"Why? Why am I locked out of this?" She gritted her teeth. "Hold on." Then her fingers quickly danced around a newly opened window. "There. It says we slowed down."

"Well, that's what you had thought, right?" Tony asked.

"Yeah, but it also looks like Nelson was trying to manually command in some new system patch. Yeah, that's weird. The system is preparing to run an update." Hackett wrinkled her face up. "Did they install the new servers already? Why are they pushing the new update through so soon?" She wondered out loud.

The terminal beeped, and the lights went out again.

But in the corridor, there were no windows. No Earth and moonlight shining through. The only light came from the glowing terminal screen and its buttons. This time it was very dark.

"Are we slowing down? Are we going to shake again?" Quint stressed aloud.

"No, the update is just installing," Hackett said, checking the terminal again. "The system reboots afterward. What the heck is going on?"

A loud clatter came from down the dark corridor and around its corner.

Tony, the kids, and Hackett all went silent.

"What was that?" Quint asked.

Hackett craned her neck out and tried to adjust her eyes to the dark.

"I don't know. Probably just Nelson." She guessed. "Nelson?" Hackett asked loudly.

The sound of heavy breathing suddenly filled the otherwise silent hallway. Rough breathing.

In. Out. In. Out.

And it was getting louder. Closer.

Tony and Hackett looked at each other in the terminal's light's display. They both shook their heads in confusion.

"Nelson? Is that you?" Hackett called out again.

She slowly leaned out of the light of the terminal into the dark hallway.

"Nel..."

She saw something move in the darkness.

"Hackett!" Tony shouted.

She shoved herself backward and out of the way just as something slashed downward where her head was going to be.

Everyone screamed as what looked like claws crashed down, scraped the corridor floor, and then quickly pulled back away into the darkness.

"Go! Go! Go!" Hackett panicked and yelled at the family. She pushed them back down the dark corridor. It was like trying to wrangle floating balloons. She kept looking behind her.

The kids continued to scream.

"Where do we go?" Tony said doing his best to yank and pull the kids forward while trying to float as quickly as he could. It was difficult to herd them in zero gravity.

"As straight as you can! The hatch is just ahead!" Hackett shouted from behind the screaming kids. She turned around again to see if anything was chasing them. The light from the terminal was too far away now, making it hard to see again.

The momentum of everyone floating so quickly suddenly slammed Tony against the hatch door roughly. He groaned and then started frantically patting the door, looking for the handle. Hackett reached up from the back of the group and found the handle blindly. She turned and pulled the hatch door open.

Tony turned and pushed the kids through the door first. He and Hackett quickly followed as Hackett slammed the door shut behind her. She locked the handle into place.

The kids stopped screaming. Hooper sniffled a little. The boys were panting. Tony wiped the sweat from his forehead. Hackett was still facing the hatch door. She had her eyes shut and a death grip on the door handle.

"What. Was. That?" Tony quietly asked.

Something beeped loudly. Then the lights came back on. They were in another corridor.

Hackett's head snapped up.

"Come on. Let's get back to the command hub." Hackett said and pushed past the family.

Tony checked the kids quickly. They were all very freaked out but not hurt. Tony's head hurt again, this time from bumping into the hatch door.

"Come on guys, follow Hackett and I'll follow you. Go. Go." Tony instructed. He turned back to make sure the hatch wasn't opening.

The kids started pushing themselves after Hackett.

They quickly floated down some more corridor tunnels. Twisting left and twisting right.

Arriving at a t-shaped intersection, the command hub hatch door was in the center. Hackett pulled open the hatch door to the command hub.

Hackett saw Commander Hart floating in front of the main mission terminals.

"Commander Hart! Sir! Something's happened!" Hackett yelled. She floated to the side and let the kids into the command hub first.

Hooper floated right up to Commander Hart.

"Captain Space! There's a monster in the hallway!" Hooper shouted.

"Little girl, there are monsters everywhere." A voice growled.

Quickly twisting his body around, Commander Hart roared.

He was a werewolf.

Part IV

Hooper screamed.

The werewolf hunched itself over as it roared. Spreading its long thick arms, it flexed its large razor sharp-clawed hands. Endless fur seemed to spill out of the sleeves, collar, and legs of Commander Hart's jumpsuit.

With its long jaws hinged wide open, it bared rows of its perfectly curved fangs at Hooper. Drool floated out of its mouth and drifted up past the intensely bright yellow eyes that glared into Hooper's terrified face.

Hackett couldn't move.

"Hooper!" Tony shouted from back by the hatch door. He paddled his arms frantically and kicked his legs, trying to glide to her as fast as he could.

While the werewolf was deadly fixed on Hooper, it didn't see Quint on her left, and Brody on her right suddenly brush past her. As hard as they could, her brothers each shoved the shoulders of the bent-over werewolf.

The station's zero-gravity magnified the push from the

little boys. The surprised werewolf suddenly fell backward, away from the kids.

Tony got to Hooper, grabbed the back of her shirt, and yanked her into his arms. The boys made sharp turns in the air and flapped their arms quickly to get away.

The werewolf was flailing its arms a bit too wildly as it tipped backward into the hub's big main control panel. Claws scraped computers and terminals. Its left claws got caught inside the now broken panel. Sparks popped out. The big werewolf howled as the shorting out panel shocked and electrocuted it.

"Come on, come on!" Hackett snapped to and shouted. She started waving the family back out of the command hub.

Tony, cradling a still screaming Hooper in his arms, moved behind the boys and used his body to push them out of the hub quicker. They squeezed through the hatch two at a time.

Hackett saw the werewolf pulling its arm free as she slammed the hatch door shut.

Tony let go of Hooper and threw himself against the hatch door with Hackett, helping hold it shut. Hooper stopped screaming once Quint and Brody huddled together with her.

"Hmm." Tony hummed, genuinely impressed with how terrible this all was.

He looked over at Hackett's face. It was pale and thick with sweat. Her eyes were darting around like she couldn't find focus. She was in some kind of shock.

Tony's attention was pulled off Hackett and to the shape that appeared down the corridor to her left. He tilted his head around Hackett to see better.

Two more werewolves turned the corner.

Carefully, the werewolves inched around. They each

wore the same crew flight suit as Hackett and Hart. Dark fur everywhere where exposed skin would normally be. One hunched close to the floor of the corridor tunnel. Its face twitched savagely and snarled. The other floated upside down and used its enormous claws to carefully pull itself along the tunnel ceiling. Slowly stalking together, the two large werewolves filled the entire space of the small cramped tunnel. Their piercing yellow eyes ravenously concentrated on the family and the astronaut.

"Hackett!" Tony shouted into her face.

She suddenly snapped back to reality. She looked over to her left and saw the werewolves just as something banged against the other side of the hatch door Tony and she was holding shut.

The kids panicked again. They hadn't started screaming yet, but they were making the noises that lead up to screaming.

The werewolf Hart was trying to get out. The hatch door handle started violently shaking. Tony reached over and grabbed it. The beast on the other side was so strong, it took all that Tony had to keep it still.

They could hear Hart growling as the banging against the hatch door got more intense.

Down the corridor tunnel, the other two werewolves continued to slowly stalk towards them.

"We can't... stay here!" Tony said, gritting his teeth, trying to keep the handle from moving. "Hackett... where?"

"There's an empty module down the tunnel on your side," Hackett said, staring at the werewolves approaching from her left. She couldn't make out the names on their flight jumpsuits.

"Is it far?" Tony asked.

"Does it matter?" Hackett hopelessly mumbled.

"Take the kids!" Tony grunted. "I'll follow!"

Hackett couldn't take her eyes off the werewolves coming towards them. Snarling and growling, the werewolves inched closer and closer.

"Hackett, go! Kids, follow! Now!" Tony shouted. His hand ached, holding the door handle still with all his might.

Hackett finally pushed herself off the door and floated past Tony. She started paddling down the corridor tunnel.

"Daddy!" Hooper cried.

"Hoop, go! Boys go! I'll be right behind you!"

Quint grabbed his brother's and sister's hands. They started gliding after Hackett.

The hatch door banged again. Then again, and again.

The werewolves saw Hackett and the kids take off. They both roared angrily and started pulling themselves along faster. Scrambling closer and closer.

The door handle dug deep into Tony's palm as it tried to turn.

He turned his head over to see the werewolves speeding towards him. Galloping across the floor and ceiling of the tunnel. Roaring and barking and they snapped their razor jaws open and shut. They pulled their massive bodies at Tony.

The werewolves were suddenly right on top of him.

Tony yelped, let go of the handle, and pushed away from the hatch door after Hackett and the kids.

The handle quickly turned and the hatch door burst open, slamming right into the faces of the attacking werewolves. They howled in pain as they collapsed into the door and each other.

The Hart werewolf growled as it pulled itself out of the command hub.

Angry and confused, the other two werewolves roared

and shoved the hatch door that had just hit them. It swung right back into place. Hart, only halfway out of the hatch, got smashed and pinned as it tried to close. The were-wolves all shrieked.

Tony flapped his arms as fast as he could, pushing himself down the corridor tunnel after Hackett and the kids. He looked back to see the werewolves all in tangle and argument with each other. He swam faster.

Just ahead, Hackett had shoved the kids into another opened hatch door and was waving for Tony to hurry.

"Hurry, hurry!" Hackett repeated and held out her hand.

Tony grabbed her hand, and she helped pull him along and into the open door. It was one of the new modules added to the space station. It was empty except for leftover building materials and supplies.

Before she shut the door, she glanced and saw the werewolves quickly pulling themselves along the corridor after them. The tunnel was jam-packed with werewolves, each one rushing to get to Hackett and the family first.

Hackett pulled the hatch door shut.

She turned to see Tony floating up to her with a long titanium pole. It was part of the building materials being used to renovate the station. He shoved the pole in between the hatch door handle and the module walls.

Hackett and Tony floated away from the door, anxiously watching the handle to see if the pole would keep it from moving. The handle jiggled a little, but the pole wouldn't allow it to turn all the way. They'd locked themselves inside.

"There… it worked," Tony said, catching his breath as he hugged his shook-up children.

"Don't get too excited. They make this module and these walls of fancy aluminum." Hackett turned and looked seriously at Tony. "You see those claws? If they wanted to, they could slash their way inside here no problem. Like a can of tuna."

"Gee whiz, super great space fact Hackett. Maybe though, let's not entertain that idea too loudly in front of my kids, thanks." Tony sarcastically replied. "Also coming in here was your idea!"

"What was I supposed to do, man? Those things were right on us!" Hackett shouted back.

A bang on the hatch door interrupted the arguing. Bang. Bang. Bang.

Quint, Brody, and Hooper all jumped and screamed. Hackett floated farther away from the door and closer to Tony and the kids.

The banging stopped. It was replaced with a snarling voice coming from the other side of the door.

"Hhhaaaccckkkeeettt…"

Part V

The werewolves were calling for Hackett from out in the corridor.

"Hackett! Open this door and let us in!" A werewolf called. It sounded vaguely like Commander Hart.

The kids all huddled behind Tony. He shot Hackett a worried look.

"You can be one of us now, Hackett! Part of the… team." Another werewolf snarled. Hackett recognized Nelson's voice. She swore that she heard the werewolves cackling in between growls.

On the other side of the hatch…

… the three werewolves crowded the door.

"Open the door, Hackett! Join us!" The Nelson werewolf snarled again.

"Why are we wasting time pleading with the food? Let's tear apart the wall and finish this!" The third werewolf barked. It was Petrov, and it was not as amused by the situation as the two American werewolves.

The werewolves didn't move their fang-filled muzzles

when they spoke. Their deep, gruff voices seemed to just project out loud in the air. This limited telepathy was one of the many gifts they received when they became werewolves long ago.

"Tear apart the module walls, you fool? You truly are as thick as your mangy fur!" Werewolf Hart scolded the werewolf, Petrov. "If we tear apart the module, we could breach the station and destroy it. Then this will have been all for nothing!"

"You are the fool, Hart!" A new voice suddenly snapped.

The three werewolves turned to the side to see the werewolf forms of Volkov and Sturges skulking down the corridor tunnel towards them.

"Volkov! Sturges!" Hart shouted. "Where's Balakin?"

"Still down in storage, cleaning up the mess from slow down. Supplies fall everywhere." Volkov grunted.

"What happened with that server update? You idiots crashed the system, the station shut down on redirect, and because of that now the humans have discovered our secret!" Hart continued to yell.

"We do nothing wrong! Installation went perfectly!" Volkov defended itself. "It was software that failed! Full of bugs! We would have discovered during pre-check if you had not rushed installation!"

"I'm sick of your excuses, Volkov!" Hart shook its head.

Volkov breathed harder. It raised its head higher. It bared its fangs.

"And I... no, we... are sick of you, Hart!" Volkov's raspy voice said. "You are an incompetent fool! You have led mission straight into disaster!" Volkov floated closer to Hart in the packed tunnel. "We have new plan. New vision. And you are not in it."

"Volkov you…" Hart began.

But before it could finish, Volkov lunged at Hart.

Volkov's claws shoved Hart to the corridor floor. Volkov was strong. Hart's yellow eyes went wide as Volkov's mouth opened his razor-sharp jaws.

Hart howled in pain.

The other werewolves looked at one another. Quickly, a few of them got worked up into a frenzy. Three more werewolves joined Volkov and attacked the helpless Hart.

Only one werewolf had not joined in. Its ears folded down, it was nervous and horrified at the chaos going on.

"Volkov! No! This was not plan! What have you all done? Stop!" The werewolf Petrov pleaded.

Volkov's head snapped up.

"We are creating a new world, Petrov!" Volkov snarled. "You will join us!"

"Never, Volkov! Not like this!" Petrov declared as it perked its ears back up and bared its teeth.

"Then I'm sorry my friend…." Volkov replied.

The two werewolves dived at each other in the cramped tunnel.

They were entangled for just a few moments. Snarling and biting. Scratching and yelping.

Volkov raised its head in victory and howled loudly. The newly formed pack joined in and howled along.

"A new world!" Volkov excitedly shouted. "We shall be masters of new world! Masters who do not just eat the scraps that are fed to them! We hunt! We run free! Free in the land of The Always Night!"

The werewolves all howled in celebration again.

"Let us finish installation of software and programming of new coordinates. We shall take this station to the moon! The always moon! And there… we will live forever!" Volkov roared.

317

"The Always Night!" They all howled.

"Now. Sturges and Rogov? Get to command hub. Begin charting the coordinates to the moon. Also, destroy all communications with Earth. We are on our own now. And find Balakin!"

"Yes, Volkov." The werewolves snapped to and floated off to get to work

"What about the sweet little snacks locked inside of here?" The Nelson werewolf licked its chomps and asked Volkov.

"Leave them. They not go anywhere." Volkov replied slyly. "We shall be hungry when we get to our new home." It snickered. "Come. Let us finish running updates on system and finally complete installation."

The werewolves crept away.

On the other side of the hatch…

… Hackett had tears floating off her face. Tony had his arms around the terrified children. They had heard everything.

"H… h… how?" Hackett finally said.

"Well, I wouldn't feel so bad anymore about being left out all the time," Tony said to Hackett. "It's not that they didn't like you, they were just werewolves."

"I still like you, Hackett," Hooper assured the astronaut.

"But… how? I mean… this whole time?" Hackett turned and asked.

"It is genuinely impressive that you've been up here this whole time and didn't know that all your co-workers were monsters," Tony said, letting the kids float freely again. "I mean, I ignore a lot of things these kids do, but I doubt I could miss them being werewolves a bunch of times during our day."

"They always disappear. Every time we pass the moon. They all just vanish." Hackett said, still in shock.

"You think they will turn back into human beings when we can't see the moon anymore?" Quint asked Tony. "Wait. How does that work again?"

"That's a brilliant question, Quint. How does the whole moon and werewolf thing work? Doesn't it have to be a full moon? Like, is it full all the time out here? That doesn't seem right. Is that how the moon works?" Tony wondered.

"I don't know! I know you need silver bullets to kill werewolves." Quint added.

"Yeah, yeah!" Tony said, excited that he remembered that too. "They hate silver!"

"Like mommy!" Hooper said.

"No, baby. Mommy likes silver jewelry." Tony corrected.

"No, she doesn't," Brody said.

"Kids, yes she does. For years now, I've gotten her lots of silver jewelry for her birthday and Christmas."

The kids all shook their heads.

"Nope," Hooper said.

"Sorry, Daddy." Quint put his comforting hand on Tony's shoulder.

"What?" Tony said in embarrassment. "She doesn't like silver jewelry? Why didn't she ever tell me? Well, then what kind did she say she liked?"

"White gold." All three kids said at the same time.

"What the heck is white gold???" Tony shouted.

"You got any silver stuff on this ship?" Quint asked Hackett.

"You know how heavy and expensive silver is, kid? This whole place is just plastic, titanium, and aluminum." Hackett replied, rolling her eyes.

"What about your tools? Anything silver?" Tony wondered.

Hackett shook her head no.

"Dang it! Stupid cheap space program." Tony muttered.

"Quint's money is silver color." Brody perked up and said.

Quint reached into his pocket and pulled out the assorted coins he'd stolen from his father.

"That is a super good idea buddy, but unfortunately, they don't use silver in money coins anymore. If we had some really old coins, those would have silver in them." Tony said to the kids.

"Well, can I have that money then?" Hooper asked, holding out her hand.

"Daddy? This quarter says Nineteen Sixty-Three, is that old enough?" Quint said, examining the floating money.

"I'm not sure. I don't know exactly when they stopped using silver." Tony floated over and plucked the quarter out of the air. "Do you know?" Tony asked Hackett.

She shook her head no.

"I'll hold on to it I guess, but I'm not sure it will work. Even if it did, I don't know what I'd do with it. Flick it at them? Thanks anyway, Quint. And good idea, Brody." Tony said and pushed the quarter into his shirt pocket and buttoned it shut.

"We can hide here until they are persons again," Brody suggested.

"We could do that buddy, yeah," Tony said to Brody.

"Didn't you hear them? They're using the upgrades to move the station to the moon. The farther away from Earth the station is, the longer it takes to circle the Earth. Which means we're exposed to the moon for much longer than normal." Hackett suddenly snapped. "And even if we miraculously lived through the trip to get there, there's no way we can survive being on the moon. We can't go to the moon."

"But wait, how do THEY survive then? I don't get it." Tony said refusing to drop it. "Doesn't it have to be hanging in the sky? Like they can be werewolves by being on the surface of the moon? How does that work?"

"It doesn't make a lot of sense, Daddy." Quint agreed.

"It doesn't make ANY sense, right? I am so confused." Tony said.

"Will you idiots stop!" Hackett said, gritting her teeth. "We have to get to the supply transport you all came here on. It's a drone ship, so it will pilot itself back to Earth. All we have to do is undock it and manually maneuver it out into open space. And I can do that from one of the terminal tablets. But we have to do it like... now. If the station rises too high, the drone won't have the thrust or fuel to get us back to Earth."

Tony looked at the kids. They all nodded to him they understood.

Tony took a deep breath.

"Okay. It's a plan. So where is this terminal tablet you need?" Tony asked.

"There's one in the lab. I left it charging there this morning." Hackett said.

"Where's the lab?" Tony asked.

"Across the station. On the other side." Hackett winced as she said.

"Oh. Okay. No big deal. You just left your smart-phone thing charging in a room across a space station full of werewolves!" Tony got louder. He rubbed his face. He got quiet for a few seconds. "Even if we sneak over to the lab without those things catching us, will it even work? Even with them upgrading the systems?"

"It will! It runs on totally different software. Installed by mission control on Earth." Hackett assured Tony.

"Are you impressed I even thought about that? Pretty smart, right?" Tony said, raising his eyebrows.

"Yeah. I'm blown away by your attention to detail." Hackett replied, grinding her teeth. "How are we going to get to it though? Those werewolves are everywhere!"

They all got quiet again.

"We go in the back door when Hooper is napping," Brody said.

"What's that mean?" Hackett asked.

"When they play outside while Hooper naps, I make them come in the back door so they don't wake her up," Tony replied. "That's another very good idea buddy, but we can't just walk outside and go around to the back door."

"Actually…" Hackett said.

Part VI

The most valuable resource known to humans is not water or gold or decent Wi-Fi. It's quiet. Stay at home parents dream about quiet. Vivid, detailed, and widescreen fantasies about things just being and staying quiet.

Tony knew parents back on Earth that would pull their heads off to experience the quiet he currently was. Tony also would have relished this silence, if he wasn't busy being more terrified than he'd ever been in his life.

Tony was walking in outer space.

They had snuck to one of the station door airlocks. It wasn't far from where they had been hiding, and the coast had been clear the whole way. They didn't make a sound.

Hackett grabbed one of the spacesuits hanging by the door and began to quickly inspect it. After she ran through a very brief safety check, almost too brief Tony thought, she quietly walked him through putting it on. As Tony stepped into and pulled on layer after layer, he immediately started having anxiety.

Tony gave his kids a look, and they read his mind. Each

of his kids wordlessly floated up to his head and hugged him tight around his neck. He kissed each one of them and fought back tears. When they were done, he nodded to Hackett.

Hackett put the large helmet over his head and twisted it. Then she pressed some buttons along the side of the helmet and on a keypad that was over his wrist. He felt the pressure change within the suit right away.

Hackett then turned to the big sliding doors and pressed a button. When the button turned green, she lifted the release handle. The doors slid open with a hiss. Hackett gave Tony a gentle shove inside the airlock. There were two sets of sliding doors. His kids waved to him as the first doors shut.

"When you're walking around outside a space station, don't let go," Hackett whispered into the radio.

"And they said your job is hard," Tony said sarcastically into his radio headset. "I'm holding as tight as I can."

Tony was pulling himself along the side of the station. Reaching whatever was sticking out of the station that he could get a grip on. All while trying very hard to not look anywhere else. He wasn't sure if space vertigo was a thing, but he wasn't going to risk it.

"Well, normally when we go outside, we get tethered to the ship, but all that equipment is at the other airlock. So, you're going to have to make sure you hang on," Hackett told Tony.

Luckily, there was plenty for Tony to reach for. The Worldwide Space station was essentially a series of strapped together boxes. The boxes and other various parts came from about eight different countries, and they all had different design aesthetics. It was ugly, but it was working out in Tony's favor. There were lots of chunky ledges and thick angles to grab onto.

"How are my kids?" Tony asked, reaching over to a pole and shimmying himself forward.

"They won't stop asking questions, so I assume they're fine," Hackett said, annoyed. "Why is it that I got stuck in here with them when I'm more experienced out there?"

"Because if those things get you or if this plan doesn't work, I don't have the first clue of what to do to get them back home," Tony said. "You're more useful in there than slipping out into space or getting eaten by a werewolf. You just walk me through what I'm supposed to do to get this tablet you need."

"Fine," Hackett said. "But I'm not changing any diapers."

"Oh, for… look at them, Hackett. Do they look like they still wear diapers?" Tony said as he swung over and reached for a gigantic bolt sticking out of the side of the station. "Are you sure it's okay for us to be on the radio like this?" Tony asked.

"It's fine. I made a closed channel just for us," Hackett assured him. "Just concentrate on getting yourself to the other airlock."

"Sorry for worrying about the monsters hearing us and coming to get you," Tony said, grabbing another ledge and dragging himself forward. "You're hiding right?"

"Yes, we are hiding. We are all in another empty module and the door is jammed shut. It's fine. Shut up. It's fine. I'm like, seriously, the best nanny ever," Hackett sharply told Tony.

Tony pulled himself farther along. It was difficult to do while wearing the thick spacesuit gloves. Sometimes it felt like Tony had gripped onto a box or a bar, but when he double-checked, he saw that he wasn't even close.

It was a slow process of reaching out with his left hand, grabbing, and double-checking. Once Tony knew he had a good grip, he pushed off of whatever his right hand had a hold of and then pulled forward with his left hand. He'd switch hands and repeat the process with whatever he could hold on to next. His feet did a little work, but Hackett had told him the less he moved his entire body the better.

"This is taking forever," Tony mumbled. "How long is this thing?"

"About three hundred and fifty-five feet. Almost the length of a football field. You've been on a football field, right?" Hackett asked.

"Oh yeah. Big time. I was the quarterback of the Springfield Wishful Thinkers. We went to state," Tony replied.

The station started to shake. Tony could see poles and instruments on the outside of the station wobble.

"Uh, Hackett?" Tony said, hugging onto the side of the station.

"Whoa, hang on!" Hackett said over the radio. "We're moving. They have entered the new coordinates. The thrusters are firing. They're moving the station to the moon."

The shaking settled down, but Tony could still feel the vibrations in the station.

"Okay, we don't have long before we're too far out of Earth's orbit for the supply transport to get us home. You have got to get going." Hackett instructed.

"Got it. How long have we got?" Tony asked, staring to pull himself along again.

"Pretend just a minute. Only a minute left, every minute, from now until we leave. That's how fast you have to be moving." Hackett said

"Okay, okay. Here I go," Tony replied as he reached for another bolt.

He wordlessly dragged himself across the moving space station. Concentrating on where he was grabbing and what he was reaching for as he side-stepped along. Hand over hand, he pulled himself closer to the other side as quickly as he could. It was like trying to scale the side of a cliff, and the Earth waited below like the ocean. Tony's loud, labored breathing was the only thing he could hear inside the heavy helmet.

After only another few minutes, he was finally at the other airlock.

"Hackett? I made it. What now?" Tony said, out of breath. He positioned himself so he was next to the sliding doors.

"Next to the door is a button and a release handle. Push the button to start the airlock. When the airlock is ready, the button's color turns green. Then lift the handle and the outer airlock doors will manually slide open. Get inside the airlock and it will do the rest for you. The outer door will shut, the airlock will equalize air pressure, and the inner doors will open. Don't take your helmet or your suit off, though, because you won't be in there long," Hackett instructed.

"Which way is the lab?" Tony whispered once he was back inside the station. Whispering seemed appropriate again since there could be werewolves anywhere.

"It will be the first module on your left. The first hatch door," Hackett whispered back.

Tony floated over to the hatch door and opened it slowly. He leaned in and looked around, checking for werewolves before he floated inside. The lab was dark and empty. The only light coming from the computer screens and LCD's hanging on the walls. He entered the room, quietly shutting the hatch door behind him.

Even in the low-lit room, Tony saw that the lab module was the biggest room he'd seen on the station. Wire cabinets and lockers that held containers and binders lined the high walls. The LCD screens mounted on the walls were scrolling data. In the back of the room was a stack of mini-refrigerators with clear doors, showing containers and beakers inside. Two rows of very wide tables ran the length of the room. The tabletops had desktop computers bolted down on them, along with some other scientific equipment that Tony did not recognize.

"Where's the tablet, Hackett?" Tony whispered.

"It should be on the table in the back. That's where I left it charging. It looks just like the tablets you have at home. It's about... wait..." Hackett stopped. "... ugh, no! For the last time, it doesn't have any cool games on it, kid," Hackett told one of Tony's kids.

Tony smiled as he floated to the back of the room. At the end of the table on the right, there was a small touch screen tablet plugged into a battery brick on the table. Tony picked it up and unplugged it. The screen lit up and its lock screen said 'Charge Complete'. Tony unzipped the thick pouch on the front of his spacesuit, where the astronauts usually stored tools on their walks, and slid the tablet safely inside.

As he zipped the pouch shut, he heard the hatch door handle suddenly turn.

"Hackett, they're coming!" Tony whispered in terror.

"Hide!" She whispered back.

The only place Tony saw that he would fit was under the tables. He quickly ducked underneath them, with no idea if his thick space suit would stick out or not. He spun around and floated up as high as he could, his face looking at the underneath of the table. He scrunched himself up and hugged the underneath of the tabletop, as the hatch door opened.

Two werewolves floated inside the lab. It was Sturges and Rogov. Their sharp hind paws swung to the ground. The lab was one of the few places on the station tall enough to float upright.

"The airlock opened again! I told Volkov that someone should watch them!" The Sturges werewolf barked. Its voice projected in the air, without having to move its fanged snout. It sniffed loudly.

"I smell nothing either," The Rogov werewolf said. "We should check the terminals and make sure that useless Hackett isn't floating around sabotaging anything,"

Tony guessed he was hidden well enough under the table for the creatures to not be able to see him at first glance. His suit must also mask his scent, as he could smell himself inside of it, and he stunk. If they could not smell his sweaty, anxious body odor then it was either the suit hid it or their noses were broken. He tried to keep still and breathe as quietly as he could.

The werewolves floated over to the computers. One was at the table on the left and the other went to the table Tony was hidden under. Tony held his breath as a werewolf maneuvered itself between his table and the wall. The werewolves hunched over the desktop keyboards and with their large clawed fingers they tapped away at the keys.

Tony glanced over and saw that they had left the hatch door open. Without hesitating, he used his fingers to pull himself along the bottom of the tabletop, trying to be as quiet as he could. The werewolves continued to type.

"Come here and look at this!" The werewolf at his table shouted at the other.

Tony stopped moving.

The other werewolf floated to Tony's table. He watched as the hairy legs that stuck out of the space-suit kicked their way closer. The legs went around his table and joined its crew mate at the computer that faced the wall. They were both standing on Tony's right side.

"Here, look at this."

"Did you run the debug command and see what it said after?" The werewolf remarked on what was shown to it.

"Of course, I did!" The other one said.

"Let me try!"

While the two werewolves fussed with the computer, a nervous Tony quickly got farther away from them before they looked under the table. He pushed himself to the left, floated low out into the open aisle, and underneath the other table.

He froze for a moment and looked over at the were-wolves' legs again. He didn't see or hear any kind of reaction. He started using his fingertips again to pull himself along the bottom of the table, closer to the hatch door. When the top of his helmet reached the end of the table, he looked over and saw there were about six feet of open space between where the table stopped and the hatch door was. He would be fully exposed if he went for it, and the werewolves looked over.

"It says it needs an admin to log in. What's your pass-word?" One werewolf asked the other.

"I'm not telling you!" It snapped back.

"Oh, relax! Like your data is so important!"

While the werewolves argued, Tony pushed as hard as he could off the table. He spun back around midair and with arms stretched out as a superhero flew towards the hatch door. He grabbed hold of the door's frame and pushed up and out, launching himself through.

He was almost out when his foot banged against the side.

The werewolves jerked their heads over to see Tony escaping the room.

"There's one!"

"Get it!" The werewolves growled.

As they started to wildly glide themselves to the door, Tony slammed the hatch door shut and kicked the handle as hard as he could to jam it.

He swam as quickly as he could down the hall back to the airlock. The lab's hatch door handle shook as the werewolves frantically tried to open it.

Tony pulled the airlock button. He waited for it to turn green. The handle on the lab door shook violently. Tony stared at the button, waiting for it to turn green. The werewolves banged on their side of the hatch door. The button finally turned green. He grabbed the release handle and lifted it. The inner doors slid open, and he pulled himself inside. As the inner airlock doors automatically shut, he saw the lab hatch door burst open and the two werewolves spill out, snarling and growling.

The system changed the pressure in the airlock as Tony took huge gasps of air. He had made it, but it was close. His heart was racing.

The light on the button went green and the outer doors opened up. The stars and Earth greeted him again. Tony carefully leaned out and grabbed a ledge. When he felt he had a good grip, he swung himself out into space and pushed back up against the side of the station. The outer doors closed.

"Hackett, I made it out," Tony shouted into his radio headset. "But they saw me. You all need to make sure you're safe because they'll be coming your way!"

"Did you get the tablet?" Hackett asked.

"Yeah, I got it! It's in my pouch!"

"Get here as quickly as you can! We're fine for now! But you have to hurry!" Hackett assured him.

"You and the kids have to stay hidden, Hackett! They saw me! They know where I am! They're going to be coming to your doors! They're coming for you!" Tony shouted.

Tony pulled himself along as quickly as he could. He tried to retrace his path, grabbing ledges, bolts, and bars that lined the outside of the station. His face was covered in sweat. His heart beat faster. His stomach was in knots. He didn't know what to do when he got to the other doors. The werewolves would surely be waiting for him.

He had made it about a quarter of the way from the airlock doors.

Then he heard something howl.

Two something's howl.

He stopped and slowly turned to see the airlock doors shutting again.

Gripping the outside of the station with their sharp claws, hung the two werewolves.

Without spacesuits.

Without helmets.

The werewolves could survive in outer space.

"Pickles," Tony said.

Part VII

The werewolves howled in outer space.

Their shrieks seemed to echo inside Tony's helmet.

Tony turned away from the werewolves and started pulling himself along faster. He was skipping his safety checks and just grabbing a hold of anything he could.

The Sturges and Rogov werewolves dropped to all fours and used the claws on their hands and feet to grip and move along the sides of the station.

Tony looked behind him to see them moving like spiders across a wall. Their yellow eyes burned straight ahead at him. With their pointy ears bent back and their razor-sharp teeth exposed, they snarled and growled as they chased him. They were so much faster than Tony was.

"Hackett? Hackett!" Tony shouted as he stretched out and grabbed a hold of a bar. "Werewolves can breathe in space! Werewolves can breathe in space! It doesn't make any sense, but they're out here and they're chasing me!"

"What? They're out there with you?" Hackett said in disbelief.

"Yeah, and they're really fast! Get to the airlock now! I don't know if I can outrun them, but if I get there before they do, I'll toss the tablet in the airlock first!"

"This can't be happening," Hackett said.

"Hackett, get my kids, and move now!" Tony yelled, reaching for another ledge.

Tony looked behind him and saw the werewolves were getting closer. One of them was crawling along the top of the station while the other stuck to the side. They snarled and growled as they pursued him.

Tony grabbed the ledge. Instead of pulling himself along and switching hands on the ledge like he had been doing, he pushed off the ledge and propelled himself forward. He quickly flew forward about ten feet. He felt himself drift farther away from the station. He reached out and grabbed on to a junction box that was jetting out. Slamming his upper body against the box, he stopped himself from going any further. It was risky, but it worked. Tony took a deep breath, and he pushed forward off of the box.

Tony let himself fly forward for a little longer. As he saw the gap between him and the station widen, he suddenly threw his arms out and grabbed a hold of whatever he could. He slammed into the station again. He turned around. While he had moved along the station much faster, the werewolves were still quickly gaining on him. He pushed himself down the station again.

He let himself go farther. He was quickly gliding down the length of the station. He stuck out his left hand and paddled himself along the station faster. He was moving now. He watched as the station appeared to be slowly getting farther away from him. Feeling he was cutting it too close; he reached his hand out to grab onto something.

But there was nothing to grab. He had floated out too far from the station. He was going to drift out into space.

He panicked and swung his arms and his legs, trying to push himself back towards the space station. But all that did was spin him around. Now he had turned around and was facing the curve of the Earth and the blanket of stars that separated it and the moon. He had no idea how far from the station he was. All he could see was the endless abyss of outer space. He suddenly thought of his wife's smile.

He was jerked back to the station by a clawed hand. The werewolf Rogov grabbed Tony by the back of his suit and slammed him back into the side of the ship. It roared fiercely at the glass of his helmet. Then it tossed Tony upwards to the top of the station.

The werewolf Sturges snatched Tony's leg and swung him down like a hammer onto the top of the space station. Tony bounced around hard inside his suit as he crashed against the station. The werewolf flipped Tony onto his back. It slammed its claws down into the station on both sides of Tony's helmet, pinning him. Then Sturges howled in excitement.

"Thanks for the hunt," The Rogov werewolf's voice said as it climbed onto the top of the station with them. "Feels good to stretch our legs," Rogov's voice said, laughing.

Even for space-breathing werewolves, it's hard to hear someone sneak up on you in outer space. So Rogov didn't see his crewmate Balakin suddenly float up behind him. Balakin hit the werewolf in the back of its head with a large wrench.

Balakin was human. He was suited up wearing one of those jetpack suits. It was a backpack propulsion rig that astronauts used when working in space. It shot gas out of a series of nozzles to propel its wearer around. Balakin used it to quickly thrust himself around to the front of the dazed Rogov. Balakin hit the werewolf again with his wrench, this time knocking it upwards and off the space station. Rogov flipped off the side of the ship and out into space.

The werewolf Sturges turned to see its pack member float off into space. It roared in rage and straightened itself up, ripping its claws out of the station to attack Balakin.

"Oh, don't let go," Tony said as he kicked the now unattached werewolf as hard as he could.

Sturges yelped as it floated straight up into space. It swung its clawed arms down furiously, trying to grab a hold of something and slash at Tony. But it floated up higher and higher away from the station. It roared louder in anger and fear.

The two werewolves floated out into space in two different directions. They would float forever.

Balakin slid his wrench into his front pouch and quickly flew himself over to Tony. He reached down and helped Tony to his feet. Tony gripped Balakin's arm as he got himself upright.

"You're a human?" Tony said, recognizing the Russian who was at the supply dock with Hackett when he and the kids had first arrived.

"Yes! I did not know my crew all werewolf! I am newest and they never let me hang out with them. Only do work. I thought they were doing hazing me!" Balakin said into his headset. "I was down in supplies with Petrov when he suddenly turn into werewolf! Then Nelson and Rogov become werewolves too! I run to airlock and take suit. I've been hiding out here since! Then I see them chase you!"

"Well, thankfully you were here because you saved my life! Thank you! But we've got to get back to airlock right away. Hackett needs this tablet to undock the supply transport and get us home," Tony said, patting the pouch on his chest. "We don't have much time, because this whole thing is floating out to the moon!" He quickly explained.

"Hackett is not werewolf? She is alive?" Balakin seemed to say with relief. He smiled for a moment and then shook his face serious again. "Hang on tight. I fly us there."

Tony gripped Balakin's arm as the Russian blasted forward towards the airlock doors. They were only going about as fast as a grocery store's electric shopping cart, but it was still so much faster than Tony could shimmy across the station.

"Did you know werewolves could breathe in outer space?" Tony asked Balakin as they flew.

"No. But, curses very powerful magic," Balakin said concentrating. "Those two back there floating will have big surprise when they can't see moon anymore."

"Wait, is that how it goes? None of this makes any sense." Tony asked, still confused by how werewolves worked.

"Curses very powerful," The Russian repeated in a deadly serious voice.

Tony rolled his eyes and just accepted he'd never know.

Balakin propelled them right up to the airlock doors. Tony reached out and pushed the button. When it turned green, he lifted the release and the outer doors slid open. Balakin boosted them forward into the airlock and the doors shut behind them.

"Daddy!" Tony heard his kids say.

When the inner doors opened, the kids flew away from

Hackett and into the airlock to hug their dad. Tony squeezed them all back tightly.

"Balakin? Volya, is that you?" Hackett said in shock.

"Hello, Rebecca, are you okay?" Balakin said, taking his helmet off.

Hackett's eyes welled up, and she swayed forward and hugged him.

"I thought you were a werewolf too!" Hackett said, suddenly remembering herself. She broke the hug and floated backward.

"Not me!" Balakin replied.

"Where are the werewolves?" Hackett suddenly remembered.

"Doing gymnastics through space, probably wishing they packed some Dramamine," Tony said, taking his helmet off. He unzipped his front pouch and pulled out the tablet. He handed it to Hackett. "That's it?" Tony.

"Yes!" Hackett said, taking the tablet. "Now come on we have to get to the supply transport. We're getting too far away from Earth. Come on!" Hackett started floating down the corridor tunnel.

Balakin had slipped his propulsion rig off. He kept hold of his big wrench. He followed right behind Hackett.

"Daddy, why did you take so long?" Hooper asked Tony.

"Don't ask. Go, baby girl. Go follow Hackett," Tony said as he took his gloves off. "Be careful, there are two more werewolves!" Shouted up at Hackett.

"Great counting!" Hackett replied halfway down the corridor.

"Come on Hooper, let's go!" Quint shouted and grabbed her hand.

Keeping the rest of his spacesuit on, Tony pulled Brody into his arms followed the group.

"Daddy? Can we please be done with outer space?" Brody asked Tony as he fiddled with his blanket.

"Absolutely, buddy. We're going home now," Tony replied.

They turned left and went down a new corridor. After that, they took a right turn down another tunnel. They sailed along as quickly as they could. There was no sign of the werewolves the entire way. That they could see.

"The supply transport is just through this hatch door," Hackett said as she arrived at a new door.

She turned the handle and pulled it. She held the door open as the group passed through. Tony recognized it from when he and the kids had first arrived. They all started floating down the long hallway to the supply transport doors.

"Hey, Hackett!" Balakin floated up next to her. "Maybe when we get back to Earth, we go and get coffee together?"

Hackett turned her head and glared at him.

"You are an absolute idiot, you know that, Balakin?" Hackett faced forward again and yelled. "Because now, one of two things is going to happen. Either, you're going to get killed by those things because you asked me out. Or, we get trapped in some unhealthy, PTSD motivated, going nowhere relationship that neither of us will smart enough to leave. You are an idiot."

"Grown-ups are dumb," Hooper said to Quint.

"I know," Quint replied.

Suddenly, something roared. Something roared behind them.

They all jumped and spun around.

A werewolf had followed them.

Part VIII

"Yeah… that figures," Tony pursed his lips and said.

The werewolf had crawled through the hatch door behind them. It roared again. The howl echoed through the corridor tunnel.

Brody covered his ears and Tony held him tighter.

"It's Nelson," Hackett mumbled.

"Someone just throw it a dog treat and let's go!" Hooper shouted.

"Okay, that's funny," Tony admitted.

"Nelson! Just let us go!" Hackett yelled at the werewolf.

"You will pay for what you've done to Rogov and Sturges!" The werewolf Nelson roared again. Everyone covered their ears this time.

"Stop! Nelson! Stop! No one is going to try to stop you from taking the station to the moon! Just please, let us go!" Hackett pleaded.

"Nothing will stop The Always Night! We will live forever!" Nelson barked, raising her claws in the air.

"Okay! That's it!" Tony snapped at the werewolf. "You're going to have to explain this to me! NONE of this makes ANY sense! Live forever on the moon? How's that going to work? How are you going to eat, stupid?"

"Volkov and Kane have big plans," Nelson hissed.

Hackett, Balakin, and Tony all glanced at each other when the werewolf said the billionaire's name.

"Kane? Nathan Kane?" Hackett asked.

"The dude with the billion dollars, Daddy," Quint whispered.

"But that's later," the werewolf's voice boomed, "right now, we'll just feast on YOU!"

The werewolf Nelson launched itself and charged at them. Baring its entire mouth full of fangs, it snarled and growled as it quickly shot at them.

"Get into transport!" Balakin shouted. He raised his wrench as he floated back down the hallway to meet the attacking werewolf.

"Volya, no!!" Hackett screamed.

"Hackett, open the doors!" Tony shouted at her.

Balakin swung the wrench at the werewolf. But Nelson ducked and backhanded Balakin. He dropped backward, letting go of the wrench. The werewolf grabbed Balakin out of the air and held him down onto the corridor floor.

The werewolf bent over, opened its enormous jaws, and moved closer over Balakin's head.

Hackett hit it in the face with the wrench.

The werewolf Nelson fell off of Balakin. Hackett hit it again. The werewolf yelped and fell backward farther. Hackett hit it again. The werewolf soared backward each time, howling in pain and confusion. Hackett bashed the werewolf with the wrench over and over, pushing it back toward the hatch door.

When they were right up against the hatch door, Hackett used the wrench to stuff the werewolf back through the door. The werewolf squeezed through and

Hackett reached over, quickly slamming the hatch shut. She slid the wrench into the handle so it would not turn. She turned around and floated back to Balakin, catching her breath.

"You owe me a doomed relationship," Hackett said, grinding her teeth and helping Balakin straighten himself up. "Let's get out of here."

Tony and the kids moved out of the way as Balakin started turning handles and knobs at the supply transport doors. Hackett began tapping at her tablet, and Tony saw buttons and lights illuminate on and around the doors.

The inner doors slid open with a loud hiss.

"You sure that doesn't have games on it?" Brody asked Hackett, pointing to her tablet.

"Buddy, no," Tony interrupted. "Let's not bother them. They need to get these doors open," He said as he moved the kids up against the corridor walls and out of the way.

Hackett ignored them and tapped some more on the tablet. Another set of lights on the door went green. Hackett nodded to Balakin. He turned another set of handles and cranks.

The second set of doors slid open.

A werewolf dived out of the transport, tackling Tony to the corridor floor.

The kids all screamed.

"Daddy!" Quint shouted.

The werewolf Volkov scratched at Tony with its massive claws. The thick spacesuit took most of the damage, protecting Tony's skin, but now it was torn open. Volkov swiped its claws over Tony's suit again, tearing more and taking some of Tony's shirt away too.

"You owe the Always Night blood!" The werewolf's voice growled. Volkov's bright yellow eyes burned Tony with rage. It slammed Tony into the floor, again and again, its claws beginning to scratch and dig into his chest. Tony had both his hands on Volkov's huge wrist, holding it back and trying to push its clawed paw away from his chest. But the werewolf was so strong.

Hackett started shoving the hysterical kids into the supply transport.

"No! Daddy!" Hooper cried.

Balakin floated to Volkov and tried to push the werewolf off of Tony. Volkov grabbed Balakin by the shirt and raised him. Volkov furiously howled and tossed Balakin over into Hackett. They crashed into each other and fell through the transport doors. Tony grit his teeth as he tried to push up against the werewolf's claws.

Tony saw something in his peripheral. Something floating to the left of his head. His eyes briefly glanced over to something shiny.

Quint's old quarter must have been torn out of Tony's front pocket. Tony took the chance and pulled one hand away from the werewolf's wrist. Claws immediately started sinking into Tony's chest. Tony gasped in pain and snatched the quarter out of the air.

"Hey!" Tony choked up at the werewolf.

Volkov stopped howling and bent down.

"Does THIS make sense?" Tony said.

Tony used the quarter like a knife and slashed it sideways across the werewolf's face.

Volkov screamed and jerked backward. It let go of Tony and grabbed its face. Tony saw the monster's face sizzling and could smell burnt hair.

Tony turned to his right and saw the end of Brody's blanket dangling in mid-air. He reached over and grabbed the blanket. Once he had it, the kids and Balakin yanked on the other end and pulled Tony into the supply transport.

As soon as his feet cleared the doors, Hackett quickly tapped at the tablet's screen and the transport's inner doors closed.

Tony turned to see Volkov thrashing its body wildly in the air. It was holding its face and howling in pain.

The kids smothered Tony in hugs.

"Hold on everyone, I don't know how bumpy this is going to be," Hackett told everyone. She poked at the tablet again.

There were loud crunches and a series of hisses. Everyone inside tumbled over as the transport clumsily lurched backward.

"We're undocked now. I'm moving us out into open space." Hackett twisted her fingers around on the tablet. They all felt the transport slowly move. "There, we're away from the station. The drone navigation system should activate and we should start moving," Hackett said, sitting back up.

Nothing was happening.

"Hackett?" Tony said nervously.

Nothing was happening.

"Come on, come on," Hackett whispered over and over.

The boosters suddenly fired loudly, and the transport started moving again.

They all yelled in celebration.

"It worked!" Balakin shouted.

The kids hugged Tony again, and he squeezed them all tightly.

The supply transport was heading back to Earth

Tony, his kids all snuggled in his lap, tilted his head back against the transport wall, and closed his eyes. He was worn out. He thought of something and his eyes popped open again.

"When we get back, I'm not going to get a bill for ruining a two hundred-billion-dollar space station, am I?"

"Doubt it. Sounds like there's something shady going on down there between Nathan Kane and the program," Hackett replied.

"You mean that there's probably a secret club of billionaire werewolves back on Earth?" Tony asked.

"You surprised?"

"Not really," Tony said and sadly put his head against the wall again.

Balakin scooted across the transport and slid next to Hackett.

"Sorry I drank your coffee," Balakin apologized.

"Shut up," Hackett said. She reached over and held Balakin's hand.

"Hey, did you hear what I said to that werewolf back there?" Tony looked up, smiling. "I said to it, 'Does this make sense?'. Get it?" No one responded. "Because I cut it with a quarter? A quarter? Cents. Make cents?" Tony said, still smiling.

No one responded.

"Daddy, no," Hooper said, shaking her head.

"Ugh. Fine." Tony huffed.

And he pouted, just a little bit, the entire way back to Earth.

DAYS LATER...

The two werewolves sat in the station's observation module.

"Volkov! It won't be long now!" Nelson's voice said,

looking out at the giant moon getting closer and closer. "We shall land soon!"

"Yes." Volkov leaned forward. Its face had a deep scar across it, pink from where the fur and flesh had burned off. "Finally. Years of waiting and years of planning. Our new home. We soon call for the others. We shall rule a superior new world! We shall rule for eternity in The Always Night!"

And the two werewolves howled at their new home.

The End

PART VI

FullTimeTony and the Sister Sigil

∞

The Sisters walked.

When The Sisters walked, all you heard was the screaming.

The witches burned my home! The witches took my livestock! The witches blinded me! The witches stole my child!

But the mistake everyone made was calling The Sisters witches. They had not been allowed to call themselves witches for a very long time.

Because as chaotic as witches seemed to be, they were still an organization. A collective of creatures with common ideals and goals. There were, of course, different groups and factions. But they all lived under the same dark order of existence. That meant there were rules. It meant there were standards. It meant there were boundaries.

The Sisters belonged to no one except The Sisters. They committed monstrous acts against the humans, as well as their fellow witch. They were hateful creatures, loathed and feared by all the known Mortal Realms and ancient Ghost Worlds. The Thousand Dimensions were terrorized for centuries.

So the witches banished The Sisters.

Banished them to a shadow inside another shadow. Into a pocket of another pocket. The witches sent The Sisters away to a dark corner of reality where they could no longer hurt anyone.

But remember, the witches had rules. They had a muddled faithfulness to the order of things. It was crucial to their magic. Some things had to just be.

So once a year, The Sisters were allowed to crawl out of their hole. Allowed to go wherever they wished for a single night. They had until dawn.

For one night a year, the screaming would start again.

The Sisters walked.

"DADDY? HOW DOES IT LOOK?" Hooper asked Tony.

"Hooper, it looks amazing!" Tony smiled. He was standing in the open garage and had just finished rearranging his modest toolbox. He slid the toolbox behind some old paint buckets to keep it away from little fingers.

The four-year-old Hooper had spent the last hour drawing on the driveway with her sidewalk chalk. She'd covered about every inch of the long driveway with a drawing or scribble. You couldn't stand on the driveway without standing on some colorful chalk artwork. There were flowers, rainbows, and smiley faces everywhere. She'd written out preschool-age looking numbers and letters. Lots of drawings of dinosaurs and robots and unicorns.

"I love it!" Hooper said, batting her eyelashes proudly.

"It truly is a masterpiece..." Tony said, looking at a beautiful drawing of a butt driving a car.

"I know!" Hooper jumped up. "I can't wait for Mommy to see."

"I just know she'll love it!" Tony told her.

"But Daddy you will tell her I drawed it and not the boys!" Hooper said, demanding sole credit be given to her and not her two brothers.

Quint and Brody were playing in the yard instead of drawing. They had bikes, balls, and other outside toys laying all over. It looked like a tornado had blown through and tossed the contents of Tony's garage everywhere.

"We will, Hoop. We'll tell her you did it all by yourself," Tony assured her. "You know, sometimes when an artist makes a painting or piece of art, they sign their name at the bottom."

"They sign it at the bottom?" Hooper said. "Oh! Okay!"

Hooper bent down and picked up a big nub of pink chalk and walked to the very edge of the driveway. With chalk coated hands she brushed her hair out of her face and crouched down.

"Daddy? How do you spell 'By Hooper'?" she asked with chalk now smeared across her forehead.

"Well, by goes B...Y..." Tony spelled.

"B...Y...," Hooper marked out a large lower case b and then y. "And Daddy, please can you help me spell Hooper?"

"Oh, you know how to spell your name," Tony said, pulling his phone out to check the time.

"Ugh!" Hooper whined. Some days you just wanted someone to spell your name for you.

Spelling it out loud, the little girl wrote out her name as large as she could. She loved to draw and color so lately they had started practicing writing her name.

"I'm done!" She stood up. "It says: 'By Hooper'!"

It did. The only thing wrong was the 'e' in her name was backwards.

"Pretty good, my little artist! Hey! Mommy will be home from work soon. I need a helper to make dinner with me. Let's go inside," Tony said.

Quint and Brody came running around from the backyard.

"Whoa," Quint said when he saw the driveway.

"Holy macaroni!" Brody said, also in awe of Hooper's epic work.

"Hooper, did you make this all by yourself?" Quint asked.

"She sure did. All by herself. See? She signed it at the bottom." Tony showed him.

Quint walked down to the end of the driveway to check out the signature.

"Hooper, your 'e' is backwards again." Quint pointed out.

"Hey! Ugh!" Hooper scowled and folded her arms. She got upset whenever she made a mistake. She got even madder when someone pointed one out to her.

"Hooper, it's okay! It's no big deal, Quint," Tony tried to defuse before she blew. "She's still learning! Hooper is working very hard. Her 'e's are backwards now but she'll get them eventually."

"Sorry Hooper. This is pretty awesome!" Quint told his sister.

"I like these robots here, Hooper!" Brody said.

"Yeah! There are the mommy robot and the daddy robot and the brothers robots and the Hooper robot! And they are going to the car wash restaurant!"

"Cool, Hooper!" Brody crouched down to look closer.

"Daddy?" Quint walked over and said, "You think we should like, find something to cover up the driveway for the night time? You know? So it doesn't wash away if it rains real hard?"

"Rains?" Hooper's head shot around. "Like a storm?"

"Oh no. Hoop," Tony raised his hands, "it's not going to rain."

Hooper was scared of thunderstorms. Honestly, her brothers were too. There were always big emotions whenever it stormed. Right now though, she was more concerned about her artwork.

"Daddy! Is the rain going to wash away my pictures? Daddy I don't want it to rain! I don't want the rain to wash away my drawings! Daddy!" Hooper said getting worked up.

"Hoop, I don't think it's supposed to rain tonight. I think your drawings are going to be okay," Tony said.

"But Daddy, when it rains my drawings will erase!" Hooper shouted.

Tony raised his phone and tapped at the screen.

"Look. The weather says no rain tonight." Tony bent down and showed her the app on his phone. "See? It says no rain tonight or tomorrow or the day after. Your drawings aren't going anywhere for a few days, okay?"

"Oh! Good!" Hooper cheered up.

"Alright my friends, let's go inside and you can help me get dinner started before Mommy gets home. By the time you all are done washing your disgusting hands we should be able to eat at about ten o'clock tonight." Tony picked up the rest of Hooper's chalk and put it into a bucket.

"I'll go first!" Quint said, taking off into a run.

"No, me!" Brody followed.

The boys both darted off into the house.

"Hey! Come back and pick all these toys up!" Tony shouted and pointed to the toys spread all over the yard.

The front door slammed shut.

"No problem boys, I'll take care of it. No, no, I want to do it," Tony muttered, shaking his head. "I'll do it later," he said to himself.

"Daddy? I'm sorry my 'e' is backwards," Hooper said walking along with Tony.

"Oh, you don't have to be sorry. Like I told Quint, you're still learning. I think you are working so hard to learn to write your name. And if we keep practicing, you're going to get better and better."

"Yeah, I will just do more practice," Hooper agreed.

"Come on, let's make dinner," Tony said.

The two of them went inside. Tony made dinner by himself.

IN THE LIGHT of the moon, two shadowy shapes appeared. Lumbering. Shuffling. Lurking.

The Sisters walked.

A flying bird, out too late on this night of all nights, dropped out of the sky as The Sisters hobbled onto the street.

Horribly aged, their bodies were ravaged by thousands of years of spells and sacrifice. Rotted, scarred flesh hung from their malnourished faces and limbs. Long green nails poked out of their twisted fingers and bare toes. What few teeth remained in their chapped, dry mouths were broken and dull. Their clothes were ragged and filthy. They were shrouded in cloaks of rough burlap with hoods pulled up, covering their balding heads.

One Sister, hunched over, pulled herself along with a

thick broken branch used as a walking stick. She dragged her useless, festering leg behind her.

The other Sister had a grimy cloth wrapped low around her head, covering up where she used to have an eye. She carried a large sack slung over her back and it was filled with fresh ingredients they had collected on their one night out. Stocking up for another year imprisoned. A bag filled with dreadful playthings so they could pass the time with unspeakable horrors.

The Sisters stood in the light of the moon…and streetlights.

"This place smells of burnt metal!" Sister Trixsue said in a jagged voice. She turned her head and spit black goo out onto the street. "The humans have replaced their masters with the machines again. Its false stench is everywhere. There is nothing natural left of this world anymore. Why are we here, Sister Ruthella?"

Those had not always been their names. But over the long centuries they had forgotten them. They had many names. These were the last names they could remember and over time they would forget these. They weren't even sure they were actual sisters. They had tried to murder each other several times over the years, when their minds were cloudy with confusion or in rages of mania. Perhaps they were family after all.

"Because Sister, we have spent most of our night collecting supplies and have barely eaten," Sister Ruthella gruffly replied as she pulled her leg behind her. "I wish to feast again before our time is up."

"Yes, but we do not know this worthless place," Sister Trixsue hissed back. "In which of these dwellings do sleeping children lie? We have no time or strength to search each one," she said, annoyed. She adjusted the sack on her back.

The Sisters looked around the neighborhood at the quiet, dark houses. After a moment, Sister Ruthella's mouth turned into an evil grin.

"Oh dear, dear Sister," she said giddily as she used the branch to scoot herself forward another step. "You must have forgotten. In all our years and in all of time and existence, there is one thing that children never fail to do," she said as she extended her long boney finger. "Children always make themselves known." She pointed at Hooper's driveway art.

"Yes!" Sister Trixsue cackled. "You clever beast! There are children there!"

"Yes! Come Sister, the night is almost over. Let us eat once more before we retreat to our prison."

The two Sisters stalked down the street to the driveway. They marched with hungry anticipation.

"Hurry up, you absolutely hideous crone!" Sister Trixsue shouted.

"Who are you calling hideous, you disgusting wretch? I'm moving as fast as I can!" Sister Ruthella used her stick to drag herself along.

They reached the edge of the driveway.

"Well you're not moving fast en...no!" Sister Trixsue looked down and cried. "No! It cannot be!" She threw her wrinkled hand over her mouth and stepped back from the driveway.

Sister Ruthella felt it before she saw it. She felt the air change. The air in front of her had become thicker and stronger. Then, she looked down and saw it.

"How is this possible?" Sister Ruthella whispered.

She slowly reached out. Carefully, she moved her hands closer to the edge of the driveway.

Her mangled hand hovered over the words: By Hooper.

Then, as if she had thrust her hand into a fire, Sister Ruthella shrieked and pulled her hand back. She howled as she watched smoke waft off her singed hand.

Sister Trixsue pointed to the backwards 'e' in Hooper.

"It's the sigil!"

And then she roared in rage.

HOOPER'S EYES JERKED OPEN.

She sat up in her bed. She thought she had heard a lion or something. She reached over, grabbed one of her stuffed animals, and squeezed it tight.

She didn't hear anything anymore. Maybe she was making it up.

She took a big breath. She slid over and hopped out of bed. Slowly, she tiptoed over to her window.

Her second floor window faced the front yard and the driveway. She slid her blinds over just enough for her to look through. She hesitantly peeked out of the window.

She saw two creatures standing down at the end of the driveway.

"IT'S A PROTECTION SIGIL! But why is it here?" Sister Trixsue shouted.

"How should I know?" Sister Ruthella said as she used her stick to balance herself. "That is a very strong magic. Surely the one who inscribed it dwells inside. Forget this house. Let us take another before our time runs out."

"But look, these are the scribbles of a child." Sister Trixsue observed. She suddenly grinned. "I want these ones. They shall taste especially sweet."

"Of course they will, but the sigil! We cannot get to the

house! We cannot pierce the protection of the sigil!" She used her branch to point at the backwards 'e' again.

"Simple fool!" Sister Trixsue scolded. "We can and we shall. We just need to be clever beasts," she said, patting the top of Sister Ruthella's head.

HOOPER LET GO of the blinds and ducked down under her window. Her eyes wide, she took deep, panicked breaths.

Those things didn't like something in her drawings. Something where she wrote her name.

Hooper started to breathe a little slower. As long as her name was on the driveway they couldn't get her, she thought.

Then she heard a loud crack of thunder.

She gasped and popped back up, peering out the window again.

THE SISTERS HAD JOINED HANDS. They had their eyes shut. They were both mumbling words in a long forgotten language.

The wind started to blow. A bolt of lightning lit up the sky. Then another loud boom of thunder.

The rain started off slowly. The Sisters started chanting faster. They started chanting louder.

The rain started to pour harder.

Wind. Lightning. Thunder.

The chalk on the driveway started to wash away.

The Sisters opened their narrow dark eyes. They turned to each other and smiled.

Wind. Lightning. Thunder.

The thunder startled something in the house's window.

The Sisters looked over and saw Hooper standing there.

The Sisters smiled.

HOOPER'S DOOR BURST OPEN!

"Hey!" a voice said.

She spun around.

"Hey Hooper, we got woke up by the storm," Quint said.

"Yeah, you want to snuggle together so we are not scared?" Brody asked her while he twisted around his worn muslin lion blanket.

Hooper didn't respond. She just took big heavy breaths. She was terrified.

"What's the matter, Hooper? I know the storm is pretty scary, but we are okay inside," Quint walked over and told her.

"There are some things outside," Hooper managed to tell Quint.

The thunder rumbled.

Quint slowly walked over to the window. He pulled open the blinds all the way.

At the edge of the driveway, The Sisters stood pointing at Quint and screeching with laughter.

Quint ducked down under the window.

"Pickles!" he said.

TONY SAT UP IN BED. The storm had woken him. It was a loud one tonight.

He heard something knock over. Sounded like it came

from Hooper's room. He suddenly remembered he'd promised Hooper it wasn't going to rain tonight. That stupid, lying weather app on his phone was going to get him in trouble now.

He leaned over to his sleeping wife.

"Hey? You awake?" he loudly whispered. "I think Hooper is awake because of the storm. Should I go check on her?"

His wife was out cold.

"Oh you want to do it? That would be great."

Still sleeping deeply.

"You know? Why don't you let me check on her? No, no, I want to do it."

She didn't budge. He kissed her forehead.

"Love you."

Tony scooted out of bed and quietly walked out into the hallway. He scrunched his face up when he noticed the boys' bedroom door was open. Then he saw that Hooper's door was open too. He leaned into her room, wondering what the heck was going on.

The kids were all sitting underneath Hooper's window. They had her big blanket covering their heads. The blinds were pulled wide open.

"Uh, what's up?" Tony asked curiously.

They jerked the blanket off their heads.

"Daddy! There's witches! Or something! Outside!" Brody announced with his lion blanket wrapped around his eyes.

"He's right Daddy. There's some ugly monster ladies outside making it rain. They're trying to wash off Hooper's chalk drawings on the sidewalks so they can come get us!" Quint explained.

"Yeah, they don't like my name!" Hooper added.

"Okay, okay, okay. Let's all take a big breath. I'm going

to look outside and see what's going on," Tony said as he walked to Hooper's window.

Tony peered outside into the stormy night. It was dark and the heavy rain made it hard to see. He squinted his eyes and looked around. He suddenly jumped back and quickly turned to the kids.

"Whoa! There's weird old ladies out there!" he said, startled. "What the heck are they doing?"

"They're washing off Hooper's name. Once her name washes off they can come into the yard!" Quint repeated.

"They're not coming into the yard," Tony said.

"Why? What are you going to do, Daddy?" Quint asked.

Tony didn't respond. He just stood there clicking his tongue while he thought about it. All three kids stared up at Tony.

"I don't know!" Tony finally blurted out. "I just kind of said that to say it, okay?" He rubbed his face. "Okay. How about this? You kids run to my room and get in bed with your mother. I'll go downstairs and out into the rain and chase away the daughters of the American revolution," Tony said as he walked out of the room.

"Don't! Daddy, don't go!" Hooper begged after him.

But he was already going down the stairs and to the front door. He got his shoes on and grabbed an umbrella out of the coat closet. He complained to himself the entire time.

He decided to go out through the garage door. He thought maybe if he just opened the loud garage door it would scare the crusty boomers away. He opened the entry door, clicking the garage door button as he stepped inside. As the heavy door slowly pulled itself open, Tony saw that the rain was almost torrential, falling fast and hard and blowing all over. His umbrella was worthless as the rain soaked him immediately.

"Excuse me! Ladies!" Tony shouted from just outside the garage door. He hoped the strange women could hear him over the loud storm. "Excuse me!" he shouted again.

THE DRIVEWAY WAS a wet rainbow of running colors. The vibrant water flowed down into the street, running past The Sisters filthy feet. The Sisters looked back down at the sigil. They could no longer see it. The air suddenly felt thinner and exposed. It worked. The rain had washed the sigil away. And the protection it cast was also gone. The Sisters began to cackle again. They looked back up at the kids still in the window.

They stepped forward onto the driveway.

"HEY! NO. NO!" Tony shouted at them from the top of the driveway. He was practically screaming over the pounding rain. "You two stay right..."

The Sisters each raised an open hand. Then, both at the same time, they closed their hands into fists. Like turning off a faucet, the rain immediately stopped. From heavy downpour to now nothing. The wind, lightning, thunder, and rain seemed to just vanish.

...there," Tony finished. He took a step back and looked around. It was jarring to experience such a drastic change in the weather.

Everything was drenched in water. The yard was a muddy mess. The quiet night air was filled with the sounds of countless drips and drops falling from trees and houses.

"Uh, excuse me," Tony called again, now that it was quiet.

The Sisters' heads jerked over to look at him. It made Tony jump again. He finally got a good look at the women and understood why his kids were so frightened. The first only had one eye and the other's leg was barely hanging on.

"Hi there." Tony cleared his throat and wrapped his umbrella back up. "Pretty crazy rain, right? Good timing on the hand thing when it stopped. You two should make a weather app!" Tony nervously joked. "Uh, say, I really appreciate you all coming by and scaring my kids to death, but if you don't mind we'd like to go back to sleep now. So could maybe just…hang out somewhere else? I'd really appreciate it, thanks."

The Sisters didn't respond. Instead, Sister Ruthella started to slowly hobble towards him, dragging her leg behind her.

"Come on, lady. Can you just get out of here? Why don't you go walk the mall like a normal person your age?" Tony said, getting annoyed. He really didn't want to call the cops. Then he remembered he'd left his phone inside.

The old woman stopped shuffling after only a few steps. She looked up at Tony and flashed him a crooked smile. Then she lifted her branch up and drew her arm back behind her. She threw the branch straight up into the air, like a javelin.

Tony watched as the branch corkscrewed high in the air and then curved over in his direction. It landed with a thump on the wet driveway about halfway between him and Sister Ruthella. The branch stood vertically, straight up and down. Tony saw no puncture or break in the concrete. Standing upright on its end, the branch was perfectly balanced.

Sister Ruthella clapped her hands one time. The thick branch suddenly began to grow. It smoothly stretched up taller and taller. As it grew, the branch also started to split lengthways down the center at the top and at the bottom. The splitting stopped before it could meet in the middle. The branch looked like a skinny letter H. Once it had sprouted to twice the size of Tony, the bottom two halves widened themselves like legs.

Tony stared in disbelief. Sister Ruthella made a motion with her hand that looked like she was scooping something out of her other open palm. Tony snapped back to attention when he saw the top two halves of the branch bend down and try to grab him. Tony dropped his umbrella and threw himself to the side, landing sloppily on the wet driveway.

"Showing off, Sister Ruthella?" Sister Trixsue said, rolling her eye.

"Quiet, you hag. We so rarely get a chance to have some fun. Go get the children. I'll take care of the father," Sister Ruthella barked.

Sister Trixsue dropped their sack of goodies on the street. She began walking into the yard towards the children's window.

Sister Ruthella punched her open palm. The branch creature waddled over and then drove one of its makeshift arms down onto where Tony was laying. Tony rolled out of the way, just missing the branch arm as it slammed deep into the driveway where he'd been. Small chunks of concrete burst out from where the arm landed.

"WE GOT TO GO HELP DADDY!" Quint said, staring out the window.

"Yeah, let's go!" Brody agreed as he tied his lion blanket around his waist.

"No boys! Don't go!" Hooper pleaded with her brothers.

But they didn't listen to her.

"Hooper, get Mommy! We'll help Daddy!" Quint said as he followed Brody out of the room.

The boys hopped downstairs and opened the front door.

They left Hooper alone.

AS THEY GOT outside they saw their dad roll out of the way just in time as the branch monster's arms lunged down at him again. They turned to the right and saw the other scary woman had stopped walking through their muddy yard and was smiling at them.

"Oh my little dearies! I was just coming to see you!" Sister Trixsue sang to them.

"Brody, this was a really bad idea," Quint admitted.

"Boys! Get out of here! Go back inside!" Tony yelled as he got to his feet.

Sister Ruthella used her finger and flicked the middle of her open palm.

The branch monster swung at Tony and knocked him down again.

Sister Ruthella tapped her palm.

Tony barely managed to dodge it striking the ground again.

"Maybe we should go get Mommy," Brody calmly suggested.

In the yard, Sister Trixsue put her thin clawed hands over her face.

As the boys went to go back inside, a huge projection of Sister Trixsue's face suddenly appeared in front of them. The front door slammed itself shut. Her floating head roared fiercely exposing a mouth filled with sharp fangs. The boys screamed.

They turned to run but her shrieking floating head was behind them too, this time with a snake striking out where her tongue would be. They continued to scream as they spun around to see Sister Trixsue's giant head everywhere they looked. It was like a hall of funhouse mirrors. The heads all roared and cackled. Some chomped their jaws toward the boys and others spit spiders out of their mouths.

The boys turned and yelled and turned until they collapsed onto the ground. They landed in some muddy grass. They had panicked themselves into the middle of the front yard. Quint and Brody looked up. The heads were all gone. Instead, Sister Trixsue stood only a few feet from them, laughing.

"Hello little dearies," Sister Trixsue waved.

The boys started screaming again as Sister Trixsue began to slosh through the mud towards them. She had her arms out and was flexing her sharp fingers. She was moving closer and closer. She cackled and called to the boys.

Then she tripped over Quint's bike and landed face first into the mud.

Quint looked around. He remembered they didn't put away the toys they brought out that afternoon. He'd left his bike in the yard. There were toys and balls all over.

"Brody, look! The toys! Daddy must have forgotten about them!" Quint told Brody.

Sister Trixsue furiously lifted her mud covered head out of the grass. Long brown strands of muck dripped off her face as she opened her mouth and snarled at the boys.

A basketball bounced off of her head and knocked her face back into the mud.

The boys were on their feet. They started to grab any toy they could reach and hurl them at the evil woman.

Brody threw a plastic bucket and small shovel.

Quint picked up Hooper's tricycle.

TONY SCOOTED AWAY as the branch monster's thick arms punched into the concrete. The thing was strong, but it was also kind of slow and lumbering. Tony scrambled to his feet. Controlled by Sister Ruthella, the big branch began to stomp towards him again.

Tony saw his umbrella lying on the ground not far away. He'd have to go around the monster to get it. The thing had a wide reach. It was one of the few times in his life he wished he had learned how to play sports. Playing offense seemed relevant at this moment.

He decided to just go for it and ran wide around the monster. The branch monster swung its arms, missing Tony by a half-inch. Tony ran over and reached down, scooping the umbrella up.

He turned around and quickly lifted the wrapped umbrella. He used it to block the monster's arm from coming down on top of him. It was so strong.

At the end of the driveway, Sister Ruthella pushed her finger harder into her palm. The monster seemed to be getting stronger. Tony could feel the umbrella start to snap. He couldn't hold it back. Sister Ruthella giggled.

Standing at the edge of the grass, Brody threw a small metal dump truck as hard as he could and clocked Sister Ruthella right in the nose. It was a good throw. Her finger left her palm as her hands involuntarily reached up to her hurt nose.

Tony felt the branch monster start to go limp. He shoved the umbrella up as hard as he could and pushed the monster away. As the monster tumbled back, Tony turned the umbrella around and used the curved end to hook its stick legs. Tony ripped the branch monster to the ground.

It fell lifeless on the driveway. It was just a dead branch again.

Brody ran over to Tony. Tony crouched down and scooped him up. Quint was right behind him and grabbed Tony's waist.

"Don't ever pick up your toys again," Tony said, hugging the boys.

SISTER TRIXSUE STOOD up and rubbed her muddy, aching head. She pulled a hula hoop from over her shoulders and stomped over to Sister Ruthella.

"Enough games!" she shouted.

"I've got them!" Sister Ruthella said, twirling her finger in the air.

The dead branch on the driveway suddenly floated into the air. It hovered over to Tony and the boys and started to wrap itself around them like it was rope. It squeezed them tightly.

"Daddy! It's squishing me!" Quint said.

"Ow!" Brody shouted.

The Sisters started to walk toward them. Stretching their arms out. Flexing their sharp fingers.

The boys started to scream again.

"Which one of you little dearies wrote the sigil?" Sister Trixsue asked. "I want to save you for last!"

"Leave them alone!" Tony shouted over the screaming.

"Shame on you for trying to keep us away!" Sister Ruthella hissed.

"We didn't write on the driveway!" Quint yelled.

"I did," Hooper said.

The Sisters turned and saw the little girl standing in front of the garage.

"You get better if you practice," Hooper said.

Then she dropped the wet paintbrush and stepped to the side. She'd written a huge 'Hooper' across the driveway. With Tony's paint.

And her 'e' was backwards.

"Nooo!" The Sisters cried.

The Sisters' bodies started to twist and crunch like crushing aluminum cans. Their bodies were violently jerked into the air off the driveway. The Sisters shrieked. They spun through the air and landed with a few bounces before slapping onto the street with a crack.

The branch tied around Tony and the boys dropped stiffly to the ground. Tony set Brody down. Hooper joined the three of them as they slowly walked to the end of the driveway.

The Sisters withered in pain on the street. They moaned and howled. They scratched at the pavement. They were hurt so badly that they didn't notice how light it got. They didn't notice that the sun had risen.

"Daddy look!" Brody pointed.

Walking down the street were three women.

"Stay back," Tony warned and put his arms out.

One woman was dressed in a perfectly pressed black pantsuit. She wore thick glasses and had her blond hair in a high tight bun. Her tall heels clicked loudly on the street as she walked. The brown haired woman next to her was wearing nurse's scrubs and worn out sneakers. She was texting on her phone. The last woman was wearing sunglasses, yoga pants, flip flops, and a sweatshirt that said 'Cabernet Then Slay'. She sipped from a to-go coffee cup.

The three women walked to the beaten up Sisters lying on the ground. They looked down and shook their heads in disappointment. Then each woman raised a hand and wiggled her fingers.

The Sisters began to levitate in the air. They hung like they were on an invisible rack. They whimpered as they floated. The nurse and the one with the coffee stepped behind The Sisters and began to walk them like dogs back down the street.

The woman in the black pantsuit watched them walk away. Then she turned around and picked up The Sisters' sack of supplies. Before she started to follow, she stopped and looked at the family. She smiled and nodded at the little girl standing next to her father and brothers.

"Hooper, right?" The woman said.

"Yes?" Hooper said.

"We'll be in touch," the woman said. And then she turned and walked back down the street.

They turned the corner and then they were gone.

"What's that mean?" Quint asked.

"I don't even want to know," Tony said.

"Daddy, did you like my name?" Hooper looked up and asked. "My 'e' is still backwards, I know."

"Hoop? It's maybe the best written name I've ever seen. Especially the backwards 'e'." Tony leaned down and kissed her head.

"Great job Hooper!" Quint said.

"Yeah, it looks amazing!" Brody agreed.

They all started walking back towards the house.

"Sorry I used your paint, Daddy. The driveway was too wet for my chalk," Hooper apologized.

"What are you going to tell Mommy about that?" Quint asked, looking at the big paint job.

"I'll tell her somebody else named Hooper did it," Tony said. "Now come on, let's go make some coffee."

"We can have coffee?" Brody asked.

"Sure," Tony said.

Hooper smiled proudly at her work.

The boys took off. They each jumped over the huge 'Hooper' with the backwards 'e' painted on the driveway. The brothers ran into the house. Tony jogged after them.

The sister walked.

THE END

PART VII

FullTimeTony and the Forever Gone

While they sat and waited, he made a list in his head.

TONY'S TO DO LIST:
   1. Pick up Hooper's medicine.
   2. Help Quint with his 'all about me' school project.
   3. Head back home.

HE HAD to make lists now. When he started staying home with the kids, Tony quickly realized he could not keep track of all the things he had to get done. So he began making lists. Now, almost five years later, he could barely function without them.

"I should say that I love to play soccer."

"Quint, this project is about things that you like and do. I've never seen you play soccer in your life," Tony said.

"Yeah, I'm not really into soccer, but I feel like I need to add more sports." Quint justified.

"Put something about video games, then. Video games are a sport now. You play those."

"Yeah, but I want people to think I do more, you know, physical-type sports."

"Buddy, write about the real you. Don't write a paper about yourself that's just full of things you think people want to hear." Tony said sweetly.

"Yeah? I guess so." Quint admitted.

"Trust me, you'll have plenty of opportunities to lie about that kind of stuff later in life when you fill out job applications and online dating profiles." Tony said.

"Really?" Quint looked over at Tony.

"Oh yeah. Tons." Tony snorted and nodded his head. He thought for a moment. "That kind of lying is actually really important when you get older." Tony stopped and clicked his tongue. "Actually, it's not a bad idea to practice now. Put baseball instead of soccer. I've seen you hit things with sticks. That counts. Write that you play baseball."

"Cool!" Quint smiled and wrote it down in a badly creased notebook he had taken out of Tony's backpack. "I'll say I'm like, great at doing slam dunks!"

"Heck yeah! Wait… is that right?" Tony paused.

"I sHaLL FeAst oN yOUr sOULs!!" a demonic voice snarled.

"Daddy, she's doing it again." Brody casually tugged on Tony's arm.

"I heard her, bud. Hopefully, we're almost done." Tony looked at Brody and said.

"But how many minutes, Daddy?" Brody said as he fidgeted with the muslin lion blanket he carried everywhere. "This is very boring for me."

"I know. I know." Tony said and gave him a squeeze. "Pretty soon."

"YoUR hEAdS wiLL rOaSt oN sPiKes iN ThE fiReS

oF yOUr worST niGhtMarES!!!" the demon voice said again.

"Yes, Hooper. Fiery spikes. We know." Tony rolled his eyes and looked over at Hooper.

Hooper was a few feet down from where they were sitting. Her eyes were glowing blood red. Her face was all broken out in rashes and hives. In between yelling disturbingly graphic threats in a bloodcurdling voice, she growled in a low hum and bared her newly formed fangs. She had bright neon green chains tied tightly around her tiny body. They promised Tony that the mystically enchanted chains were strong enough to restrain Hooper and the space demon that had possessed her.

"Not too much longer, okay, Hoop?" Tony shouted over at the creature that his daughter had turned into.

"I sHaLL bREaK thESe cHaiNs aNd teAr YOu ApARt aTOm bY AtoM!!!" Hooper looked over and hissed at her father.

"Yes! I know you can! You can do anything you want, Hooper!" Tony assured her. He was over her demonic dramatics, but still wanted to be encouraging to his daughter.

"Daddy, how do you spell 'world champion'?" Quint asked Tony.

An explosion suddenly went off.

FIRE BURST through the ceiling of the sewer tunnel. Brody's hands leapt to his ears at the noise. Rock, dirt, and sparks rained down into the underground shaft and splashed into the murky water. Tony and the boys jumped up from where they had been sitting on the walkway, trying to avoid the dark sewer water that was spraying up at them. As the smoke and dust cleared, their eyes adjusted to the bright light that was pouring into the once dark tunnel.

A cluster of figures and shapes dropped through the opening into the underground shaft. They splashed down, quickly hustled over to the wide walkway that ran the length of the sewer, and climbed up out of the water. Two of them stayed down in the water and pointed their weapons up at the newly created hole, making sure nothing was following them.

The group was a wide variety of species from all over the galaxies. The two guarding the entrance were stone creatures the size of football linemen. The Triangle was the shape of a triangle and used her stick thin arms and legs to pull herself awkwardly out of the water. A family of four, who resembled two-foot tall Earth mice, helped one another up onto the walkway.

Another seemed to be a shapeless wet jelly blob that was spilling itself onto the ground and then lunging itself forward again like an accordion. The one who seemed to take charge after the initial breakout was Vedra. He looked the most human, but had solid black eyes and his hairless skin was the color of a gold speckled eggshell. A small, chunky robot floated in the air alongside Vedra. The boys called it Crocky, because it looked exactly like Tony's slow cooker back home.

"We've got to move quickly." Vedra said as he approached Tony. He carried a worn pickaxe in one hand and a metallic cylinder the size of an empty paper towel roll in the other. Hanging around his chest was a bandolier filled with round balls that had provided the explosion.

"So much for getting in and out quietly." Tony pointed his chin at the enormous hole in the sewer.

"Getting in was easy. Out, not so much." Vedra explained as he caught his breath. "We broke into the medical lab, no problem. But as soon as we found what we needed, the alarms went off. They flooded the place with Cyber Guards. We held them off by barricading the door, but that was our way out. So, we made our own exit."

"That actually sounds really amazing." Brody remarked.

"Did you get it?" Tony anxiously asked Vedra.

Vedra lifted the metallic cylinder and handed it over to Tony.

"This is it." Vedra said.

Tony looked intensely at the tube in his hands, turned it back and forth.

"This will fix her?" Tony asked.

"It should work, yes." Crocky answered in a static and tinny voice. It sounded like a living walkie-talkie.

"It should?" Tony said, very frustrated.

"Buddy, she stared down a Demon Dog! Everybody knows you don't stare into a Demon Dog's eyes! Its demon jumped out of the beast and right into your daughter! What's inside there cures possession, but who knows if they have ever used it on one of you humans before?" Crocky snapped back.

Tony shook his head. Only Hooper could catch herself a space demon.

"Okay, uh. Right. So, what do I do with it?" Tony finally just asked.

"Twist the tube to open. The cleansing crystal is inside." The floating robot echoed.

Tony carefully unscrewed the metallic tube. Removing the top half of the tube revealed a bright purple crystal shard.

"That's beautiful. Is that medicine?" Brody craned his head up to see what Tony was holding.

"It's magic will draw out the demon. Remove the

crystal from the protective tube." Crocky bobbed up and down. "Then, take the crystal and slowly slide it across your daughter's forehead."

"Will it hurt her?" Tony asked the floating robot.

"More than having a demon inside of her?" Crocky barked in its distorted voice.

"We must hurry. More Cyber Guards will be here soon." Vedra anxiously reminded the group.

Tony inhaled sharply and removed the shimmering purple crystal from the tube. It was the size of a carrot and had an uneven weight to it. He walked over to the still sitting Hooper. She was rotating her head side to side and gnashing her fangs at the empty air. He knelt down and turned her chained body toward him.

"Hoop, this will fix you. I need to do this, so sit still, okay?" Tony said to his daughter.

"GEt tHAt tHiNG aWay FrOm mE!!! i wiLL tEAr DowN oBLIVion AnD eRAsE yOU fROM exisTaNCE!!" The Hooper demon shouted back at Tony.

"Oh yeah? Then who's going to get you juice boxes?" Tony snapped back.

Quint and The Triangle each grabbed one of Hooper's shoulders and steadied her. Tony gently placed the thick end of the purple crystal against Hooper's broken out forehead. Then he slowly slid the crystal over her brow from left to right. As he moved the crystal across, he noticed its bright color pulse. Hooper shrieked and howled as it moved. Quint and The Triangle held her as still as they could.

When it had gone all the way across her forehead, he gently pulled it away. He looked down at his daughter. She was still a demon.

"HaAHaHAhAhaHA!" Hooper's deep laugh echoed. "SOrRy, fLEshbAG!" She cackled.

"It didn't work!" Tony said angrily, jumping to his feet. "You said it would work!"

"It takes more than one application, slick!" Crocky blurted. "Does medicine on Earth work in one dose? Or do you have to take it multiple times?" The robot said mockingly. "Drawing the demon out all at once would kill her, so you have to do it in small doses. You'll need to do it KOLMITRI every UNTWOD!"

"I don't know what that means!" Tony yelled.

"Three times! Once every thirty minutes." Crocky recalculated in Earth.

"Thank you." Tony said and sighed. He looked down at Hooper. Her face had cleared up slightly and her eyes were not as bright red.

The crystal in his hand suddenly felt a little heavier. Looking at it, the purple color was slightly duller. He saw something moving around inside. Moving it closer to his face, he saw there was a tiny creature swimming around in it. Grossed out, he slid the crystal back into its tube and twisted the lid back on.

"Okay. Three doses total, one every thirty minutes. We can handle that. Can you set me a timer or something?" Tony asked Crocky as he put the metallic tube in his backpack.

"I can." Crocky bobbed up and down.

"That means, Daddy, she'll need it again in a half hour." Quint informed Tony.

"Thanks Dr. Quint." Tony acknowledged.

"Doctor? Hmm… medical training." Quint said out loud to himself. He nodded, opened his notebook, and started writing something down.

TONY MADE a new list in his head.

. . .

TONY'S TO DO LIST:

1. Give Hooper the purple crystal thingy two more times every thirty minutes to get rid of the space demon inside her.
2. Help Quint with his 'all about me' school project.
3. Get back home.

PLASMA BLASTS SUDDENLY RAINED DOWN through the hole in the ceiling. The two stone men guarding the opening yelled something in their language.

"They're here!" Vedra said, and ran towards the stone men. The Triangle and the mouse family followed him. The jelly blob stayed behind and slithered next to Tony and Crocky.

The stone men returned fire with their stolen plasma rods, the mechanized nightsticks blasting laser beams at the Cyber Guards advancing down upon them. Tall, thin, and polished to a high shine, the now lifeless metallic robots fell through the opening and into the sewer water.

Tony held his hands over Brody's ears as the weapons echoed in the tunnels.

"Get back!" Vedra was in the water at the opening, dodging another falling Cyber Guard. The stone men stopped firing and got out of his way. Vedra pulled a round ball from his bandolier, threw it up into the hole, and jumped back.

The jelly blob creature quickly formed up into the

shape of a thick translucent wall and moved in front of Crocky, Tony, and the kids.

Another thunderous explosion boomed through the tunnels. Fire and smoke rushed out of the opening. After a few seconds, the ringing from the bombing stopped and so had the shooting.

"We can't stay here. We have to move." Vedra said as he picked up more of the destroyed Cyber Guards plasma rods. He handed the weapons over to the mouse family and The Triangle. "Come on. Everyone down this way." He directed. The mouse family and The Triangle led the way.

"Uh, thanks." Tony said to the jelly blob as it formed back into its normal pile shape. It plopped itself down the tunnel walkway with Crocky and the rest of the group. "Okay, boys, let's follow everyone else. Be quick and stay together, okay?" Tony said to Quint and Brody. "You too, Hoop." He said, picking up the loose end of Hooper's green chain.

"i'D rATheR ReMAin heRE iN THiS bEAUtifUL FiLtH!" Hooper snarled back at him as she stomped ahead of him.

"I hope no one finds out I was walking my daughter like a dog." Tony said, holding the green chain. "Can I take these off of her?" He yelled up at the group.

"I wouldn't," Crocky replied.

Hooper turned around and looked at Tony with her monster eyes and sharp fangs. She raised her eyebrows menacingly.

"Maybe we'll let that magic crystal kick in a little more." Tony concluded.

Vedra waved the group down the walkway. He joined Tony's pace. The stone men heaved themselves out of the sewer water and onto the walkway. They kept watch on things behind them.

ˮTHESE TUNNELS WILL LEAD to the planet's Flightway Beam System. That's a particle transporter. It's the quickest way to get you back to your planet. It will phase you right there in just a few seconds." Vedra told Tony.

"Okay." Tony said, only half understanding what Vedra was talking about.

"Where did they pick you up?" Vedra asked.

"I don't know, exactly. We had just finished doing… a thing…" Tony rolled his eyes. "… and they grabbed us on our way back to Earth." He turned to Vedra. "Thank you for all your help. For getting us back and for finding that crystal for Hooper and everything."

"No, no. We must thank you. Or rather thank your heroic daughter. Her bravery in staring down that Demon Dog gave us just the distraction we needed to make our escape. We've been toiling away at that work camp for a long time. We are very grateful they assigned your family to our little chain gang." Vedra smiled. "Your daughter has given us the chance to take back our freedom from this terrible place."

"I don't know if I would call having a bad temper 'brave' but yeah she got us out of that." Tony said. "What was that? What is all of this? A prison planet?"

"Not a prison. Their public relations team works very hard to clarify that this is not a prison." Crocky floated back to them. "We are all technically contracted employees."

"Contracted employees? Who works at gunpoint? Guarded by killer robots and huge monster dogs? They kidnapped us!" Tony shouted.

"Sounds like a typical first day to me, partner! Now that you've survived orientation, welcome to Moc, Inc.!" Crocky cackled.

"What are you talking about?" Tony ducked under the floating robot.

"This planet is Moc. It's believed to be one of the lost Alpha Planets." Vedra took over. "Alpha Planets were the first planets in existence, and since Moc was there at the beginning of everything, it carries within it leftover energy from the creation of the universes. Powerful energy. But for billions and billions of years, Moc stayed hidden. So this power lay dormant. Hidden within the planet's core, it was inactive and useless. Until a few hundred years ago…"

"Oh great. A story." Quint said to Brody, rolling his eyes.

"Aw, man! There's ALWAYS a story." Brody whined in agreement.

"… when The Company found it. They soon figured out how to awaken Moc's energy. By feeding it. While surveying the planet, they cracked Moc's crust, and as the debris tumbled down into the pit, the energy suddenly came alive. The more things The Company threw into the pit, into the planet's core, the stronger the output." Vedra explained.

"Like a fire." Tony said.

"The more you stoke it, the more you feed it, the hotter it gets and the larger it grows." Vedra nodded. "Now imagine that the heat you produce could power an entire planet. Or an entire galactic system. An Alpha Planet's energy has that power. This is how all of creation could survive those first few infinities. Alpha Planets were engines that kept the universes running."

"So, The Company that we 'work' for, figured out how to hook the engine up to other planets." Tony concluded.

"Moc became Moc, Inc. The Company's engineers extracted the energy from the pit and pipelined it out to other planets and systems. Siphoning it out all over the sector, it became the number one source of power in this system. But as wealthy as that made them, it also created a production problem." Vedra said.

"They needed to be constantly feeding the pit to keep up with demand." Crocky bobbed up and down as its voice popped. "The planet's forests, mountains, plains, and deserts would all have to be mined down and thrown into the pit. They even figured out a way to divert the rivers, lakes, and oceans to the pit!" Crocky said. "It was an around the clock job. At first they bussed in low-income workers and planetary immigrants. It was hard labor and only the most desperate would do it. Tearing down an entire planet's ecosystem to feed to a pit? It's grueling and dangerous." Crocky's voice crackled.

"The most dangerous conditions you could imagine." Vedra continued. "Mining a planet down to its bare bones. No safety regulations, no breaks, no mercy. People get hurt and killed every day. Workers getting trapped in the forest mines. Lives taken in mountain demolition. Desert shifts that last months before you get relieved. Workers dropping to the ground because of hunger, wounds, or exhaustion."

"And it is never good enough! Quotas rising every day! Every hour! The demand for the planet's energy is growing higher and higher!" Crocky said.

"Kind of like last summer when I did my lemonade stand, right Daddy?" Quint, who is never not listening to adults talk, turned around and chimed in. "My lemonade stand was so popular I had to have Brody and Hooper help me. There were people lined up! Cars around the block!"

"Quint, there were cars around the block because you had slowly inched your lemonade stand out into the middle of the street. It forced people to buy something so they could get around you." Tony said, rolling his eyes.

"Daddy, I'm telling you it's ALL about location!" Quint insisted. "It's okay. You don't get it, you're not great at business like I am." Quint turned back around. He narrowed his eyes. "Hmm... great at business." He nodded, opened his notebook, and started writing something down.

"It keeps getting bigger too. The pit has grown in size. Once it was just a crater, now, it's an endless canyon that runs the length of the planet. A crack in the world. Bottomless and always hungry. But now, there's nothing left of the planet to feed it. So, The Company is charging planets to let them dump their garbage here. Thousands of worlds have their planet's trash transported here to be fed to the pit. That's what they had us digging. There are mountains of it up there." Crocky buzzed.

"This story is... very long." Brody declared.

"The Company used their money and power to get the intergalactic rights laws rewritten." Vedra angrily said. "So now they can fly around the universe and legally enforce contracts onto anyone they pick up. Like you and your family. Like most of our friends here with us." Vedra pointed to everyone else in the line. "They had military engineers develop the Cyber Guard robots for them to keep order. They contracted the Forbidden Shadow Priests to conjure the Demon Dogs and other monsters to keep us constantly in fear." Vedra's face went from angry to sad. "They auto-renew our contracts anytime they like. Adding years. Years before any of us can leave and see our families again. And when that date arrives, if you're still alive, they renew the contract again. Anyone who could stop them gets paid off. They use their power to make sure that you can never leave." Vedra's eyes welled up.

"How long have you been here, Vedra?" Tony asked.

"A long time. My son… he got very sick and my family got in some financial trouble trying to afford his treatment. We had to put off some bills so we could pay for his medical care. I missed payments on the energy bill to the Company." Vedra looked away. A tear broke free. "And if you can't pay for your power, you can work for it."

"dO yOU ThiNK ThEY'rE hIRing MaNAgERs? MaYBe i caN pUt IN aN AppLICatiON?" Hooper snarled.

"Hooper, that's enough!" Tony snapped at the demon girl. "Vedra, I'm sorry. Your son, is he…?" Tony hesitated.

"He's better now. I hope to see him again, someday." Vedra said. "We all have similar stories." He motioned to his friends in line. "We all hope that when our contracts finally end, we walk out of here. Not get carried out."

THE MOUSE FAMILY started squeaking loudly. They were pointing at an upcoming fork in the sewer tunnel. Up ahead, the shaft was going to split in two different directions. Everyone stopped walking.

"This is where we part ways, my friend." Vedra said.

"I will guide you down that tunnel to sneak you to the Flightway Beams." Crocky told Tony. "It's time for you to go home, fella."

"But wait? Everyone is going, right? This is your chance to get out of here." Tony asked.

"We're going through the other tunnel." Vedra pointed. "It will take us to the main corporate headquarters. If we hurry, we can make it in time for a worker shift change. We're going to free more of our friends up there. If we can get enough numbers on our side, we can try to end this madness."

"But, they know you're out here running around.

Shooting at their robots. You took out their dog monster and blew up their med lab. They're going to be expecting you!" Tony said to the group.

"Then we shall not disappoint." Vedra grinned proudly.

The small group of revolutionaries all cheered.

Tony grabbed Vedra by the arm. "Vedra, your son? Your family? This is your opportunity."

"But if I have even the slightest chance of giving everyone that same opportunity, then that is what I must do." Vedra exclaimed.

Tony let go of Vedra's arm.

"And if you somehow free them up there? Then what? The work stops? The pit stops being fed? How many planets are going to lose power? What about them? You're just going to shut their lights off?" Tony asked.

"They had perfectly good power before The Company offered theirs. It will be messy and inconvenient, but they can find it again." Vedra replied. "Don't worry. You've done enough, friend. It's time for you to get your family back home safely."

Tony looked at the two tunnels. Then he looked at the group. The mouse family was so thin you could see their rib cages. The Triangle anxiously jumped at every noise and movement around her. The two stone men seemed more weighed down with anger than their own rocky bodies. The jelly blob... was a jelly blob, but it was probably sad.

"Come on, we've got to help them! For my charity work!" Quint said, holding up his notebook.

"DeSTroY eVErytHinG!!!" Hooper snarled.

"Yeah, Daddy! You love shutting off lights at home! It's your favorite." Brody smiled.

"It is not my favorite! But nobody else…" Tony stopped and shook his head, refusing to get into it.

Tony looked at the two tunnels. He sighed.

"Okay, then. Let's get fired."

TONY'S TO DO LIST:

1. Free imprisoned workers.
2. Overthrow evil corporation.
3. Give Hooper the purple crystal thingy two more times every thirty minutes to get rid of the space demon inside her.
4. Help Quint with his 'all about me' school project.
5. Get back home.

TONY WAS in awe of a planet so disgusting that its sewers smelled better than the surface.

They snuck out of a drainage pipe that jutted out of the side of a garbage hill. Crouching low, they cautiously sidestepped down the uneven and loose trash until they reached a ridge overlooking Moc Inc.'s corporate head-quarters. A bizarrely shaped skyscraper with abnormal angles and peaks that defied architectural physics stood before them. It was a gray monolith reaching high into the putrid green sky.

"Daddy, it smells like throw up out here." Brody whispered.

"The sky looks like it, too." Quint added, looking up.

Tony squinted up. The destruction of the planet's ecosystem, along with the exhaust of constantly incoming and outgoing galactic garbage ships, had turned the sky a disgusting shade of green. Tony didn't want to think about how toxic the air was.

Trash surrounded the strange building on all sides and spread as far as Tony could see. The waste had taken the place of the dirt, trees, waters, and mountains that were fed into the pit. The entire planetary landscape was garbage, with an ugly gray building sticking out of the middle of it, and big ships entering the planet to dump more trash every minute.

The giant structure's shadow loomed over a clean and neatly organized airstrip. Tony watched a steady stream of flying transport ships arrive from all directions of the planet and descend onto long runways. The bus-shaped transports floated down and loudly screeched to a halt at big shelters built alongside the lanes. Crowded inside each of the shelters were long queues of depressed Moc Inc. workers waiting to board. Cyber Guards supervised as exhausted and injured employees unloaded from the buses and replaced with the weary new ones.

"Who knows how long those shifts will last?" Vedra appeared next to Tony. "Days, weeks, months? You never know when they will put you on those transports."

"So what's your plan?" Tony asked.

"BLoW iT uP!" Demon Hooper hissed.

"We start with one transport. Overtake it after it's unloaded and free everyone. Then rally and arm our liberated friends and move onto the next. Two become four and four become eight and so on." Vedra answered as he safely checked the plasma rod he was holding.

"That's if… you can take over the first one." Tony warned.

"Have faith, buster." Crocky's hollow voice buzzed behind him.

"So what do you want us to do?" Tony anxiously asked.

"LeT Us rUN bLiNDly InTO tHE oPEn ArMS oF DEAth!!!" Hooper growled.

"Or… or… I was thinking we could stay up here and guard this area. Right here." Tony gestured.

"We should go down there and distract those robots while everyone else sneaks up on the first bus." Quint stared down at the runways and suggested.

"That's exactly what I was thinking too." Vedra said and waved the rest of the team over to him.

Tony turned to Quint and shot him a dirty look. Quint leisurely lifted his school notebook up and shook it.

"Creative management and team-building skills." Quint smiled.

"I hope you get an F." Tony whispered to Quint.

"That bus. Right there." Vedra pointed to a transport that had just landed. It was shutting its engines down, and in moments, the workers would disembark. There were six Cyber Guards standing outside the transport, supervising the unloading. "Tony, wait until they have everyone off and then you and your kids go distract those guards. There will have been a high alert update to their systems that you escaped. So, taking you into custody is a priority and will override their current assigned operation. While you do that, the rest of us will go around and take them out from behind. When the shooting starts, get behind the shelter and hide."

"Wait, are we sure they're JUST going to take us into custody? Or are they going to shoot us on sight?" Tony nervously asked.

"It's hard to say."

"Well, good luck, chum!" Crocky added. Then it

hovered low to the trash pile as Vedra, the stone men, the mice family, the blob, and The Triangle all crawled away.

"Doesn't anyone else want to be on our team?" Tony whisper-shouted. "Anyone? Someone with a shooty stick?" Tony scowled. "Fine."

"What are we going to do, Daddy?" Brody asked as he anxiously twisted his lion blanket in his hands. The sewer and garbage had made it even filthier than usual.

"I don't know yet, buddy." Tony reached over and tied the blanket over his shoulders like a preppy sweater. "We need to distract those robot guards. We have until the bus is almost empty to think of something."

"i aM NoT gOiNG!" Hooper said in a bratty growl.

"Yes you are, Hoop." Tony said and tugged on her neon green chain, pulling her closer.

"nOPe. NoT HaPPeNinG. WHy sHOUld i HELp yOU fLEShY tHIngS?" She ranted.

"We should sing The Butt Song to them." Brody suggested.

"i wOUld rATheR... WaIT... wHAt'S tHE BuTT sONg?"

"You should know, demon. The monster you possessed wrote it." Tony told her.

ACHING bodies shuffled slowly off the transport bus. Beings of all types, from all over the universes, marched orderly out of the transport's exit doors and into the shelter to await further instructions.

"Hurry. Single file. Let's go. Move it." A Cyber Guard's robotic voice called out to the exhausted employees. Along with two other Cyber Guards, it supervised the disembarking. They posted three more Cyber Guards outside the shelter, waiting to begin the loading of the next group of workers.

"Hey! Excuse us?" A little voice called out as the last worker stepped off the transport.

The Cyber Guards all turned.

A tall man and three young kids stood on the runway next to the shelter.

"We would like to sing you... a little song!" Brody giddily shouted. "Hit it Quint!"

"Halt. Do not move." The Cyber Guards all spoke in the same cold clanging voice. "Escaped employees located."

"Ohhh... I've got a butt! And you've got a butt! Everyone's got a butt!" Quint and Brody sang and danced. Tony waved his arms and swayed. Hooper just stood and scowled.

"Halt. Do not move. Escaped employees located. Operation objections updated. Take employees into custody for immediate performance review. Priority Red." The Cyber Guards lifted their plasma rods and took a step forward.

"Please respect my butt, and I'll respect your butt! Respect every butt you see!" The boys giggled as they sang. Hooper continued to scowl, but she unconsciously started tapping her foot along to the song.

"Halt. Do not move. Priority Red. You have abandoned your work station without management authorization. You are to be taken into custody for immediate performance review." The Cyber Guards continued to step towards the family.

"When everyone respects everyone's butt, we'll live in har-mo-nyyy!" They stretched their arms out as they belted out the big finish.

"Halt. Do not..."

The transport bus exploded.

The fiery blast knocked backwards Tony and the kids.

It destroyed the three Cyber Guards closest to the bus along with it. Then, jumping directly through the raging flames, the two stone men each smashed a Cyber Guard to the ground. The only still standing Cyber Guard wobbled back and forth as Vedra suddenly appeared behind it. He raised his plasma rod at the disoriented robot and fired.

Tony winced as he quickly sat back up and checked on the kids. They all seemed surprised, but they were just fine.

"That was awesome." Quint smiled.

"Man, those guys love blowing things up!" Brody said, rubbing his elbows.

"Yeah, they sure do." Tony said as he helped Hooper up.

"cAn'T i wATch tHEm BUrn a LiTTLe wHiLE lONgeR?" The little girl growled as Tony set her down.

"No, sicko, we've got to go! Come on!" Tony said, as he herded the three kids over to the back of the shelter.

The employees who were waiting in the shelter cautiously stepped out and looked around at the damage. Some were in shock. Some seemed delighted. A bulky creature with horns and three eyes walked towards Vedra and his friends.

Vedra bent over and picked up the fallen Cyber Guard's plasma rod. He held it out to the creature. The creature looked at the weapon. The crackling of the bus's flames punctuated the silence between the two workers. As the seconds passed like centuries, Vedra looked reassuringly into the creature's eyes. Finally, it nodded, and Vedra nodded back. It took the plasma rod from Vedra and raised it high over its horns. Turning to the sizable crowd of employees, it shouted loudly in its language.

The crowd enthusiastically responded to what it was

saying. They picked up the weapons that lay on the ground. They got louder and louder. Rage and passion fueled the crowd into a fury. The fourteen revolutionaries had now become forty.

Suddenly, a unit of Cyber Guards appeared. They shot at the frenzied mob. The crowd scattered to avoid the initial blasts, but immediately regrouped and started fighting back.

"We'll split up! We will handle this. You take a group and go free some more! Then move on to the next one!" Vedra shouted at his new three eyed horned brother.

The creature nodded. It took a chunk of the crowd with it and they ran down the runway to the next transport.

"Entertaining, including musical performances." Quint was writing in his notebook.

"Daddy, I'm hungry." Brody told Tony, as they all crouched around the corner of the shelter. Then he turned and put his little hand over Tony's mouth. "And don't say, 'hi hungry'!" He said angrily.

"Okay, okay." Tony said, pushing Brody's hand away. "I've got some granola bars in my bag, I think." He slid the backpack off his shoulders and unzipped it.

Another transport bus exploded down the runway. Then another further down. More and more plasma rods were being fired. The rebelling workers were gaining more and more numbers. The entire airstrip had turned into chaos and noise.

"wHAt Is A graNOLa bAr?" Hooper licked her chapped lips.

"Hooper, you always say you don't like these." Tony told her as he handed the snacks over to Quint and Brody.

"Yeah Hooper, you hate granola bars." Quint told her as he removed the wrapper.

"yOU kNOw NOThinG abOUt mE, yOu liTTLe sWINe!" Hooper snarled at Quint.

"That's enough!" Tony yelled at her. "Okay then, would you like one?"

"yEs."

"Can you say please?"

"cAn yoU BreAThe wiTH nO noSE?!" she snapped.

"Will you cool out? Here. Take a bite." Tony said. He held it out for her to take, but then remembered they chained her up. "Oh sorry. Uh, here." He pulled a chunk off, tossed it in her razor-sharp mouth, careful not to lose a finger.

As an explosion went off next to it, one of the stone men picked up The Triangle and tossed her like a Frisbee. She sliced through a dozen Cyber Guard reinforcements like they were weeds. Mid air, she grabbed one of the carved robots' plasma rods and started firing as soon as her stick legs hit the ground. A bus transport crashed down onto the runway in a tremendous burst of fire.

"tHeSE aRE dELIcIOUs. wHaT aRE THEy mADE oF? BoNE and BRaiNs?" She said with her mouth full.

"What? Gross, Hoop. No, it's like sugar and then granola coated with more sugar to hide the granola taste. And candy." Tony told her.

"i EnJoY thEM vERy muCH." She chewed. She opened her mouth for another piece.

"That's really weird, because when you don't have a demon in you, you hate them. You scream at me whenever I offer one to you. Is this the cure for picky eaters?"

"See what else she'll eat, Daddy!" Brody laughed.

"Yeah, now I wish I had brought some vegetables." Tony said.

The mouse family took down another Cyber Guard. Two of them grabbed the legs, and the other jumped on its torso and head. They wrestled the robot to the ground as it short-circuited. Another transport exploded in the distance. The jelly blob had grown to the size of a bounce house and absorbed another Cyber Guard. The giant Jell-O mold slithered by with guards floating around inside it like marshmallows.

"This is really loud, Daddy!" Brody said, pulling his lion blanket off his shoulders and holding it over his ears as makeshift headphones.

"I know, man. I know. Come here." Tony said, and he pulled all three kids closer to him. The fighting sounded like it was getting more and more intense. He tried to crane his neck around the corner to see what all was going on, but he was afraid to stick out too much.

As he hugged his kids tighter, Tony heard a terrifying roar. He looked down the runway and saw a pack of Cyber Guards remove the neon green chain from the collar of a giant Demon Dog. Freed, it hunted towards the shelter. Tony immediately looked away to avoid accidentally making eye contact with the beast.

"Boys, don't look. It's another one of those monster dogs. It's coming this way. Do. Not. Look in its eyes. You got me?"

"Yes, Daddy." The boys said, suddenly quite scared.

It was like a Rottweiler the size of a monster truck. A magnificent beast with glowing red eyes that bared a mouthful of fangs when it snarled. It had thick, dark fur, all matted and stained. It trampled through the fighting, chomping down at both the brave and the fleeing. The shooting was lessening. Tony could hear the panic and fear coming from the rebelling workers. They screamed as the creature clawed and gnawed at them.

It was getting closer. Tony didn't want to take a chance on it finding them. He scanned around, looking for another place to hide, and settled on getting off the runway entirely.

"Okay, gang. We're going back to the garbage hills. Straight ahead. As fast as you can, got it?" Tony told the kids. "Hooper, I'll help you. Okay? Ready?" They got to their feet. Tony picked Hooper up and tucked her sideways under his arm like a duffel bag. "Okay… one, two, three!" And they took off running.

Now out in the open, they made it about ten steps before the Demon Dog spotted them. An easy meal. Ignoring the plasma rifle blasts the rebels were pelting it with, the monster leapt high into the air. It landed hard on the roof of the shelter. The building immediately collapsed like a paper bag under the beast's weight.

Tony and the boys stopped running when the Demon Dog roared at them.

"Stupid, Tony." He said woefully. "Boys. Don't look. Don't turn around." He frantically tried to think of something. He knew he had just gotten them all killed.

Growling, the Demon Dog slowly stalked toward them.

"Oh, kids. I am so sorry."

"PuT mE DoWN." Hooper snarled.

Tony looked at his daughter.

"Daddy? Put me down." She sweetly said in her normal voice.

Scared and confused, Tony did as she asked, gently setting her down on her feet. She turned around and faced the Demon Dog. She tilted her head slightly to the side and took a few steps toward the beast.

"siT." She commanded.

The Demon Dog opened its massive jaws and let out a terrifying roar at the little girl.

As if she'd flicked on her high beams, Hooper's red eyes suddenly blazed brighter. Her hair floated up and blew wildly around. Her chained little body bent forward as she produced an insane, ear-piercing shriek. The demonic blood-curdling scream paused the fighting throughout the runway, as employees and robots froze at the evil sound. The noise dropped Tony and the boys to their knees as they threw their hands over their ears. Her howl was no ordinary loud noise. It was alive with torture and violent pain. It was the cry of thousands of consumed souls and centuries of hate.

The Demon Dog leaned back. It lowered and tucked its massive head, trying to escape the little girl's cry. Trembling and shaking with fear, the monster stumbled and tripped over itself. Hooper stopped shrieking. The terrible scream hung in the air for a few seconds afterwards. As they took their hands off their ears, Tony swore he could hear the echo cackling before it finally faded away. Quint and Brody looked at each other wide eyed.

"nOw… siT!!!" Hooper shouted at the Demon Dog again.

The giant monster immediately got on its stomach. Dominated, it lowered its head in terror.

"Partner! The chain! Tie it up!" Crocky blurted from behind the Demon Dog.

"What?" Tony said.

"Your girl's green chain! Use it on the Demon Dog!" Crocky and The Triangle quickly rushed over as the fighting resumed.

Tony looked over at Hooper. Breathing heavily, her raging red eyes were still staring intensely at the beast. Tony slowly walked towards his daughter.

"Hoop? You okay?" Tony cautiously told her.

"jUSt A SCaReD liTTLe pUP." She growled, still staring.

"Hey… we need your chain. If I take it off of you, can

you be good? Like, would we be safe?" Tony kneeled next to her.

Her head jerked over towards Tony. He jumped and fell backwards.

"dO yoU hAVe MOre gRaNOLa baRs?" She wheezed.

"Uh… yeah. I have some more." Tony said, getting back up.

"i WoULd LiKe sOMe MoRe. PLeaSE."

"Sure. Yeah. You can have some more. If you promise to not hurt us." Tony said, picking the loose end of her chain up off the ground.

"i AGrEE tO YOur tERms." She said as her red eyes dimmed and her hair floated back down to normal.

Tony carefully unwrapped the heavy glowing green chain off of her. As he peeled the last of it away, she stretched. Tony heard her tiny bones crack, and she rubbed her arms. He handed the mystical chain over to The Triangle and Crocky. They carried it over to the still cowering Demon Dog. The beast whimpered as The Triangle anxiously clipped her half of the chain onto its collar. Crocky wrapped its end around the bumper of an overturned transport bus that was burning nearby.

Tony handed Hooper another granola bar.

"tHanK yoU." She said, taking a bite. "wE sHaLL REneGotiAtE wHEn yOu RuN OUt, sKiNbUcKeT."

"Good job, Hooper!" Quint ran up and told her.

"Yeah, you are so great at screaming!" Brody added.

"Let's be careful, it's still dangerous out here." Tony said, herding them together as explosions went off nearby.

Tony saw Vedra and the mouse family appear. Running out of the riot, they joined Crocky and The Triangle at the chained up Demon Dog. Vedra held a broken off Cyber Guard head in his hands. He was saying something to Crocky, but Tony couldn't hear over the noise of the fighting. The Triangle suddenly put her hand to her mouth in shock. Everyone in the group turned and looked at Tony and his kids.

"What's going on?" Quint asked as the group hustled toward them.

"Probably everything is great and there are no other issues." Tony said through gritted teeth.

"My friend, we discovered something. Bad news, I'm afraid." Vedra said, out of breath, stopping in front of Tony. He had a cut across his speckled bald head that was bleeding down his face.

"It's not going well, is it? There's so many Cyber Guards, we're outnumbered, aren't we?" Tony guessed.

"Oh no, we've almost completely retaken this airstrip. There are many more of us. We're going to finish up here and then take the transports to the worksites. We need to free our friends who are in the middle of their shifts. It won't be long now." Vedra smiled. For a second, his face lit up with joy. He didn't let it linger, though, exchanging his brief happiness for concern as he held up the Cyber Guard's robot head.

"What is it?" Tony reluctantly asked.

"This was a captain. We hacked its directory to find the locations of the worksites. But we found something else. It seems there's a phase two no one knew about. The Company knows that garbage won't sustain their numbers, so it seems they've been looking at relocation."

"Relocation?" Tony didn't understand.

"Since they've used up all the natural resources here, they want to move the corporation somewhere where they can... start again." Vedra struggled for words. "They want to feed a new planet to Moc Inc."

"Don't say it." Tony balled his fists up.

"The data says that they chose a new location this morning. A new planet."

"Don't say it." Tony pointed at Vedra's face.

"A planet called Earth."

"And, you said it." Tony rubbed his face.

"All the workers going on strike just put the second phase into action. They've already begun the process." Vedra said with regret.

"Earth? But aren't we like, trillions and billions and gazillions light years or something away from Earth?" Quint asked.

"We sure are, ace." Crocky answered. "But somehow, they must have found out about it."

Then, Tony suddenly remembered back to when they arrived here and saw himself shouting:

"We're from Earth! Haven't you idiots ever heard of it? Earth!"

"What's the matter, Daddy?" Brody asked as Tony bent over and started groaning.

"Are you okay?" Vedra wondered.

"Pickles." Tony said, standing up straight again. He took a deep breath. "Okay. But that's going to be impossible, right? Moc, Inc. is an entire planet. They can't move this entire planet next to Earth."

"If they've changed their Flightway Beam System to transport on a larger scale, it is possible." Crocky calculated. "It would take an unfathomable amount of power to move a planet. Which… is something Moc, Inc. has plenty of."

"So what do we do?" Tony asked.

"We can sabotage the Flightway Beam System. Get to its control center, upload some deconstructing code, and blow it up so it can't finish the transfer." Vedra suggested.

"Then how do we get home?" Quint nervously asked.

The Triangle put her arm reassuringly around his shoulders.

"If we time it just right, we can rush you through the System before it self-destructs." Vedra assured him.

"We'd have to be fast." Crocky said.

"Real fast." Vedra agreed.

"So where is this control center?" Tony asked.

"Up there." Vedra pointed up to the towering skyscraper. "Top of corporate headquarters."

"Okay. Let's go." Tony said.

"Right." Vedra turned to The Triangle. "Spread the word of what's happening. We need contingency plans in place in case we fail. Everyone's going to need to get off the planet quickly if this doesn't work. Tell them to work faster to free everyone and then get loaded onto as many transports as they can."

The Triangle nodded. She turned and gave Quint a loving hug.

"Goodbye, Triangle." Quint said sadly, squeezing her tighter.

"Let's get to a transport." Vedra directed.

"I'm sorry buddy, we've got to get moving." Tony tapped Quint.

"sORry tO SPoiL tHe MOMent, bUt i wOULd liKE aNOtheR gRAnoLA bAr!" Hooper snarled.

TONY'S TO DO LIST:

1. Help sabotage space teleporting machine.
2. Keep evil corporation from feeding Earth to their energy pit.
3. Hurry to the space teleporting machine before it's destroyed.

4. Give Hooper the purple crystal thingy two more times every thirty minutes to get rid of the space demon inside her.
5. Help Quint with his 'all about me' school project.
6. Get back home.

THEY WERE SITTING in the back of one of the transport buses, bouncing around as it bumpily hovered into the sky when Crocky started beeping.

"Time for your daughter's second treatment, boss." Crocky told Tony, then returned to the front of the transport where Vedra was piloting.

"Thanks." Tony called out and slid his backpack off his shoulders. He removed the metallic cylinder and unscrewed the top. He lifted the large purple crystal out of the tube and sidestepped down the center aisle over to where Hooper was sitting. She was looking out of a window and holding a granola bar in each hand. "Hoop?" He leaned down.

"wHaT?" she said, a chunk of granola falling out of her mouth.

"Medicine time, kiddo." Tony told her. "Now, sit still, okay?"

"BuT…" she protested. But Tony didn't give her the chance and dragged the purple crystal from left to right across her forehead. "Arrrggg!" She growled and squirmed. He put his other hand on her shoulder to steady her.

Tony felt the crystal getting heavier as it made its way slowly across her forehead. It pulsed brightly as it was being applied. When he finished, he pulled the crystal away, and it stopped flashing. Now, its purple color was much duller than before. Tony looked into the crystal and saw whatever had been swimming around inside it was larger. It took up most of the space inside and looked like a chicken ready to bust out of an egg.

"Daddy?" Hopper said in a sleepy voice.

"Hoop? Hoop, are you okay?" Tony said excitedly and leaned forward. Her face looked clearer of rashes and pock marks. Her eyes were still red, but it was more of just a glaze.

"Daddy, what is happening?" Hooper said, confused. "What is… gOINg oN?" she suddenly belched. "CaN'T geT riD oF Me YeT, pOPs!" The hoarse voice said. "Who said that?" Hooper switched back.

Tony shook his head and put the crystal back into its tube. He screwed the lid back on and tucked it into the backpack.

"Daddy, why am I eating granola bars?" Hooper asked in her normal voice. "bECauSE wE liKE tHEm noW!" she answered herself in her growl and took a bite out of each one.

"Now there are two Hoopers?" Brody was kneeling in his seat, looking at them from over his headrest.

"Yeah, I don't get it either, Brody." Tony walked by him and turned him around so he was sitting. "I think we're getting closer to normal Hooper though."

"That's good, Daddy. Two Hoopers are so many Hoopers." Brody told him and fiddled with his blanket.

"I think so, too." Tony said. He continued to walk down the bus's aisle towards the front. Bouncing around as it roughly cut through the sky, higher and higher. Tony passed Quint, who was sitting with his legs pulled up to his chest, scribbling into his notebook balanced on his thighs. "What are you adding now?" Tony asked him.

"Road trips." Quint motioned around the bus. "Travel. That kind of thing."

"Good thinking. Keep up the excellent work." He smiled at Quint.

Tony kept shuffling towards the cockpit where Vedra and Crocky were. In the front seats of the bus, the family of mice creatures had found a first aid kit onboard and were patching one another up. One had a dressing around her leg and another had her arm in a makeshift sling. They were wrapping the third mouse's waist tightly. The last mouse was fixing her own ear with gauze and preparing a bandage. Tony leaned up into the driver's seat, his head next to where Crocky floated. As he looked out the windshield, he finally saw it for the first time.

"Whoa." Tony said, not finding any other words. "Is... is that it?"

"That's it." Crocky said.

Trying to reach the top of the colossal corporate building, the transport bus had climbed so high into the green sky that you could finally see the infamous energy pit of Moc, Inc. It was the most massive thing Tony had ever seen. A crack in the world. It was so long that Tony couldn't see where it began or ended, it just went on and on. From this height it looked hundreds of miles wide, but Tony knew it would probably be more if they were closer to it. There were huge conveyors and cranes positioned all alongside the pit, constantly dumping trash down into it. In between its cliffs, running down the center, was a thick, churning white light. Pure energy flowing like a river of lava.

"That's terrifying." Tony finally said, still staring down at it.

"That's power." Crocky told him.

"Found it." Vedra said, pushing a button on the

console. "The scan's finished and I've located the Flightway Beam System's control center." He touched some more screens and flicked some switches. Tony saw that the mouse family had bandaged up the cut across Vedra's head. "Right there." Vedra pointed out the windshield at a section of the building near the very top.

"Okay, good. Great." Tony said. He squinted at the area Vedra had pointed at. "Where do we land?" He asked.

"Well... yeah, that's the thing. There's really no simple way to do this." Vedra replied. He turned to Tony. "You may want to go sit down." He warned.

"Why not?" Tony mumbled. "Kids! Hold on to something!" Tony turned and shouted as he hustled back to a seat by Brody and Hooper.

Vedra sped the transport up, and it jumped faster into the air. Tony fell into a seat across from Brody and pulled the boy over next to him. The bus transport leveled out when Vedra reached the height he was looking for. They carefully circled around, and Vedra positioned the bus directly at the skyscraper.

"Here we go!" Vedra shouted, and then jammed the flight stick forward.

The mouse family huddled together and squeaked loudly.

"Woo-hoo!" Quint raised his arms.

The transport bus sped faster and faster at the building.

"Oh no! This one's going to hurt!" Hooper yelled. "oH YeAH! tHiS ONe'S gOiNG To HuRt!!!" she yelled again.

Tony pulled Brody in tight and tensed his body up as the transport bus crashed into the building. Everyone bounced into the air as the bus violently burst its way through the walls. Sparks flew and glass shattered as the crushed transport flipped on its side and scraped across the control room floor. As momentum gave out, they skidded to an abrupt stop.

Tony was on his side, covering up Brody. The little boy's eyes were as wide as half dollars, and he had a death grip on his lion blanket. He looked up at his dad and scowled.

"Wasn't my idea." Tony told him. They were lying on the walls of the bus, which had now become its floor. Tony carefully crawled to his knees, trying to avoid the jagged metal and broken glass. He called out for his other two kids.

"Quint? Hoop? Where are you?" Tony shouted.

"I'm good." Quint fell out of his sideways seat and gave the thumbs up.

"Here, Daddy." Hooper coughed. "That was terrible… nO! iT WaS aMAziNg!"

"Anyone hurt?" Crocky floated back.

"I don't think so." Tony answered as he gathered up Hooper.

"That's good. Because I don't think they're happy to see us!" Vedra said, pointing out the shattered windshield at the Cyber Guards gathering around the destroyed bus.

Without hesitation, the mouse family all dived out of the broken windows with their plasma rods blazing away at the Cyber Guards. Following their lead, Vedra rolled out of the front window, tossing one of his grenades as his plasma rod fired. The bomb exploded and blew away an entire platoon of Cyber Guards. Vedra and the mouse family ducked behind various chunks of the broken wall, trying to eliminate the remaining robots.

"Come on, friend-o's! Out this way!" Crocky announced and led Tony and the kids out of the transport bus through a hole in its bottom.

They crawled out just as the shooting stopped. With all

the Cyber Guards taken care of, Tony helped his kids to their feet, and Vedra hustled over to the bank of computer terminals. Crocky joined him as Vedra started hitting buttons and typing commands. Vedra ripped a piece of the computer open and yanked out a set of cables.

"Start uploading the code." Vedra told Crocky as he connected the cable to the floating robot. "I'll see if I can slow the system down to buy us some time."

"Uploading now." Crocky told him.

The kids wandered around as the mouse family patrolled the destroyed room. Against the side wall was a tall elevator door. Suddenly, the buttons lit up and beeped. The mice panicked, loudly squeaking and backing away.

"What is that?" Tony asked.

"Executive elevators. They're here to supervise the planet's transfer to Earth." Vedra looked nervous.

"Who? Who's coming to supervise?"

"Managers." Vedra gulped.

The elevator doors opened and three giant shapes slowly glided out onto the control room floor. They had no faces or what you would call a body. Dark as night, they were blank angular creatures that constantly shifted and altered their shapes, like shadows produced by a flickering fire. They stretched about twelve feet tall and towered over the mouse family that were pointing weapons up at them.

"Okay, those things are freaky looking." Brody pointed and said.

"Managers. They get rich off of the work we do. To show off status and power, they upgrade their bodies as much as their wealth will allow." Vedra continued to type into the terminals. "Eventually, they get rid of their body entirely and have their consciousness uploaded into shape shifting planes of floating dark matter. It's very fashionable in the corporate world." Vedra explained the creature's otherworldly appearance.

The Manager in the middle lifted what Tony assumed was an arm to what Tony assumed was its head. Suddenly, there was clanging footsteps coming from down a hallway entry. It had called more Cyber Guards. Everyone scrambled to hide as the robots entered the room. The mouse family turned back to Vedra and squeaked something. He took his grenade bandolier off his shoulders and slid it across the floor to them. A mouse snatched the bandolier and dragged it along as they all shot. They ran towards the attacking Cyber Guards, driving them back into the hallway. One of Vedra's grenades flew into the crowd of robots.

"Kids! Down!" Tony shouted.

They all took cover again as the bomb blasted the Cyber Guards completely out of the control room. The mouse family squeaked loudly as they charged ahead. Blasting away at the Cyber Guards, they chased them down the hallway and out of sight.

Everyone stood back up. The Managers hadn't moved an inch during the brief skirmish.

"I need more time," Crocky's voice squawked.

"So do I." Vedra added. He lowered his voice and pulled Tony closer. "They can call for more Cyber Guards and who knows what else. You need to buy us some time." He told Tony.

"Buy time? How? I'm betting The Butt Song won't work on..." Tony froze when he saw The Managers had moved. They were now standing directly over his kids.

The shapes and angles of the dark figures changed slowly and smoothly as they examined the children. Their bodies produced a constant humming white noise. The one in the middle spoke, its voice a jumbled mess of uneven sounds that clattered together. The kids looked at each other, confused.

"Excuse me, but what are you saying?" Hooper asked. "YeAH YoU LAva LaMP lOOkinG weirDo, nO onE CAn uNDerStaND yOU." Her less subtle other half assisted.

The Manager spoke again. It was a noise that stopped and started. Sounds stumbled over one another, like frantically scanning radio stations, never staying on one for more than half a second. The noise got more and more chaotic before it finally seemed to find the right frequency.

"… reach out… touch base… personal brand…" Its voice was a distant whisper that echoed between loud bursts of static. "… it is what it is…"

The kids looked at each other again.

"It is what it is?" Quint wrinkled his nose.

"… circle back…" the one in the middle said.

"… circle back…"

"… circle back…" the other two echoed.

"… reach out… touch base… it is what it is…" the middle one whispered again.

"Like, what is I? Are you asking who we are?"

"… hit the mark… bottom line… we have an 'ask'… reach out… values… culture… bring to the table… at this time…"

"You gotta be kidding me." Tony said. "Zillions of miles from Earth. Far beyond space and time. An entire universe of different species and cultures. And still, all bosses still talk the same way."

"Uh, well I'm Quint. And uh, I guess I bring to the table, I mean, who I am is uh…" He anxiously squeezed the rolled up notebook in his hand. His eyebrows raised in realization. He opened his notebook. He read aloud. "My name is Quint and here are some things all about me."

"Keep working. Quint's given me an idea." Tony told

Vedra and Crocky. He smoothed his hair and smiled as he walked over to the kids and the creatures. "Mr. Quint? I'm sorry, did I miss the meet and greet?" Tony said in a fake, schmoozing voice. "So sorry, I'm late, I had to put out some fires."

"... put out some fires... networking... touch base... engagement..." The Manager replied.

"How you doing fellas, I'm Tony, Mr. Quint's personal assistant. This is his core team, Mr. Brody and Ms. Hooper. They handle brand management and metrics." Tony said with his hands on the kid's shoulders.

".... brand... metrics... triage... all-hands..." The Manager's attention grabbed, its changing shape stood up straight.

"That's right." Tony continued. He gently took Brody's lion blanket from him and winked. "Look, all of this is time-sensitive so I'm just going to drill down and cut to the chase." Tony turned to The Managers, folding the blanket. "Mr. Quint can see that you're having some, well, staffing issues at the moment. We see you've got all hands on deck out there. Now, don't worry, we know how it is." Tony leaned down, putting Brody's blanket around Quint's neck. He tied it. "Too many balls in the air. Motivation gets off message. Team-building exercises and workshops are no longer yielding. Looks to us you may need to try something else to move the needle." He finished adjusting the boy's crude new necktie.

".... mission critical... hard stop... circle back..."

"... circle back..."

"... circle back..." the other two Managers repeated.

"... forward planning... pivot... new normal..." The Manager said changing shape again.

"We see that. You're undertaking a complete company wide relocation? In this economy? You sure you're in the black enough for that? Looks like to us, you're bleeding capital." Tony put his hands in his pockets and clicked his tongue. "I tell you what. Why don't we just pull the trigger? Mr. Quint is ready to make you an offer for the whole thing. Lock, stock."

"… buy in… integration… unpack… optics… analytics…" The Manager replied.

"I think once you see what Mr. Quint can bring to the table, you're going to find it's an easy win." Tony said and motioned for Quint to hand him his notebook. Quint handed it over. The other two kids were not sure of what was going on and just quietly watched. Behind them, Vedra and Crocky continued to upload and reprogram as fast as they could.

"… unpack… optics… analytics… data-driven…" The Manager asked again.

"Let's see, here's just a taste." Tony opened the worn notebook. "As a leader in creative management and team-building skills, Mr. Quint has run several successful independent juice bars, the most popular in the region. My friend, they literally stop traffic!" Tony said enthusiastically. "What else?" Tony flipped a few pages. "As a former successful athlete himself, he's still heavily invested in the local franchise teams. Mr. Quint is very active in high-profile humanitarian and charity activities. He's traveled the world as an internationally famous entertainment superstar." Tony closed the notebook dramatically. "I didn't even mention that he's a tenured medical expert! I mean, what else do you want? You guys get to dump a sinking ship and get rich doing it. Mr. Quint is your white knight."

Quint wiggled the knot in his tie and beamed with pride.

"… check the right boxes… intuitive… influencer…

efficiency… engagement… diversity…" The Manager in the center rambled. "… win-win…"

"Oh yeah, I think it's definitely a win-win." Tony nodded. "Here, why don't you run this upstairs to the big guys. See what they think. We could get this deal done and have some margaritas sitting in front of us by sundown." Tony held out Quint's notebook.

The Manager in the center didn't reply. It just stood there, shifting its shape. It stuck an angle out and was about to take the notebook. Suddenly, it stopped.

"… hard stop… content… disruptive… synergy… in the weeds…" It pulled its shape back into place. "… put a pin in it… table discussion… circle back…"

"… circle back…"

"… circle back…" the other two said.

Tony gulped, realizing it was rethinking the proposal. Still holding out Quint's notebook, he could feel his hand sweating. If these things called in any more Cyber Guards, they would be done for. He glanced back at Vedra and Crocky. They were still working. He had one more idea.

"Fine. You know what?" Tony pulled the notebook back and tucked it under his arm. "It's my fault. I didn't know you guys weren't looking to move up." Tony said in a disappointed voice, "This proposal is a golden ticket to some real organic growth within The Company. It shows some real buzz and bleeding edge. I mean, anyone who brought the big guys this gift wrapped, would surely shoot to the top in no time. Especially if you thought of yourself as some kind of subordinate." Tony casually scratched his nose and tried to subtly point at the two Managers on the ends. "You could leapfrog the ones in front of you. Bypass the usual chain of command. Why wait? You cold just take what's yours." Tony said.

"... values... frictionless... core competency... disruptive..." The Manager spoke.

"... circle back..."

"... circle back..." the other two Managers suddenly said. "... back-of-the-envelope idea... table the conversation..." The Manager on the left said.

"... hand holding... take action... take offline..." The one on the right continued.

They grew two sharp angles out of themselves and drove them into The Manager in the center. Tony stepped backwards and pushed the kids away. The Manager wailed and spasmed as its dark body filled with blue light. Tony and kids covered their eyes as the light got brighter and brighter and The Manager screamed louder and louder. Its entire shape filled with light, and then it popped like a bubble. The light faded away. The Manager was gone.

Their sharp angles formed back into themselves. The one on the left extended a block out at Tony.

"... buck the trend... game changer... forward planning... new normal..."

Tony cautiously handed over the notebook. It greedily snatched it from him.

"... paradigm shift... reach out... bring to the table... crunch the numbers..." The Manager on the right told him.

"You do that. Why don't you go present the proposal?" Tony cleared his throat. "We'll be here making some calls and checking in."

"... checking in..."

"... checking in..."

"Yep, right here. When you get your answer, why don't you circle back and let us know."

"... circle back..."

"... circle back..." they said, then they glided back to the executive elevators.

"Look forward to working with you, gentlemen." Quint said in a grownup voice.

The Managers entered the elevators, and the doors shut. After a second, the kids let out a loud cheer of victory.

Tony let out an enormous sigh of relief. He felt like he was going to throw up.

"Daddy that worked! You did it!" Quint jumped up.

"No buddy, it was you. I got the idea from you." Tony said, hugging Quint and kissing the top of his head. "Great job."

"You're the boss now, Quint!" Brody patted Quint on the back.

"Yeah, I always wanted to own a power company." Quint said proudly, taking Brody's blanket tie off and handing it back to his brother. "You can be vice president!"

"Oh yeah, that sounds amazing." Brody snuggled the blanket.

"What about me?" Hooper asked. "cAn wE Be JAniToRS?"

"Of course!" Quint laughed.

"We got it!" Vedra suddenly shouted. "It's done."

"You stopped the transfer?" Tony ran over to them.

"No, but we've slowed it down. I've just finished uploading a deconstruction code into the Flightways Beam System," Crocky said as Vedra unhooked it from the computer. "Its navigation programming is going to corrupt and eventually short circuit."

"And when that happens the system will fail to the point of self destruction." Vedra finished. "It's going to blow itself up."

"But there's time to get us out first, right?" Tony asked.

"Just barely, pally. But we have to get to the actual transport units right now." Crocky said, floating past him.

"Where do we go?" Tony asked, waving the kids over to him. "Is it close?"

"Let me see." Vedra said typing into the computer. "Oh."

"No, no, no. Don't 'oh'. Please, don't. Where is the teleporting thing?" Tony barked.

"It's on the other side of the pit." Vedra grimaced. "All the way on the other side."

"And how are we supposed to get over there?" Tony shouted. "Your park job kind of trashed our ride!" Tony pointed to the crashed transport bus.

"I know! I know! Hold on!" Vedra typed some more on the terminal. "Okay, here. This will work. Under the building, there's a maintenance junction. They have a small rail station." He turned back to Tony. "There's a track that runs across the pit. A bridge. They use it to send supplies over to the other side. We can take that across."

"You're sure?" Tony stared at him.

"We will get you home, my friend. I promise." Vedra said.

"We can take this down, buddies!" Crocky hacked the executive elevator doors. They beeped and slid open.

"I get to push the button!" Hooper yelled. "nO fAiR! i wANt A tURn!" She yelled again.

The kids all ran into the elevator.

"Come on. We must hurry." Vedra said. He led Tony to the elevator.

"You know, Vedra, now that you're out of a job, if you need a reference for your resume, just let me know." Tony told him.

"No, I think I shall retire." Vedra said, stopping to pick up two new plasma rods. "What about you? I heard the way you talked to those Managers. Sounds to me like you've got some experience in the corporate hustle?" He checked the weapons. "Talking in meaningless circles, selling them something they don't need, turning them against one another." They stepped into the elevator.

"What, those things? That's not a corporate hustle. That's just parenting." Tony replied.

The elevator doors shut.

TONY'S TO DO LIST:

1. Cross a very dangerous bottomless energy pit.

2. Hurry to the space teleporting machine before it's destroyed.

3. Give Hooper the purple crystal thingy one more time to get rid of the space demon inside of her.

4. Help Quint start his 'all about me' project over again.

5. Get back home.

THEY COULD FEEL the heat before the elevator doors opened.

"Daddy, it's so hot down here!" Brody moaned as they stepped out.

The elevator had taken them beneath the planet's surface, a few miles below the edge of the pit. Nestled on the cliff's side, the maintenance junction was a station built right into the hollowed out rock. Walking off the elevator into a sauna, they stepped onto a platform. Tony saw the rail bridge that would take them across the pit. Tony thought the bridge's track was probably around twelve feet wide, about a single highway lane. He looked to his right and saw that the elevated bridge stretched far out of the station and ran to the other side of the pit. It seemed to be held up by an engineering magic trick.

In the station, hovering a couple of feet off the tracks, were heat scorched mine carts lined up in a row. Just ahead of the carts were a few open air vehicles that looked like old time railway trolleys. The kind you had to pump the lever up and down to get to move. These hovering ones looked a bit more advanced.

"iT's nOT thAT baD." Hooper said, fanning her hand in front of her face. "It's really bad." She said again.

"Just hang in there, we're almost home." Tony told her. He leaned over to Vedra. "We're almost home, right?"

"Yes, the Flightways Beam System is directly across from us, on the other side of the pit." Vedra pointed. "They buried it down here to prevent escapees from easily getting to it."

"I can't see that far, so I'll take your word for it." Tony squinted down at the bridge. He looked around the station. "No guards?"

"Probably up top, fighting." Vedra told him. "Come on. Let's get moving. We have little time." He ushered them onto the trolley in the line's front. Crocky had already floated on board and was remotely linking himself to the navigation.

"I'm in control, amigos! Let's hit the road!" The robot squawked.

"All aboard!" Quint called out as he stepped onto the trolley. Everyone was going to fit, but it was going to be a cramped ride. And with no doors or safety bars around them, a dangerous one. Tony made the kids scrunch together and sit crisscross applesauce on the vehicle's floor. He knelt behind them, putting his arms as far around them as he could to act as some kind of protection from falling out. Vedra kneeled behind Tony, and

Crocky bobbed up and down in front, controlling the trolley.

"Here we go!" Crocky shouted and the trolley lurched forward. Slowly, it crept towards the edge of the station. Tony squeezed the pile of kids in front of him. The seconds right before the trolley left the safety of the platform was the most scared he'd been all day. The trolley rolled smoothly onto the suspended bridge. It was unnerving to ride so openly and exposed on such a high bridge. It terrified Tony they'd slip out and fall. The suspended bridge was also too thin to give Tony any peace of mind. The trolley could easily drift off the sides.

Despite Tony's anxieties, Crocky was doing a good job of maintaining steady control of the vehicle as it hovered over the tracks. The trolley rolled along, hitting the speed of a full throttled golf cart. The breeze produced by the zooming trolley offered no relief from the temperature, instead it just blew hot air on everyone's faces. The farther they traveled over the bridge, the hotter it got. The blazing heat generated from the pit's energy blasted up at them like a furnace.

Tony wiped his slick forehead and looked down into the pit. The bright, white fiery light inside seemed to swirl and churn. The rhythmic and choppy waves of energy mesmerized Tony as it crashed over itself. For a few calm minutes, he fixated on the wonder.

"You're sitting on my hand, Hooper!" Quint yelled.

"Ugh! Sorry! I'm getting squished!" Hooper defended herself. She shoved her shoulder into him. "sCOOt oVeR biG bUtT!"

"Everyone! Stop!" The squirming kids snapped Tony out of his daze.

"Yes, we must be very safe, my little friends. Not a good idea to have an accident out here." Vedra warned them.

"If one were to fall into the pit, you would be gone forever."

"Forever? Gone?" Brody repeated with wide eyes.

"Even if the heat didn't get you, no one knows if the pit has a bottom. You could fall for eternity." Vedra said and wiped the sweat off his bald head. "Or it could convert you into more energy. No one knows for sure, but it's not good."

"Did everyone hear that?" Tony squeezed them. "Let's not get eaten by the pit. Sit still. We're so close to getting home."

A plasma blast ricocheted off the back of the trolley. The vehicle briefly wobbled and swerved before Crocky got it back under control. Tony and Vedra turned around and saw another trolley many miles behind them, leaving the station.

"I've got to stop saying things out loud." Tony said.

"We need to go faster!" Vedra yelled, twisting around and lifting his plasma rod.

"I'm trying! I'm trying!" Crocky panicked.

Tony looked harder and saw the shapes of Cyber Guards driving and hanging off the pursuing trolley. Standing tall in the back were the other two Managers. Their black shifting shapes stood out boldly against all the white light.

"Quint, I don't think the deal went through." Tony turned forward and gathered the kids together tighter.

"Pickles!" Quint cussed as Tony leaned over to shield them. "Well, they can have fun being the CEO of sucking."

More plasma blasts went off all round their trolley. Crocky expertly avoided them as he found a little more speed for the fleeing vehicle. Vedra returned fire rapidly at the attackers. One of his shots knocked a Cyber Guard off its trolley and down into the pit.

"… circle back…"

"… circle back…" The Managers angrily grumbled.

"How much farther?" Tony shouted up at Crocky.

"We're a little over halfway across, but there is still a lot to go, comrade!"

More blasts scattered all around them. The trolley shimmied and shook, but kept on going. Vedra continued to take aim and shoot back, hitting another robot.

"… team building… all-hands…" A Manager ordered the Cyber Guards. The robots immediately switched to firing their weapons all at once.

"Incoming!" Vedra yelled as he saw a thick wave of plasma blasts arching through the air towards their trolley.

The blasts rained down around the trolley. There were too many of them for Crocky to maneuver around. Zig-zagging too aggressively, the vehicle swerved sideways and tipped over. The trolley flung its passengers forward into the air, just as a cluster of plasma blasts collided with it. Tony didn't hear the explosion. Everything went silent.

Airborne, he struggled to maintain his grasp on the kids as the impact's force pulled them away. They drifted apart from him. His brain frantically tried to process flying, getting a grip on his kids, and where they were going to land. If they were going to land.

"… tee up… drill down… move the needle…" A Manager instructed.

The Cyber Guards sped up their trolley faster.

Quint and Brody landed first. They hit the bridge hard and rolled. Tony was clutching Hooper by the back of her shirt and yanked her into his arms just as he spun onto his back and slammed down onto the bridge. Pain shot him back upright, rushing through his body as he pushed Hooper off of him. He quickly refocused and looked for Quint and Brody. He saw them a few feet ahead, getting to their feet, rubbing their knees and elbows.

"Boys! Are you okay?" Tony shouted as he shakily got up.

"Help!" a voice called out.

"Daddy!" Quint pointed at the space between them. Vedra had fallen off the side and was desperately trying to get a hold of something. Tony dived over and grabbed Vedra's hand before he slipped further off the bridge. Gritting his teeth, Tony struggled, trying to pull Vedra up. As he got higher, Vedra threw his leg back onto the bridge's ledge and helped push himself along. Tony dragged him the rest of the way. They got to their knees and gasped for air.

"Thank... you." Vedra managed.

"They're coming, sport!" Crocky appeared. He had a big dent on his side.

"Run kids, run!" Tony yelled.

They sprinted as fast as they could down the rest of the track. Its end was in sight, but there was still a lot of bridge to cover on foot. Tony tried to scoot the kids along faster. Farther and farther they ran.

Plasma blasts scattered all around them. Vedra looked behind him and saw The Managers were getting closer, making their way to the burning wreckage of the crashed trolley. Vedra suddenly realized he no longer had a weapon.

"The little kids!" Tony called over to him. Vedra scooped up Hooper, and Tony grabbed Brody, his blanket flapping behind them like a cape as they ran faster. Quint put his head down and sprinted harder. Everyone's feet pounded the tracks, pushing themselves forward. More plasma bursts exploded in the air and on the ground next to them.

Crocky beeped. Hooper's alarm. Her last crystal dose.

Tony wheezed, trying to process what was happening. What should he do? Could it wait? Would they catch up to them first? Would they miss their window before their ride home exploded? He sped up next to Vedra.

"Trade me!" He yelled. Panting, they slowed to a jog and then came to a stop.

"You sure?" Vedra gulped.

"I don't know what I'm doing." Tony told him. "Here, take him and keep going." He set Brody down and reached into his backpack. Vedra put Hooper in front of Tony and picked up Brody. They ran off, trying to catch up to Quint and Crocky.

He took the metallic tube out. It had small dents in it from their crash. He quickly unscrewed the lid and tossed it aside. Turning the tube upside down, he let the dull purple crystal drop into his hand. He glanced over at the Managers approaching. They were right up on the burning trolley wreckage. He pulled Hooper closer.

"Hold still, baby." He told her. She was crying.

"Daddy?" Hooper blubbered. "DoN't StOP rUNNing."

Tony dragged the purple crystal across her forehead. Hooper winced in pain but didn't make a sound. Halfway across her forehead, the rash and scarring on her face faded completely away.

The Managers crashed through the flaming wreckage of the trolley. Flame and debris flew everywhere as they continued to rush forward.

Hooper's eyes were no longer red as he pulled the crystal off the end of her forehead.

"Daddy!" She smiled.

His arm holding the crystal sank to the ground. Suddenly, he could barely lift it. Looking at the now dark and cloudy crystal, Tony saw it had cracks running along the sides. It shook.

"Run, Hooper, run!" Tony told her. She took off.

Closer and closer, The Managers gained on him. The crystal cracked more. It shook harder and harder. Between the weight and the shaking, Tony almost dropped it. Instead, with all the strength he had left in him, he threw the crystal as hard as he could at the attacking trolley. The crystal twirled as it flew. The Managers got closer. The crystal shattered on the tracks a few feet in front of them. Tony turned and ran away. A purple mist flowed out of the broken crystal. As the mist thickened and spread, it took shape. It grew arms and claws... and glowing red eyes. An astral version of the demon rose in front of the speeding trolley.

"... circle back..."

"... circle back..." The Managers said.

When they drove into the demon's purple essence, it wrapped itself around the vehicle. Tony turned around to see the trolley rise high into the air and then slam back down onto the bridge. The vehicle exploded in a burst of fire. The demon ripped a robotic Cyber Guard apart. A Manager was trying to crawl away from the evil mist and burning flames, but a purple arm reached out and dragged it back. Tony faced forward and kept on running. He could hear the furious roar of the monster and the terrified screams of its prey.

Tony felt the bridge move. He heard another explosion. He looked back and saw the misty demon violently tearing into a Cyber Guard. The surrounding bridge burned. As the demon slammed a Manager down, Tony felt the bridge shake harder. He stopped. There was a loud crack.

"Daddy! What's happening?" Quint yelled at Tony. They also stopped running when the bridge moved. Unsure of what was going to happen, Vedra set Brody down next to Quint and ran back to hurry Hooper along. Crocky hovered above the boys and they watched closely.

The demon pounced on a Cyber Guard, and there was an even louder crack. The bridge around the chaos suddenly broke. Snapping under the weight of the demon and its carnage, the bridge collapsed. The demon roared as it slid down the fallen piece of bridge, the burning trolley and remains of the Cyber Guards and Managers tumbling along with it. The hanging piece of bridge broke away completely and everything on it fell down into the energy pit. The bridge stopped shaking, but it was now missing an enormous chunk of itself. Tony's half of the bridge remained stable.

Boom! As he jogged towards the others, powerful geysers of hot air started popping up along the sides of the bridge. The pit was loudly erupting with bursting gusts of heat. Boom! Tony had to throw his arms over his face as the blistering energy blew over him. It was like the pit was burping after a satisfyingly enormous meal. Boom!

"The self destruct?" Tony waved the hot air away from his face and asked Vedra when he caught up to them. His sides were throbbing from all the running. "Are we going to make it?" He huffed, taking huge gulps of air.

"It's going to be close!" Vedra shouted over another loud boom of energy hiccups.

"Come on." Tony herded the three sweaty kids together and pushed them forward Completely drained, they struggled to keep going.

"I'll get there first and get the machine prepped!" Crocky floated back between them. Then he rocketed forward, past everyone else, and down the rest of the bridge.

On they ran, getting closer to the other side. Soaking wet with sweat and caked in grime, they exhaustedly pushed forward. The end of the bridge was finally in sight.

"Keep going, Hooper. Good job, Quint." Tony tried to motivate. Brody had fallen behind them. He was worn out and lazily dragging his lion blanket between his little legs. "Brody, come on, buddy. Hurry."

"I'm coming, Daddy. I'm coming." Brody whined.

"You're going to get tangled up in that blanket, buddy! Pick it up."

"Here, Daddy, you hold it." Brody balled the blanket up.

"No Brody, don't throw it!"

Boom!

Another huge gust of air erupted. The hot wind grabbed the blanket and blew it up into the air.

"No." Tony whispered.

"Daddy! My blanket!"

"No!" Tony jumped to grab it as it sailed above him. But it was too high.

Boom!

Another burst went off and tossed the blanket higher and to the left. Twisting like a kite, it spiraled over the side of the bridge.

"Daddy! Get it, Daddy! Get it!" Brody cried.

Tony ran to the edge of the bridge as the blanket floated far past where he could reach. Tony dropped to his knees and stretched himself out as far as his body would safely allow. The blanket slowly sank lower and lower down into the pit until it blended into its white light.

Tony turned back to Brody.

"No! No! My lion blanket! Daddy, my lion blanket! It's gone! Daddy, my lion blanket!" Brody wailed.

Tony scrambled over and lifted him up. He started running again. Brody dug himself into Tony's body. He could feel the boy thrashing in his arms.

"Daddy! No! Daddy! I don't want it to be gone! I don't want it to be forever gone!" Brody cried hysterically. He reached behind Tony, grabbing desperately at the empty air. Tony squeezed the boy tight and ran faster.

SHE UNLOCKED the front door and stepped inside.

"Hello?" she sang out. There was no response. "Hel-lo?" She said again, setting her bag down. "Nobody missed me, huh? Oh, I see. Fine." She remarked as she shook her heels off and let them clatter on the floor.

So, they weren't home. The van was in the driveway. Maybe he walked them to the playground. She looked at her phone and didn't see any texts about it. She messaged him she was home and asked what they were up to.

She walked into the kitchen and opened the fridge to get her water bottle. As she chugged her drink, she saw the bag of tortilla chips laying on the counter. She guessed it was going to be tacos tonight. She set her water bottle next to the bag and messaged him again, asking if he wanted her to get them started. While she waited for him to respond, she debated opening the bag of chips now for a pre dinner snack. The debate was short as she ripped open the bag and had some.

As she took another sip of water, a very bright flash of light flickered through the windows. Weird, she thought. It was clear outside. No clouds. Why would there be light-ning? The front door opened.

"Hello?" she sang and walked to the door. She saw them and stopped. "On no? What happened?"

Quint and Hooper said nothing. They looked terribly sad and had tears running down their cheeks. Tony stood there, his face drained of color, clutching a loudly sobbing Brody in his arms.

"What's going on? Is everything okay?" She went to Tony. She tried to pull the bawling child off of him, but his body was incredibly tense. His face was buried in Tony's shoulder. "Hey? Hey?" she said softly to Brody and rubbed his back. "What's the matter, baby?"

Brody heard her and finally let go of Tony. He spun around, his face a wet, snotty mess. He jumped into her arms and started crying even harder.

"Oh, my goodness, Brody. Baby, what happened?" She asked sweetly.

"It's gone, Mommy! It's gone!" He wailed. "It's gone, Mommy!"

She hugged her boy tight and rocked him side to side as he cried uncontrollably. She looked over at Tony, her eyes desperate for answers.

"I was trying to do too much." Tony's voice quivered. "It just got away from me." He began to cry.

She reached her arm out and pulled him to her and Brody. Quint and Hooper threw their arms around their parent's legs and squeezed.

"It just got away from me." Tony cried.

TONY'S TO DO LIST:

    1. Get Anna.

THE END.

PART VIII

Next Time

NEXT TIME

"We've been searching for you a lot time, Princess Hooper!" The fairy said.

"You know, the is not as much fun when the floor is literally lava."

"Can we keep him?" Brody pointed to the Frankenstein.

"Uh, ask your mother."

"Why would someone steal the world's supply of yellow fish crackers?"

"I'm sorry if I disappointed. TV and movies in the 80s promised me that living with an alien would be way more wacky than this."

"Is this what you do all day while I'm at work?"

COMING SOON:

LIVE. LAUGH. RUN.

FULLTIMETONY SEASON TWO

Author's Note

I started a stay-at-home dad blog about a year into staying home with the kids. It was supposed to force me to write and give me a void to scream into about what I was experiencing, both good and bad. But I got three entries in when I realized that I had no advice or tips when it came to parenting (Feed them and keep away from fires) and my days were not exciting enough to document (Three spit ups in one afternoon! Target had a sale! We saw a cool looking bird!) and finally, that it was becoming yet another social media personality that I simply did not have the energy to maintain.

It was much more fun to make things up. So the kids and I went to other planets, fought ancient evil monsters, and ran away from werewolves. And I got to make really dumb jokes. I took the opportunity to work some stuff out about parenting with anxiety and having a child with Autism Spectrum Disorder. I wrote about the spectacular highs and depressing lows of being a stay-at-home parent. I've been smiling since I started writing these. It is a dream made reality. With dumber jokes.

But I didn't do it alone.

I've had an army of people supporting me while I did this and also cheering me on my whole life. So if it's okay, I would like to thank just a few very special people who helped us travel through time and space. I promise I won't be long and then you can be done.

Barbara Burgess is the reason you are reading this. She held me down and beat the stories out of me with loving motivation and inspiration and one of those bats with the nail in it. She's the one who got them off the blog and into more people's hands. She sends texts at like two-thirty in the afternoon that just say "Let's Gooooo!" and make you want to take the world on. I am honored to have her friendship and her help with these. I also want to thank the rest of my fellow Pilgrim Fowl Press criminals, Annette Williams McCann and Matt Dyer. Two brilliant and supportive artists who have talent that makes me rage with jealousy.

My wonderfully supportive family is just scary enough to be afraid of if I don't mention them. My parents, Richard and Karen Gruenwald, this is all their fault. Also the amazingly encouraging and kind Kerry and Kathy Buckingham. I want to thank my sisters and brothers: Amanda Gruenwald and Luke Imeson, Jacky and Brandon Bottomley, Johnathon Gruenwald, Brad Buckingham, Traci and Aaron Gaspar, and Jamie Buckingham and Justin Baker. And of course, my little buddies Wes and Joey. I love you all so much.

I have the best friends in the universe. They are always there for me and I am so lucky to have them in my life. I love and appreciate all of you. But I would like to give special thank you's to Joe Vargo and Katherine Lamb, Clarissa Doehler, Jared Sinclair and Katerina Ntourou, Pat

Boyle, Zak Etschied, Steve Freeman, and Dave Roden and Tracy Boylan (I finally did it, Colonel).

And finally to Jill, W, D, and P. Thank you for putting up with me putting up with you. I love you all so much.

If you're reading this, you also mean the world to me. Thank you so much for going on adventures with us. I hope you will join us next time.

Be good. Help each other out. I'll see you tomorrow.

- Tony Gruenwald, writing standing up at his kitchen counter probably while someone asks for more juice, Summer 2021

About the Author

Tony Gruenwald is a stay-at-home dad to three kids in Minnesota. His wife is awesome and his kids are just okay. He is the author of the FullTimeTony short stories. You can find more at https://fulltimetony.wordpress.com.

Made in the USA
Monee, IL
01 March 2022